Hallelujahs From Two Continents For Kate Charles and
A Drink of Deadly Wine

KATE CHARLES
A DRINK OF DEADLY WINE

THE MYSTERIOUS PRESS

Published by Warner Books

A Time Warner Company

First published in Great Britain in 1991 by Headline Book Publishing PLC.

MYSTERIOUS PRESS EDITION

Cover illustration by Richard Newton
Cover design by Diane Luger
Hand lettering by Carl Dellacroce

The Mysterious Press name and logo are trademarks of Warner Books, Inc.

 Mysterious Press books are published by
Warner Books, Inc.
1271 Avenue of the Americas
New York, NY 10020

 A Time Warner Company

Printed in the United States of America

Originally published in hardcover by The Mysterious Press.
First Printed in Paperback: December, 1993
10 9 8 7 6 5 4 3 2 1

For Simon

Author's note: I have taken a few ecclesiastical liberties for which I hope I will be forgiven. St. Anne's Church, Kensington Gardens, does not exist, nor does St. Dunstan's Church, Brighton. I have also elevated two towns to cathedral cities for reasons of plot: Selby Abbey of course exists, but is not a cathedral, and likewise Plymouth has been elevated.

Thou hast shewed thy people heavy things:
thou hast given us a drink of deadly wine.
                                    Psalm 60:3

Prologue

Keep me from the snare that they have laid for me:
and from the traps of the wicked doers.

                                        Psalm 141:10

Emily put her head around the study door. "The children
are ready, darling. Shall we go?"

With an effort, Father Gabriel Neville smiled at his wife.
"You and the children go on ahead. I want to have a last
look at my sermon—people will be expecting something
special today!"

"And I'm sure you won't disappoint them. See you in a
bit, then."

As the door closed behind her, the smile faded from
Gabriel's face, and he stared unseeing at the piece of paper
in his hands. An ordinary piece of paper, with no distin-
guishing marks. He could throw it on the fire and get on
with his life, with his career. But the words that were
written on that paper were already incised on his heart, and
the threat behind them would not go away.

Ugly words, words full of hate, and malice, and hurt. His
carefully ordered world . . .

A shaft of morning sunlight broke through the study
window, and his desk was momentarily dappled with pools
of color from the inset pane of stained glass. Cool blue

lapped his sermon notes, while a finger of red touched the smooth rock paperweight. The past . . . he would not allow himself to think of the past. Gabriel shuddered and reached convulsively for the silver-framed photo of Emily and the children. A beautiful family— any man would be proud. Lovely Emily, with her glossy dark hair and her glowing brown eyes. Viola and Sebastian, the twins. People often stopped Emily on the street, astonished by their beauty. Beauty in duplicate it was, with their perfect heart-shaped faces, Emily's shining dark hair and his sapphire-blue eyes. He gazed gratefully at them. The past, threatening to crowd in on him, was held at bay by their smiling faces. The present, yes, the present was all that mattered—that, and the future.

He looked around the study as he contemplated his future. When the time came, he would be sorry to leave this place; of all the rooms in the vicarage, this was his favorite, his sanctuary. All was in order: his books, lined up alphabetically on the oak shelves; the mantelpiece with its carefully arranged treasures; the beautiful Queen Anne desk, polished to a mellow sheen and clear of all save the sermon notes and the photo; the Persian carpet, its colors still rich and vibrant despite its great age. It was all of a wholeness, just like his life.

And now this. Gabriel opened the top drawer of his desk and thrust the folded paper in, then hesitated. No one else should be opening his desk drawer—the children knew they were not to enter his study, and the daily would never look inside his desk when she polished it, but it didn't do to take chances. He fiddled with a bit of wood, and a secret drawer slid silently out. The paper thus safely dealt with, Father Gabriel Neville prepared himself to go to church.

PART I

Chapter 1

*Take the psalm, bring hither the tabret: the merry
  harp with the lute.
Blow upon the trumpet in the new moon: even in
  the time appointed, and upon our solemn feast-day.*
Psalm 81:2–3

In the moment of expectant pause before the entry of the
procession, Emily looked up from her prayers. The church
had never looked better—Gabriel would be so pleased. The
six silver candlesticks gleamed on the high altar and the
figures on the newly cleaned rood screen virtually shone.
Even the stained-glass windows, begrimed by London traffic, had been cleaned for the occasion, and were jewel-
like in their brilliance. The sun streamed through; it
seemed a good omen after several weeks of almost unrelieved
rain.

The Feast of St. Anne, the church's annual Patronal
Festival: It had always been the highlight of Emily's year, as
long as she could remember. As a small girl growing up in
this church she'd loved the sights, the sounds, the smells of
this day—the cloth-of-gold, the choir, the incense. She
loved the banner carried in procession, the one with St.
Anne, mother of Our Lady, teaching the young Mary to

read. That banner, weakened by age, was now only brought out once a year, on this feast day.

She drew in her breath in anticipation as the doors at the northeast of the nave opened and the procession entered. Sebastian, making his first appearance as boat boy, walked solemnly beside the thurifer. He'd been looking forward to this day for a long time. Emily felt Viola tense beside her, and gave her shoulder a little squeeze of sympathy.

The thurifer swung the heavy silver thurible straight in front of him, releasing an aromatic cloud of smoke. By the time the choir entered, behind the crucifer and acolytes, it was becoming difficult to see. But there it was—the banner. And there, just ahead of the Bishop, resplendent in cloth-of-gold, was Gabriel.

Beautiful Gabriel. That first time, ten years ago it was, she hadn't even seen him at first, so entranced she'd been with the banner. But once she'd seen him she hadn't taken her eyes off him for the rest of the service. Gabriel had been thirty then, but looked younger. His was the heartbreaking androgynous beauty of a Burne-Jones angel: tall and slender, luminous pale skin, high cheekbones, long straight nose, deep-set eyes, startling in their blueness and fringed with dark thick lashes, lips that were soft and rounded without being full. His hair was auburn, wavy and worn a fraction longer than the current fashion, but it suited him so completely that it never occurred to anyone to criticize it. And now, after ten years, he was little changed, his hair perhaps shorter but without a touch of grey, his face smooth and unlined, his figure slim as ever. As he passed by, Emily smiled at him with love.

Involved in his own observations, Gabriel missed her smile. The church looked splendid, he thought—full marks to Daphne, who was chiefly responsible, and to all the ladies who'd worked so hard cleaning and polishing. He'd have to remember to thank them. The procession passed under the rood screen; each person moved smoothly to his appointed place. The servers were doing uncommonly well—he'd have a word with Tony later to compliment him. Now he smiled at Tony as he brought the book forward for the collect; the young man returned his smile discreetly. Sebastian, clutching the silver incense boat, was behaving beautifully, conscientiously following the thurifer's every move. It was a shame that Viola had taken it so hard, but she had to understand that there were still certain things that girls couldn't do.

As the choir began the Gloria and he settled into his seat, Gabriel's eyes moved over the congregation. His thoughts, so carefully under control until now, moved back inexorably to that piece of paper. He finally articulated to himself the terrifying question: Who had sent it? Who had crept up to his door early this morning and slipped the envelope through the letter-box? Who could hate him that much? And most frightening of all, who could possibly know about that terrible time in Brighton, so long ago?

He collected himself during the readings, concentrating very hard on the words, and prepared himself for the sermon. The choir chanted the psalm set for the day; its words reinforced his calm.

Blessed are all they that fear the Lord: and walk in his ways.

For thou shalt eat the labors of thine hands: O well is thee, and happy shalt thou be.

Thy wife shall be the fruitful vine: upon the walls of thine house.

Thy children like the olive-branches: round about thy table.

Lo, thus shall the man be blessed: that feareth the Lord.

The Lord from out of Zion shall so bless thee: that thou shalt see Jerusalem in prosperity all thy life long.

Yea, that thou shalt see thy children's children: and peace upon Israel.

As he stepped into the pulpit, Gabriel was well in control. The congregation settled back with a collective sigh for one of his famous sermons. He was justly famed, for he was a spellbinding speaker. Although he was a scholar of some note, with an impressive intellect, his sermons were never dry exercises in scholarship. He had a gift for making the most abstract and esoteric concept understandable, and in a way that made his listeners feel that they not only understood it, but had known it all along. With his compelling beauty and his eloquent and charismatic delivery, it was said that no one had ever slept through one of Father Gabriel Neville's sermons. Today he spoke movingly on the subject of Grace, the literal translation of the Hebrew name Anne.

As he preached, he made eye contact with the congregation, one after another, though their presence barely registered with him: Emily, near the front, gazing at him with rapt love, with Viola beside her; the churchwardens, flanking the aisles; Lady Constance, in her customary pew on the left; Daphne at the back; the Dawsons, their usual disapproving looks softened by his rhetoric.

One of his gifts as a preacher was knowing when to stop, and he sat down leaving his listeners wanting more. The choir sang the Credo, the Intercessions were made, the Prayers of Penitence said, and the Bishop stepped forward for the Absolution.

Forgive us all that is past . . .

The Mass. The Bishop was celebrating, so Gabriel could stand to the side and let the familiar words of the Prayer of Consecration slip through his mind like rosary beads through his fingers. With angels and archangels . . .

The Agnus Dei soared high into the polychromed roof as Gabriel took the silver chalice and moved to the rail. His mind was numb, the twin questions beating a painful tattoo in his head: Who hates me? Who knows?

They came forward and knelt one by one, and he looked searchingly at each one as he proffered the chalice. The servers knelt first. Ahead of Gabriel, Sebastian gazed up suitably awestruck as the Bishop's hand rested momentarily in blessing on his dark head. Old Percy "Venerable" Bead. "The blood of Christ." Who knows? The two youngsters, Johnnie and Chris. "The blood of Christ." Who hates me? Tony Kent. "The blood of Christ." Who knows? Lady Constance, the next to receive communion from the Bishop, as was her due. "The blood of Christ." Who hates me?

Miles Taylor, down from his perch in the organ loft. "The blood of Christ." Emily. The Dawsons, two little grey people, together as always. "The blood of Christ." Who knows? Daphne Elford, solid and comfortable. "The blood of Christ." Who hates me? The churchwardens at the end, Wing Commander Cyril Fitzjames and Mavis Conwell. "The blood of Christ." Who knows? Who hates me? Who knows? Who knows?

Chapter 2

Thou shalt hide them privily by thine own presence
from the provoking of all men: thou shalt keep
them secretly in thy tabernacle from the strife
of tongues.

                                      Psalm 31:22

The Bishop had managed to arrive and robe with a minimum of fuss, but after the service he found himself the object of Percy Bead's hovering ministrations. "Right Reverend Father, let me take your mitre. If I may say so, it's a lovely one." Percy's short fingers lingered over the rich gold embroidery. "May I help you with your cope? We have to take particular care with this gold set."

"It's a beautiful Mass set—one of the finest I've seen in a long while. You're very lucky to have it."

Percy, characteristically, took that as a personal compliment and beamed. "Yes. It was a gift from Lady Constance Oliver, just after her husband died, so that goes back a long way. We'd never be able to replace it today. You just can't get materials like that any more." He grew confidential. "There aren't many left in the church who remember back that far. I'm one of the old ones, you see. Me, Lady Constance, Cyril Fitzjames."

Percy Bead, known to all as "Venerable," was possessed of strongly held opinions about everything, and he never hesitated to share them. The Bishop, who had only recently become Area Bishop, realized that this could be a valuable asset on his periodic visits to St. Anne, Kensington Gardens. He measured up the old man, squat in his black cassock. "I suppose you've seen quite a few Vicars come and go."

"Oh, yes, I've seen them all. We had a grand tradition here in the old days. Mind you, we manage to keep things up a lot better than they do most places nowadays." His disapproving sniff conveyed a great deal. "You've got to hand it to Father Gabriel—he does insist on maintaining standards." A crafty look crossed his face. "Of course, he might not be here that much longer. With the Archdeacon retiring . . . some people think he's about due for a promotion."

The Bishop smiled noncommittally. He'd been right— there was speculation in the church. They'd be looking for an announcement soon. How would the news be received? Ten years was long enough for a priest to stay in a parish. Would Gabriel Neville's departure be mourned?

The other servers, awed by the Bishop's presence, stayed out of the sacristy, so their conversation had been conducted in some privacy. But at that moment Mavis Conwell, one of the churchwardens, bustled in and hurried up to the Bishop. "Your Worship, it's so wonderful to have you here today!" She grabbed his arm. "Come along and have some sherry—I'm sure there are people you'd like to meet."

She walked with him to the church hall. "Actually," she said confidingly, "I'm glad to have a chance to have a word with you. Did you see the *News of the World* last week?"

The Bishop permitted himself an ironic smile. "No. I'm not a regular reader of that publication. But I've heard about the fuss." Indeed, it would have been difficult for anyone to have been unaware of the "Pervie Precentor of Plymouth" scandal, rocking the Church of England for the past week.

Mavis, impervious to the irony, went on, "Well, of course I don't read the *News of the World,* either, but I know people who do. And I think it's just disgusting."

"What's disgusting, Mrs. . . . er, Conwell?"

"That people like that are allowed to remain in the Church. Honestly! That's what's wrong with the Church today—there's not enough plain talk about what's right and what's wrong. And for a man of the cloth—a man of God—to tell a journalist that he has fantasies about choirboys— well! I know what I'd do with people like that."

The Bishop replied mildly, "And what would you do, Mrs. Conwell?"

"Why, kick them out of the Church, of course! Just think about our young people, and the example that's being set for them. They're being corrupted and led astray by all these . . . people, and the Church is making it easy."

Attempting to change the subject, the Bishop asked, "Do you have children?"

A look of pride transfigured her plain face. "I have a son, a good boy." She frowned. "But if I ever thought that anyone . . . well, their life wouldn't be worth living." She was not easily diverted. "What I really wanted to say was that we're very lucky here at St. Anne's. Father Gabriel may not always speak out as frankly as I'd like about these things, but he's a good family man himself—not like so many of those priests you hear about." Here she stopped in her tracks, faced him, and lowered her voice confidingly, fixing him with her gimlet eyes. "There are rumors . . . well, everyone says that he may be made Archdeacon soon. And I just want you to know that I for one think it's very important that our new priest, when we get one, should be a family man."

Taken aback, the Bishop replied, "You know, don't you, Mrs. Conwell, that I don't have the patronage for this appointment?" His natural discretion asserted itself. "Even if there were going to be a vacancy, and certainly no announcement has been made about that, the gift of the living belongs to Lady Constance Oliver."

Mavis Conwell was undeterred. "Yes, but surely you have some influence. I'm sure that Lady Constance would listen to you. She knows how I feel, but if she were to hear it from someone like the Bishop . . ."

"I'll keep it in mind," he replied noncommittally, resuming his progress towards the church hall.

Most of the congregation had already gathered there, and were standing about in small groups, sipping sherry and dissecting the service according to their own particular interests.

In one corner, Miles Taylor, the organist, was holding forth to Wing Commander Cyril Fitzjames. "You just have no idea what I have to put up with," he asserted earnestly. "You churchwardens just have to parade around with your staffs—or is it staves?—and look dignified. I have to hold the entire service together. *And* cope with priests who can't sing. We don't realize how lucky we are with Gabriel—he has a beautiful voice. But did you hear the Bishop? Sheer agony!"

Cyril Fitzjames made the appropriate noises of sympathy, though his attention was elsewhere. No one actually listened to Miles Taylor any longer. He'd been organist at St. Anne's for several years now, but had run out of original conversational topics within the first few days. It must be said that he was a man of considerable musical talent, and had raised the standards at St. Anne's noticeably. And he was not without charm, after an eccentric fashion. Many of the elderly ladies at St. Anne's had been captivated by this young man's manner—they of course thought of him as a young man, though he must be over thirty. Tall, lanky and sandy-haired, he seemed to be all arms as he gesticulated wildly through every conversation.

"Of course the choir sounded all right—they know the Byrd four-part Mass backwards—though I can never understand why Gabriel insists on all that ancient stuff! It's just not moving with the times! There's so much good music being written these days that's never performed, because of old-fashioned priests who won't let a chap get on with his job! Now, at Selby..." He lifted his arms dramatically, exuding a faint whiff of cigarette smoke. "If I've told the Vicar once—" He broke off and looked around suddenly. "Where is the Vicar?"

Sensing the opportunity for escape, Cyril said quickly,

"I'll go and look for him," and shambled off. Miles, temporarily thwarted, shrugged and went outside for a cigarette.

Emily chatted with the Sacristan, Daphne Elford, her mind only half on the conversation. Just after the service, Gabriel had slipped up to her and whispered that he had a terrific headache and was going home. Poor Gabriel, the stress of the service had obviously been too much for him, though he had always enjoyed it in past years. Maybe this was different, knowing that it was probably his last.

"Aren't you required in the sacristy? Putting away the vestments and the silver, and all that?" Emily asked.

Daphne snorted. "You'd never know I was Sacristan, the way Venerable Bead takes over after Mass. He makes me feel like a trespasser in the sacristy, so I just stay away until after he's gone. Especially with the Bishop—he's acting like he's his personal property."

Just then Emily noted the Bishop, pinned in the corner by the earnest Mavis Conwell. "Oh, the poor Bishop, he'd be better off with Venerable Bead—look who's bending his ear."

"No doubt telling him that the Church of England is going to the dogs. Perhaps I'd better rescue him and see that he meets a few people," Daphne suggested.

The Bishop was drowning in a barrage of words, now centered chiefly on the weather. "It's been a dreadful summer. When Craig was younger and my husband was alive we used to have some lovely holidays at the sea, but this year—why, I was hardly out of the hotel for the whole fortnight, it rained so much. It's got something to do with the ozone layer, I think, don't you?"

He was saved the necessity of a reply by the welcome intervention of Daphne, bringing him a glass of sherry. Mavis hung on doggedly for several minutes, then admitted defeat and marched over to where her friend Cecily Framlingham stood with the Dawsons. Cecily, a tall, hatchet-faced woman in her early fifties, was describing the difficulties she'd encountered in finding the flowers she'd wanted for today's service. "You'd think, wouldn't you, that in the middle of summer you'd be able to get white roses? But there just aren't any to be had this year. And I did so want some for in front of the statue of Our Lady of Walsingham. White roses are just the thing for Our Lady. Crysanths just aren't the same. I told my Arthur..."

"It's the ozone layer," Mavis interjected. "I was just telling the Bishop..."

Roger Dawson wrung his hands. He had a perpetually disgruntled look on his face. "It doesn't really matter what flowers you use, as long as Our Lady of Walsingham is stuck in that corner where no one can see her. It's a disgrace. I shall tell the Bishop—"

"I really think that red roses are better for Our Lady," interrupted Julia Dawson earnestly, her receding double chin quivering with emotion. "They represent her suffering—the Sacred Heart, you know."

"But white roses represent her purity," explained Cecily. "It's most important. Remember that sermon that the Vicar preached last year about Our Lady? How her purity was..."

"Where *is* the Vicar?" queried Roger Dawson. "I haven't seen him since Mass."

"Purity!" announced Mavis triumphantly. "Now *that's* a quality that's lacking in the Church of England today! If only the Vicar would have the courage to preach about that! He should have been up there today denouncing that disgusting 'Pervie Precentor' instead of talking about... whatever he was talking about. How can we expect proper standards to be upheld when clergy—even respectable married clergy—close ranks around their own? It's cowardice, I say."

Meanwhile, in their favorite corner near the drinks table, the servers were also finding the "Pervie Precentor" a fascinating topic of conversation.

In keeping with his position as head server, Tony Kent was as usual the spokesman for the group, and the leader of opinion. In his late twenties, Tony was also the oldest of the servers, with the notable exception of Venerable Bead: Most of the servers were in their late teens or early twenties. Tony was a handsome young man with grey-blue eyes and straight, fine hair worn in a floppy fringe; well educated and articulate, he was a teacher of history and geography.

"Poor old Norman Newsome—you've got to feel sorry for him," he stated. "Though talking to that journalist wasn't the smartest thing he's ever done."

Venerable Bead, who had just joined the group after his self-imposed toils in the sacristy, nodded vigorously. "I've met Norman Newsome, you know—last year, or was it the year before, when the Society of the Most Holy Blood had its annual do at Plymouth. He celebrated at the service, and he was brilliant. Biretta, lace down to his knees, and the liturgy... well, the man really knows what he's doing. It would be a crime for the Church to lose a man like that."

"What will happen to him? Will he resign?" These questions were from the young ginger-haired server named Johnnie—or was it Chris? No one but Tony ever seemed to remember which was which. Close friends and always together, they were referred to indissolubly as "Johnnie 'n' Chris" by those who knew them, and the "dark one and the ginger one" by those who did not.

"Hard to say," ventured Tony. "The Dean says he won't force his resignation, but the pressure is pretty strong. I don't know if he can hold out against it."

"If he does resign, he'll never get another job in the Church of England," Venerable stated.

The dark one—Chris—added, "But it's not as if he's actually *done* anything! How can they hound him out of the Church just because he's had fantasies? I mean, who's perfect? The first stone, and all that?"

Tony shook his head. "It's not what you think—or even what you do—that matters. Most people"—he shot a look at Mavis Conwell, still holding forth to her friends—"most people don't really care, as long as they don't have to know about it. Some, of course, make an occupation out of knowing other people's business."

Emily caught the end of this as she approached the cluster of servers, and exchanged smiles with Tony. "Morning, Mrs. Vicar," he said, tugging on his floppy forelock. "To what do we owe this favor?"

Emily played along, greeting him with a royal flourish. "I don't want to interrupt anything, but I wanted to tell you all how excellent the serving was this morning. I didn't see a single mistake, and I know Gabriel really appreciated the care you've taken."

"Where is Gabriel?" asked Venerable, looking around. "I haven't seen him since he left the sacristy."

"Oh, he's gone home with a headache." Emily tried to look unconcerned. "I suppose the pressures of the service—with the new Bishop and everything—must have caught up with him. And of course things are very difficult for him now, between curates. All the workload is falling on him."

"Well," said Venerable, with a cagy expression, "I suppose the pressure really is on, with the Archdeacon retiring. The Bishop must be taking a very close look at Gabriel right now."

Discreet as always, Emily changed the subject quickly. "Thank you especially for looking after Sebastian. He's been looking forward to this day for a long time. I hope he didn't give you too much trouble."

"Oh, no, he was as good as gold. He knew he wouldn't dare misbehave, and I don't think he would have wanted to," replied the thurifer.

"Well, he's certainly pleased with himself now," Emily said. "Next week he's going to want to be the crucifer!"

"I think he might find the cross just a bit heavy for him," laughed Tony. "But I'm sure he won't be boat boy forever. Was Viola upset to be left out?"

"Dreadfully. I've always told her she can be anything she wants to be. So now she wants to know why she can't be the first female server at St. Anne's."

Venerable bristled angrily. Before he could speak, Tony interposed, "Can you imagine what the Dawsons would say?"

Emily laughed, "They don't even approve of *me*, you know. Married clergy are definitely not the thing, in their book."

The Bishop was at that moment enduring a session of hearing the Dawsons' views on the sad state of the Church of England, and most particularly Anglo-Catholic worship at St. Anne's. Their main grievance, as far as he could tell, was that Father Neville failed to treat the Walsingham Cell of which Roger was clearly the leader, with the due respect and deference it deserved, or indeed to accord it any preeminence among Church organizations. Mary Hughes, a gentle spinster of the parish, joined them and tried to turn the conversation in a more positive direction. "Don't you think we're fortunate to have such a good choir—and such a gifted organist?" she asked. The Bishop nodded and she went on, "And of course there's that clever little machine on the organ." Before the Bishop could respond, an extraordinary-looking old woman hobbled up and confronted them. "It's Beryl Ball," Mary Hughes whispered warningly. "Don't pay any attention to what she says."

Beryl Ball was, as always, very smartly dressed in the cast-off clothes which she purchased at the jumble sales of the fashionable London churches. But the overall effect was just slightly bizarre, set off with the bright green moonboots which she always wore. She fixed the gathering for a moment with a stare, her eyes magnified alarmingly behind thick spectacles. Then she startled the Bishop by thrusting out her false teeth with her tongue, and settling them back into place, before she spoke. "It won't do you any good, you know," she announced. "I can tell that you want me, but I'm telling you right now that I'm pure. No man has ever touched me, and no man ever will." She looked at the Bishop challengingly, defying him to deny it. "I've been in this church for a long time, and every Vicar who's been here has wanted me, but I've kept myself pure." She lowered her voice, shooting a look at Emily. "Not that I wasn't tempted by this last one. Oh, he was a beautiful young man, and he didn't half want me. I very nearly gave in to him. But then *she* came along and stole him away from me. No better than a prostitute, is that one. She came between me and the Vicar, and that's no mistake." Her expression was pure venom. The Bishop gazed with re-pelled fascination at the magnified eyes with their dilated pupils.

Mary Hughes tried to intervene. "Beryl, now you know that's not true..."

Beryl Ball turned on her fiercely. "Shut up, Mary Hughes! Everyone knows that you wanted him for yourself! All the women wanted him, but he wanted me, until that whore made him marry her!"

The Bishop opened his mouth, then shut it again. He knew it wasn't true, but what sort of man was this who inspired such passionate feelings? What sort of man was he about to recommend to be Archdeacon?

Chapter 3

O go not from me, for trouble is hard at hand:
and there is none to help me.

Psalm 22:11

After the splendors of the morning service, and later Solemn Evensong and Benediction, the seven-forty-five Low Mass was a welcome relief. Gabriel conducted the service quietly, his head still throbbing with a dull pain behind his eyes. This wasn't like him, to feel unwell. Not like him, either, to dwell on negative feelings. What shall I do? he thought. There's no one I can talk to, no one who can help me. No one who would understand. If only I could confide in Emily, and she could tell me what to do... And then a name came into his mind unbidden, and resounded there. David. I must talk to David.

The congregation was small, but Lady Constance was there as she usually was. After the service, Gabriel waited for her to finish saying her rosary in the Lady Chapel, and approached her as she rose to her feet. She was an imposing woman, rather tall and with a stately carriage. Her silver hair was immaculately waved above her fine-featured face, delicate fair skin webbed with the tiny lines of old age. "I want to apologize to you for this morning," he began. "I'd intended to have a glass of sherry with you and the Bishop, but I got a terrific headache during the service, and had to go straight home."

She looked closely at him, noting the faint purple marks of pain under his eyes. "I hope you're feeling better now," she said with concern.

He smiled with an effort. "I tried to get some rest during the afternoon, and of course Emily did her best to wave her magic wand and make it go away. She fixed me some foul-tasting herbal brew, and kept the children quiet—and that was quite an accomplishment, believe me."

"Your wife is a treasure. I hope you realize that," said Lady Constance with a smile.

"My greatest asset," Gabriel agreed. "I don't know where I—or the parish—would be without her."

A good choice . . .

It was probably because he was so unaccustomedly thinking about the past that when Emily's face appeared in his mind's eye, it was not the self-assured Emily of today he saw, but the Emily of ten years ago, at their first meeting.

Cyril Fitzjames, churchwarden even then, brought her over to him with a faintly proprietary flourish. "Father Gabriel, I think you should meet Miss Emily Bates. Her father is an old friend of mine." Shy, quiet Emily, just down from Cambridge with a First in English. She looked up at him, her small heart-shaped face framed by sleek wings of dark hair, her dark eyes glowing with a quick intelligence, and with something more . . .

Was it from that moment that he had determined the shape of his future?

The future, the past . . .

David.

* * *

Gabriel hesitated for a moment before the Sacristan's flat. He occasionally turned up for a quiet drink after the evening services, so Daphne wasn't likely to be suspicious of ulterior motives. But how exactly was he going to bring up the subject of David, without making it seem forced? He'd have to play it very carefully, make it look like her idea somehow. He rang the bell deliberately.

Daphne's round face creased with pleasure as she opened the door. "Why, Gabriel! Do come in."

Daphne's flat was as homely and welcoming as she was; Gabriel felt instantly at ease in its comfortable shabbiness. He sank gratefully into an armchair and accepted a drink with thanks. Having women fussing around him was a constant feature of his job, and one Gabriel could very well have lived without, so Daphne's matter-of-fact treatment of him was always a welcome relief.

She wouldn't be described as feminine in any conventional sense: Short and plump without any of the curves that might once have softened "plump" into "voluptuous," Daphne had a blunt, open face and roughly cut grey hair with no pretense of style. Her manner, too, said, "Here I am—take me for what I am, or leave me." And yet there was an essential vulnerability about her that tempered the honesty into something even more appealing. She could be counted on never to be small-minded, petty or judgemental. Gabriel, in common with most people, liked her very much.

He sipped his whisky for a few moments before speaking. "I didn't have a chance to tell you this morning how much I appreciated all your hard work in getting the church ready for today. Everything looked absolutely splendid."

"I can't take all the credit. You know I had a lot of help."

"Yes, but I also know that you won't let anyone else touch the silver. You must have worn your fingers to the bone polishing it all."

"Not exactly," she replied, holding up stubby hands for inspection. "But it does seem to multiply on these occasions." She looked at him thoughtfully. "That reminds me—I thought that Mavis Conwell was going to give us a new silver alms dish in memory of the late, lamented

Richard. It must be nearly a year since he died—has she said anything about it lately?"

"No. Strange, isn't it? After he died, that was all she could talk about, but I haven't heard a word about it for several months now."

"Well, the old one will do for the moment. I don't suppose we can press her on it."

They sat in companionable silence for several minutes. Thank God Daphne's not one of those women who feels she has to fill every second with conversation, Gabriel reflected.

Daphne spoke at last. "Have you heard anything from David lately?"

Gabriel smiled to himself. This was going to be easier than he'd thought.

"David Middleton-Brown? Not really. Of course I had an acknowledgement of the flowers for his mother's funeral, but nothing else. How is he doing? I'd meant to write him a proper letter of sympathy, but I had the Area Synod meeting that week, and the PCC . . ."

"I don't think he's handling it very well. You know David." She smiled fondly. "She was a terrible old harridan, his mother, but she was all he had. It must have been hell for him, living with her, but he needs to be needed. Now he's got nothing, no one."

"Have you spoken to him?"

"You know that David hates the telephone; never uses it unless he absolutely has to. No, I had a letter from him just yesterday. It was typical David: polished prose, all terribly light-hearted, but between the lines a real cry for help. I wondered if we might be able to help him—you and I."

Gabriel was cautious. "How? I realize you've known him much longer than I have, but I wouldn't have thought that he'd welcome help from either one of us."

"Oh, I don't mean . . . Wait, I'll explain my idea," Daphne replied. "He seems to be at a real loose end at the moment. Apparently he'd booked a long summer holiday so he could take his mother to the seaside for a month. And now . . . well, he certainly doesn't want to go to the sea by himself, and his firm says he must go ahead and take the holiday, since they've planned the workload around him already—you know how inflexible solicitors can be." She paused consideringly, then rushed ahead. "I was wondering if we might invite him to come here for a while. I know he's refused our invitations before, but maybe under the circumstances . . ."

Behind the carefully maintained noncommittal expression, Gabriel was jubilant. This was going far better than he could have hoped. "You think he'd come?"

"Well, he might. If I were to write to him and invite him, and you were to write at the same time . . . We couldn't make it seem like we were trying to do him a favor, or he wouldn't come. Maybe if we could let him think we needed him to do us a favor . . ." She considered, then went on. "We could say we needed his help in sorting out something in the sacristy. Something to do with the silver, that required his expertise . . ."

"No good. You taught him practically everything he knows about church silver. Why would you need his help?"

"These old eyes aren't as good as they used to be on the hallmarks," she chuckled. "And you do him an injustice—he knows much more about silver than I do. But no. I've got it. The Comper crypt chapel. You know how long that project has been hanging fire! Lady Constance has offered to fund the repairs to the polychrome walls and roof, in her brother's memory. We've even been granted the faculty for the work. You know the only reason it hasn't been done yet—we need to be sure we're doing it exactly right."

"And who better than David to advise on that?" Gabriel finished. "I must admit, that will be pretty irresistible bait for him. He'll protest, say he isn't qualified, that he doesn't know any more about Comper or polychrome or gilding than the average man in the street—but he'll come." He paused and took a sip of his drink before considering the next difficulty. "Where will he stay?"

"Of course he can stay here. I have an extra room."

"Will he think that's proper?"

Daphne smiled wryly. "I'm an old woman. He's an old friend. Why shouldn't it be proper?"

"That's settled, then." Gabriel was silent for another minute, thinking. This might be the most difficult part. He continued, slowly, "One more thing. I'd appreciate it if . . . well, that is, I'd rather it looked like he was visiting *you*, not me." She looked at him, inquiring. "I can't really explain, but I just think it would be better if the parish didn't know generally that we knew each other. In fact, it might be better if the letter inviting him came just from you, and I kept out of it entirely. Would you mind?"

She was puzzled but compliant; Daphne had long ago learned not to ask Gabriel—or David, either—too many questions, especially when she wasn't sure she wanted to know the answers. "I won't say a word. Would you like another drink?"

Gabriel rose with a satisfied smile. "I'd love one, but I'd better not. I'd better be on my way—you have a letter to write, and the sooner the better."

Chapter 4

These wait all upon thee: that thou givest them meat in due season.

Psalm 104:27

The lounge bar of the country pub was almost empty, but Emily chose a table in the back corner and sank into the chair with a sigh, exhausted after the morning's task of delivering the twins to her parents for a short visit. "Sit down Lucy. I don't know about you, but I'm absolutely starving."

"Don't you want to order a drink?"

"I'd love to, but I'm driving, so I'd better not. Just an orange juice and lemonade, I think."

She watched her friend order the drinks, then thread her way back to the table balancing one in each hand. Lucy managed to perform even such a mundane task with unnatural grace. She sat down and pushed her hair back from her face with a characteristic gesture.

Lucy Kingsley's hair had, in childhood, been bright red; now, in her thirties, it had faded to an attractive strawberry blonde. But it retained all of its natural curl, and it fell to her shoulders in a cascade of waves and ringlets. She had a long white neck, and her coloring was of the peaches-and-cream sort that so often accompanies that particular shade of hair; she accentuated her very English type of beauty by dressing in pastel-colored floral Laura Ashley prints.

She faced Emily across the table and raised her wine glass. "Cheers, Em. Now, what's up? Why the sudden invitation to accompany you on this mission? Did one of your men-friends stand you up?"

"Don't be daft. Let's order first—I'm really famished." Emily applied herself to the menu. "I'm going to be really wicked and order the kind of thing I'd never let the children have. A huge plate of fried scampi and chips, I think," she said to the waitress who had materialized beside their table.

"And I'll have the avocado and smoked chicken salad."

"That doesn't sound like much, Luce. Aren't you hungry?"

Lucy shook her head, then smiled mischievously at Emily. "We could have eaten at your parents', you know. Your mother positively begged us to stay for lunch."

Emily grimaced. "Very funny. You don't know what it's like to have a mother who can't cook. I love my mother very much, but I have no illusions about her culinary abilities. She's the only person I know who can ruin a cheese sandwich."

"Then how can you leave your children there?"

"I'll admit it's difficult. But they're only six—too young to suffer any permanent damage from bad cooking." She laughed. "Of course when I was their age, I had no basis of comparison—I thought everyone cooked like that. School dinners were an absolute treat for me!"

"But Viola and Sebastian know better. You're a good cook, Em. They're used to a pretty high standard of food."

"Thanks to you." She smiled reminiscently. "It seems like such a long time ago now—those days when I was first married, and didn't have the first idea what to do in the kitchen. And you offered to teach me. I don't know how I would have managed without you, Luce."

"You could have kept the housekeeper. After all, Gabriel got by somehow before he married you." Lucy added, "Anyway, I seem to recall you telling me that *his* mother was not exactly brilliant in the kitchen."

Emily laughed. "I never knew her, of course, but I have it on good authority that she never even knew where the kitchen was!"

"Not impossible in that sort of grand house, I suppose. Poor little Gabriel, only the cook to blame for a deprived childhood." Lucy rolled her eyes. "How is the Angel Gabriel, by the way?" she added ironically.

"All right." Emily was silent for a moment, moving her glass around and leaving damp circles on the polished wood table-top. "Men... you know what they're like."

Lucy studied her bent head, certain that she was getting close to the reason for today's invitation. "All too well. What's he up to now?"

Emily's laugh was affectionate but bemused. "He's been in a real strop the last day or two. There's just no pleasing him."

"What's brought it on? A week of the children's summer hols?"

"I don't think so." She reflected. "There was only one day last week when it didn't rain, and he went with us to Kensington Gardens. Viola insisted on looking at Peter Pan, as usual, and Sebastian wanted to sail his boat on the Round Pond. Gabriel was fine that day—he really seemed to enjoy it."

"And since then?"

"Well, I've managed pretty well to keep the children out of his hair when he's had work to do. He worked ever so hard on his sermon for the Patronal Festival yesterday." She shook her head. "He's overworked since the last curate left, of course, and the new one won't come till the end of the summer. But I'm sure it's all this pressure over the Archdeaconry. I think he felt that yesterday was the big test.''

"And was it?''

"Probably. The Area Bishop was there, of course. You know how these things work. The position won't be vacant for some months—the end of the year, I think—but I'm sure they're already close to taking a decision, and the Bishop of London will want the Area Bishop's recommendation. It's really no wonder Gabriel felt pressurized. He wants that job very badly.''

"How soon will he know?''

"Probably not for a month or so. The sooner the better, as far as I'm concerned,'' Emily declared. "Gabriel can be obsessive, but he usually handles it better. That's why I think this promotion must be very important to him.''

"What exactly has he done?'' Lucy touched her friend's arm, and added facetiously, "He hasn't been beating you, has he? I didn't really think the Angel Gabriel would resort to physical violence!''

"Hardly,'' Emily laughed. "Oh, look, here's the food.'' For a few minutes she concentrated on the scampi in silence, then continued, "You know that Gabriel is never ill. He prides himself on that—always says it's all in the mind. Well, yesterday, after the service, he went home with a headache! I've never known him to have a headache. He even missed having a sherry with the Bishop, so he must really have felt rotten.''

"That does sound like stress. Then what?''

"I brewed him up some of my herbal headache remedy— it's an infusion of lavender flowers, lemon balm and a few other bits—and the way he complained you would have thought I was trying to poison him! Honestly!''

"Was he any better today?''

"No, that's the point. I don't think he slept very well, and this morning he was singularly uncommunicative.''

"He was meant to go with you to your parents', I take it.''

"Yes, he was having a day off to take the twins to Mum

and Dad's. I was really looking forward to having a quiet day with him after the big weekend. I thought that after a decent interval with my parents, we could escape and maybe go somewhere on the way home—somewhere in the country where we could have a nice long walk, if the weather was decent. But this morning he shut himself in his study, and only put his head out long enough to say that he had some very important work to do, and would I mind if he didn't go along?''

"So that's where I came in," Lucy mused, twisting a corkscrew of hair around her finger.

"Yes. I just couldn't face the prospect of an hour in the car, with the children scrapping in the back seat, and I didn't think you'd mind keeping me company, Luce. Gabriel suggested it, in fact."

Emily missed the quick flash of antagonism in her friend's eyes, as Lucy carefully controlled herself and said neutrally, "I suppose he thinks I haven't got a proper job, so it doesn't make any difference." She added more warmly, "I'm glad. We don't very often have a day out together, Em, and I think we should make the most of it. He won't be expecting you back for a while yet, will he? Where shall we go after lunch?"

Chapter 5

He chose David also his servant: and took him away from the sheep-folds.

Psalm 78:71

As usual it had been a long night, and there was nothing to get up for. David Middleton-Brown looked up at the ceiling, his mind blank. Gradually the noises of the postman—the advancing steps, the clink of the gate, the clatter of the letter-box, the retreating steps—seeped through to his consciousness, and gave him an excuse to get out of bed.

I hate holidays, he thought grimly, slipping into his dressing-gown. And the only thing worse than staying at home for a holiday is going away. He padded quietly down the hall, pausing without thinking to look into his mother's room. The curtains were wide open and the white counterpane stretched smoothly across the bed. The room was empty, empty even of the force of her strong personality. David would have sworn that that, at least, would have survived her death, would have left an imprint on this room.

"I don't know why I bother," he murmured to himself as he descended the stairs. "It's probably just bills. And advertisements for double glazing."

Indeed, as he stooped to retrieve the pile of envelopes, he recognized an electricity bill on the top. He shuffled through quickly: another bill, a newsletter from the Kempe Society, a brochure for the Wymondham Choral Society's next season, a catalog from an antiquarian bookseller, some communication from the Law Society. He paused as an envelope with Daphne Elford's distinctive, nearly illegible handwriting emerged from the pile. You'd never know from her writing that she'd been a school teacher, he reflected idly. The next envelope . . . his heart lurched involuntarily as he recognized the elegant pen strokes. Gabe, he thought. My God, Gabe.

With characteristic self-control, David carefully laid the letters, unopened, on the hall table and went into the kitchen to make himself a pot of tea. He concentrated almost obsessively on the ritual, willing himself not to think. He filled the kettle and switched it on, retrieved the teapot from its shelf, took a mug from a hook—Mother wouldn't approve; she insisted on a cup and saucer—and got out the little silver milk jug, bought for next to nothing years ago at a junk shop on one of his jaunts with Daphne. But he found no milk in the fridge and had to avert his eyes from the pile of post as he made his way to the front door. The milk bottle stood in a puddle of water on the porch. Damn, he thought. Another wet day.

By the time he'd returned to the kitchen and filled the milk jug, the kettle had nearly boiled. He poured a bit of water into the pot and swirled it around, then reached for the tea canisters. Two spoons of English Breakfast and one spoon of Darjeeling, a legacy from Mother. She liked her tea made properly, and wouldn't have a tea bag in the house. As he poured the boiling water over the fragrant leaves, her words came back to him. "Nasty things, tea bags, and not good for you, either. Mark my words, David. Someday they'll find out that the paper in tea bags gives you cancer."

David put the things on a tray and carried it through to what his mother had called the sitting room. This room strongly reflected her taste, and he'd always hated it. The crocheted white doilies that to her had indicated refinement were everywhere, on the chair arms and under the lamps. The lampshades were of a nasty pretentious sort, scalloped rose-colored satin with little silky pink tassels. A monstrous television set had pride of place, a bland cyclops straddling the corner. Much as David had complained about having a television in the room, she had insisted. "If you can afford to have a nice big television, what's the point in hiding it away somewhere where no one can see it?" That's what I'll do this holiday, he decided suddenly—change this ghastly room. And that television will be the first thing to go. As a first step he unplugged it, and immediately felt better.

It was time. He went into the hall for the post; while the tea steeped he looked at the Choral Society brochure—a nice program, he thought. He laid it aside and poured the tea, then fetched the letter-knife from the ornate bureau in the alcove beside the fireplace. The fireplace—that was another of his mother's great prides. At terrific expense she'd had the efficient and homely coal fire bricked up ("So dirty, don't you think?") and a gas fire with a marble hearth and "real flame-effect" logs installed. David despised its synthetic perfection.

He resumed his seat and opened Daphne's letter with mild curiosity. His correspondence with her was intermittent, but had continued over nearly twenty years, and he'd heard from her several times since his mother's death.

> Dear David,
>
> You may be surprised to hear from me again so soon, but I have a problem and I hope you may be able to help me with it. I've told you about St. Anne's Comper crypt chapel—I've probably mentioned that in recent years it's suffered rather badly from damp, and the paintwork is peeling from the walls and the roof. Lady Constance Oliver—I'm sure you've heard me speak of her—has offered to pay for the repairs and restoration, but no one here has the expertise to advise on what needs doing. We want it done properly, and I don't know where to begin to find the craftsmen, materials, etc. Even if you could only stay for a few days, I'd really appreciate it if you could come and have a look, and let me know what you think. Any time would be fine—my spare room is always free, and you can stay as long as you like. A few days in London might do you good! Let me know...

It tailed off, and was signed, Affectionately yours, Daphne.

He reread it thoughtfully. She'd almost had him taken in, until she gave herself away with that last bit about a few days in London doing him good. A put-up job, that's what it was. Good try, Daphne old girl, he said to himself. I've got to hand it to you—the Comper chapel is a masterstroke! He'd write tomorrow and decline. Still, a Comper chapel... it would almost be worth going. Almost.

He took a sip of tea, then gulped down half the mug. Out of the corner of his eye he could see it—Gabe's letter. It hadn't gone away, wouldn't go away. He couldn't put it off forever. David picked up the stiff envelope and forced himself to study it for a moment. If Gabe's fluid script weren't so distinctive, he might not even have recognized it, so infrequently had he seen it. Letter writing had never been Gabe's style, and the annual Christmas cards were always addressed and signed by Emily. Ten years, he thought. Ten bloody years. With a swift slash he opened the envelope, and extracted the letter. It was written on heavy notepaper with the letterhead of St. Anne's Vicarage. There were only a few lines. He willed his eyes to focus on them, his brain to absorb them.

> Dear David,
>   You should be receiving a letter from Daphne, asking you to come and advise us on the restoration of the Comper chapel. She doesn't know that I am writing this, asking you to please consider coming. We really could use and would appreciate your help with this. But there's another reason that Daphne knows nothing about. Something's come up and I don't know where else to turn. Please come, David—come soon. I need you. Don't let me down.

It was signed simply, G.

David sat still for a long time, the blood pounding in his head. Through all the pent-up emotions of ten years which now raged in him—the pain, the hurt, the love, and, yes, the anger—shone that brief sentence, like a shaft of sunlight through a storm cloud, piercing in its sweetness. I need you.

Gabe needed him. Years ago he'd needed Gabe, but Gabe had never needed *him*. Gabe had loved him—of that he was sure. It was that certainty alone that had kept him going through much of the last ten years. But needed him? Never. No more than the planet Jupiter, cloaked in beauty and mystery, needed the tiny moons that spun around it.

Gabe needed him. If he left now, he could be in London by lunchtime. He felt in his dressing-gown pocket for his car keys; the utter ridiculousness of this action returned him to reality.

And with reality came the realization that things had changed in ten years. Emily. No matter how or why Gabe needed him, Emily would be there.

David rose and started upstairs, unaware of what he was doing, his thoughts now centered on Emily. How could he go; how could he bear to meet her? Through ten years of imaginings she had grown in his mind to a selfish, grasping monster. How else to explain the inexplicable? She had cold-bloodedly trapped Gabe into marriage, that was clear. It was against his nature. Therefore he was an innocent victim, a lamb to the slaughter, and she was a scheming bitch. It was the money, he supposed, and the position; maybe she even fancied him—he couldn't blame her for that. But why, Gabe? Why?

As he'd done so many times before, he tried to imagine her, this woman who had captured Gabe. She must be attractive, at least in a superficial way. A Sloane Ranger type, he supposed. Blonde. Probably a lot of hair. Long red-lacquered fingernails. Hard, calculating eyes set in a pretty, vacuous face. She was supposed to be bright, something of an intellectual even, he'd heard, but he didn't believe it. Street-smart, more likely, with an eye to a good thing.

So great was his loathing of this unknown woman that he'd gone to every length to avoid meeting her. He'd declined the invitation to the wedding—of course! that was pain beyond enduring—and all subsequent half-hearted invitations from Gabe to come for a visit. He'd even refused to visit Daphne in the two years since she'd been at St. Anne's, insisting instead that she come to him for their periodic reunions; he'd had his mother's bad health as an excuse, and Daphne had never questioned that. And of course he was too proud to ask Daphne about Emily, to try to find out what she was really like. How could he face Emily now?

He was facing himself now, staring at his own image in the dusty mirror. Dusty? He looked around with surprise to find that he had gone past his own room and climbed the narrow stairs into the attic room.

This room, shabby as it was, had been his only real refuge from his mother; she had been unable for years to negotiate the steep steps, little more than a ladder really. David hadn't been up there since she died—there was no more need to escape.

It was also the room which evoked the strongest memories of Gabe, and he knew, looking down at the letter still clutched in his hand, that those associations had drawn him here now. Gabe had visited this house just once, for a week's holiday, against David's better judgement. But his misgivings had been unfounded, and the week had been magic. Mother had adored Gabe. Gabe was always charming even without trying, and he'd made a special effort to be captivating that week. Even Dad, who had rarely said anything, had been drawn out by his easy manner into actual conversation, day after day.

And night after night . . . they'd been together in this room. Mother had never been one for having people to stay, and there was no spare room for that purpose. So David had given up his room to Gabe, and had moved into the attic. There, night after night, Gabe, loving him, wanting him, had crept silently up the stairs, in spite of David's initial frantic protests. There under his parents' roof, in the house of his childhood, though he was approaching thirty he felt like a naughty schoolboy, terrified of being caught.

But they hadn't been caught, and the joy was all the sweeter for the fear. It was in the early days of their love, when everything was new and each discovery brought a fresh sense of wonder.

Candlelight. Gabe, boyish, sprawling on the bed. Laughing up at him, his eyes in shadow, his soft lips curved, his hair glinting on the pillow. The arms, outstretched, inviting . . .

Their behavior, during those enchanted candlelit nights, had been reckless, certainly; possibly even irresponsible and unwise. But an older and wiser David could not regret the most complete happiness he'd ever known. He could only regret that it had ended.

David gazed again at the mirror. He no longer felt like a schoolboy, and he recognized, with the shock of one who usually looks into a mirror without seeing, that it had been a long time since he'd looked like one. His face, never particularly handsome (why had Gabe loved him?) was at least beginning to look what people kindly called distinguished, with that hint of grey at the temples, while the fleshy pouches under his eyes spoke of long tiring days and sleepless nights. And his body, though still reasonably trim, had lost the suppleness of youth.

Gabe will be ten years older, too, he realized suddenly. Funny. He'd always pictured him looking just as he had then, perpetually beautiful, untouched by time. He found himself wondering exactly what he would find when he arrived in London, as he knew he must. Gabe needed him.

Chapter 6

Thy tongue imagineth wickedness: and with lies
thou cuttest like a sharp razor.
Thou hast loved unrighteousness more than goodness:
and to
talk of lies more than righteousness.

Psalm 52:3–4

"So, what did you do today, all on your own?" Gabriel asked his wife over their evening meal on the following day, Wednesday.

Emily considered. "Well, this morning I made a couple of batches of jam for the fête. If I make some every day for the next week, and maybe bake a cake or two for the freezer, it won't be so awful at the last minute."

"How about this afternoon? You were out, weren't you?"

She made a slightly guilty face. "Yes, I went down to Kensington High Street for the summer sales. It's so difficult to do the sales properly with the children along, so it seemed a good opportunity. Lucy met me along the way, and we had a nice tea at the Muffin Man afterwards.''

"Did you buy anything?"

"Mostly things for the twins. I got them some lovely cotton jumpers at Marks and Spencer's—they've quite grown out of the ones they had last year."

"You miss the children, don't you?" Gabriel smiled sympathetically.

She looked at the empty chairs. "I really do. It's so quiet in the house without them, especially when you're away in the evening. But I mustn't be selfish—my parents do so enjoy having them to stay, and spoiling them with little treats."

Gabriel consulted his watch. "Well, I won't be out long this evening. I need to pay a call on that new family in the parish, but the churchwardens are coming by at eight for a meeting about the Quinquennial Inspection, so I should be back by then."

Emily grimaced. "You'd better be. For heaven's sake, don't leave me alone with that appalling Mavis Conwell. I can't be held responsible for what I might say to one of her frightful remarks."

"I'm sure that Cyril will be on hand, more than happy to come to your rescue as your knight in shining armor." Gabriel's smile was tinged with malice.

Emily stuck her tongue out at him affectionately. "Poor old Cyril—he can't help it. Anyway," she added, "I don't make fun of all the women who are in love with *you*."

"Except Beryl Ball."

"Except Beryl Ball," she conceded readily. Glancing at the clock, she asked, "Have you got time for a coffee?"

"Just about. I'll probably get offered one later, but it's always best not to count on it."

Emily rose and went to the kitchen. Gabriel sat quietly, abstractedly drawing designs on the tablecloth with the tip of his knife, a small frown between his brows. The phone bleated in the hall and he jumped, startled.

"Stay there—I'll get it," Emily called, then put her head

round the door a moment later. "It's Daphne, she says she wants a quick word."

"Ah." In a few strides he was in the hall, picking up the receiver. He tried to keep the eagerness out of his voice. "Yes, Daphne?"

"Oh, hello, Gabriel. I've been out all afternoon and just got home to find a reply from David in the second post."

"And?"

"He's coming. On Friday, he says. I just thought you'd like to know."

He closed his eyes and sighed, then said, "Thanks. That's good. Will he come straight to you?"

"Yes, I expect it will be sometime in the afternoon. I'll probably take him over to the church and show him the crypt chapel."

"Why don't you give me a ring when he's arrived, and I'll meet you there?"

"Fine. I'll talk with you then."

"Thanks, Daphne. I'm sure it will do him good to have a change of scenery."

"Right. Ta."

Gabriel replaced the receiver and felt his shoulders relax. David's coming, he told himself. He'll get to the bottom of this somehow. Everything will be all right.

He returned to the dining room and accepted the steaming cup of coffee with the first real smile he'd given his wife in days. "Thanks, my love."

* * *

Gabriel hadn't yet returned when the doorbell sounded, a few minutes before eight. Emily went to answer it with a sinking heart. If I'm lucky it will be Cyril, she thought—I can cope with him, anyway. But on the doorstep, under a dripping umbrella, stood Mavis Conwell. As Emily beckoned her indoors, Mavis's small eyes, fractionally too close together, swivelled round to see if she were indeed the first to arrive. "Am I early? Father Gabriel said eight."

"I'm very sorry, Mavis. He's not back yet. He went out

on a pastoral call about an hour ago. Can I offer you a coffee?'' Emily took the proffered umbrella and the wet raincoat with a cordial smile.

"Thank you, Emily, that would be very nice.''

"Why don't you make yourself comfortable in the drawing room?'' she suggested. But Mavis followed her into the kitchen and watched her fill the kettle.

"Actually,'' Mavis confided, "it's nice to have a chance to chat with you. It seems like I hardly ever see you to talk to.''

"I'm usually around,'' Emily replied, with a vague wave of her hand. "But I suppose there are always people who want to have a word with the Vicar's wife.''

"Exactly,'' Mavis rejoined. "And it's just lovely the way you try to make time for all of them.''

Emily opened a cupboard and took out the sugar basin. "That's all I can do.''

"No, you go far beyond that. For example, I think it's just wonderful the way you've been counseling that head server, Tony Kent. Not everyone would have the courage.''

Frankly puzzled, Emily frowned. "What do you mean?''

"Well, everyone knows he's a''—Mavis lowered her voice conspiratorially and glanced around—"you know, a homosexual.'' She almost hissed the word. "And for a woman like you, with a small son, to counsel him—well, that's what I call an act of real Christian charity.''

"Counsel him?''

"I've seen you talking to him after church on Sundays, and I do think it's very brave. Someone must have the courage to tell these people that what they're doing is an abomination before God. I'd do it myself, but I'm sure he'd listen more to you, being the Vicar's wife and all. And a bit nearer his age,'' she added.

"But Tony is a friend,'' Emily protested, baffled.

"Of course he is, dear,'' Mavis agreed smugly. "They say that we have to befriend these people before we can really help them. He *does* want to be helped, doesn't he?''

"I think he's perfectly happy the way he is.''

Mavis was horrified. "It will probably take you an awful

lot of counseling then. But do be careful. I mean, you never know what you might pick up from these people. Not to mention the danger to Sebastian.''

Emily didn't know whether she wanted to laugh or to scream at her, but she controlled her expression and said mildly, ''I don't think Sebastian's in any danger. And I don't know what you think I could catch from Tony.''

''Oh, I didn't mean AIDS, though on that score I don't think you can be too careful, do you? But, well, I don't know... Those people go to such horrible places...''

Emily took a deep breath and deliberately changed the subject. ''How is Craig? I haven't seen him for quite a while.''

Mavis beamed. ''He's just fine. I know he doesn't come to church very often—it's not 'his scene,' as he says, but he's a *good* boy. No harm in him.'' Unwilling to let the subject drop, she went on, ''Quite a one for the girls, is my Craig. I'm just so glad that I have no worries on that score.''

''But what about the girls? Don't you worry about them?''

''Girls these days can take care of themselves. They're all on the Pill, aren't they? Anyway, I'd rather have him get a girl pregnant than to be . . . the other way. I just thank God that I have a manly son!''

Emily was saved the necessity of replying by the pealing of the doorbell. ''Excuse me a moment, Mavis. That must be Cyril.''

Wing Commander Cyril Fitzjames stood on the doorstep, smiling fondly at Emily as she opened the door. ''Good evening, my dear,'' he boomed, smoothing his hair carefully across his head. Although he was quite bald on top, he had cultivated a very long piece of hair on the side of his head with which he endeavored to disguise the fact; the parting started just above his right ear. The effect was never very convincing, and at times was frankly bizarre, but it satisfied his vanity.

He stepped inside, shaking the rain from his mac like a big wet dog. Emily had often thought there was much that was dog-like about him, from his appearance to his devotion to her. He was a large man, and in his prime had been impressive, with his broad shoulders and erect carriage. But the muscle had gone to fat and the military bearing had become a stooped shamble. He had a jowly, heavy face with drooping eyelids and liver spots, and his hands, large and mottled with age, had a slight tremble. Emily took his mac and offered her cheek for the inevitable kiss.

"So what's this meeting tonight all about, my dear?" he bellowed. "Gabriel didn't say. You'd think a chap had nothing better to do than come out in this rain for a blasted meeting."

"Oh, something about the Quinquennial Inspection, I think he said."

Mavis appeared at the kitchen door, clutching her coffee cup. "What's the Quinquennial Inspection?"

Cyril smiled condescendingly. "Ah, Mrs. Conwell! When you've been churchwarden as long as I have, you'll know what the Quinquennial Inspection is, all right!"

"Well, what is it?"

"Quin—that's five, if you remember your Latin. Every five years the diocese comes in to make sure that everything is shipshape. Looks over the building, goes over the books." He gave a short, barking laugh and wagged his finger at her roguishly. "So, if you've been pinching money, you're sure to get caught, my girl!" He broke off as the door opened and the Vicar blew in on a gust of rain. "Ah, Gabriel, my dear boy! Let the meeting commence!"

It wasn't until much later that Emily discovered the coffee stain on the hall carpet, but she managed to get most of it up so that it hardly showed.

Chapter 7

I have considered the days of old: and the years that
are past.
I call to remembrance my song: and in the night I
commune with mine own heart, and search out
my spirits.

Psalm 77:5–6

Driving across the Fens alone was depressing even at the
best of times, David reflected, and this wet summer day was
anything but the best of times. The low clouds were unbro-
ken, the rain unremitting, and there was no compensating
warmth in the air. In spite of his resolution not to dwell on
the past, David found himself remembering a happier time,
driving back to Brighton with Gabe beside him at the end of
a lovely week. The drive from Brighton to Norfolk at the
beginning of the week had been tense, fraught with his
anxieties about the wisdom of the enterprise, and the leaden
sky had threatened snow. But at the end of the holiday
they'd both been basking in the warm glow of their love. It
was an afternoon in mid-winter and the Fens had never been
more beautiful. In a cloudless sky, dusk was closing in
early; the horizon glowed like a creamy iridescent pink
pearl. Each twig on every tree—thousands, millions of
twigs—stood out in stark relief, like intricate black lace,
against the nacreous sky, and the black birds perched in the
trees were silent. David and Gabe had been silent, too.

David groaned now with frustration as a lumbering farm
vehicle pulled out in front of him from a side crossing. He'd
never get to London at this rate. He was unused to London

38

traffic: It had been years since he'd lived there, as a student and as a trainee solicitor, and in the intervening years the evening rush hour seemed to have begun earlier and earlier. By the time he'd negotiated the M25, then Finchley, St. John's Wood and Paddington, it was nearly teatime and he was in a black mood when he pulled in front of Daphne's flat.

Daphne had been watching for several hours from her vantage point at the window, the latest P. D. James novel unopened on her lap. In the morning she'd cleaned her flat, bathed, and taken special care with her appearance. Silly old woman, she'd grumbled wryly to herself, but she'd still put on a new coral-colored jumper with her best summer skirt. She realized as she sat looking out the window, that her motives in asking David here had not been entirely unselfish, but that uncomfortable knowledge did not prevent her from taking pleasure in anticipating his arrival. Self-knowledge did not always come easily to Daphne, but once it was achieved, she didn't shrink from its implications.

As the ancient brown Morris ground to a halt outside, she resisted the impulse to go outside and meet him; she remained in her chair and counted to ten after the bell went. But any potential awkwardness in their meeting was dispelled as she spontaneously burst out laughing at the sight of his grim face.

"I don't know what's so damned funny," he said peevishly.

"You," she chuckled. "You look like you've lost your last friend. Oh, David, it is good to see you."

He glowered, but unbent sufficiently to kiss her cheek with affection as he came through the door. "Any chance of a cup of tea? It's been a hellish trip."

"I'll put the kettle on." She retreated to the kitchen and he followed automatically.

"Nice place you've got here," he remarked, looking around with interest. "This comes with the Sacristan's job?"

"Yes. I'm very fortunate. Rents are sky high in this part of London, that is if you can even find rental property. I don't know where I would have gone when I retired and left the school if this hadn't come up." She looked at him, hesitating. He usually accepted gratitude with bad grace.

"Have I properly thanked you for finding me this job? I wouldn't have ever known about it if you hadn't been such a thorough reader of the classified adverts in the *Church Times*, and I probably wouldn't have had a chance of getting it if you hadn't written such a nice letter of recommendation to Gabriel."

He was embarrassed. "I'm glad it's worked out for you. I didn't say anything that wasn't true." He paused. "How is . . . Gabriel?" he finally asked, the unfamiliar name enunciated with an effort.

"Overworked and a bit distracted these days, to tell the truth. I don't know if I mentioned that he's likely to be appointed Archdeacon in the near future. That probably accounts for it."

"I haven't seen him in over ten years, you know."

Daphne looked at him speculatively; she'd often wondered about that, but knew better than to ask. Finally, as if reading his mind, she said, "I wonder if you'll find him much changed. I've only known him a couple of years, but he is very well preserved for his age!" She added sincerely, "Of course, you're not so bad yourself."

David shrugged philosophically. "I'm not the boy you used to know, am I? But at least I've still got all my hair, even if it is a bit grey around the edges."

Daphne warmed the teapot and tore the cellophane off two new packets of Twinings' tea. "I remembered," she said somewhat self-consciously. "Two spoons of Earl Grey and one of Assam. No tea bags. Milk, no sugar."

He laughed, delighted. "I hope you haven't forgotten the English Breakfast and Darjeeling for tomorrow morning!"

"No, and I haven't forgotten the Scotch for tonight, either."

He smiled, but his thoughts were suddenly sober: I shall probably need it by then.

* * *

Gabriel paced impatiently at the west end of the church, glancing at his watch. Daphne had phoned a quarter of an hour ago to say they were on their way. They were certainly taking their time about it.

As they walked along to St. Anne's, David had the curious sensation of moving in slow motion, like a fish swimming upstream. Daphne's flat was not far from the church, but their route led them from her quiet street on to a very busy main road, the pavements clogged with people in a hurry, the thoroughfare bumper-to-bumper with rush-hour traffic. Then suddenly they turned off the main road, and St. Anne's Church was a short distance before them. The rain had stopped, at least for a time, and David's first glimpse of St. Anne's was in a watery sunlight. Daphne chatted about the building's architectural merits, pointing out a buttress here and some tracery there with the specialized knowledge off a passionate amateur, knowledge that he shared and surpassed. He half listened and responded in kind.

Nearing the door, some instinct informed her that this meeting should not be witnessed. "You go on in and say hello to Gabriel. I'll . . . uh, check the notice board in the north porch to see if there's anything I need to know about, and I'll be in directly."

He stepped into the Pre-Raphaelite gloom of the church's interior, blinking for a moment as his eyes adjusted to the dim light, and came face to face with Gabriel. For a very long moment the two men regarded each other, the silence suspended like a crystal between them.

He hasn't changed, was David's first coherent thought, after the flood of inchoate emotion. Damn it, it's not fair. He looks exactly the same. How can I stop loving him when he's just the same?

Gabriel observed him with mixed feelings, this relict of a long-ago past. After the anticipation of the last few days, he now felt an odd detachment. This man had once meant something to him—for a time had meant everything to him— but now he seemed a stranger. Older, greyer; lines around his hazel eyes. But then at last David spoke, and the illusion of strangeness dissolved; the dry voice, the ironic self-deprecating smile instantly recalled the David of old. "So where's this famous Comper chapel I've come all this way to see, Gabe?"

Gabriel flinched almost imperceptibly at the name. "No one calls me that," he said in a soft, controlled voice. "No one else ever has. Perhaps it would be better..."

"I'm sorry... Gabriel. It just came out." David looked away, the pain almost too great to bear; he'd foolishly thought that Gabe no longer had the power to hurt him.

Daphne joined them at that moment. "You're looking uncommonly smart today, Daphne," Gabriel greeted her in quite a different voice. He was surprised to see her blush—something he would not have thought possible.

"You've never seen our church, David?" He assumed the comfortable official role of Vicar and tour guide as they strolled about; he pointed out the Morris & Co. windows and the Burne-Jones reredos in the Lady Chapel, the Bodley rood screen, the Bainbridge Reynolds metalwork, before leading the way down the spiral staircase which led from the Lady Chapel into the crypt.

David caught his breath, his attention truly captured at last. "Why, it's stunning! Absolutely stunning!" The three of them stood silently for a moment, drinking in the blue and gold richness of the chapel. After a while, David went on, "This is even better than the one at St. Mary Magdalene, Paddington. I can't imagine why it's not better known."

"But as you can see, the damp has really got in. Here," Gabriel pointed, "and over here. And here on the roof, the gilding is flaking off. Something really needs to be done."

"Yes, well. I suppose that's what I'm here for. Not that I know any more about it than either of you. I learned everything I know from Daphne."

"Don't be daft," she interposed. "I may have got you started, but you passed far beyond my knowledge a long time ago."

"And I learned everything I know from *you*," Gabriel finished. "So no false modesty will be tolerated."

"Everything you know?" David dared, shooting him a significant look. "I thought it was the other way around."

Gabriel ignored the implication. "Everything about church furnishings, certainly," he replied neutrally. But while Daphne was inspecting a bit of peeling paintwork, he said rapidly, in a low voice, "I must talk to you. Tomorrow. Come to early Mass. Seven thirty."

* * *

After a simple supper, David and Daphne sat companionably in the overstuffed chairs of her living room, drinking and reminiscing. The rain was again beating a steady tattoo on the window, and in spite of the season she'd lit a small fire against the chill of the night air.

David sipped his whisky appreciatively. "I've always blamed you for my taste for whisky. I don't think I'd ever tasted good whisky before I met you."

Daphne smiled, and he regarded her fondly. To him she seemed little altered in twenty years. She had appeared old to him then, or perhaps timeless, with her cropped grey hair and her comfortably shapeless figure. Strange to think that he was now as old as she'd been then; the intervening years had somehow narrowed the gap between them.

A bright summer morning, full of promise. His cases packed, the guidebooks endlessly perused and marked. A fortnight in the churches of the West Country ahead. Then Daphne's arrival, the confused explanations and excuses. A holiday in shambles, a friendship mortally wounded. Rejection. . . .

David looked at her again, wondering. They'd never spoken of it since. But why the hell not, he decided. "Why did you cancel that holiday? Why wouldn't you ever tell me what happened?"

Daphne regarded him over the rim of her glass. "You really don't know?"

"No. Why should I?"

She lowered her glass and looked at him gravely. Seeing him sitting there, so much the same David and yet so different, was more painful than she would have thought possible; she'd convinced herself that she'd got over these feelings years ago. But now she felt as though her heart would break all over again, as the light from the fire caught the burnished glints in his hair. "It was all a long time ago."

A late summer afternoon, sunlight slanting through the clerestory windows of the church, motes of dust dancing. The smell of the flowers she was arranging. The muted murmur of voices in the chapel. "I hear they're going away together again. Doesn't she realize how ridiculous it looks?" "Obviously not, the silly old cow." "Why, he's only half her age—if that!" "She's obviously besotted with him. Well, you can't blame her for that, but honestly!" Shock, automatic denial, then . . . sleepless night, agonized realization . . .

She took a quick gulp of whisky to fortify herself, then said rapidly, "People were talking. I decided it wasn't a good idea to leave you open to that."

David stared, incredulous. "But there was nothing to talk *about*! It's ludicrous even to suggest it! You were—well, you weren't young, and I was scarcely more than a boy, and . . ."

The hand that smoothed back her hair hid the pain in her eyes as she repeated softly, "It was all a long time ago." When it came to revealing the secrets of her own heart, her characteristic honesty would take her this far and no farther.

Chapter 8

O worship the Lord in the beauty of holiness: let the whole earth stand in awe of him.

Psalm 96:9

Although the bed in Daphne's spare room was more comfortable than his narrow bed at home, David had not slept well. At six o'clock he lay awake, listening to the rain on the window and replaying in his mind everything Gabe had said to him yesterday, everything he'd said to Gabe. He'd had rather too much whisky last night, and felt that he needed some fresh air; he got up, opened the sash, and leaned out, drawing in deep breaths of damp, smoggy London air. Was Daphne an early riser? He thought she was, and couldn't face the prospect of cordial chit-chat and English Breakfast tea (with one spoon of Darjeeling), so he shaved and dressed quietly, found his umbrella, wrote her a quick note, and slipped out of the flat. It would be an hour before he could decently turn up at St. Anne's, but Kensington Gardens were just around the corner, and he spent an hour walking in the rain, thinking about yesterday, about Gabe, about today, about . . . Emily. Today would probably be the day he'd have to confront her, or tomorrow at the latest.

When he arrived at St. Anne's, still half an hour before early Mass, the door was unlocked, though no one else seemed to be about. Yesterday, in the emotion of meeting Gabe again, David had absorbed only a general impression of the church, even during their tour. Now he decided to explore it himself, and to concentrate on its features.

David's extensive knowledge about churches, their architecture and furnishings, was something that he had acquired on his own, through reading and through many years of visiting churches, as well as from Daphne, whose shared interest in churches had been the basis of their friendship. He was passionately interested in the subject, and he often wished that he could have made some sort of career for himself in that field. But his mother would never have approved, and somehow at the time it had been easier to take the path of least resistance and to read law.

His family had never been a churchgoing one, and David's first exposure to any church had been as a young boy on a school visit to Wymondham Abbey, the ancient monastic church in the town where he'd grown up. It had been a case of love at first sight; he'd wandered away from the other, bored children, entranced by the beauty of the church, hungry to explore it on his own and to learn more about it. The massive Comper screen, with its nearly life-sized figures of saints and its impressive canopy, had stunned him

with its splendor, and had inspired his special interest in the
work of Sir John Ninian Comper.

David had returned to that church again and again as a
boy, first just to soak up the sense of beauty that was so
lacking elsewhere in his young life. But eventually he'd
begun to attend services; there a beauty of a different kind
gripped him, and faith was born. Thus David's faith, born
in beauty, was inextricably bound up with his interest in the
church buildings themselves and his response to them. His
God was a God of beauty; it was inconceivable to him that
God could be worshipped in an ugly building.

He had found Gabriel a kindred spirit in this respect.
Although Gabriel's knowledge was not so extensive as
David's, he, too, was moved by the beauty of the Anglo-
Catholic approach to worship, and the awe and reverence
which it inspired. His sense of his vocation for the Church
was strong; David had always envied him that, and envied
him as well the strength of character which had driven him
to follow that sense of vocation in spite of a fair amount of
opposition from his wealthy, aristocratic family.

David wondered now, as he explored St. Anne's, how it
was that he had never been there before, especially as its
Comper chapel was so splendid. He and Daphne had spent a
lot of time visiting the churches of London, all those years
ago, when he'd been a student. It was a lovely church—
Gabe must be very happy here, he thought.

Eventually he became aware that people were arriving; it
must be nearly time for Mass. Early Mass was held in the
Lady Chapel, and was attended by only a handful of the
faithful, David noted as he slipped into a pew near the back.
There was an imposing-looking elderly woman towards the
front, and a man and a woman, both in grey and looking
very alike—both had the corners of their mouths turned
down, permanently it appeared—in the middle. Wandering
around the edges, trying first one seat and then another, was
a rather odd old woman, dressed very smartly but wearing
enormous padded moon-boots. An elderly man in a black
cassock, small and squat with a beaky nose, small bright
eyes and bushy white hair and eyebrows, bustled up to the

altar and lit the candles. David knelt and tried to pray, but was distracted by the wonderful Burne-Jones reredos, the huge central panel depicting the Annunciation. Mary's face was averted, perhaps from the temptation of the terrible beauty of the angel. The Angel Gabriel . . .

When the Vicar entered, and the odd woman moved yet again, David realized that she was positioning herself to get the best possible view of him. Maybe she's not so crazy after all, he observed wryly. She's got good taste in men, anyway. Gabriel looked splendid in a silvery-green chasuble, and David had forgotten how movingly and how reverently he had always celebrated the Mass.

After the Mass, Gabriel waited at the door to greet his small congregation. The little grey couple rushed away, presumably home to their breakfast, and the odd woman was not far behind, with a last, fond leer at Gabriel. David lingered on his knees while the elegant old woman spoke with the Vicar, but as their conversation became prolonged he decided that his devotion was too conspicuous, and joined them at the door.

Gabriel welcomed him with a smile. "Lady Constance, you must meet David—he's a friend of Daphne's. David Middleton-Brown, this is Lady Constance Oliver."

Lady Constance extended her hand and gave him a searching look. "You must be the clever one that Miss Elford was telling me about: the one who's going to see to our chapel for us. We're so grateful."

"I don't know what she's been telling you about me, but I'm not a bit clever," he protested with his self-deprecating smile.

"I shall judge that for myself, thank you, young man. You must come to supper some evening. You and Miss Elford. Monday?"

David glanced at Gabriel, who gave an imperceptible nod. "Thank you, Lady Constance, I shall look forward to it very much." He bowed slightly as she turned away.

Gabriel watched until her back was out of sight, then turned to David. "Come home with me for breakfast. Then we'll talk." David waited at the north door while Gabriel went to the sacristy, returning a moment later in a black cassock and carrying an umbrella.

"Does your... does Emily know that you're bringing a guest to breakfast?" David asked as they walked the short distance to the vicarage.

"No, but she won't mind."

I'll bet she'll be just thrilled to meet her husband's old lover. Or maybe it's something she's used to, he thought bitterly.

He knew he hadn't been the first for Gabriel, as Gabriel had been the first—and only—for him. Not that Gabriel had ever been promiscuous; one relationship at a time was more his style. Gabriel had never actually told David the details of the experiences he'd had before they met, but he knew that there had been a few. Gabriel's sexual education had probably started very young; at the exclusive, expensive boarding school where he'd been sent as a boy.

The vicarage was a large brick Victorian house, just across from the church and built at the same time. David looked approvingly at its spacious aspect as they approached; in a moment they were inside. "Come on through to the kitchen." Taking a deep breath, David followed Gabriel through the door as he announced, "Darling, I've brought someone home for breakfast."

The woman who turned, smiling, from the cooker to face them was so opposite to David's expectation that he almost cried out in protest, "But where's Emily?" He tried to assimilate her appearance, to make it fit somehow with the calculating character he was sure she must have, but his mind just wouldn't take it in. Small-boned and delicate in her dressing-gown, she wore no makeup; her dark brown hair, cut close at the nape, curved forward at chin length to frame her face, with its small pointed chin and softly rounded cheeks, a face dominated by large, warm brown eyes and transformed by the look of love she turned on her husband. An enchanting face, without artifice and without guile. There must be some mistake.

"Darling, this is David Middleton-Brown, an old friend

of mine, and a friend of Daphne's. He's come to stay with her for a visit.''

The smile of welcome that lit her face was entirely sincere; she was glad to see her husband, and she was glad to see his friend. "David! How lovely to meet you at last! I've heard Daphne speak of you so often.''

"Oh?'' was all he could say.

"In fact, don't we have you to thank for having Daphne here at all? Didn't you recommend her to Gabriel for the Sacristan's job?''

"Well, yes. I knew she was looking for something to do when she retired from teaching, and when I saw Gabe . . . Gabriel's advert in the *Church Times*, I thought . . . well, why not?''

"How thoughtful of you. We're entirely in your debt, then— Daphne is absolutely wonderful.''

"Well, she does know her stuff.''

"So do you, from what she tells me. Anyway,'' she added impulsively, "it's lovely to meet an old friend of Gabriel's. Maybe you can fill me in on what he got up to before I met him!''

David stared at her aghast, at a loss for words. She doesn't know, he thought. She probably thinks we went out looking for girls together.

She noticed his stricken expression. "Is something the matter?'' she asked with concern.

"No. That is, well . . . I mean, you're not what I expected,'' he blurted.

She laughed delightedly and put her arm through Gabriel's, looking up at him; the unself-conscious intimacy of the gesture hurt David more than he would have imagined possible. "Darling, what have you been telling this man about me? You didn't tell him about the second head, did you? I forgot to put it on this morning.''

Gabriel's answering laugh was strained, as he looked from one to the other of them, from Emily's animated face to David's curiously blank one. "I told him . . . that you'd give us some breakfast.''

"And so I shall, in just a minute. Why don't you go into

the breakfast room and sit down, you two. Have some tea while you're waiting—the kettle's just boiled."

David sat down across the table from Gabriel and made an effort at conversation. "The children. Aren't they up yet?"

"They're not here. Didn't I say? They've gone to Emily's parents in St. Albans for a week or so. They'll probably come back spoiled rotten. You know how grandparents are."

"I thought . . . well, I suppose I had the impression that Emily's parents lived around here. I don't know why."

"Oh, they used to. Emily grew up in this parish. But when her father retired a few years ago, they wanted to move out of London. They like it in St. Albans, but they quite miss the grandchildren." Gabriel poured the tea. "Do you take sugar, David? I don't remember."

"No, thanks."

It wasn't English Breakfast, but it was hot and strong, and as he sipped it David felt himself reviving a bit, regaining his equilibrium. In a few moments his breakfast was before him: eggs, bacon, sausages, tomato, sautéed mushrooms, fried bread. And then there was toast and homemade marmalade. Just the sort of breakfast he loved and so seldom got—his usual fare was cornflakes—but he found he wasn't very hungry.

Emily sat down beside him. "When did you come down from . . . Norwich, isn't it?"

"Just outside. Wymondham. Yesterday."

"Oh, Wymondham, that's right. How long have you lived in Wymondham? You were in Brighton at the same time as Gabriel, weren't you?"

"Yes, I . . . knew . . . Gabriel in Brighton. But I grew up in Wymondham, and went back to look after my mother, when my father died. That was nearly ten years ago."

"Wymondham is somewhere I've always wanted to see. The abbey is supposed to be splendid."

"It is splendid. You must come up to stay some weekend," he found himself saying, totally against his will.

"We'd like that very much, wouldn't we, Gabriel?"

"Of course."

"Perhaps in the autumn, if you really mean it," she went on. "We could leave the children with my parents for the weekend. I don't imagine you're up to entertaining six-year-old twins, are you?"

The thought filled him with utter horror, but he replied politely, "I'm sure I could manage, if you wanted to bring them." He couldn't resist adding, "This time I'd have a proper guest room to offer you, Gabriel."

"Oh, have you been before, darling? I hadn't realized."

Gabriel shot him a warning look. "Yes, once," he said lightly. "Twelve or thirteen years ago—I'm surprised I've never mentioned it to you."

David addressed himself to Emily, enjoying Gabriel's discomfiture in spite of himself. "He was a great hit with my parents. My mother thought he was quite the nicest young man she'd ever met. She always hoped he'd come back one day; in fact, after my father died, she had his room converted into a guest room, just in case 'that lovely young clergyman' came again."

"And you never went. Gabriel, that was very naughty of you. And now your poor mother's dead," she went on with feeling. "David, I *am* sorry. How long has it been?"

"Almost two months." David hated facile sympathy, but Emily's warmth nearly brought tears to his eyes. He changed the subject abruptly. "Do you usually have a bigger congregation than that for your weekday Masses? Or is that the norm?"

"Generally a few more than that, but the weather does discourage some people. We've got quite an elderly congregation, by and large, and a lot of them don't like to come out when it's wet."

"Who was there?" Emily asked with interest.

"A most peculiar old woman," David stated. "She kept swapping seats."

"Beryl Ball." Emily laughed. "She has to make sure she has the best view of Gabriel."

Gabriel nodded. "Lady Constance, of course. She's invited David and Daphne to supper on Monday."

"My, but you're the honored one! I shall want to hear all about it. You must remember everything she serves so you can tell me."

"I'll try."

Gabriel continued, "Aside from that, it was only the Dawsons. And Venerable serving, of course."

They chatted back and forth, amiably, about church affairs; David stopped listening and became involved in his own thoughts. Seeing Gabe in this cozy domestic situation was infinitely more painful than the scenario he had imagined, the "marriage of convenience" he had so desperately wanted to believe in. But confused as his emotions were, and unsure as he was about Gabe's true feelings, two things were clear to him: she doesn't know—not about Gabe and me, not about any of it; and, she really loves him. Crazy as it seemed, and with no real basis—he still had no idea why Gabe had sent for him—he suddenly found himself terrified for Emily.

He looked down and discovered that although he'd had no appetite, he had, in his abstraction, eaten every bite of his breakfast. "Would you like some more?" Emily was asking. "No?" She jumped up. "Then I'll leave you two old mates to talk about past times. I've got cakes to bake—the fête is a week from today, you know!"

Chapter 9

I will acknowledge my sin unto thee: and mine
unrighteousness have I not hid.
I said, I will confess my sins unto the Lord: and
so thou forgavest the wickedness of my sin.
Psalm 32:5–6

Gabriel ushered David into his study and into the most comfortable chair; he himself sat in the swivel chair at his desk. There followed a few seconds of uncomfortable silence as Gabriel, face averted, fingered first the paperweight and then the silver-framed photograph. "Here are the twins," he said abruptly, handing the photo to David.

"You have a lovely family, Gabriel," David stated gravely and without a hint of irony. He was wary, expecting anything and prepared for nothing.

Gabriel hesitated. "What . . . do you think of Emily?"

"I think she's lovely," was the sincere reply.

Gabriel's relief was visible. "I'd always hoped that you and Emily could be friends," he said awkwardly, looking out of the window. "Perhaps it's not too late."

Yes, David reflected, why not? He and Emily had a lot in common. They both loved the same man. The only difference between them was that Emily had Gabe, and he had . . . his memories. His mouth twisted bitterly at the cliché, so true and so uncomforting.

Gabriel turned back towards him. "I was very sorry to hear about your mother, David. Please accept my sincere sympathy on your loss."

The formal words, so devoid of real feeling, ignited a small spark of anger on his mother's behalf. It wasn't just him that Gabriel had deserted. This man had deliberately charmed his mother, won her over completely, and then abandoned her for the rest of her life. For the last thirteen years she'd been comparing him, David, unfavorably with the absent Gabriel, and blaming him somehow for Gabriel's failure to return. "She asked for you on her deathbed," he said softly. "She could never understand why you didn't come back as you'd promised."

Gabriel looked away again. "Then she never knew . . . about us?"

"No, of course not." He gave a short, dry laugh. "Not that she wouldn't have believed me capable of any depravity under the sun. But not the blameless Gabriel. Funny, isn't it? Why I didn't even know . . . what I was . . . until I met you?"

Gabriel made no reply; he clenched his fist around the paperweight and gazed out of the window. David looked at his exquisite profile and the words were wrenched out of him without his volition, words so heavy with pain that Gabriel flinched visibly. "There's never been anyone but you, Gabe. Never."

"I don't want to talk about it."

"What *do* you want to talk about, then? What am I doing here? Why did you send for me?"

Faced with the uncomfortable reality of David, Gabriel wondered about that himself. Was there any chance that David could actually do anything to help? Sending for him had been little more than grasping at straws: he realized that now. But it was too late to turn back.

Gabriel took a deep breath and turned to face him. "It was an impulse, really. I just didn't know where else to turn."

"But what's the problem? And how can *I* help?"

"I've had a letter—a threatening letter. I suppose you'd even call it a blackmail letter, though it doesn't ask for money. And I thought . . . well, I suppose I thought perhaps you could help me find out who wrote it," he finished lamely.

"How? I'm not a detective or a policeman. I'm only a humble country solicitor."

"But people talk to you, don't they? It's one of your great gifts—the ability to get along with so many different sorts of people, and to make them say things they wouldn't ordinarily say. That was my idea, I suppose: that you could go around and talk to people in the church, and see if you could work out who sent it. Anyway," he added, "when you've seen the letter, you'll understand why I couldn't possibly show it to anyone else."

"How do you know it was written by someone in the church?"

"It must have been. I don't see how it could be anyone else."

"Can I see the letter? I'm not promising anything, but if it will make you feel better to let me have a look at it . . ."

Gabriel released the catch of the secret drawer, as he'd

done so many times in solitude during the past few days, drew out the folded paper and handed it to David, then sat impassively as he read the typed lines in silence. Gabriel knew the ugly words off by heart.

> I know about Peter Maitland, and what you did to him. You are responsible for his death, as surely as if you had killed him yourself. You are a disgrace to your sacred calling, and have brought dishonor on yourself, the Church of England, and St. Anne's. If you do not resign your living and leave the priesthood by the Feast of Assumption, I will see that your wife, the Bishop, and the national newspapers know about Peter Maitland and how he died.

David read it through several times and still the words made no sense to him. Peter Maitland. The name meant nothing at all. Peter Maitland. Dead? What did it all mean? He raised puzzled eyes to Gabriel's still face. "Peter Maitland? Who is . . . was . . . he?"

Gabriel hardly knew how to explain. Things had always been so simple for David, he thought. His approach to life and love had always been very uncomplicated: He had loved Gabriel, and that was all there was to it. He had never been able to—would never be able to—understand Gabriel's more complex needs, never be able to understand that his love for David had represented only a part of his nature, and that there was another side of him that had needed something else. David wouldn't understand about Peter, any more than he understood about Emily. He would have to be as factual as possible, remove the emotional content from the story he was about to tell.

And so Gabriel's voice was entirely matter-of-fact as he related the story; he might have been reading Emily's grocery list for all the emotion he displayed. "He was a boy I knew in Brighton. You never knew him. I met him . . . well, it doesn't really matter how I met him. He was young, inexperienced—but he pursued me—he thought he was in love with me. Maybe he was. I thought it was a lark. Things were . . . well, things had got a little stale, a little predictable . . . between you and me, and I was ready for a bit of excitement. It was fine at first. I was intrigued by him—he was very beautiful, very eager. But he didn't know how to handle it. He wanted more and more. He didn't understand that making love to him was . . . fun, but it just wasn't that important to me. I was afraid that he might become indiscreet. I told him I wouldn't see him again. He wrote to me, asked me to meet him on the beach one night. He said if I didn't come he'd kill himself. I didn't go. I thought he was just being dramatic to get my attention. Two days later his body washed up. I read about it in the newspaper. There were no signs of foul play, as they say, and the inquest recorded a verdict of accidental death. My name was never mentioned. I knew it wasn't my responsibility—it was his own choice. I was guilty of bad judgement and foolish behavior, nothing more. But it hit me pretty hard, I don't mind telling you, and I wanted to get away, to have a fresh start. I pulled every string I could to get out of Brighton. My spiritual director . . . well, I was lucky enough to get the living of St. Anne's very quickly. So I came here, I met Emily. I started again. There's no point in living in the past, David.''

David remembered reading somewhere that men who have limbs blown off in battle don't feel a thing at the time; the only way for the body to cope with such intense, immediate pain is to postpone it. With great detachment, he thought that the mind must be the same. He heard Gabriel's terse words, he understood their meaning perfectly well, and yet . . . Later on this is going to hurt, he realized. Later on, when I've absorbed it, I will wish I were dead.

He had no consciousness of speaking; he heard his own voice from far off as though it were coming from another room. ''Emily. What does she say about this?''

Gabriel's face and voice finally registered emotion. ''Good Lord, David! How could you even imagine that she could know about it? She just couldn't cope with it!''

What about me? ''Then how do you propose to explain to

her what I'm doing? My going about asking questions won't work if people know that I know you. Emily knows that we're friends—what's to stop her telling the whole parish?''

"I'll have a word with her—that won't be a problem. Emily can be very discreet."

"I can see you've made a good choice for your wife." David closed his eyes briefly, then continued. "There's not much time. The Feast of Assumption is only two and a half weeks away. Do you have any idea who might have written the letter?"

Frowning, Gabriel replied slowly, "I haven't thought about much else all week. And I'm at a total loss. First of all, there's the question of motive. Who could hate me that much, and why?"

"And?"

"I just can't think. That's where you come in, really. Maybe you can catch someone in an unguarded moment."

"But that's not the only question, is it?"

"No, and this is the real problem." Gabriel spread his hands, palms up. "You see, until a few minutes ago, I have never told a living soul about Peter Maitland. Who could possibly know?"

* * *

After David had gone, Gabriel sat for a very long time, looking out of the window. Eventually there was a tap on the door.

"Oh, David's gone, has he? I was going to offer you some coffee." Emily entered the study, encircled her husband with her arms, and laid her cheek on the top of his head. He pulled her on to his lap and kissed her, lightly at first but with increasing urgency; presently he murmured, "Forget the coffee, my love. Let's go upstairs."

Chapter 10

*For it was not an open enemy, that hath done me
this dishonor: for then I could have borne it.
Neither was it mine adversary, that did magnify
himself against me: for then peradventure I would
have hid myself from him.
But it was even thou, my companion: my guide,
and mine own familiar friend.
We took sweet counsel together: and walked in the
house of God as friends.*

Psalm 55:12–15

David had left his umbrella at the vicarage, but he was
oblivious to the soft rain which fell as he walked blindly
through Kensington Gardens. There were many more people
about than there had been earlier that morning, in spite of
the weather; however, no one gave a second look at the
solitary man, hands jammed in his pockets, who walked
back and forth, up and down. At one point the thought
crossed his mind that Daphne might be wondering where he
was, might have breakfast—or lunch—waiting for him. But
he knew also that Daphne would never ask questions, and
so he walked on.

After a while, he left the park and wandered instead
through the streets of Bayswater, up the main roads through
bustling crowds of people, past greengrocers and gourmet
delicatessens, antique shops and wine merchants, fast-food
take-aways and pizzerias, and then around the back streets,
past row upon row of terraced houses, bleak in the rain.
Ordinarily he would have taken a great interest in the

multifaceted personality of London, but today he was completely unaware of his surroundings.

Without conscious thought, he found himself eventually back in front of St. Anne's for the second time that morning. After a moment's hesitation he went in, realizing suddenly that he was quite wet. The church seemed empty, though someone was playing the organ softly; David thought the piece sounded like Messiaen. A lingering scent of incense mingled with the smell of fresh flowers and the lemony tang of furniture polish. With no sunlight to illuminate them, the stained glass windows looked muddy, the faces lifeless. But a spotlight on the rood screen emphasized its rich colors while casting distorted shadows high up on the chancel wall of the crucifix, with its limp tortured figure, and the mutely agonized postures of Our Lady and St. John. David genuflected to the altar and the flickering Sacrament lamp, then crossed into the Lady Chapel. He automatically went to the votive rack, felt in his pocket for a coin, and lit a candle for his mother. She wouldn't have approved of such popish nonsense, he knew, but it made him feel better to have done it.

When he turned around at last, he discovered with a start that he wasn't alone in the chapel. A sharp-featured woman with drab grey hair was looking critically at a half-finished flower arrangement on a large pedestal. She added another spray of greenery with a stabbing motion of ill-concealed hostility. David would have fled, but she caught his retreat out of the corner of her eye and turned to speak to him. "It's no good, is it?" she demanded.

"It looks just fine to me. Of course, I'm not much of a judge," he replied diplomatically. "What seems to be the matter with it?"

"I just don't have enough flowers. The Vicar's wife was supposed to bring in some from the vicarage garden, and help with the arranging, I might add, but she hasn't shown up!"

David felt absurdly defensive on Emily's behalf. "I'm sure there must be a good reason," he offered. "Perhaps some emergency..."

The woman snorted dismissively. "This younger generation just has no sense of responsibility. As my Arthur says, a man's word should be his bond. If you say you're going to do something, you must do it."

David, seeing that this conversation was leading nowhere, said, "Well, I think the flowers look fine," and made his escape towards the stairs down to the crypt chapel. But before he'd reached his goal, an absurdly tall, thin man with enormous round gold-rimmed spectacles came hurtling towards him from across the chancel. "I say, you don't have a fag on you, do you?" the man accosted him fiercely.

"I beg your pardon?" David replied, startled.

"A cigarette!" the man repeated, a little more loudly, as though David were deaf.

"No, I'm sorry. I don't smoke."

"Damn. My wife must have pinched mine from my jacket pocket, and I'm absolutely gasping for a smoke!" The man, towering above him, flung out his arms in a massive gesture of despair. "Wives!" he groaned dramatically. "Are you married?"

"No, I'm afraid not."

"Well, if you're smart you'll keep that way. Wives—they're more trouble than they're worth!" And with that the man turned and sprinted back across the chancel; shortly the tones of the organ were once again heard.

David stared after him a moment, bemused, then went down the steps to the crypt. The sound of the organ faded gradually as he descended, and when he reached the chapel he felt a welcome solitude surrounding him in the blue and gold silence. The gilded angels on the riddel posts of the altar, and the serene saints in their niches, were his only companions. He knelt.

For a long time his mind remained mercifully blank, empty of thought and empty of emotion. But suddenly, blindingly, it was all there. All the knowledge, all the pain that his mind had been suppressing in the hours—how many?—since this morning. As he replayed in his head all that Gabriel had said, the terse sentences exploded one by one like fireworks in his mind, illuminating corners that had been dark for over ten years. It explained everything. Why had he been so blind at the time? Why had he not sensed Gabe's boredom with their relationship, understood his need for excitement? How had he failed to read all the signs? It must have been his inexperience, his natural inclination to take people at face value, his belief in the uniqueness and completeness of their love—for both of them. All the pieces fell into place; the inexplicable was explained. Gabe's absences, his excuses, his gradual withdrawal. Those few terrifying weeks of alienation and silence, and then . . . Gabe was gone. Practically overnight, gone from his life with scarcely a word; the first communication he'd had from him had been the wedding invitation, a few months later. All these years he'd lived with the fear that it was his fault somehow, that he'd failed Gabe, hadn't loved him enough, and now . . . was he free of blame? If he'd understood Gabe half as well as he'd loved him, would all this have been prevented? "There's no point in living in the past, David."

That was easy enough for Gabe to say. Gabe, who had an enviable present and a bright future. But David's past was Gabe, and his present was . . . emptiness. His future? He didn't even want to contemplate that. His impulse was to flee right now, back to Wymondham, back home. But was there any escape from the pain? Or, for that matter, from the love? Could he stop loving Gabe now, even if he wanted to?

He lost track of time as he stayed on his knees, trying to work out what to do. Did he owe it to Gabe to stay and help him, to make up for the way he'd failed him? Or did Gabe deserve to be abandoned to his fate? And what about Emily? She was truly the innocent party in all this—she must be protected. But Gabe had married her—let him deal with it. She was Gabe's responsibility, not his.

A soft step on the stairs tore his eyes from the crucifix on the altar and he half rose, looking at the door, as Emily tentatively entered. "Oh, it is you, David," she greeted him. "Cecily said that a man had come down here, and I thought it might be you. I didn't mean to disturb your prayers."

"Oh, that's all right, Emily. I had finished." He smiled at her. "So you finally made it with your flowers? That woman wasn't very happy with you."

Emily looked embarrassed. "I was . . . delayed."

"I told her that probably something had come up at home."

She bit her lip to suppress a smile. "Yes, you could say that. But I've made my apologies, and I think I've been forgiven. Cecily's a bit intimidating, but I'm used to her. I hope she wasn't too hard on you."

"Not at all. But that chap—I think he was the organist—"

She laughed. "Oh, no, Miles hasn't been having a go at you, has he?"

"He was trying to scrounge a cigarette. I thought he was a bit peculiar."

Emily shook her head. "Don't worry about Miles—he's perfectly harmless. Just a bit obsessive, that's all. And he smokes like a fiend."

"He's a good organist."

"Yes, very good. He was the organist at Selby Cathedral, before he came to us." She made a comical face. "According to Miles, everything at Selby was absolute perfection. He almost expects you to genuflect when he mentions the sacred name of Selby."

"If it was so wonderful, why did he leave?"

Emily laughed again, "Oh, here he has so much more scope for complaint! And complaint is what he lives for."

David marvelled at the sympathy that there was between them, as she sat down next to him. "Gabriel's very lucky to have a wife who can share his work," he said impulsively.

She smiled and looked thoughtful. "But he doesn't really have what I'd call friends. That's why I'm so glad you've come. I think it will do him a world of good to have you to talk to."

"He talks to you."

"Yes, but that's not quite the same. There are some things that I can only tell my friend Lucy, and I'm sure there are some things that he'd only tell another man. You're good for him, David." She regarded him earnestly. "I can tell a difference in his mood already, since you've been here. He's explained to me that you're on a little private mission, and you don't want people in the church to know that you're friends. But I must tell you how grateful I am for your friendship, and how glad I am that you're here."

Although his better judgement told him to get in his car and drive away while there was still time, as he met her brown eyes, David knew that he had no choice but to stay.

Chapter 11

O remember not the sins and offenses of my youth:
but according to thy mercy think thou upon me,
O Lord, for thy goodness.

Psalm 25:6

The remains of a veritable orgy of Sunday paper reading were strewn about the sitting room. Daphne, sated, looked over the tops of her half-moon reading glasses at David, nearly asleep in his chair. "Are you ready for some tea?"

"Mm." He roused himself a bit when a fragrant mug of Earl Grey appeared in front of him several minutes later. "Sorry, Daphne. All of a sudden I just couldn't keep my eyes open." He yawned. "It was that excellent lunch, I'm sure—I suppose I ate too much. And you shouldn't be waiting on me like this, cooking for me, and bringing me tea. I'm perfectly capable of helping, you know."

Daphne looked horrified. "But you're my guest! I wouldn't dream of allowing you to help! Anyway, it's a pleasure to have someone to fuss over, for a change. I must admit, I don't usually bother with a proper Sunday lunch for myself."

"But how can you manage for the rest of the week, without leftover joint? Not that you've got much left over this week! It's a good thing we're going to Lady Constance's tomorrow."

"I wouldn't be surprised if you're asked out every night," Daphne teased him. "There seems to be a great deal of interest in the parish in that handsome young man who's come to take a look at the crypt chapel."

David grimaced. "Not very handsome, and not very young, but thanks anyway, Daphne."

"Miles Taylor seems to look on you as almost a personal protégé. He was going around telling everyone this morning that *he* discovered you."

David shook his head. "You certainly have a few odd characters at St. Anne's. The churchwardens, for instance—they're a strange pair, aren't they?"

"Cyril is an old dear, but I'm afraid he's a bit past it. He's gotten more and more vague over the last few years, but he won't even consider giving up the wardenship."

"Was it my imagination, or was he following Emily around the church hall after the service this morning?"

Daphne laughed indulgently. "That's not exactly a well-kept secret. He's adored her for years, or so I've heard. She's very patient with him."

"Well, he seems a harmless sort, anyway. There's something a bit terrifying about the woman."

"Mavis Conwell? Well, I'll admit, she's not exactly tact personified."

"I get the feeling that people don't like her much."

"That's probably a fair statement. She puts a lot of people's backs up with her comments sometimes. She's fairly renowned for her insensitivity."

"How on earth did she ever get elected churchwarden, then?"

"It was a sympathy vote, I suppose. Her husband died about a year ago, and she was at a loose end and really wanted the job—something to keep her busy, or maybe it was the prestige, or the power, that she wanted. There's certainly still a bit of both connected with being churchwarden, isn't there? Anyway, when the Annual Parochial Meeting came round, I don't think anybody else was that keen to do it, except perhaps Roger Dawson, and his wife is Mavis Conwell's friend, so he stepped aside. But a few people have lived to regret it, I dare say. Anyway, I try my best to keep out of parish politics. I'm only the Sacristan."

"You don't usually go to the eleven o'clock Mass, do you?"

"Not generally." She grimaced guiltily. "I must admit, I usually stay home and listen to the *Archers Omnibus* on Sunday morning! The Sacristan's job is really a doddle, with Venerable Bead always around wanting to take over. I polish the silver and look after the other bits during the week, though he takes care of early Mass every day, so I don't even have to deal with that. I usually go in on Saturday night and get things laid up for the eleven o'clock, and let Venerable have his fun clearing up afterwards. It all keeps him happy!" She shook her head. "I prefer the seven forty-five low Mass in the evening, anyway. But I must admit I'm glad that I've got it over with this morning and don't have to go out tonight."

"Then you're not going to Solemn Evensong and Benediction?" David asked.

Daphne raised her eyebrows. "You should know that SE and B has never been my style. I didn't think it was yours, particularly."

"Oh, well," he said, slightly shamefaced, "it isn't really, not in my own church anyway. But I think I'll go along, just the same, to see what it's all about."

She laughed. "David, I do believe that you're a spiritual thrill-seeker. Pass me your cup—it looks like you need more tea."

* * *

Solemn Evensong and Benediction might not be his favorite, but David had to admit that it was done very well at St. Anne's. The music was superb, the serving was flawless, and of course Gabriel handled the whole thing beautifully.

After the service, as he rose from his knees, David was approached by a young fair man dressed in a cassock. "Hello, we haven't yet been introduced. I'm Tony Kent."

"David Middleton-Brown. You're the head server, aren't you? I must congratulate you on your team of servers—I think they're the best I've ever seen."

Tony beamed; he took great pride in his servers, and spent much time training and rehearsing them in the complex choreography of the Mass. "It's very kind of you to say that. A lot of credit has to go to the Vicar—he sets very high standards. Fortunately, we're not short of volunteers, so we can pick the best." He paused, then went on impulsively, "Listen David, why don't you join us at the pub? We usually have a pint down at the Rose and Crown after SE and B. How about it? I'll buy you a drink."

"The magic words. Yes, why not?"

"Terrific. I'll be with you just as soon as I can get out of this gear."

David wondered briefly about the wisdom of falling in with this high-spirited young crowd, as they chattered their way down the road to the Rose and Crown. But it was all in the interest of information-gathering, after all, and he felt that he could use a drink.

They quickly settled in the corner of the pub with their drinks. Most of the young men were drinking pints; his double whisky made David feel far removed from their generation. But they welcomed him readily.

"Where are you from, David?" the young ginger-haired chap asked.

"Wymondham, near Norwich."

"The abbey?" inquired Tony with interest. "I'll bet the serving there is of pretty high standard."

"Yes, it's not bad."

"Were you ever a server there?"

David twisted his glass around on the table. "A long time ago," he admitted. "When I was in my teens—a little younger than most of you. And I served for a while at . . . a church in Brighton."

"Oh, our Vicar did a curacy in Brighton," interposed the dark-haired one called Chris (or was it Johnnie?). "At St. Dunstan's, I think."

"There are a lot of churches in Brighton," David said quickly—almost too quickly. "And I was there a very long time ago."

"You're not *that* old! You talk like you're about as old as Venerable Bead!" said the ginger-haired one.

David welcomed the opportunity to change the subject.

"Is he the old chap? Where is he now? Or does he stay away from these gatherings?"

"He insists on doing the seven forty-five low Mass," Tony explained. "He'll be along as soon as it's finished. Gabriel never lingers long over the seven forty-five."

"Before he gets here, tell David the story of Venerable and the Bishop," urged one of the young servers who hadn't spoken before.

Johnnie and Chris both leaned forward eagerly. "Yes, you must hear this one," the dark-haired one began.

The ginger-haired one continued. "It was a visit by the Area Bishop a few years ago."

"Not the one we've got now—he's new."

They tossed the narrative back and forth between them. "This one was a veritable prot—a real evangelical."

"He didn't even like to wear a mitre . . ."

"He wore a little, apologetic one—it looked more like a tea-cosy!"

"Anyway, the Bishop pulls up in front of St. Anne's in his car."

"It was a really ordinary car, too—a Sierra or something."

"He gets out of his car. You can only just about tell that he's the Bishop and not the chauffeur . . ."

"Because he's wearing a purple shirt with a dog-collar."

"Not even a cassock!"

"Well, Venerable's been hanging around the west door, waiting for the Bishop."

"He's all dressed up in a cassock and cotta . . ."

"With a couple of feet of lace on it at least!"

"Old Venerable goes dashing out . . ."

"Just as the Bishop's getting his case out of the boot."

"And right there in the middle of the road . . ."

"He goes down on one knee!" they both roared together.

"And grabs the Bishop's hand . . ."

"And kisses his ring!"

"You've never seen anything like the look on the Bishop's face!"

"Pure horror!"

"Then Venerable says, 'Your Worship, let me take that,' and grabs for the Bishop's case."

"But the Bishop won't let go . . ."

"And the case goes flying into the road!"

David joined in the contagious laughter. Tony shook his head at the two ebullient storytellers. "Poor old Venerable, he'll never live that one down."

Presently, David looked around and said, "It looks like it's time for another round. I'll buy." His head full of drink orders, he made his way towards the bar.

Before he reached his goal, he encountered a most unlikely patron of the Rose and Crown—it was unmistakably Mavis Conwell, with her close-set sharp eyes, her inexpertly dyed rusty-black hair, and her rat-trap mouth. She was looking around with a furrowed brow, and didn't see him at first. But just as he thought he might slip by unannounced, she grabbed his arm. "Mr. Middleton-Brown!"

"Good evening, Mrs. Conwell." He thought with a sinking heart that she was going to expect him to buy her a drink.

But his fears were unfounded. "I'm looking for my son—my boy Craig. He hasn't been home this afternoon, and I thought maybe he'd come down to the local. But you don't know my Craig, do you? So that's no help. And I'm certainly not going to ask *them* if they've seen him," she added, with a malevolent look at the servers in their corner. She lowered her voice and looked earnestly at David. "Would you like a word of advice? Stay away from *them*. Everyone knows what they are, and if you're seen with them, people might think you're . . . well, like that." She bared her teeth in a smile. "And I know you're not."

David regarded her with bafflement; he didn't have any idea what she was hinting at. "It's very kind of you to take such an interest in my reputation, but . . ."

"Even the Vicar knows better than to be seen with *them*, and no one would ever think of saying that the Vicar was . . . like that. He leaves it to his wife to counsel them. A very wise man, our Vicar."

"Well, it was nice seeing you, Mrs. Conwell. I'm sorry I

can't help with your son. I hope you find him," he said, disengaging himself and continuing towards the bar, desperate by now for another drink. He found her attitude towards the servers inexplicable: They exhibited youthful high spirits, certainly, but nothing more sinister than that. What was the woman going on about?

The servers greeted his return with increased hilarity. "Trying to pick up women, are you, David?" laughed the ginger-haired one.

"Couldn't you do any better than Mavis Conwell?" the dark-haired one added.

"She was looking for her son, she said."

"Oooh, the manly Craig," said the ginger-haired one.

"What is this Craig like?" David asked curiously.

"He's a very nasty piece of work," Tony replied. "She thinks that the sun rises and sets in him, as you might have guessed, but he's a right little bastard."

"Who do you suppose I've just seen on my way in?" interrupted Venerable Bead as he plodded up to the table, drink in hand. "Mavis Conwell! She was going on again about Norman Newsome. She thinks he ought to be kicked out of the Church. Imagine—a man with such a gift for liturgy!"

"And such an eye for choirboys," added Johnnie wickedly.

Tony looked stern. "Boys, this is all very funny, I'm sure, but we have a guest tonight. What will he think of us?"

"Not at all," said David. "It's all been most . . . illuminating."

Chapter 12

*Yea, because of the house of the Lord our God: I
will seek to do thee good.*

Psalm 122:9

Having resolved to spend the day on Monday on his ostensible mission of the crypt chapel, David found himself in an absurdly good mood. The servers' high spirits of the previous evening had been contagious, and after all he was engaged in work in which he had a passionate interest. So he pottered about the chapel contentedly all morning, making notes on a pad of paper and whistling something that sounded curiously like Byrd's "Ave Verum" under his breath. Of Gabriel and his problem he thought not at all.

The only interruption to his concentration came when Percy Bead, hearing suspicious noises coming from the chapel, made his way down the stairs to investigate.

"Oh, David, it's you."

"Good morning, Mr. Bead," David greeted him cheerily. "Lovely day, isn't it? It actually looks as though we might get some sun."

"Call me Venerable, please. Everybody does."

"Do you mind that?"

"It's an honorable title," the old man chuckled. "There are some, our Vicar for one, who would give a great deal to be called Venerable," he added slyly.

Recalled unwillingly to thoughts of Gabriel and his responsibility to him, David decided to make the most of the voluble old man's presence.

"And do you think that's likely to happen? That he'll be named Archdeacon?"

"I don't know why not. He's served ten years at St. Anne's—that's a long time in this diocese. He's well regarded by the powers-that-be, I think."

"What sort of reputation does he have?" David asked curiously. "In the diocese, I mean."

"I know a lot of the bigwigs—I get around, you know," explained Venerable with a falsely modest smile. "Father Gabriel is considered to be a hard working priest—a good parish priest—and something of a scholar. He's written a couple of obscure theological books, you know."

"No, I didn't realize that," David replied, surprised. He knew, of course, that Gabriel would excel at anything to which he applied himself, but somehow he'd never imagined him getting involved in the finer points of theology. "And what about the congregation? What do they think of him?"

Venerable was not the least suspicious of this line of questioning; to him this type of clerical gossip was the most natural thing in the world. "His sermons are famous—he's the best preacher I've ever heard, and I've heard a few! Personally, he's very well liked. Loved, I'd say. Especially by the ladies, who can't resist those blue eyes!" he added with a chuckle. "My wife—God rest her soul—used to say that no man ought to have eyes like that! And more charm than a man ought to have! It's a lucky thing for him he's got a wife—and I have to say, he didn't waste any time finding one after he got here—or he'd have ladies on his doorstep day and night."

"Then he didn't have a wife when he got here?" David asked ingenuously.

"No indeed. One or two people even thought he might be . . . not the marrying sort, if you know what I mean. But he soon proved them wrong. Almost indecent haste, it was. But they make a lovely couple, don't you think? Or haven't you met the Vicar's wife?"

"Yes, I have. I've found her very . . . pleasant."

"Emily's a good sport. She's always been nice to the servers—and she and Tony are good friends."

"Tony seems a very nice chap," David remarked.

"Oh, Tony's the best. He really knows about serving. Of course, I've taught him a lot, but he's got a real gift for it. He keeps the other chaps in line."

"He's not married?" David asked.

"He may as well be: He's got a boyfriend, if that's the correct term, that he lives with. Ian—that's the chap's name—often joins us down at the pub on a Sunday night, but he didn't come last night. He's not a churchgoer, so you won't see him around here."

"I quite enjoyed myself last night," David admitted. "I haven't laughed so much in years."

Venerable smiled in a paternal way. "Yes, the boys are a lovely bunch. We do have some good times." He didn't seem to find it at all unusual to include himself in their ranks.

"Mavis Conwell warned me about being seen with the servers. I didn't understand what she meant—they seemed fairly harmless to me."

The old man's eyes snapped. "Oh, she thinks just because Tony... that we're all that way! But she's wrong! Poisonous old..." He pursed his lips virtuously. "But I'm a Christian man, and I won't say what I think of her. Well, I'd better get back upstairs. The church wants tidying up after the weekend. People *will* come in and disturb things."

* * *

In the early afternoon, David decided to clear up a few obscure points by paying a visit to the reference collection of the Conservation Department at the Victoria & Albert Museum. He would cut through Kensington Gardens, he decided, skirting the Round Pond and emerging near the Albert Memorial, where he could cross Kensington Road and head down Exhibition Road to the V & A. It was a rather pleasant day, and he found himself walking slowly through the park, reflecting on the state of his inquiries to date.

On the whole, he decided, while he'd met some interesting people and learned some fascinating things, he had made no progress at all in finding the blackmailer. No one seemed to have any negative feelings about Gabe . . . rather the opposite, in fact, he reflected somewhat sourly. The man was apparently universally loved by his parishioners; no one would say a word against him. Perhaps his best bet would be in following the other line of inquiry: trying to discover who, by some means, had found out about Peter Maitland. It was all very well for Gabe to say that no one could have done; but someone clearly had. Probably the boy had talked to somebody, and mentioned Gabe's name, and somehow it had got to the ears of . . . whom? David wished that he could talk it over with someone; Daphne's common sense would be a great help in sorting out the options, but of course that would be impossible. Gabe would never agree, and he couldn't really blame him.

He dashed across Kensington Road, barely escaping death under the wheels of a red double-decker bus coming from the right, and a taxi coming from the left. After catching his breath, he noted a small florist's shop in a side street. He'd have to remember that on his way back—he must pick up some flowers for Lady Constance. Freesias, it would have to be—carnations just wouldn't do for someone like Lady Constance. He'd better get some for Daphne, too, while he was at it.

* * *

"Tell me a little bit about Lady Constance," David requested as they walked the short distance from Daphne's flat to the exclusive square, surrounded by tall white houses. "She's a widow, I assume?"

"Yes, for many years, apparently. Her husband was a wealthy industrialist—his family made their money from Victorian sweat-shops, I would have thought. It was their conscience-money that built St. Anne's."

"Oh, really?"

"Yes, it was her husband's grandfather or great-grandfather who founded and built the church and obviously he was willing to pay for the very best. Lady Constance has continued to take a close personal interest in St. Anne's—

we've been very lucky. Whenever we've needed money for anything, from new vestments to cleaning the rood screen, she's been more than generous. And of course most of the silver has been given by the Olivers, through the years.''

"Does she have any money in her own right?''

Daphne considered. "No, I don't think so. I believe that her father was some impoverished baronet, with hundreds of years of history but no money. But I'm not really sure about that.''

A maid opened the door as soon as he'd rung the bell, at eight o'clock sharp; they were ushered into the entrance hall of the Georgian house, as gracious on the inside as it was impressive on the outside.

Lady Constance met them at the door of the drawing room. "So nice to see you, Miss Elford, Mr. Middleton-Brown. Oh, freesias, how very lovely. My favorite. Thank you so much.'' An old gentleman rose as they entered the room. "Mr. Middleton-Brown, have you met Wing Commander Fitzjames?''

"Yes, we met briefly on Sunday. How nice to see you, Wing Commander.''

"My pleasure, my boy. Do call me Cyril. Good evening, Daphne. You're looking charming tonight, if I may say so.''

Invitations to sup with Lady Constance were not commonplace, and Daphne had made a real effort. Although she'd entertained fleetingly—then rejected—the radical notion of visiting the hairdresser, she had actually set her hair on rollers, and the result was not unbecoming. She had applied a bit of makeup, and was wearing her best dress; the dress had been bought several years ago for a nephew's wedding, and although its cost had seemed at the time, on her teacher's salary, somewhat excessive, it had seldom seen the light of day since. She'd felt slightly foolish taking the extra trouble with her appearance, but now was relieved that she'd done so—at least David wouldn't be too ashamed of her.

Lady Constance, of course, was her usual picture of unselfconscious elegance, in a well-cut dark dress and pearls. Sherry was offered and accepted, and there was the inevitable slight hesitation before polite conversation was initiated.

"Have you always lived in London, Lady Constance?" David inquired.

"My girlhood was spent in the country," she replied. "But I've lived in this house since my marriage, and I'm afraid I've become a real Londoner. One does become spoiled by all the amenities—the galleries, the concerts, the ballet, and of course the shops. One misses it all dreadfully, I fear. I've only been away from London once for more than a short holiday, when I looked after my brother in his final illness. I tried to persuade him to come here, where he could be properly seen to, but he just wouldn't leave his parish, even at the end. Lewes is not a bad place, but it was such a relief to get back."

"Oh, I remember!" Daphne exclaimed. "That must have been my first summer here, two years ago. There was all that problem with the fête because you weren't here to open it!"

Cyril gave a loud, throaty chuckle. "That fête! What a disaster! At the PCC meeting, when we realized that we had no one to open the fête, everyone had their little idea about who should be asked. The argument went on for hours, as I remember it, and afterwards everyone thought that someone else was taking care of it, but in the end no one did, so no one showed up on the day to do the honors!"

"And it rained," Daphne added.

"Didn't it just!" Cyril chortled. "Absolutely teemed, all day. Had to have it in the church hall, and of course no one came that didn't have to."

"The 'fête worse than death,' Father Neville still calls it," Lady Constance said with a wry smile. "I'm sure he still holds me personally responsible."

"You *will* be doing the honors this Saturday, I assume?" Cyril laughed.

"Oh certainly. I wouldn't miss it. I do hope we have good weather this year. It's so much nicer when the teas can be held in the vicarage garden."

In due time they moved to the dining room. "Just a simple cold supper," Lady Constance apologized. "I do hope you don't mind." The "simple cold supper" included asparagus vinaigrette and smoked salmon, as well as a bottle of fine vintage wine, and finished with an exquisite homemade sorbet, so David minded not at all.

"I'm curious," Cyril said, as they neared the end of the meal. "How did you and Daphne get to know each other?"

"Oh, we go back a long way, don't we, Daphne?"

"Over twenty years," she confirmed.

Lady Constance looked interested, though her good breeding prevented her from asking any probing questions. Cyril, though, had no such inhibitions. "Where did you meet?"

They looked at each other and laughed. "In a church, of course!" Daphne replied. "Here in London."

"I was at university, and Daphne was teaching. We found that we had a mutual interest in churches—architecture, furnishings, the lot—and we became great chums. I was a young ignoramus—I loved it all, but I didn't know much about it—and Daphne knew so much. She took me under her wing. We did quite a bit of traveling, exploring..."

"And before I knew it, he had passed me by!" Daphne added ruefully.

"Which brings us to the crypt chapel," Lady Constance interposed. "What do you have to tell me about that, young man?"

David pulled some papers out of his breast pocket. "I must warn you that I'm not a professional," he said with a self-deprecating smile. "I've never done anything like this before. But I'm tremendously excited about it." He indicated the papers. "I've brought a few notes to show you. I must tell you I'm very impressed by the chapel. It was done fairly early in Comper's career, before he reached his mature genius, but it shows all the marks of his style, in the very best sense of that term. His characteristic use of blue and gold, the lavish, not to say reckless, application of gold leaf, the wonderful angels..." Soon he was involved in technical detail about paint and gilding, fabrics and embroidery.

Lady Constance asked intelligent questions but mostly listened, impressed by his expertise. At last she said, "You clearly know what you're about. Go ahead and engage whatever craftsmen you need to do the work, and I will happily pay the bills. All I ask is that you supervise the work to make sure it's done properly."

David nodded, satisfied.

"And now, Miss Elford, don't you think we ought to leave the gentlemen to their port for a while?"

After the ladies had gone, David said conversationally, "I understand that you've been churchwarden at St. Anne's for a long time."

"Donkey's years, my boy. I've seen Vicars come, and Vicars go."

"I've heard rumors that Father Neville might not be around much longer."

Cyril sighed lugubriously, and shook his head. "I dread the thought. Don't get me wrong, my boy. He's a jolly good priest, and I like him very much. But I just can't imagine life around here without . . . Mrs. Neville. Emily."

"You've known her a long time?"

"Practically all her life, I suppose. I remember her as a little girl—a tiny little thing she was. Her father and I were great friends. He lives in St. Albans now—I don't see him very often. But in those days . . . well. As I say, she was a lovely little thing. Enchanting girl, Emily Bates. And then, after my wife died it was, she came back from university, and I was just bowled over! She was still tiny and delicate, but she'd grown into the most exquisite young woman." He looked at David over his wine glass; his rheumy old eyes were filled with misty tears. "I had a bit more to offer in those days. And I thought—well, I don't mind telling you, my boy, I had my hopes."

"What happened?"

He shook his head again, more slowly. "He came. Gabriel Neville came. No other man stood a chance against him. I don't blame her, mind. But . . . well, I had my hopes," he repeated forlornly.

David topped up the port glasses and made meaningless comforting noises. He realized with a start that this old man was the first person he'd found who actually had a reason to hate Gabriel. The oldest motive in the book . . . But what could he possibly hope to gain by driving Gabriel (and

Emily) away from St. Anne's? And how could he know about Peter Maitland?

Chapter 13

Let his children be vagabonds and beg their bread:
let them seek it also out of desolate places.
Let the extortioner consume all that he hath: and
let the stranger spoil his labor.

Psalm 109:9–20

"Isn't it dreadful," David commented, buttering a morsel of toast and heaping it with marmalade. "I haven't been able to get myself up for early Mass yet this week."

"I shouldn't feel too guilty about it," Daphne replied as she poured him another cup of tea. "After all, it is your holiday."

"You should know by now that 'guilt' is my middle name," he said lightly. "I can feel guilty about anything. Sins of omission, sins of commission—they're all grist for my mill."

"So what are you going to do today?"

"Get to work making arrangements about the chapel, I should think. I say, Daphne, I couldn't talk you into making some phone calls for me, could I?" He looked slightly sheepish; she couldn't help laughing.

"I'll be glad to do what I can, but don't you think it would save a lot of time and effort for you to talk to these people yourself?" she said sensibly.

"I suppose you're right," he agreed reluctantly. "Maybe I could nip around and see some of them in person."

She shook her head in affectionate amusement. "Suit yourself. But don't forget that Tuesday is the day that they serve lunches in the church hall. You might enjoy coming—if you think you can stand another session with the inmates of St. Anne's.''

"Perhaps I will put in an appearance," he said. "Though I don't suppose I can expect gourmet fare."

"Quiche and salad, most likely. But it's usually very good. It's all homemade, and the sweets are generally excellent."

"You've convinced me. I'll catch up with you at lunchtime, then."

* * *

David entered the church hall, balancing a plate of quiche in one hand and an incredibly rich and delicious-looking sweet in the other. He was relieved to see a number of familiar faces in the crowded room, though, naturally enough on a weekday, there was a dearth of men. They mainly seemed to be concentrated at one table, and he started towards them. Venerable Bead was conversing earnestly with Tony Kent— David remembered that Tony was a teacher, and would be on his summer holidays—and Cyril Fitzjames sat with them, not joining in and evidently not even listening. David instinctively followed Cyril's gaze to another table. Yes, there was Emily, and with her Gabriel, and Daphne, trying to catch his eye and gesturing towards an empty seat. He sighed and made his way over to join them.

"David, sit down quickly!" Daphne greeted him. "I've had to fend off all sorts of people from your seat. I've just been telling Emily about our evening with Lady Constance."

"Hello, David," Emily put in. "She's got me drooling over the smoked salmon."

Gabriel acknowledged him with a nod. "Daphne tells me you've been hard at work over the chapel."

"Yes, it's a slow time of year for the workmen, and I think they'll actually be able to begin work by next week sometime."

"That's splendid news," Gabriel said heartily. "And now, if you'll all excuse me, I want to get home and start on my sermon for Sunday. I can't afford to leave it to much later in the week, with the fête coming up. See you later, darling," he added to his wife; they all watched his tall cassocked figure leave the room before resuming their conversation.

"Oh, the fête," Emily grimaced.

"Well, it can't be as bad as the 'fête worse than death,'" Daphne observed comfortingly.

Emily came back quickly, "No, but I'll still be glad this time next week when it's a 'fête accompli.'"

David laughed in appreciation. "What are your responsibilities?"

"Well, in the afternoon I have to oversee the teas in the vicarage garden, though I should have quite a few helpers. And in the morning I'm lumbered with the jam stall as usual. Lucy's offered to help me with that, fortunately. That way I can start getting organized for the teas in plenty of time."

"Is this one of Lucy's quiches?" Daphne asked, as she took a bite.

"No, it's one of mine, which means it's still Lucy's recipe," Emily replied. She explained to David. "My friend Lucy's a superb cook. She taught me how to cook when I got married. That sweet you've got is one of her specialties."

He eyed it with anticipation. "It looks wonderful. Just the sort of thing I shouldn't eat. Can't I meet this gourmet chef?"

"Oh, she's not here today. If you want to meet Lucy, you must come to the organ recital tomorrow. That's something she never misses—Lucy's a real music lover."

"Then I shall definitely come. Is this something that happens every week?"

"Yes, every Wednesday at lunchtime."

A woman approached their table, looking anxious. Initially David didn't recognize her, then realized that he'd never seen Julia Dawson without her husband before; she looked incomplete somehow. Her face reminded him of some nocturnal woodland animal, with its wide, startled-looking eyes, its long, pointed nose, and its receding chin. She didn't really look exactly like her husband, he decided: Roger Dawson had more resemblance to a predatory creature, a wolf perhaps, with his sharp, prominent teeth. It was their identical curdled-milk expressions and the overall greyness of them that gave that impression of likeness; both had straight, iron-grey hair, an unhealthy greyish tinge to their skin, and a way of moving that was both self-effacing and obtrusive. Julia Dawson was dressed in an unseasonal murky-colored jumper, as she sidled up to Emily purposefully.

"Have you been baking cakes?" she asked, with an intense quiver in her voice, completely out of proportion to the question.

"Oh, yes," Emily affirmed. "But my freezer's getting full, I'm afraid. I don't know if I'll have room for the ones I did this morning."

Julia stood stock-still, her face registering horror. "But that's terrible! What are you going to do?"

"Put them in someone else's freezer, I imagine."

"I can put them in *mine*. I can get them right now, if you're finished here." She looked at Emily's empty plate. "Running the cake stall is such a *responsibility*. You just can't imagine."

Emily rose, with a regretful smile for David and Daphne. "I'll see you tomorrow at the organ recital, then."

"She won't see me," Daphne stated as Emily departed.

"Why not? Don't you like Miles Taylor?"

Daphne looked at him shrewdly. "I'm not one of the old ladies in his fan club, if that's what you mean. He knows I haven't got any money, so he never bothers being nice to me."

"Are you saying . . ."

"I'm saying that he makes a great fuss over some of the old ladies, and they all adore him." She smiled blandly, inviting him to draw his own conclusions.

The two empty chairs at their table were now being claimed by Cecily Framlingham and Mavis Conwell. Mavis barely acknowledged their greeting; Cecily, too, virtually ignored their presence, but chatted volubly to Mavis. "It's too crowded today. I just don't know where all these people come from. I suppose it's this nasty weather that brings people indoors. It's just ruined the flowers, the frightful weather we've had this summer. I simply don't know what we'll have to sell on the flower stall at the fête." She turned to Mavis. "What have you got in your garden that might do?"

"Oh, I don't know," she replied offhandedly. "Not much, I suppose."

"How about the lobelia? Or the dianthus? I wish your antirrhinum were better this year. Maybe some of that artemisia—people like that for drying, don't they?"

"You can have whatever you like."

"We can always try to sell some of Arthur's marrows, if the worst comes to the worst. The rain doesn't seem to be doing *them* any harm."

Mavis made no reply. Frustrated by her friend's lack of response, Cecily tried a topic calculated to engage Mavis's interest. "Did you see that Norman Newsome has resigned? Arthur read it in this morning's newspaper."

Mavis' reaction to this bombshell was less than gratifying. "Oh, really?"

"Yes. Apparently the Dean decided there was no smoke without fire, if you know what I mean. That's what you've said all along, Mavis. No smoke without fire."

David, intrigued by her uncharacteristic silence, observed Mavis out of the corner of his eye as he ate—with great appreciation—his sweet. She seemed to be watching the entrance; she gave a little start and David raised his head in time to see a young man hesitate for a moment at the door, then slouch towards her. He was a well-built and good-looking young man, with coal-black hair worn very short, but there was an indefinable weakness around his mouth, and his posture was appalling. The manly Craig, David concluded, as he reached the table.

"Craig," his mother said flatly.

"Mum, where's the ten quid I asked you for? I need it now." He spoke in a low, urgent voice.

"I haven't got it, Craig. I told you I didn't have it." She looked frightened.

"But I need it! Well, give me a fiver then."

She scrabbled in her brown vinyl handbag, looking for

loose change. A couple of pound coins appeared, and a few odd coppers. "This is all I've got. You can have it."

He looked at the proffered coins with scorn. "Is that the best you can do? That's not much bloody good, is it?" His voice was low, but it carried.

"Craig, please! Not in church!" she hissed in an agonized whisper.

"Maybe I can help," Cecily interposed, pulling a five-pound note out of her handbag. "Consider it a loan, Mavis."

Craig took it from her, inspecting it with care. "I'll expect the other fiver tonight, Mum. Don't forget," he muttered ungraciously, and, glowering sullenly, turned and made his way out.

Most people who were close enough to hear anything of this exchange were looking down at their plates in embarrassment, but Beryl Ball, who had just come into the room, observed his departure with frank enjoyment.

She shuffled up to their table. "That's a fine boy you've got, Mavis. Quite a high-spirited lad." She nodded, smiled, and thrust her teeth out with her tongue.

David couldn't help raising his head and looking at her. She was dressed all in yellow, with a large-brimmed yellow hat. He stared involuntarily at the glassy-eyed canaries perched on its brim, as if ready to burst into song, or soar into flight.

"What are you looking at?" she challenged him loudly. "I know that look—you want me, don't you? Well, you can't have me! If I don't give in to the Vicar, I certainly won't give in to you! I've kept myself pure for over fifty years, young man! I have never been touched by a man!" With a majestic toss of her head, which sent the canaries bobbing, she turned and hobbled out of the room. Mavis took advantage of the distraction to escape, with Cecily close behind her.

David looked at Daphne with a bemused smile. "Well, I must say. You certainly put on a good show for visitors at this place. And I thought I was going to have a quiet lunch!"

Daphne shook her head. "Anything to keep you amused. It looks as though you're ready for a cup of tea. Shall I get it? Or would you rather have a coffee?"

"Tea would be lovely, thanks." He watched her make her way to the table with the urn. She stopped to speak to a woman who had just come in, and David observed the newcomer with quiet amusement. Barbara Pym, he thought. She looks exactly like someone out of Barbara Pym.

She was a large woman, tall and well upholstered though not fat. All of her clothes were just a bit too small for her; her dress encased her body tightly, and stopped just short of the knee, where a lace petticoat peeped out coyly, and she wore a white vinyl raincoat, also very tight and a bit shorter than the dress. Her face, topped by tightly permed white hair, was large and round, like an undercooked dumpling, with small features and pale gooseberry eyes. Her shoes were an old-fashioned brown, and as she approached with Daphne he noted that she walked slightly pigeon-toed, with small mincing steps that seemed quite out of keeping with her substantial frame.

Daphne introduced them. "Mary, this is my friend David Middleton-Brown. David, Miss Mary Hughes."

"Hello, David, it is so nice to meet you." Her voice was also unexpected: it was precious and slightly breathless.

"My pleasure, Miss Hughes. Are you joining us?" David rose gallantly and pulled out a chair for her.

He was rewarded with a look of extreme gratitude. "Oh, thank you. You're most kind." She sat down and leaned toward him confidingly; he got a not-unexpected whiff of Pears' Soap. "I do hope that Beryl hasn't upset you. Daphne tells me that you've had a little encounter."

"I've been assured that she's harmless," he replied.

"Oh, she is. I've known Beryl since we were girls together, if you can believe it!" She giggled in a coy way. "We were confirmed together in this church. That's been a few years ago, of course."

"Has she always been . . . like this?"

"Oh, Beryl has always been a bit peculiar, if you know what I mean. I suppose you've heard about all the men who have been in love with her. I wish I could tell you it was true!''

"You mean it's not?" Daphne was disillusioned, if not surprised.

"No, indeed. But she's always had a fixation about clergymen. All men, really—it's quite dreadful. '*Sex*,' " she whispered furtively. "It's unhinged her mind. Not having any, I mean." She blushed at her own candor.

* * *

"A whisky before bedtime is something Mother would never have approved of," David said, stretched out on Daphne's sofa.

Daphne refrained from saying that Mother was no longer around to approve or disapprove of anything that her son did. From her own observations, Daphne had concluded that Mother had done much more of the latter than the former, and not to her son's benefit. "Well, I approve heartily," was all she said.

"Tell me about Mary Hughes. She's so Barbara Pym."

"Yes, isn't she? One of her 'excellent women' types, but we have a lot of those at St. Anne's."

"What's her story?"

"I don't think there's that much to tell. Spinster, obviously. She looked after her aged parents until they died a few years ago. They left her well cared for financially, so she can now devote herself to the church and other 'good works.' She still lives in the house where she was born. She's a very well-meaning person, and usually gets lumbered with all the jobs that nobody else wants."

David pondered the events of the day. "I know I've promised Emily to go to that organ recital tomorrow, but in the morning I fancy getting away from it all. Do you realize that we haven't looked at a single London church since I've been here? How about it, Daphne? It's been years since we've done a London church crawl. You can show me your favorites. Let's get an early start. Well, a civilized start," he amended.

Chapter 14

Therefore will I praise thee and thy faithfulness, O God, playing upon an instrument of musick: unto thee will I sing upon the harp, O thou Holy One of Israel.

Psalm 71:20

Wednesday morning had passed too quickly; David and Daphne agreed to continue their leisurely progress through the London churches on the following day, and David arrived at St. Anne's in good time for the organ recital.

Mary Hughes handed him a program at the door. "This is your first time, isn't it, Mr. Middleton-Brown? You're in for quite a treat, I can tell you."

He glanced down the list of pieces. "Mm. Sounds very nice. A most ambitious program. Mr. Taylor is a very accomplished organist, I believe."

"Oh, yes, he's wonderful!"

He was surprised to see a sizeable audience gathering in the nave. There were many people he didn't recognize, and he assumed that the weekly event must draw in many regulars from outside the congregation.

Emily was waiting for him inside the door. "Here you are, David. The best seats are going fast!" She led him up the aisle and selected three seats. "We'll save one for Lucy."

"Is it always this well attended? I'm amazed to see so many people here on a weekday!"

"Oh, definitely. See that group over there?" She indicated a section of the prime seats, distinguished chiefly by the uniformly white heads of the inhabitants. "Lucy and I call that the Fan Club. They're all here every week."

David looked around curiously. "Is Miles's wife here?"

Emily laughed. "The mysterious Mrs. Taylor? Not a chance!"

"What do you mean?"

"Would you believe that no one at St. Anne's has ever seen his wife? Lucy and I think that he keeps her hidden away, so as not to damage his mystique with the Fan Club. The old ladies love him, you know."

David nodded. "So it would seem." He went on, "This really is an impressive crowd. Do you get many people from outside the church?"

"Well, there are quite a few people who work around here who come regularly, and then there's always the odd tourist who wanders in."

"You ought to charge admission."

"That's what Miles says. We do take a retiring collection, but he thinks that's not good enough."

An expectant hush had fallen; a few of the more eager members of the Fan Club were craning their necks towards the chancel. Mary Hughes abandoned her post at the door and hurried up the aisle to her seat amongst the Fan Club.

"Looks like Lucy's going to be late," Emily whispered.

Lucy slipped into the church halfway through the Bach Prelude and Fugue and decided to stand at the back until the end of the piece. She spotted Emily, with the empty seat beside her; on her other side there was a man she'd never seen before. She observed him with interest and wondered who he was.

During the applause at the end of the fugue, she moved to claim her seat beside Emily, and whispered introductions were made. There was just time enough for Lucy to get a quick impression of the man Emily said was called David Middleton-Brown. He was quite ordinary looking, distinguished by no particular beauty of form or feature. He appeared to be of an average height, and had brown hair, dusted with grey at the temples, and pleasant hazel eyes. But it was a nice face, Lucy decided—above all a kind face.

The recital continued. The final piece was a very dissonant and somewhat formless work that David found much more difficult to appreciate than the Bach. After he'd finished, the lanky organist descended into an eager crowd of admirers; Mary Hughes was in the forefront. "I didn't realize that Miss Hughes was such a great fan," David remarked, as they stood up.

"Definitely," Emily replied. "She thinks that our Miles is the 'bees' knees.'"

He turned to Lucy for the first time. "Emily tells me that you come every week. Don't you count as one of the Fan Club?"

She laughed. "No, not I. The man's organ playing is superb, but . . . well, he's just not my type. For that matter, I don't think I'm his type, either."

"Then that is his loss," David said gallantly, feeling a bit foolish as he said it. She smiled at him almost conspiratorially as Emily asked her a question about jams, and for a moment the two women were involved in a technical discussion of boiling points and pectins. Though he hadn't given her a great deal of thought prior to this meeting, Lucy wasn't really what he'd expected, David decided, watching them with their heads together, one dark and one rosy. He'd thought she'd be much like Emily, he supposed, but the two were very different, and not just in coloring. Emily was wearing what David had come to recognize as her preferred everyday garb—jeans and a loose cotton jumper—whereas Lucy was elegant in an ivory lawn blouse with a delicate antique lace collar and a calf-length flowered skirt in shades of willow green and apricot. There was something so graceful in the way she pushed her hair back from her face with her long tapering fingers. That incredible aureole of hair! She wasn't a girl, David realized. The network of tiny lines around her greeny-blue eyes told him that she would never see thirty again. But the quality of her beauty was not dependent on youth.

"Do forgive us, David," she said, turning to him with a charming smile. "We've been very rude, talking about jams

like that! But this fête seems to be overshadowing everything that happens around here at the moment.''

"Why don't you both come back to the vicarage and have
some tea?" Emily suggested. "Gabriel's out this afternoon,
and with the children away it would be nice to have some
company."

"That would be very nice," David accepted. "I don't
think Daphne's expecting me back just yet."

Lucy looked regretful. "I'm sorry, Em, but I really can't.
I started a painting this morning, and I must get back to it.
I'll tell you what, though—could you both come to me for
tea tomorrow afternoon? It might be finished by then, and
you can tell me what you think."

"Super, Luce. David, how about you?"

"I'd love to come, thank you."

"Lovely. I'll see you both tomorrow, then. It was very
nice to meet you, David." She smiled as they parted at the
church door.

"And you." His eyes followed her involuntarily as she
walked down the street and around the corner.

Emily tugged at his arm. "Come on, David. You can't
get out of having tea with me so easily."

He smiled down at her. "That's the farthest thing from
my mind."

In a few minutes they were settled in the drawing room at
the vicarage, sipping tea. "Have some of this cake, David."
She pulled a slightly guilty face. "If Julia Dawson finds out
I've been raiding the fête cakes . . ."

"She won't hear it from me," he assured her. "You can
consider it advance advertising. It's absolutely delicious,
and when the great day comes I intend to buy one exactly
like it."

"You'd better get there early, then. The cakes sell out
quite quickly."

"I'm sure I'll be there early. Seriously, is there any way I
can help on Saturday? I suppose all the stall assignments
have been fixed for months, but if there's anything I can
do . . ."

"Thanks, David. I'm certain that no volunteers will be

turned away! If you'd be willing to go where you were needed . . ."

"Yes, of course. I'll leave myself entirely in your hands." He looked around the drawing room with interest; it was the first time he'd been there. "This is a lovely room," he said. "Have you decorated it? Or was it like this when you moved in?"

"No, it was awful when I came—very dark and gloomy. It had been that way for years, I think, and Gabriel hadn't really been here long enough to do anything about it. But I couldn't bear it. It was my first try at decorating, with lots of help from Lucy."

"I suppose she's good at that sort of thing?"

"Very. Wait till you see her place—it's stunning."

"Did I understand correctly that she's some kind of artist?"

"Oh, yes. She does watercolors. Didn't I tell you? But they're not the sort of thing you'd expect. She'll show you some of her work tomorrow, if you're interested. Lucy's extremely talented. Her things are very much in demand, in certain circles—she makes quite a nice living from it, too."

He absorbed all this information in silence. "Does she live alone?"

"She's not married, if that's what you mean," Emily replied with a knowing smile. "She was married once, when she was quite young, but I don't think it lasted very long, and she never talks about it."

"Not even to you?"

"Not even to me. Lucy is a wonderful listener—people are always telling her their problems—but she very rarely talks about herself."

"Then she must be in much demand at St. Anne's. There seem to be a great many talkers there, and very few listeners."

"She doesn't spend a great deal of time at St. Anne's, to be honest. She's very much on the fringe."

"Why is that?"

Emily shrugged. "I'm not really sure. Her work, I

suppose—it keeps her quite busy. And her father was—still is—a Vicar, so maybe she's all churched out.''

"Do you think she feels ... well, would being divorced make any difference, as far as St. Anne's is concerned?''

Emily considered. "No, I don't think the divorce thing really bothers her much. A few of the congregation would mind about it: The Dawsons, for example, wouldn't approve at all. But Lucy wouldn't care if they approved or not— she'd think that was their problem, not hers.''

"It's easy to cast the first stone, isn't it?'' David mused. Emily looked at him questioningly, and, afraid he'd betrayed something, he quickly changed the subject. "Well, I'm looking forward to our tea tomorrow. I'm going out with Daphne in the morning, and don't know when I'll be back. Shall I stop by for you, or just meet you there?''

"It will be easier for you if you don't have to worry about me. I'll tell you how to get to Lucy's—it's not far.''

Chapter 15

Thou hast loved to speak all words that may do hurt: O thou false tongue.

Psalm 52:5

That evening, David felt a bit unsettled and restless, for no reason he could put his finger on. He tried to read the newspaper, and found it boring; he even attempted to watch television, something he rarely did. Finally he suggested to Daphne that they go out for a meal. "Forget about cooking tonight, why don't you. Let me take you out, Daphne. Do you have a favorite place?''

"We could get a Chinese take-away, and eat it here,'' she suggested.

He grimaced. "No, I'd like to go out. What's the matter—are you ashamed to be seen with me in public?"

"Oh, all right. I just thought . . ."

"Come on, then, Daphne. Where shall we go?"

"There are several pizza places down along Kensington High Street, if you like. Cheap and cheerful."

"It doesn't have to be cheap and cheerful. I'm quite happy to take you somewhere nice, if you like. You've been spoiling me—let me spoil you for a change!"

Daphne pulled a face. "Pizza is also quick, and I've just remembered that I promised to call and see Mavis Conwell this evening. We could stop there on the way back, if we don't take too long over our meal."

"Mavis Conwell? Whatever for?"

"I'm not sure," she replied. "She rang this afternoon, and was quite insistent that I come to see her. Or at least she wanted to see me, and I suggested that I go along there, rather than have her come here. I thought I might never get rid of her if she came here."

"Yes, at least we can make a speedy exit. She didn't give you any idea what it was about?"

"No. Just said she wanted to see me, and it had to be tonight. Well, we'll soon find out."

"Right, then. Let's go have a pizza, and maybe a bottle of wine, to fortify us for the loathsome Mrs. Conwell. Perhaps if we're lucky we'll have another glimpse of the manly Craig . . ."

* * *

The Conwells' house was a small terrace, in a street surprisingly close to St. Anne's and the splendid homes that surrounded the church. Property values in this part of London were so high that it was still worth a considerable amount of money, David surmised; he wondered what the late Mr. Conwell had done for a living.

Mavis opened the door to them quickly, almost as if she'd been waiting. Perhaps she'd seen them coming from a window.

"Oh, Daphne. Thank you for coming. And you've brought Mr. Middleton-Brown with you." She smiled her fierce, false smile at them. "You'd better be careful, Daphne. People will start talking about you. You wouldn't want that, would you? I mean, having a man to stay with you in your flat! Some people might think there was something in it! Of course, if anyone said anything like that to me, I'd set them straight for you." She looked back and forth between them speculatively, showing her teeth.

David could feel Daphne tense beside him; she was so furious that she was unable to speak. He had never known her to be at a loss for words, and marvelled at Mavis's ability to get at her.

"Good evening, Mrs. Conwell," he said smoothly. "I'm so sorry to come along without being invited, but we've just been out for a meal."

"Come in," she beckoned. "Have you been to someone's house, then? I know you were invited to Lady Constance's on Monday. Cyril told me. I'm sure that lots of people are jealous of Daphne, having you all to herself." She smiled at him again, coyly this time. "Especially when there are other eligible women around who are closer to your own age!"

He was repelled by her implication, as she stood there grinning at him, and he felt incensed on Daphne's behalf. When neither of them spoke, Mavis ushered them into the room on the right of the entrance hall. It was a small sitting room, neat as a pin.

"Would either of you like a coffee?" Mavis offered.

David nodded, out of a desire to get rid of her for a few minutes rather than from a need for coffee.

Daphne nearly exploded when she'd left the room. "Of all the damn cheek!" she whispered fiercely.

David put his hands on her shoulders to calm her, and pushed her down into a chair. "Down, girl. Consider the source."

He moved around the room, pretending to examine things, and tactfully allowing Daphne a moment to collect herself.

It was obvious from the condition of the room that Mavis

was a house-proud woman. Everything was in its place, and dusted meticulously. He picked up a "Souvenir of Brighton" ashtray, with a picture of the Royal Pavilion stamped in the center. "How tasteful," he murmured. More promising was a photo on the mantelpiece. He strolled over and examined it: In a plastic frame, the manly Craig sulked petulantly on a beach somewhere. Mavis also had a large television set, similar to the one at home in Wymondham. In many ways, David reflected, looking around the tastelessly tidy room, Mavis was like his mother. That didn't bear thinking about.

Craig in the flesh was nowhere in evidence, David noted with regret. He might have provided a diversion from Mavis's relentless awfulness. And from what David had seen on the previous day, the boy seemed to have a dampening effect on her that couldn't help but be an improvement.

By the time Mavis returned with the coffee, Daphne had regained a semblance of her usual manner. She still looked a little white around the mouth, but at least she was able to speak. "What was it you wanted to see me about, Mavis?" she asked in her blunt way, unwilling to spend any more time than was necessary with this odious woman.

Mavis tried to look offhand. "Oh, it was nothing, really. Nothing important."

"What, then?" Daphne demanded.

"Well, I just wondered about something. The church books—they're usually kept in that drawer in the sacristy. But . . . well, they aren't there now."

"No, they're not," agreed Daphne, perversely forcing Mavis to be more direct.

"Well, where are they then?" Mavis finally asked. Her attempt at appearing disinterested was not very successful.

"You know the Quinquennial Inspection is coming up. Gabriel's asked me to lock them in the safe until then. To make sure they don't fall into the wrong hands," she added with a look at Mavis's anxious face.

"But I'm a churchwarden. I have a right to see them," Mavis insisted.

"Of course you do. No one said you didn't. You know where the safe key is kept, don't you?"

"I'm not sure. You showed me once, but . . ."

"It's in the vestment cupboard, the one nearest to the safe. On a hook. Would you like me to get the books out for you tomorrow?"

"Oh, no, thanks. I just wondered. Just in case . . ." Mavis bit her lip and was silent for a moment, then changed the subject quickly. "Did you hear that Norman Newsome has resigned? That's one way to get that kind of filth out of the Church of England. The *News of the World* has done us a great service, don't you agree?"

Chapter 16

O sing unto the Lord a new song: for he hath done marvellous things.

Psalm 98:1

Thursday was a day in which bursts of heavy rain had alternated with brief and glorious sunny spells. For once, none of the churches that he and Daphne had visited had been locked, so David was in a rather cheerful mood as he walked in the sunshine to Lucy's house. She lived in a small mews, just south of Kensington Gardens, and with Emily's directions he had no difficulty finding it. The narrow house had a minute garden in front, imaginatively laid out and immaculately tended.

"Hello, David," she greeted him, opening the door with a welcoming smile. She was dressed in primrose yellow today, and the effect was an entirely different one from Beryl Ball's yellow ensemble, he noted with approval. She led him into a small sitting room, flooded with the afternoon sun; it seemed to be full of fresh flowers.

"What a very lovely room," he said impulsively. It had

none of the grandeur of Lady Constance's drawing room, or the one in the vicarage, but it was totally in harmony with itself and with its owner, reflecting her sense of gracious serenity in every detail, and he appreciated its warmth and its integrity.

"I'm glad you like it." She smiled. She had a deliciously enigmatic closed-lipped smile which David found enchanting. "Please sit wherever you like." He chose a small but comfortable armchair covered in flowered chintz. She left him looking around the room and returned a few minutes later with a tea tray, which she perched on an overstuffed footstool.

"I hope you don't mind too much," she said, curling into a chair. "It seems that it will just be the two of us this afternoon. I suppose I should give you the opportunity to escape, if you want to."

"Not at all. But what's happened to Emily?"

"She rang me this morning—apparently she'd forgotten she'd promised Julia Dawson that she'd join her in a cake-baking session all afternoon. She was sure we'd understand. It doesn't do to upset Julia Dawson, after all." She rolled her eyes.

"And I think that Julia Dawson is rather easily upset," he observed. "Well, it's Emily's loss, but I think we can manage without her."

She poured the tea into antique china cups. "It's Earl Grey. Would you fancy a slice of lemon instead of milk?"

"That sounds lovely for a change."

She passed him his tea, then produced a plate of delicious-looking finger sandwiches. "These are prawn and avocado, and the others are smoked salmon and cucumber. Rather monotonously fishy, I'm afraid."

"They look marvellous. Emily told me that you were a gourmet cook."

"Emily flatters me. I just enjoy pottering about in the kitchen, that's all. And I love good food," she added.

He savored the sandwiches, noting that there were more delicious-looking things on the tea tray—several sorts of cakes and pastries. "I could easily get spoilt by this kind of treatment. I'm usually lucky to get a biscuit out of a tin with my cup of tea." He felt vaguely disloyal to Daphne as he spoke, but the feeling was dispelled by Lucy's warm smile.

"Maybe it's about time you were a bit spoilt. I don't think it will do you any harm at this stage."

A small marmalade-colored cat crept from under the sofa and looked hopefully at the sandwiches. "Sophie, I don't think so," her mistress said mildly.

He extended his hand tentatively toward the cat, who sniffed it, then, satisfied, jumped on his lap and immediately began purring loudly.

"Sophie is quite fussy about laps. You should feel very honored."

He stroked the cat's warm fur, eliciting even louder purrs. Her contentment communicated itself to him, and together with the tasty food, the afternoon sun, the cozy room, the smell of fresh flowers, and the congenial company, produced in him a feeling of great well-being. The empty house in Wymondham, the clamor of egos at St. Anne's—they all seemed very far removed.

"You seem used to cats, David. Have you got one?"

"No. I always thought I'd like to have one, but Mother would never allow animals in the house. She's dead now, so I suppose I could get a cat if I wanted to."

"Has it been very long since she died?"

"No, only about two months. I still haven't got used to living without her."

"I don't know anything at all about you, David. Where do you live?"

"Wymondham in Norfolk. It's a market town, quite near Norwich. A lovely town, really, with a beautiful abbey church."

"And what do you do in Wymondham?"

"Well, I work in Norwich, actually. I'm a solicitor. Nothing special. It's just a job, and a pretty tedious one at that." He sighed.

"And have you always lived at home . . . with your parents, your mother?"

"Not always. I read law at the University of London, and

my first job was in London. But my father died about ten years ago. I was living and working in Brighton at the time. My mother . . . well, her health wasn't good. It seemed like the only thing to do at the time, to move back home. It's a very boring story.''

"I'm interested," she said firmly. "You're an only child?''

"Yes. My parents married quite late in life. There was only me.''

He found himself talking at length about his childhood, telling her stories only dimly remembered and never before shared. She listened intently, twisting a lock of hair around her finger and asking questions to draw him out. When the mantel clock gently chimed six, he looked at it in surprise.

The cat was still on his lap, but the sandwiches and the cakes had all been consumed. He smiled a little self-consciously at Lucy. "I seem to have done a lot of talking, and a lot of eating. Look at the time! I really should be leaving you in peace. But you promised to show me your paintings. Will you?''

"Of course, if you'd like." She rose, and he regretfully deposed Sophie and followed her out of the room and up the stairs. "I've made the second bedroom into a studio," she explained. "It's in the back, so it gets the northern sun— when there is any, that is—and I've had a skylight put in. This time of year I can work well into the late afternoon in natural light.''

There were several paintings in various stages of completion about the room. The medium was watercolor, but her works were far from the bland impressionistic flower paintings he'd halfway expected. The paintings were stylized and highly individualistic, featuring abstract motifs repeated in clear colors. It was obvious that she had a great deal of talent and skill, and David could see why her work was in demand. "Why, they're brilliant!''

"Surprised?" she asked wryly.

"Not at all. But . . . well, they're just so unusual. Wherever do you get your ideas?''

"That's a well-kept secret, but I think I can trust you!'' She smiled. "Most of my inspiration comes from the good old Victoria & Albert. I'll never run out of ideas as long as the V & A is right around the corner! All those patterns, all those incredible designs." She pulled out a sketchbook filled with pencil drawings of Egyptian antiquities, Indian textiles, Chinese porcelain.

"Well, for whatever it's worth, I'm impressed."

She led him back downstairs.

"How long have you lived in this house?" he asked. "You've done it up so beautifully."

"Oh, about twelve years now. It's taken most of that time to get it fixed up to suit me."

"How do you ... well, don't you hate living alone?" David blurted.

"Well, I'm used to it," she replied candidly, pausing at the foot of the stairs and looking up at him. "And, after all, what choice do I have? It's just one of those things." She laughed and added without a trace of self-pity, "You know what they say, and I'm afraid it's true: By the time you get to my age, all the good blokes are either married or gay." Pushing back her hair, she went on, "But I'll tell you what I *do* hate, and that's eating alone. If you don't have any plans for this evening, David, how about doing a lonely spinster a favor and staying for a meal?"

"I'd love to," he replied instantly.

"It won't be anything special," she warned. "Just whatever I've got on hand."

"You can't talk me out of it that easily."

"Good." She led him into the kitchen at the back of the house. It had been extended and fitted to her specifications. He looked around, impressed once again.

"It will be a privilege to watch you at work in this place. You will let me watch, won't you?"

"You do talk rubbish sometimes, David." She laughed affectionately. "You won't be watching, you'll be helping."

Chapter 17

Mavis Conwell fitted the large key into the sacristy door and turned it with great care. No one was in the church at that time on a Thursday evening, she knew, but you couldn't be too careful. There was enough illumination coming in the window so that she could avoid turning on a light. She shut the door behind her and locked it with the key, then located the key to the safe on its concealed hook in the vestment cupboard. From the safe she drew out the large, heavy ledger book, bound in blue cloth, and carried it over to the desk in the corner.

She turned rapidly through its pages until she reached the entries she was looking for. Very deliberately, she took a small penknife from her pocket and neatly slid it down the full length of the page. There! You could scarcely tell that a page was missing. She folded the page up and put it in her pocket along with the knife, before repeating her steps in reverse. The whole operation had taken less than five minutes.

* * *

The wine was unashamed plonk, but it tasted good, and the food was delicious. Lucy, with a little help from David, had concocted a pasta dish with browned butter and feta cheese, and a big leafy salad. Served with fresh French bread and plenty of sweet butter, and followed by fruit and cheese, it was a filling and satisfying meal. They talked and laughed without a pause through the preparation and consumption of it, then returned to the sitting room with their coffee.

David was amazed to realize that the subject of St. Anne's had scarcely come up. "Emily tells me that you manage to keep your distance from St. Anne's," he began.

"Yes, well, the Angel Gabriel manages to run it pretty well without my help," she replied.

There was something in her tone of voice that piqued his interest. He looked at her guarded expression with curiosity. "You don't like him much, do you?"

She shrugged, not bothering to deny it. "No, not especially."

"Why not?"

"Emily is my best friend. She worships the ground he walks on. I think he's a ... well, I won't say it."

David was intrigued. Was it possible that Lucy was one of those women who cherished an unrequited passion for the Vicar? Somehow he couldn't imagine it. "But why?"

She shrugged again. "For one thing, there's something ... unsettling ... about a man of forty who only looks half his age, don't you think?"

"That's hardly a reason to dislike him, Lucy. I wish I looked half as good as he does."

She looked at him in the darkening room. "I don't know why you always put yourself down," she said shortly. She liked his air of maturity, the nice lines at the sides of his eyes when he smiled, the hint of grey in his hair. "I like the way you look."

He leaned over and switched on a light to cover his embarrassment. "Father Gabriel," he pursued. "He ... treats Emily well, doesn't he?"

"As well as a clergyman ever treats his wife, I suppose. I know that I'd never want to be married to one. I saw what it did to my mother, and I know how hard it is on Emily to share her husband with every lunatic in the parish."

"But she doesn't seem to mind."

"She minds, all right. Do you have any idea what she gave up to become Mrs. Gabriel Neville?"

He was puzzled. "No. She was quite young when they married, wasn't she?"

"She was twenty-one, and had just taken a first-class degree at Cambridge. She'd been offered a research fellowship to go on and take her doctorate. But the Angel Gabriel put an end to that."

"Surely it was her decision?"

"But she was madly in love with him, and he didn't want to wait. They were married within six months."

He was silent, remembering.

"And then, after she lost the first baby. . ." An involuntary noise from David stopped her and she looked sharply at him. "Oh, you didn't know about that? I shouldn't talk about it, then."

"Please," he urged. "I want to know."

"The year after they were married. She carried it nearly to full term, then something happened. Well, she's so small, you see. Narrow hipped—she's built almost like a boy."

He wished that she hadn't put it quite like that.

Lucy's voice was full of pain for her friend. "The doctors said that she'd never be able to carry a baby to term. They said it could kill her to try. But she was determined to give Gabriel a child. We talked about it often. She wanted children too, of course. But I think that she felt she had failed him, and that somehow she owed it to him."

"And?" He was almost afraid to speak.

"A couple of years later she became pregnant again. They found out very early that it was twins. The doctors wanted to terminate the pregnancy. They said her chances of surviving and giving birth to two healthy children were . . . well. She was determined, as I said. She spent almost the entire nine months flat on her back. She was absolutely huge—you can just imagine. I'll give Gabriel credit—he brought in the best specialists that money could buy, and she came through it all right in the end. She nearly died, but she gave Gabriel his children, his precious Neville heirs." The bitterness in her voice was unmistakable.

"I see." He paused. "I had no idea."

"No, most people don't. She doesn't talk about it." She refilled his coffee cup from the cafetière and forced a smile. "Anyway, let's talk about something more cheerful. Any suggestions?"

"Well, I'm curious to know what you do with yourself on a Sunday, if you don't go to church? It's very difficult for me to imagine Sunday without it."

She laughed more naturally. "That's what I used to think, till I discovered a big wide world out there, outside the four walls of a church." She looked at him as an idea occurred to her. "I'll tell you what. If you want to know what I do on Sunday, why don't you join me this week?"

"Give me a hint what it is before I commit myself," he said with a smile.

"Well, first of all, I go out for breakfast." At his shocked look she went on, "Yes, I know that's terribly decadent, but there's nothing quite like eating eggs that you haven't cooked yourself! Later, I go and spend most of the afternoon at the V & A, mainly sketching. I usually take along a sandwich or something, and when I get hungry I take a break. If the weather's nice I eat it in Kensington Gardens or Hyde Park and have a little walkabout, then go back to the V & A. When it closes I come home, and fix myself a nice supper."

"You've talked me into it," he affirmed. "It never hurts to see how the other half lives . . ."

* * *

Walking back to Daphne's late that evening, David's route took him past the vicarage. He saw a light on in Gabriel's study, and on impulse he went up and looked in; Gabriel was writing at his desk. David tapped on the window. Gabriel looked up in surprise, then gestured towards the front door.

He opened the door quickly and quietly. "Emily's gone to bed early—a bit of a headache, I think. Come in, if you like."

David was suddenly awkward. "No, that's all right. I didn't mean to bother you. I was just passing by, and thought . . ."

"No bother at all. Come in and have a drink. We haven't really talked all week. I'm afraid I've been very busy this week . . ."

David followed him into the drawing room, bemused.

Gabriel was behaving more naturally towards him than he had since his arrival; he didn't quite know how to react.

"Have a seat, David. Whisky? Or something else?"

"Whisky is fine."

Gabriel took two glasses and a decanter out of a cupboard and poured generous measures of drink. "Here, David. Well, here's to . . . whatever."

He almost said "old times," David thought. Not a good idea. He acknowledged the toast with a nod.

"Well, what have you been up to this week? Meeting lots of people?"

"Yes, I've met quite a few." In a half-conscious gesture of something, he wasn't sure what, he added, "I've spent this afternoon and evening with Lucy Kingsley."

Gabriel nodded approvingly. "How nice. She's a very charming woman."

"Yes, I like her very much. She's very fond of Emily," he added.

"I believe so."

There was a short silence. "Do you know anything about . . . well, have there been a lot of men in her life?" David asked, hesitating, not sure himself why he was asking.

Gabriel considered the question. "I'm not really sure. You'd have to ask Emily. Wait, I remember there was one, quite a few years ago. I think he was actually living with her. And then, a couple of years ago, there was another one. That one was serious too, I think. She brought him round to dinner here one evening. Nice chap, I thought."

"But what happened to him?"

Gabriel looked at him blankly. "I have no idea. I don't think I ever saw him again after that. Emily would know."

A fine pastor to his flock he is, was David's quickly stifled disloyal thought.

"Why do you want to know?" Gabriel asked.

"Oh, I just . . . wondered. She seems . . . oh, I don't know. Vulnerable, but wary."

"Well, Lucy Kingsley surely wouldn't be any help when it comes to finding out about . . . the blackmail letter," Gabriel stated.

Of course. The letter. Peter Maitland. No wonder Gabriel wanted to talk—no wonder he was interested in what he'd been doing.

"Have you found out anything at all?" Gabriel pursued.

"Very little that sheds any light, I'm afraid. I've talked to a lot of people and the only person I've found who has any reason to dislike you at all seems to be Cyril Fitzjames, for pinching the woman he wanted." And Lucy Kingsley, for the way you've treated that woman, he refrained from adding.

"Cyril," Gabriel sneered dismissively. "He hardly seems a likely blackmailer, does he?"

"Not at all. But . . . well, I've been thinking. So far I've got nowhere in trying to find a motive. So I need to concentrate on the other angle. Who could have found out about Peter Maitland?" He deliberately kept his voice neutral, treating it as an abstract problem.

"No one. I told you—"

"Don't be silly, Gabriel," he cut him short. "It's obvious that someone has. If you didn't tell anyone, then Peter must have."

"Yes, I suppose so. But who . . ."

David came to an instant decision. "I don't know. But I intend to find out, one way or another. There's less than a fortnight left. Tomorrow I shall go to Brighton."

Chapter 18

Yet do I remember the time past; I muse upon
all thy works: yea, I exercise myself in the works
of thy hands.

Psalm 143:5

Friday morning dawned clear and bright, with the promise of very warm temperatures. Forgoing early Mass yet again,

David climbed in the brown Morris and set off for Brighton. Very soon he began to regret his lack of planning; the first truly summer-like day of the school holidays had brought sun-seeking families out in their thousands, and the roads were jammed with cars. Even before he cleared the London traffic, he realized that he should have taken the train. From Victoria he could have been in Brighton in under an hour and a half. At this rate he would be lucky to be there in three hours.

Telling himself that it did him no good to fret and raise his blood pressure, David tried to remain calm in the crawling queue of cars that stretched the entire length of the A23.

For the first hour or so out of London, he thought about the previous day's visit with Lucy Kingsley, replaying in his mind the conversations they'd had and trying to recapture the sense of peace he'd felt in her presence. But the nearer he got to Brighton, the more inevitably his thoughts turned to Gabe; unwillingly, he found himself remembering their time there together. This was getting him nowhere, he decided. He forced himself to consider the problem which was the reason for his journey. He must think about it objectively, as having nothing to do with himself, nothing to do with Gabe. It was about a boy who'd died, that was all. An unfortunate incident. A tragic accident. A mystery to be solved.

If he were a young boy in that situation . . . whom would he tell? In whom would he confide about the man he'd fallen in love with? He'd never found out how old the boy was. Still in school, perhaps. Would he possibly tell a trusted teacher? That wouldn't be impossible, especially if he were a bit disturbed. What teachers did David know at St. Anne's? Daphne. Well, that was pretty ridiculous. Tony Kent. He wasn't old enough—he was probably, in fact, about the same age as Peter Maitland would have been. He wasn't sure about anyone else.

Friends? He wouldn't know where to begin to look. Gabriel had been very vague about the circumstances of meeting Peter. He claimed that he couldn't really remember where they'd met or how they'd become acquainted. David didn't deceive himself that Gabriel was trying to spare his feelings—he was probably just blocking a memory that had painful associations.

This trip to Brighton had been an impulse, and not a very well-thought-out one. What could he possibly hope to discover, with only a few hours, and nothing to go on? His mood was approaching despair by the time he arrived, faced with the prospect of searching for a place to park. But luck was finally with him: As he drove along the seafront, a family with several children, sticky with Brighton rock and cotton candy, piled into their car and pulled out of their parking space.

He hadn't been back to Brighton since . . . then. Not since his father died. There had been no reason to come back. There was his friend Graham, a colleague from work, who still lived in a Brighton suburb with his wife and family. But he and Graham had never been that close. They'd often had lunch together, and had shared an occasional drink after work; he'd enjoyed Graham's company, but they didn't have that much in common. Now they kept in touch only with annual Christmas cards. On an impulse, he thought that he might look Graham up later on, when he'd got something to go on. If he needed any sleuthing done on a local level, Graham would be very keen to help. And Graham had never met Gabe, so no awkward explanations would be necessary.

He got out of the car and walked aimlessly for a while along the beach. He scarcely noticed the thousands of people who jealously guarded their small rocky patches of ground, their pale white flesh exposed to the relentless sun. He wished it were raining. In his memories of Brighton, his memories of Gabe, it was always a day like this, a day bright with sunshine, and alive with joy. The summertime scent of Brighton—the tang of the salt air, the sickly sweet smell of cotton candy, all the mingled odors of hot bodies and suntan lotion—evoked such powerful memories. And the smell of fish and chips, redolent with vinegar. He realized that it was past lunchtime and he was hungry, and he turned his steps automatically towards his favorite fish and chip shop. Yes, it was still there, still serving steaming paper cones of succulent freshly caught fish with thick greasy chips. He ordered a large portion and ate it greedily, sitting on the beach.

The library, he decided. When in doubt, go to the library. It was a good place to start.

It took him a moment to orient himself. The library had entered the modern age, with computer terminals where ranks of card files had once stood. But eventually he located the periodicals department, still where it used to be, and found the newspaper archives, where back issues of the *Brighton Beacon* were stored on microfilm; Gabe had said that he'd read about the death in the newspaper. David thought for a moment. He didn't actually know the date when Peter Maitland had died, but he would be able to get pretty close by reconstructing his own painful memories of that time. Damn Gabe, he thought. He could have at least told me the date. And of course he hadn't thought to ask.

Spring, ten years ago. He'd start with April and see what he could find. He located the spool and wound it onto the cumbersome machine. It was like entering a time warp. The events recorded on these newspaper pages were things that he remembered, practically his last memories of Brighton. He was fascinated, and, absorbed in the past, nearly forgot what he was looking for. He found it almost by accident—a small paragraph, tucked on a back page. "Body Found on Beach." His heart jumped; he read and reread the brief account.

A body, identified as Peter Maitland, aged eighteen, was discovered early Monday morning on the beach to the east of the town. Maitland had been reported missing on Saturday. The body had been in the water for some time, and drowning appears the probable cause of death. There were no signs of foul play. An inquest will be held after a postmortem examination has been completed.

Until he saw the words, even on this distorted screen, David had believed somehow, that it was all a terrible mistake, a bad joke. There was not, had never been, a Peter Maitland, and those unthinkable things that Gabe had said were not true. Now his mind had to accept it. Peter Maitland had lived, had died. Gabe had been involved. No matter how strongly he tried to deny responsibility, he had been involved. And someone had found out.

He continued to scan the newspaper pages, one after another. A fortnight after the initial account, the results of the inquest rated a brief mention.

> An inquest has been held into the death of Peter Maitland, aged eighteen. Maitland's drowned body was found washed up on Brighton beach in the early hours of the morning of April 7. The post-mortem examination revealed no evidence of foul play, and Maitland's roommate testified that no suicide note was found. Verdict: accidental death.

Accidental death. David rewound the microfilm, replaced it carefully in its drawer, and went out for a cup of tea. The afternoon was getting on; his labors over the microfilm machine had taken longer than he'd realized.

Death notice, he thought suddenly. He hadn't even looked on the obit pages. If Peter Maitland was anybody at all, there should be a death notice. He quickly paid for his tea and returned to the library. It was nearly closing time, but he might just about manage. He relocated the reel of microfilm and turned the handle rapidly. April. Nothing on the 7th, of course, and nothing on the 8th. The 10th—there it was.

> Maitland, Peter. Suddenly on April 5, in his nineteenth year. Beloved son of Susan and George Maitland of Croydon. Funeral will be held at 10 a.m. on Monday, April 14, at St. Mary's Church, Croydon. No flowers please. Memorial gifts to the

Selby Cathedral School's chorister fund. "His voice will be heard in heaven."

For a long moment, David stared at the words. Selby Cathedral. Chorister. My God.

The librarian came by with a pleasant smile. "We'll be closing in five minutes, sir. If you don't mind finishing up . . ."

He shook himself out of his trance. "Is it possible to get copies from the microfilms?"

"Certainly, sir. I'll just pop it on this machine for you. If you'll show me what you want copied . . ."

Ten minutes later he returned to the car, photocopies of the three pieces in his pocket. As he went by a phone box he fleetingly considered ringing Gabriel, but his aversion to the telephone overcame his desire to share his incredible find. If all went well, he could be back in London in a couple of hours, with plenty of time to see Gabriel tonight.

All did not go well. The thousands of cars which had rushed, lemming-like, to the seaside that morning were wending their way back to London that night. Near Crawley, there were major road-works in progress, bringing the northbound traffic nearly to a complete halt. David drummed his fingers on the steering wheel in frustration, but to no avail. It was well past midnight before he pulled up to Daphne's; good thing she'd given him a key, he thought. Tomorrow morning would have to do. He'd set his alarm and get up for early Mass. Then he could tell Gabriel that there was a light at the end of the tunnel.

Chapter 19

*It is but lost labor that ye haste to rise up early,
and so late take rest, and eat the bread of
carefulness: for so he giveth his beloved sleep.*

Psalm 127:3

The alarm went off at half past six. Its harsh buzz came as a shock to David, who hadn't needed to set it since he'd been in London. Friday's good weather was forecast to continue through the weekend, he heard as he switched on the radio.

He lay in bed for a few minutes, savoring the thought of telling Gabriel of his discovery. He'd be relieved, grateful . . . Of course there were a few loose ends to be tied up. They'd have to contact Selby Cathedral School, confirm that Peter Maitland had been a pupil there, and a chorister, find out if he'd been there when Miles Taylor was organist and choirmaster. And after that—he didn't know how Gabriel would want to handle it. It was still a very delicate matter. But he'd done his part, and he was pleased.

Early Mass was once again quite poorly attended. The regulars were all there—Lady Constance, the Dawsons, Beryl Ball. Mary Hughes was there, too, and Cecily Framlingham, with a man he assumed must be Arthur. David barely noticed them. After the service, he hung back until they'd all filed past Gabriel at the door, with a handshake and a murmured word.

He approached, and Gabriel grasped his hand automatically. It was like an electric shock; Gabriel's hand was cool and smooth, and David realized that it was the first time they'd touched since he'd been there. Those hands—those well-known, well-loved hands . . .

He took a deep breath to collect himself and looked Gabriel in the eye. "I have something very important to tell you," he said. "Can we go somewhere and talk?"

Gabriel looked at him as if he'd taken leave of his senses. "Talk? Now? David, don't you realize that the fête will be starting in under an hour?"

The fête! How could he have forgotten so completely that today was the day? "It's important," he reported lamely.

"Tonight, then. After the fête. Come round to the vicarage tonight."

"I suppose it can wait till tonight . . ."

"Right, then. If you'll excuse me, David . . ." and Gabriel was gone.

* * *

The church courtyard was transformed. Colorful stalls had appeared, and people dashed about with armloads of assorted goods in a flurry of last-minute preparation. David stood dumbly watching, trying to get his mind in tune with what was happening. "There you are," Daphne greeted him. "It seems like I haven't seen you for about two days. You crept out this morning before I was up, but I guessed I'd find you here."

"The fête," he said stupidly.

"Yes, once a year, whether we like it or not," she chuckled. "You've been to Mass? Have you had breakfast?"

"No. It doesn't matter."

"I suppose you can fill up on cakes, in due course."

He looked at the large table which the Dawsons, assisted by a very plain teenaged girl, were rapidly covering with vast numbers of cakes. "Yes. Everyone's been busy, haven't they?"

"Frantically."

"What stall are you doing, Daphne?"

She grimaced. "The jumble stall. Bric-à-brac, they call it. Everyone's cast-off rubbish, in other words. I've been through everything—you can be sure there's nothing you'd want.''

''No unrecognized treasures? Bits of tarnished silver that someone thought were plate?''

''I'm afraid not. But perhaps you'd be interested in a 'Souvenir of Scunthorpe' eggcup, only slightly chipped? Or maybe a complete set—near enough anyway, give or take the odd piece—of genuine plastic picnic cutlery?''

''How tempting. I'll have a look later. But now I'd better report for duty to Emily and see if she has anything for me to do.''

He moved toward the stall where the two women were lining up jars of jewel-toned jams in neat rows. They were both looking extremely attractive today, he observed. Emily had given up her jeans for the day and was wearing a very flattering simple white cotton summer frock, while Lucy's dress was covered in tendrils of delicate pink and blue sweet peas. David felt a bit self-conscious, in a pleasant way, at the warmth of both their greetings. He realized, with an odd shock, that it was just a week since his first anxious meeting with Emily. Now, astonishingly, she seemed an old friend. And Lucy. . .

''Well, the weather is certainly cooperating,'' he said.

''I can't believe how lucky we are,'' Emily replied. ''It's not supposed to rain all weekend.''

''Do you have anything for me to do? I'm at your service.''

''You can help us get the jams set out.'' There were boxes of them: orange marmalade, lemon marmalade, apple jelly, strawberry, raspberry, greengage and ginger, gooseberry, damson, apricot. Then there were jars of lemon curd and chutney to fit on the stall. David wondered if the lemon curd was as good as his mother's.

''I'll have to buy a good selection to take back home with me,'' he said, when they had finished.

''Why don't you pick out what you want now, and we'll put it away for you?'' Lucy urged, handing him an empty box. ''You'd be surprised how fast they sell out.''

He filled his box and secreted it under the stall. ''Now what?''

"Why don't you go over and give Tony a hand with that sign? It keeps falling down," Emily suggested.

Tony was struggling with the large square of cardboard which announced: "Tombola—25p a ticket or 5 for 1." David held it for him while he secured it with strips of tape.

"Thanks. I needed three hands for that job," Tony said.

"How are you, Tony? I haven't really seen you this week."

"Very well, thanks. Enjoying my summer holidays. And are you having a pleasant stay? How much longer will you be with us?"

"Yes, I'm enjoying it very much. I should be here another week, at least—until I'm satisfied that the crypt chapel restoration is well under way and in good hands."

"That's good. Maybe we could get together sometime next week for a drink or something," Tony suggested.

"I'd like that," David responded, looking around at the increasing levels of activity. "Who is the girl with the Dawsons?" he asked idly.

"That's Teresa, their youngest daughter."

David looked surprised. "I didn't realize that the Dawsons had any children."

"Heaps, actually. Nick, the oldest, is around my age. Then there's Benedict, and a few more, and finally Teresa. She's the only one still at home."

David laughed, delighted. Nicholas, Benedict, Teresa. "Are all of them named after saints?"

"Of course. What else would you expect from the Devout Dawsons?"

"I would think the Dawson boys would have been servers. Have you had to deal with them?"

Tony rolled his eyes. "That's a story in itself. The two oldest boys, Nick and Ben, were apparently pretty good servers. But the youngest, Francis—well, it's quite a tale. I must tell you about it sometime."

"I can't wait."

Tony paused. "I'll tell you what—why don't you come to me for lunch next week? Then we can have a good gossip. Could you bear to pass up lunch here on Tuesday, and come to me instead?"

"I'd love to." He looked over at the Dawsons. "Teresa's no great beauty, is she?"

"The Dawson offspring are a singularly unprepossessing lot," Tony replied. "Not really surprising, considering their genetic makeup."

Emily was gesturing to him. "I suppose that's my cue," David apologized. "I'll see you later."

"Thanks for your help with the sign."

"Don't mention it."

Before he could reach the jam stall, David was waylaid by Mavis Conwell. "Mr. Middleton-Brown! We missed you yesterday!"

"Yesterday?" He was baffled.

"The final preparations for the fête—all day yesterday. Everyone was here. Everyone but you, that is." She looked accusingly at him. "No one seemed to know where you were. Have you got a girlfriend somewhere in London that nobody knows about?" she added, with a ghastly attempt at a coy smile.

He didn't bother to answer. "Emily needs me. Good-bye, Mrs. Conwell." Mavis is certainly back on form today, he reflected as he strode away.

Emily was looking at her watch. "It's just about time to begin. Lady Constance should be here any minute." As she spoke, Gabriel and Lady Constance came out of the church together and walked formally to where the ribbon stretched across the courtyard gate. An expectant hush had descended; in clear tones she made a little speech, welcoming everyone and thanking them in advance for their generous purchases in aid of St. Anne's Church. Gabriel handed her a pair of scissors and she cut the ribbon smartly, to polite general applause. Then, as the general rush to the cake stall began, she and Gabriel strolled over to the jam stall where David stood with the two women.

"Young man, I require your assistance," Lady Constance addressed David.

"How can I be of help, Lady Constance?"

"I need to visit each of the stalls and make my purchases. Will you please accompany me, and carry the things for me?"

He looked to Emily for confirmation; she nodded encouragingly. "Yes, Lady Constance, I'd be delighted to walk with you," he replied. Gabriel produced a large wicker basket and handed it to him.

"Excellent. We can begin here." She considered the array of jams while David attempted to compose himself into a suitable posture. But Lucy caught his eye, and he could have sworn that she winked at him. "Now, what do you recommend, Mrs. Neville?" Lady Constance inquired gravely.

"The apricot looks quite good," Emily replied seriously. "And Lucy's greengage and ginger is always delicious."

Lady Constance looked dubiously at Lucy, but nodded, and David put the two proffered jams in the basket. "And how about some marmalade?" Lady Constance added.

"Do you prefer thick-cut or thin-cut?" Emily asked. "The thick-cut is Mary Hughes's specialty, and I've made the thin-cut myself. Or there's some very chunky marmalade made by Mr. Bead."

"The thin-cut would be very nice, thank you, Mrs. Neville," she concluded, handing her a five-pound note. "Do keep the change."

"Thank you very much, Lady Constance, and I hope you enjoy them."

"Oh, I'm certain I will."

As they approached the cake stall, the crowds fell back like the parting of the Red Sea. Lady Constance carefully considered the large array of cakes. "I shall have one of these fruit cakes, and a lemon sponge. Perhaps a dozen rock cakes, a plate of shortbread, and . . . yes, I'll take this chocolate gateau."

"Yes, of course, Lady Constance. Is that all? Let me just show you this . . ." Julia Dawson was volubly obsequious, while her husband wrung his hands in an agitated manner.

While these transactions were taking place, David smiled encouragingly at Teresa Dawson. She hung back and looked at him with bulbous eyes, made even less attractive by her almost invisible eyelashes. She looked like nothing so much as a frightened rabbit, David decided, with those eyes, her mother's receding chin, and her father's sharp, protruding teeth; her stringy hair was even a rabbity-brown color. Decidedly unprepossessing.

Lady Constance paid Roger Dawson, and Julia turned to David, anxious to be seen to be on good terms with one who was so obviously in favor with Lady Constance. "Mr. Middleton-Brown, how very nice to see you today. We did all wonder where you were yesterday!"

He smiled noncommittally, unwilling to enter into any explanations. "Good morning, Mrs. Dawson."

"Roger and I ... that is, we were wondering ... we'd very much like to invite you to join us for a meal next week. When are you free?"

There's no escaping from this one, he told himself with resignation. "Most evenings, I should think."

"Oh, good! Would Wednesday be possible? Our son Francis will be home that night, and it would be so nice for you to meet him." This was delivered with great emotion.

"Yes. I'll look forward to it very much," he fibbed.

Lady Constance had turned to him. "Mind you put the cakes in here very carefully, young man. I don't want anything crushed."

"Yes, of course." He put the shortbread on the bottom and the chocolate gateau on the top.

The servers were manning the sideshows, and Johnnie and Chris greeted David with cheerful waves as he and Lady Constance passed by. The sideshows were beneath her dignity, but she stopped at Tony's tombola stall. The most coveted prize was a bottle of very good whisky, David noted approvingly.

"I shall have ten tickets, please, Mr. Kent," she announced, handing him two pounds. He offered her the bowl of tickets, and she pulled them out one by one. Two of the numbers were winners, and she collected her prizes—a pair of bright orange tights and a packet of custard powder—with gracious thanks. David and Tony exchanged smiles as the prizes went into the basket.

The next stop on their progress was Cecily's flower and produce stall. "Those are uncommonly fine marrows, Mrs. Framlingham," Lady Constance pronounced.

"Arthur grew them himself," Cecily volunteered eagerly.

"What a pity I don't care for marrow. Perhaps a bunch of those sweet peas, and a pound of tomatoes. Did Arthur grow the tomatoes?"

"No," replied Cecily, crestfallen. "They're from Mavis's greenhouse."

"Oh, Mrs. Conwell. I see."

Mary Hughes was at the next stall, selling handicrafts. "Good morning, Lady Constance," she said, a bit over-enthusiastically. "I have some lovely things this year." Lady Constance inspected the array of hand-knitted baby sweaters, embroidered needle-cases, and multicolored knitted tea-cosies; they all looked indistinguishable from last year's and the year before's. She tried to remember what she'd bought the previous year. A tea-cosy, probably. Or perhaps that had been the year before.

"Bedsocks," she intoned judiciously. "Have you any bedsocks?"

"Oh, yes, Lady Constance. What color do you fancy? These blue ones are nice. Or these pretty lilac ones—they match your dress!" Mary Hughes stammered, blushing at her boldness.

Lady Constance turned to David. "What do you think, Mr. Middleton-Brown? Blue or lilac?"

"I'd choose the blue, I think."

"Yes, I believe you're right. Thank you, Miss Hughes, for your help. They're two pounds fifty, I believe? Keep the three pounds."

"Oh, thank you, Lady Constance. I do hope you'll be happy with the bedsocks."

The Mothers' Union was traditionally in charge of the "nearly new" clothing stall, which was their next stop. Mavis Conwell, who, in her role as churchwarden, would shortly retire to the sacristy to begin counting the takings, was doing an early stint at the stall. She'd done some very good business already, selling a number of items to Beryl Ball. Beryl had bought several hats, an evening gown, a Harris tweed coat, and a silk dressing-gown. Now Mavis greeted Lady Constance. "You'll have a hard time making your mind up, Lady Constance. Wait till you see what we've got!''

Lady Constance tended to agree that she'd have a difficult time, but perhaps not for the same reason that Mavis intended.

"Thermal underwear!" Mavis announced. "Just look at the quality of this thermal underwear. It will keep you nice and toasty warm next winter—and it's hardly been worn! I'll bet that big house of yours is cold in the winter. I'd hate to pay the heating bills, anyway."

Lady Constance looked at all the garments strewn about by Beryl Ball in her enthusiasm. Beryl Ball's rejects of someone else's castoffs—it didn't bear thinking about. "Yes, I'm sure that will be most . . . suitable," she agreed repressively. "Could you please wrap them up?"

"Of course, Lady Constance. Thank you very much. And may I say . . ."

Lady Constance turned away without hearing what Mavis wished to impart. "Dreadful woman," she murmured under her breath so that only David could hear.

The book stall was nearly all that remained. Lady Constance passed quickly, with a delicate shudder, over a pile of detective novels with lurid covers. She inspected a complete set of the *Waverley* novels. "A bit too heavy to carry," she concluded, looking farther. She looked at a 1967 Almanac and leafed through an old medical textbook.

"Poetry?" David suggested. "How about Keats?"

"I'm too old for Keats, I'm afraid. Is there any Tennyson?"

"One is never too old for Keats!" Cyril Fitzjames protested from behind the stall. "Especially not you, Lady Constance," he added gallantly.

David unearthed an old leather-bound volume of George Herbert and showed it to her. "That's just the thing," she agreed.

"Let me buy it for you," he said impulsively.

"You're very kind, young man," she said, bestowing a rare smile.

Daphne stood behind the final stall. Business had not been good, and David could see why. The eggcup was still there, and the plastic cutlery. They were indeed among the more choice items available. There was a box of jumbled-together rhinestone jewelry, all with stones missing, and a stack of stained beer mats. Lady Constance was looking bemusedly at a framed picture of the Sacred Heart of Jesus, throbbing with three-dimensional blood, while David inspected a lamp made out of a wine bottle. "Not even a very good wine," he muttered; Daphne stifled a chuckle. Then Lady Constance pounced thankfully on a box of dusting powder, unopened—someone's unwanted Christmas gift. "This will do nicely, Miss Elford," she proclaimed. David added it to the collection in the basket.

"Well, that's over for another year," Lady Constance said to him in a low voice as they walked away from the stalls. "Would you be so kind as to help me to my car?"

He took her arm and walked with her to the elegant old Bentley, parked just around the corner. "I usually walk," she said apologetically. "But I was a bit tired this morning, and then there are these things to be got home..." She paused as her chauffeur climbed out of the car and efficiently dealt with the basket of purchases. "You really have been most kind," she continued. "I like you, young man. Will you have tea with me next week?"

"Yes, of course. It would give me great pleasure, Lady Constance."

"Shall we say Thursday, then? Perhaps you'll have something to report about the work on the chapel by then."

"I will look forward to it." He handed her into the car, and saluted respectfully as she was driven away.

Chapter 20

They talk of vanity every one with his neighbor:
they do but flatter with their lips, and dissemble
in their double heart.
The Lord shall root out all deceitful lips: and the
tongue that speaketh proud things...

Psalm 12:2–3

The jams were looking decidedly depleted by the time David returned; he was glad he'd selected his in advance. Emily was relieved to see him. "Oh, you're back—good. Would you mind giving a hand on the book stall for a while?" She lowered her voice. "Miles was supposed to help Cyril, but he hasn't shown up yet, and dear old Cyril—bless him—keeps wandering off to buy another jar of my jams."

"Or a cake that she's baked with her own fair hands," Lucy added, smiling.

"So poor Daphne's had to cover the book stall, as well as her own, half of the time."

"Where is Venerable Bead?" David asked curiously, looking about. "I would have thought he would be here in the thick of things."

"Oh, he's giving conducted tours of the church. Much more his line," explained Emily.

"Of course. I should have guessed. Well, I'm off to Daphne's rescue."

Daphne gave him a look of gratitude as he stepped behind the book stall. Cyril was just returning from the cake stall. "You're here to help, are you, my boy?" he boomed.

"Just look at this marvellous cake I've bought. Almond and cherry. Emily baked it herself."

"It looks delicious."

The morning went by quickly; David was kept busy making change, wrapping up parcels of books, and listening to Cyril's chatter. Periodically, Gabriel's black-cassocked figure appeared as he relieved them of their accumulated cash and took it to the sacristy, where Mavis remained to count it. "We're doing very well," he said on one visit. "Well ahead of last year, Mavis says."

"I used to count the money," Cyril told David when Gabriel had passed on to Daphne's stall. "That was always my job, year after year. But now they think I'm past it, so they've given it to that woman to do. Maybe I am past it, my boy. Maybe I am."

David was on the point of reassuring him when Miles Taylor rushed up to them, completely out of breath.

"Wouldn't you know!" he expostulated. "Wouldn't you just know! My alarm didn't go off this morning! Well, all I can say is, thank God it didn't happen on Sunday morning!"

"No problem, my boy," Cyril responded. "This fine young man and I have managed splendidly, haven't we?"

"Oh!" Miles drew back and looked at him, gravely offended not to have been missed. "Well, if you knew how late I'd been up last night—I was out very late indeed." He paused to allow them the opportunity to ask where he'd been, but again he was disappointed.

Cyril chuckled condescendingly. "Ah, out sowing your wild oats, were you, young man? Well, I suppose at your age that's to be expected."

Miles drew himself up to his full height and looked at him stonily, the light glinting on his round lenses. "I was not sowing wild oats! I am a married man! I was . . ."

Mary Hughes touched his arm diffidently and he spun around. "Oh, Mr. Taylor, I'm so sorry to interrupt you! But I just wanted to ask—you are doing a recital in church this afternoon, aren't you? I've been so looking forward to it. When you weren't here earlier I thought perhaps . . ."

He gave Cyril a triumphant look. "Yes, my dear Miss

Hughes," he replied expansively. "I will be giving a recital at half past four. And I shall play some of your favorite pieces, just for you."

"Oh, *thank* you!" She turned quite pink with pleasure, and hurried back to her stall.

Miles turned back to David. "You can go now," he said with a dismissive wave of his hand, then drew a cigarette out of his breast pocket and lit it nonchalantly, taking a deep drag and blowing the smoke in David's face.

David shrugged, and took his leave. "Thank you for your help, my boy!" Cyril called after him.

He stopped by the tombola stall to see how Tony was faring. Incredibly, the bottle of whisky was unclaimed. "Do you feel lucky?" Tony greeted him, holding out the bowl of tickets.

"Well, you never know. Today may be my lucky day." David fished in his pocket and found twenty pence. The first ticket got him nothing, but the second one he drew bore the number on the whisky bottle.

"Well, I never!" exclaimed Tony. "I've been waiting for that to happen all morning!"

"I suppose I owe you a drink for this," David said, tucking the bottle under his arm. "Daphne will be pleased!"

He turned around to see that Lucy had come up behind him. "Emily's sent me to find you. The jams have sold out, so we've packed up, and now she wondered if we could give her a hand setting up the vicarage garden for the teas." She didn't touch him, but there was something about the way David looked at her, about the familiar, almost intimate, way that she spoke to him, that piqued Tony's interest and caused him to watch them as they walked together to the vicarage. Maybe I was wrong about him, he speculated.

Emily was waiting for them with a plate of sandwiches. "I suddenly realized that I was starving!" she said. "And I wondered if you two would join me for a sandwich before we get down to work." So they sat in the vicarage kitchen for a few moments, eating ham sandwiches and drinking lemon squash.

"When are the children coming back, Em?" Lucy asked.

"We're going to fetch them on Monday," Emily replied, her eyes alight with pleasure. "I have missed them. They will have been gone a whole fortnight!"

"It's a shame for them to have missed the fête," David remarked.

"A shame for them, but actually much easier for me. I have so much to think about today, and they would have been bored after the first hour or so. Once they've done all the sideshows, there's nothing much for them till tea. And my parents promised to take them to the Woburn Safari Park today, so missing the fête was the last thing they were worried about!"

"Have you talked to them, then?" David asked.

"Oh, yes, every day. I'm sure that I miss them more than they miss me, but they are only six!"

"I'm sure their father misses them too," said Lucy, her face turned away from David.

"Yes, of course he does. It will be lovely when we're all together again." Emily smiled, a faraway look in her eyes.

"And I look forward to meeting these wonderful children," David said, much too heartily.

"Of course you haven't met them! How very odd that seems!" Emily looked at him with wonder.

Gabriel came through the door. "I wondered where you were."

"Just having a bite to eat with Lucy and David, darling. Have you got time for a sandwich?"

"Yes, I suppose so. I've just taken Mavis the latest batch of money." He sat down at the table and helped himself to a sandwich. "It's really going very well. The cakes have sold out, and the jams, of course. Even Daphne's managed to shift a lot of her rubbish."

"I suppose there's no accounting for taste," David remarked. Gabriel looked at him sharply but David only smiled.

* * *

The vicarage garden looked lovely. David had set up all the tables, and the women had covered them with snowy white cloths and decorated them with nosegays of flowers. Stacks of crockery were at the ready, all the cakes had been sliced and the sandwiches cut, the urns were on the boil, and all that remained was to make the tea when the moment arrived. The helpers began trickling in—Julia and Teresa Dawson, assorted members of the Mothers' Union. Roger Dawson came too, announcing that he would be happy to take the money.

"I think I can manage now," Emily said to Lucy and David. "You've both been a great help, but now you're entitled to a break. Relax and have some tea, won't you?"

They escaped gratefully, and joined the crowd that was gathering outside the vicarage garden, waiting for the gate to open. Restive murmurs of "I could murder a cup of tea right now," "Isn't it about time?" and "I'm perishing for a cup of tea," were heard on all sides. In a few minutes Emily opened the gate and the rush began.

Lucy hung back, laughing. "Let them have their tea first, if they want it so badly. I'm sure there will be some left for us in a few minutes."

"Why don't we go to Kensington Gardens for a while?" David suggested.

"Oh, yes. Why not?"

* * *

They'd gone farther than they'd intended, all the way down the Flower Walk, so they were ready for their tea by the time they returned. They found a small table at the edge of the garden and settled down with their tea and cakes, oblivious to the speculative stares they were beginning to draw from various members of the parish.

"Were you planning to go to the organ recital?" David asked, looking at his watch. "It's nearly half past four."

"Oh, I suppose so. Though it seems such a shame to go indoors when it's so glorious outside." Lucy stretched luxuriously in the sunshine and pushed her hair back with both hands. "Well, never mind."

"We can wait a few minutes more. It won't hurt to miss the beginning, will it?"

"Not at all. It's the kind of thing where people come and go, anyway."

"Then let's have another cup of tea."

"Oh, yes."

Gabriel had quite a heavy-looking bag of money when he stopped by their table a few minutes later.

"Enjoying yourselves?" he asked in his most cordial Vicar-voice.

"Yes, thank you," Lucy replied coolly. "Your wife has worked very hard to make this a success."

"I know she has. And of course the wonderful weather hasn't hurt."

Emily appeared beside him quite suddenly, looking very worried. "Oh, Gabriel, could you come? Teresa Dawson has just fainted!"

"Yes, of course. I was just taking this money to the sacristy. . ."

"I'll take it for you," David offered quickly.

"Thanks, David." Gabriel handed him the bag and disappeared with his wife.

"Finish your tea, why don't you?" David suggested to Lucy. "And when you've done, I'll see you at the organ recital."

He could hear the sound of a Franck chorale as he approached the church. Reluctant to go through the church while the recital was in progress, he walked around the north side of the building and found that the small side door was unlocked. It led directly into the corridor where the sacristy was located, he discovered to his satisfaction. He tapped lightly on the sacristy door.

"Come in, it's not locked."

Mavis looked up as he entered. On the table in front of her were piles of notes, stacks of coins, and a ledger sheet where she was entering hourly totals. "Oh. Where's Father Gabriel?"

"He had an emergency. I offered to help."

"Put the money right here," she directed. "Mind you don't knock anything over."

It was the first time David had been inside the sacristy,

Daphne's domain, and he looked around with mild interest. It was a fairly large room; in the center was the heavy oak table where Mavis sat with the money. Set into one wall was a large old-fashioned safe, and the other walls were lined with tall, upright oak cupboards for hanging copes and albs, and stacks of big, shallow drawers for storing chasubles, stoles, and linen. In the corner opposite the door there was a small desk, on which were an ancient manual typewriter, Mavis's brown handbag, and a collection of assorted prayer books and hymn books. It was a tidy, well-kept room, which David attributed more to Gabriel's influence than to Daphne's inclinations. He could imagine what Gabriel would say—it was a room for holy things, therefore it was proper that it should be kept neat.

"Father Gabriel says we're doing quite well," he said, glancing at the ledger sheet.

"Oh, yes. I've been comparing the hourly figures to last year's, and we've been well ahead all along. It's the good weather that's made all the difference. We've gone over two thousand pounds already!"

"That's very good. Well, I won't keep you from your counting any longer, Mrs. Conwell." He retreated, shutting the door behind him. Instead of leaving by the side door, he went down the short corridor which led to the church. Beryl Ball, dressed in blue, passed him with a nod and a friendly waggle of her false teeth as he went through the door.

He looked around for Lucy. She certainly wasn't with Mary Hughes and the Fan Club. Tony Kent caught his eye and gestured tentatively, but he shook his head as he saw Lucy slip in from the north porch. For an instant the sun coming in the west window behind her turned her hair into a halo of rose gold, and he drew in his breath sharply.

They met at the back, smiling silently at each other, and found two seats. Half an hour later, after a slightly flawed performance of Bach's Great G Minor Fantasia and Fugue, they agreed to call it quits and see if they could get another cup of tea before Evensong.

"Miles isn't at his best today," Lucy remarked. "He must have something on his mind." David had to agree.

* * *

Venerable Bead was weary after a day on his feet, taking group after group of people around the church. He wasn't as young as he used to be, he reflected, and he hadn't even had his tea. There just hadn't been time for such self-indulgence. He wished he didn't have to serve at Evensong, but if Father Gabriel couldn't count on him, who could he count on? He looked at his watch. Half past five. There was certainly no time for a cup of tea before Evensong. He'd have to start laying out the things for Father Gabriel any minute now— his cotta would probably need a quick press. And the candles on the altar were getting low—he'd better replace them before the service. He hoped that fool organist knew that he'd have to stop playing—showing off, more like it—quite soon to allow for the preparations for the service. He sighed, and got to his feet; with a heavy tread he made his way through the door at the northeast end of the church and down the corridor to the sacristy. He tried the door tentatively; it was locked. With another heavy sigh he retrieved his ring of keys from his pocket and fitted the large key into the lock.

* * *

The teas were winding to a close. David and Lucy had begged a final cup from Emily, and were enjoying it in the late afternoon sunshine. Julia Dawson had taken the ailing Teresa home, so Gabriel had been pressed into service clearing tables. Lucy pointed out to David how ridiculous he looked, carrying around trays of dirty crockery in his black cassock. But he bore the ignominy with the good grace of a parish priest who often has to do many tasks that he considers beneath him.

No one really saw him coming. Certainly David and Lucy did not. But suddenly Venerable Bead was there, in the vicarage garden, clutching his chest and breathing raggedly. His face was white, and large beads of sweat stood out on his clammy forehead. He staggered to Gabriel, nearly collapsing.

"He's having a heart attack," Lucy said quickly. "Someone get a doctor." David rose, then paused as the old man spoke with a great effort.

"Come!" he said. "The sacristy. You must come, Father. She's in the sacristy. Mavis Conwell. She's hanging. She's dead!"

PART II

Chapter 21

They smite down thy people, O Lord; and trouble
thine heritage.
They murder the widow, and the stranger: and
put the fatherless to death.

Psalm 94:5–6

David didn't understand why the police wanted to talk to
him—he had scarcely known Mavis Conwell—until it was
explained to him that he was the last person to admit to
having seen her alive.

To admit it. That meant that they thought someone else
had seen her later, David reasoned. Someone who wouldn't
admit it. Someone who had . . . killed her. So they think it's
murder, he told himself as they escorted him into the
sacristy.

Several hours had passed, during which the efficient
police teams had done their work: fingerprints, photographs,
and finally the removal of the body. A small crowd had
gathered in the street outside St. Anne's, as inevitably
happens when the police barriers go up, but they'd dis-
persed by now, with the departure of the ambulance. David
had remained at the vicarage, drinking black coffee supplied

by Emily, while Gabriel had joined the police in the church. And now they'd sent for him.

The sacristy looked different in artificial light than it had in the afternoon. Two policemen sat at the table where so recently Mavis had counted her money, and their notebooks and bits of paper replaced the piles of notes and coins. Both of the policemen had anonymous, kindly faces. They rose as he entered.

"Mr. Middleton-Brown? Thank you for coming. I'm Detective Inspector Pierce, and this is Sergeant Gordon. We'd just like to ask you a few questions about this afternoon."

"Of course. I understand."

A chair had been placed in front of the table. Detective Inspector Pierce motioned for him to sit and he complied.

"Now, Mr. Middleton-Brown. You came into this room this afternoon. At what time was that?"

"It was just after half past four. Probably twenty-five to five."

"How can you be sure about the time?"

"The organ recital began at half past. He was playing the first piece, the Franck Chorale, when I arrived. I'd checked my watch at about twenty past, and it couldn't have been much later than that."

"And how long did you stay?"

"Just a few minutes. Three or four at the most."

"And what route did you take to get to this room?"

"I didn't want to walk through the church during the recital, so I came around the side and in the little door."

"You found that door unlocked?"

"Yes."

"And the sacristy door as well?"

"Yes. I knocked, and Mrs. Conwell asked me to come in."

"Now, I understand that Father Neville had been bringing the money in to be counted all day. Why, on this particular occasion, were you bringing it?"

"There was an emergency at the vicarage—a girl had fainted. I offered to bring it over, to help him out."

The Detective Inspector jotted down a few notes, then looked up again. "What did Mrs. Conwell say to you?"

"She asked me why I'd come instead of Gabriel—Father Neville. I told her the same thing. That there'd been an emergency and I was helping out. We chatted for a minute or two about how much money we'd taken in—that sort of thing. Just chit-chat."

"And how did she seem? How would you describe her?"

David thought for a moment. "Very ordinary. She didn't appear to be upset or agitated. If anything, she was just a bit more subdued than usual, but she was involved in counting the money, and not really interested in conversation."

"How well did you know Mrs. Conwell?"

"Not very well at all. I first met her . . . last Sunday, it must have been. I've seen her briefly once or twice since then."

"And what seemed to be the general opinion, among people you know, of Mrs. Conwell? Was she well liked?"

"No, I wouldn't say so. She had her friends—Mrs. Framlingham and Mrs. Dawson—but most people . . . well, they tended to steer clear of her."

"And why was that?"

"Well, I think she was regarded as a gossip, and she was very judgemental about . . . people's lifestyles, if they didn't agree with her . . . moral standards."

"Very good, Mr. Middleton-Brown. Now, I'd like you to take a look around this room. Look very carefully. Does it look the same as it did this afternoon?"

David stood up and studied the room. Desk, typewriter, prayer books, safe, cupboards, table. "The money, of course. The money was on the table."

"Yes. We've recovered the money. You needn't worry about that."

"Aside from that, it looks the same to me. But I've only been in here the once."

"Well, thank you, Mr. Middleton-Brown. I don't think we have any further questions for you at this time. Father Neville would be able to tell us where you could be reached, if it were necessary?"

"Yes, he would."

"Thank you for your help."

David left the church through the north porch and walked the short distance to Daphne's.

It had been a very long day. He wasn't thinking clearly, he knew. He hadn't really absorbed the fact that Mavis Conwell was dead, murdered, and that he'd seen her less than an hour before she died.

Why? And who? He had a feeling that it was all tied up with the blackmail somehow. In a day or two he'd be able to think about it, maybe sort it out. And he had faith in the police; in his professional dealings with them he knew them to be competent, thorough, and honest. So why hadn't he mentioned the blackmail to them? They hadn't asked—but that was a ludicrous excuse. Why on earth would they ask? He hadn't been thinking clearly. He'd answered the questions they'd asked, straightforwardly, and for tonight that was enough. Tomorrow he'd talk to Gabriel. Tomorrow he'd know more, understand more. But tonight all he wanted was a drink, and his bed.

Chapter 22

In the multitude of the sorrows that I had in my heart: thy comforts have refreshed my soul.
                                        Psalm 94:19

David's sleep had been laced with nightmares of Mavis Conwell, grinning at him with a rictus-like smile, but in the morning he was no closer than he'd been the night before to understanding or even apprehending her death.

Daphne was up before him, and had brewed a pot of black coffee. He accepted a mug gratefully, but neither one was particularly inclined to talk about the events of Saturday. They sat silently for a few minutes, drinking their coffee.

"Let's go to eight o'clock Mass," he suggested. "And then . . . well, I'm not sure. I was going to spend the day with Lucy, you know, but . . . under the circumstances, maybe . . ."

"I think you should go ahead," Daphne said sensibly. "Why should you change your plans? You've said your piece to the police, and if they need you again, they'll find you soon enough. Anyway, it will take your mind off things."

"Yes, I suppose you're right. But it just doesn't seem . . ."

"Respectful to the dead? I wouldn't worry about that."

"Hm. Well, I'll try not to be back too late. Will you wait up for me?"

"If you like."

Eight o'clock Mass was a hurried affair. Gabriel's heart just wasn't in it; he looked harassed and preoccupied, and rushed through the service with a totally uncharacteristic lack of feeling. But everyone made allowances—it wasn't every day that a priest had a member of his congregation, and a churchwarden at that, murdered in his sacristy. And the silent, but visible, presence of the police during Mass was a constant reminder to everyone that this was not a normal Sunday.

Gabriel didn't even remain to shake hands with his departing congregation. "I don't suppose he can face all the questions," Daphne whispered as they left the church.

"I'm sure he doesn't have any more answers than anyone else at this stage," David defended him half-heartedly.

They parted, and David tried to shake himself out of his mood of foreboding as he walked to Lucy's house. It shouldn't have been difficult: The weather was even more glorious than the day before, a perfect summer's day. But in the back of his mind was the uneasy feeling that this death was just the beginning of even more terrible things to come. Tomorrow. Tomorrow he must talk to Gabriel. But today . . .

Realizing that it was still quite early, David took the long way through Kensington Gardens, stopping for a few moments to sit on a bench and watch the antics of the birds. The swallows were chasing each other across the wide expanse of grass, skimming over the ground, swooping and diving in perfect unison, their wings scissoring the azure sky. Kensington Gardens represented an anomaly, a bit of the country in the heart of London, a bit of peace in the midst of chaos. He looked at his watch. Nearly time. He thought suddenly how glad he would be to see Lucy. She would banish his morbid thoughts if anyone could.

Her front door was ajar, and he tapped tentatively. "Come on in, David," she called from within.

He stood in the entrance hall for a moment, looking about for any clues to her whereabouts. "I'm just about ready," she said as she came from the kitchen, pushing back her hair. "David, just look at my nose!" She stood before him, lifting her face.

"What's wrong with it?"

"What's wrong with it?" she echoed disbelievingly, moving to the mirror and peering at herself with horror. "Why, it's all red! It was that walk in Kensington Gardens before tea that did it, I think. I look just like a clown."

"Not to me you don't. I think you look beautiful," he said with sincerity. She did look beautiful, in a creamy cotton dress strewn with roses just the color of her hair.

She turned from the mirror and smiled at him. "Well, I don't know about that. But maybe if I wear a hat, you won't be ashamed to be seen with me." She rummaged in the cupboard under the stairs and emerged a moment later with a broad-brimmed straw hat, which she clapped on her head. "There! If I keep it on when we're outdoors, at least it won't get any worse. What do you think?" she demanded, facing him.

"You look beautiful," he repeated. "But I wish you didn't have to cover your hair."

"It can't be helped. Not unless you're particularly anxious to see me looking like a beetroot by the end of the day," Lucy said, going into the kitchen. She returned shortly with a large wicker hamper. "Do you mind carrying this?" He took it from her as she collected her sketch pad and a clutch of pencils from the hall table. "There now—off we go. I hope you're ready for breakfast."

"Where do you go for breakfast around here?" he asked as they walked along.

"The Muffin Man. It's not far. They do a lovely breakfast." She turned off Kensington High Street—congested with sightseeing buses even on a Sunday morning—and led him down a side street. "You wouldn't find this if you didn't know it was here," she commented as they went into the small restaurant. They found a table in the corner. It was covered with a flowered tablecloth and located under a hanging basket trailing with ivy. Lucy wasted no time. "We'll have two breakfasts—the works," she instructed a passing waitress, dressed in a pinafore to match the tablecloths.

"I've been to eight o'clock Mass," he confessed. "And I'm starving. I've been up since—well, early."

She looked concerned. "Mavis Conwell. Of course you must be upset about that. The police only had a few questions for me—I wasn't really involved. But you . . . Did you have to talk to the police last night?"

"Yes," he replied shortly, unwilling to go into details. "But it wasn't too bad. It's just . . . well, there's something about the whole thing that bothers me. But I don't want to talk about it today. I want to forget that St. Anne's exists, for the rest of the day. Will you help me to do that?"

She smiled into his eyes. "You've come to the right person." She reached across the table and gave his hand a gentle squeeze. "Oh, look. Here's the orange juice." Raising her glass, she toasted him. "Here's to today, David Middleton-Brown."

After the creamed eggs, and the toast with marmalade, and the pots of tea, they were finally ready to move on. "When does the V & A open?" David asked.

"Oh, not for hours yet. Shall we go to the park?"

"How about Hyde Park? I'll tell you what—I've always wanted to go in a boat on the Serpentine."

"A rowing boat? Oh, what fun! Can you row?"

"I suppose I can learn," he said doubtfully. "At least it will help to work off breakfast."

There were quite a few other people with the same idea, but they managed to hire one of the turquoise boats for an hour, and David somehow successfully piloted them around the Serpentine without mishap. Rowing was hard work, but he alternated with periods of lazy drifting. Lucy trailed her hand in the water and laughed tolerantly at his efforts from under the brim of her hat.

When their hour was over, they walked about for a while in the brilliant sunshine, until David declared himself unable to continue. "You won't believe it, but I'm hungry again!"

They found a secluded, shady spot of grass under a silver birch tree and Lucy discarded her hat. "You've worked hard," she said. "You're entitled to be hungry." She spread out a cloth, and began to unpack the hamper.

"I thought you said a sandwich," David remarked, eyeing all the lovely things that were beginning to appear.

"That's when it's just me. I love having someone to cook for, and a picnic is one of my favorite things." Lucy pulled out a bottle of champagne and David popped the cork as she produced two carefully wrapped long-stemmed glasses.

They had chilled watercress soup from a thermos, then little savory parcels of filo pastry filled with cream cheese, a roulade of chicken and crab meat, and other various delicacies, finishing with a mango soufflé.

"That was the nicest picnic I've ever had," David declared, when the last bite had been consumed. He lay back in the grass and closed his eyes. The grass was warm, even in the shade, the quiet murmur of the insects was soporific, and the half-bottle of champagne he'd drunk was making him drowsy.

"You just rest a while," Lucy said soothingly. She got out her sketch pad and spent some time on a drawing of David in repose. The tense expression was completely gone from his face as he rested peacefully, in that half-aware state between sleep and wakefulness. He knew that he was well-fed, and that Lucy was there. He knew that he was . . . happy. He knew . . .

He opened his eyes with a start, not at all sure how much time had passed. Lucy was working on a close-up sketch of him, and was sitting very near. She smiled at him as he opened his eyes; he reached out a disembodied hand and gently pulled on a ringlet of her hair. It stretched out, but snapped back as soon as he released it. "What wonderful hair," he murmured.

"You should have seen it when it was really red," she laughed. "When I was . . . young."

* * *

Eventually they made their way to the Victoria & Albert Museum. "My turn to do some real work," said Lucy with regret. She settled down with her sketchbook in the Islamic gallery. David made himself comfortable against a nearby pillar and watched her with fascination. He was now wide awake, but kept very still to avoid breaking her concentration. She drew rapidly, skillfully, and very quickly filled several pages. After a while they broke for a quick cup of tea in the museum café, then Lucy returned to work until closing time at six.

The sun still shone brightly as they walked slowly back to her house, David carrying the empty hamper. "It's really hot," he said. "I could use a cool drink about now."

She took off her hat and fanned herself with it. "Coming right up," she promised. "We're almost there."

"How fortunate you are to live practically around the corner from the V & A."

"Oh, I know. I love living in London. And this is such a wonderful area. There are all the museums, the shops are good, and then there's the Royal Albert Hall nearly on my doorstep."

"Yes, the Proms. Do you ever go?"

"Of course," she replied. "Several nights a week, usually. I always buy a season ticket, then if it's anything good I go and queue up. You have to get there early to get a decent spot, but if I don't have anything better to do . . ."

"Could I come with you some evening?" he asked impulsively.

"Certainly, if you like. You can take a look at the book when we get home, and see if there's anything you fancy."

Sophie was waiting for them when they came in, mewing querulously. "Oh, poor Sophie, she wants her dinner," Lucy murmured. "David, you can go in the sitting room and make yourself comfortable, if you like. I'll get you a drink, and feed Sophie. How about a Pimms?"

"That sounds lovely." He sat down in his favorite chair and put his feet up on the footstool. A moment later she'd brought him an icy drink and the Proms book; he turned to the programs for the coming week.

"Have you found anything tempting?" she asked when she returned with her own drink.

"Yes, definitely. Tuesday sounds very good, and so does Thursday. Were you going to go on Tuesday?"

"That's the all-Mozart program, isn't it? Yes, I thought I'd go to that one. A little Mozart goes down well on a nice summer evening."

"Do you mind if I tag along?"

She smiled. "I think I could put up with you."

In another minute Sophie had finished her dinner, and was curled up on his lap.

Chapter 23

The sorrows of death compassed me: and the over-flowings of ungodliness made me afraid.

Psalm 18:3

There were two glasses and a bottle of whisky on the table, awaiting his return; Daphne looked up from her book as

David came in just after eleven. "Have you had a good day?"

"Lovely, thanks."

"Do you want anything to eat?"

David groaned. "I don't think I shall want to eat for a week. I've been eating practically non-stop all day."

"Anything good?"

"Oh, yes. All of it. And I've just had a marvellous supper."

"Well, have a drink, then. Or would you rather have tea or coffee?"

"This looks good to me." He poured himself a generous whisky. "What have you done today?"

"Not much. I read the papers, had a sandwich, started reading this Ruth Rendell novel."

He imagined Daphne eating her solitary sandwich while he was indulging in culinary delights, and had a brief pang of guilt. "Anything exciting in the papers?"

"There was just a paragraph in the *Independent* about . . . Mavis."

Mavis. It was time to start thinking about Mavis. He sighed as the foreboding, the feeling of vague fear descended on him again.

"What did it say?"

She leafed through the paper and found it for him. " 'The body of Mrs. Mavis Conwell, aged forty-eight, was discovered in St. Anne's Church, Kensington Gardens, London, late Saturday afternoon. The police are making inquiries,' " she read.

"That's the *Independent* for you," he said dryly. "To the point."

"Yes, I can imagine what the *News of the World* had to say about it. 'Lonely Widow Slain in Church Bloodbath' or something like that."

"You know," he said suddenly, "it just occurred to me. If she died in the sacristy—wouldn't it have to be reconsecrated before Mass could be celebrated?"

Daphne laughed. "Full marks to you on that one. I found out this afternoon what happened: Gabriel had to bring the

Bishop in last night to do it, after the police had finished in the sacristy. The Bishop was at a dinner party, and was none too happy about being called away, or so Emily says! I must admit, I never even thought about reconsecration."

"So," David said, taking a fortifying gulp of his drink, "what do you make of this business?"

"Mavis, you mean?"

"Yes. You must have your ideas about it. After all, you read all those crime novels."

"So you're assuming it's murder."

"Yes, of course," David asserted with a nod. "It certainly wasn't an accident, and Mavis didn't seem the type to kill herself. Too self-satisfied by half. She wouldn't hesitate to suggest that entire . . . groups of people . . . should go out and kill themselves en masse, but not her."

"I think you're right," Daphne admitted.

"Then who killed her?" he posed bluntly.

"Ah, that's the real question, isn't it?"

"Well, what do you think?" he demanded.

"Of course you have to think about the two big questions: motive and opportunity. Opportunity is easier to deal with," Daphne said in a detached, mystery-fan way, making herself more comfortable on the sofa.

"I should think that's a pretty wide open field," David commented.

"Yes, in this particular case, anyway. All sorts of people were around, and any of them could have nipped in and done it."

"The sacristy door wasn't locked when I left."

"And neither was the side door, was it?"

"No, it wasn't."

"And anyways, even if the sacristy door were locked," Daphne added, "half the people in the church have a key, and the other half know where to find one. So that wouldn't eliminate anyone."

"Are you assuming it was someone from the church?" As he said it, he realized that it echoed his question to Gabriel about the blackmailer. He wished he could tell Daphne about the blackmail letter.

"Most likely. A stranger probably would have been noticed by someone, and a stranger wouldn't have known that they'd find her in the sacristy."

"Unless it was a simple robbery?" he suggested. "And she just happened to be the one there when someone went in to steal the takings from the fête?"

Daphne considered the possibility. "Now we're on to motive, aren't we? That's not impossible, in theory. There was a lot of money there, and that wouldn't be too difficult for a lot of people to have figured out. But in that case, the *modus operandi*"—she laughed self-deprecatingly at the phrase—"just doesn't fit. A casual thief might shoot someone who stood in his way, or even stab them, but hanging—no. Hanging implies that it was someone who knew her well enough that she wouldn't be suspicious. Someone who could get behind her with a noose . . ."

David shuddered at her detached tone. She'd read too many mystery novels.

"Anyway," she added, "the money wasn't taken, was it? Didn't the police tell you that it was all accounted for?"

"Well, what about other motives then?"

Daphne laughed dryly. "You know yourself in your short acquaintance with her that Mavis wasn't the best loved person at St. Anne's. There were plenty of people with reason to dislike her." David looked at her pointedly; she merely raised her eyebrows and went on. "But murder? That requires more than just dislike."

"Such as?"

"Well, if you remove money from the list . . . you're left with things like jealousy, revenge, thwarted love, blackmail, the thirst for power. Power—now that's an idea. Who do we know who desperately wants to be churchwarden?" she asked humorously. "Roger Dawson, maybe?"

He smiled, but another word in her list had inevitably caught his attention. "Blackmail," he said slowly. "What do you mean? How could that be a motive?"

"Oh, blackmailers very often get themselves murdered—in books that I've read, anyway. Blackmail is a very dangerous business. If the victim finds out who his blackmailer is, he can kill the blackmailer to protect himself. Self-preservation is a powerful motive for murder.'' Daphne talked on at great lengths about the other possible motives, but David was no longer listening. As soon as he could, he made his excuses and went to bed.

But not to sleep. He lay awake for hours as the enormity of the situation dawned on him. Mavis Conwell had been murdered. She'd been murdered by someone she knew, someone at St. Anne's. Someone she'd blackmailed. Gabriel. After his first visceral acknowledgement and simultaneous denial of the possibility, David thought about it logically. Gabriel could not have killed Mavis. He'd been at the vicarage when she was killed. He, David, had taken Mavis the last bag of money that had been delivered. Thank God for that, he thought. Thank God Gabe was out of it. Emily would be able to give him an alibi for the whole period. He'd been helping with the teas, with the clearing up. Any number of people would have seen him.

He had no difficulty in accepting instantly his instinctive feeling that Mavis had been Gabriel's blackmailer. She had the essential self-righteous mind-set, he knew. That was all the motive necessary for the letter she'd sent—ridding St. Anne's of an impure, unworthy priest. She wouldn't care that it was ancient history, that Gabriel was now a respectable and respected married man. If she'd found out . . . But how had she found out? Something nagged at his brain. It would come to him. She must have found out.

If she were blackmailing Gabriel, would she stop there? Or would she be blackmailing other people too? That must be the answer. She'd blackmailed someone else, and they'd killed her. He could imagine Mavis Conwell sitting over her typewriter, pouring out poisonous suggestions and self-righteous demands to those who had somehow offended her moral code. Someone else with a secret . . .

He'd almost made a fool of himself, he'd been so ready to accuse Miles Taylor of being the blackmailer, just because Peter Maitland had been a chorister at Selby. Clearly he had been wrong—it was a coincidence, nothing more than that. Mavis Conwell had been the blackmailer, and now she was dead.

Tomorrow. He must talk to Gabriel tomorrow. In the dark, he peered at the clock. Today.

Chapter 24

He shall deliver me from my strongest enemy, and from them which hate me: for they are too mighty for me.

Psalm 18:17

David looked out of his window at an overcast sky and decided not to go to early Mass. Instead he walked to the vicarage, arriving just after eight. Emily, dressed already in jeans and a striped shirt, answered the door. "Good morning, David. Is Mass over? Have you come for breakfast?"

"I haven't been to Mass," he confessed. "I've come to have a word with Gabriel. But I wouldn't say no to breakfast."

"Come on in, then. Gabriel's not back yet." She looked at her watch. "He might be delayed by the police. But I hope he won't be too long—we're going to St. Albans later."

"Yes, of course. The children."

"I can't wait to see them," she confided. "Come into the breakfast room, David. Would you like some cereal?"

"Yes, thanks." He discovered, improbably, that he was very hungry.

"And how about a boiled egg?"

"That sounds delicious."

"We won't wait for Gabriel. He can have his when he comes," Emily said, joining him.

When Gabriel arrived, nearly half an hour later, he was looking relaxed and happy; all the tension of the past day, of the past weeks, was dissipated. He greeted Emily with a kiss, and David with an open, friendly smile, then ate his breakfast heartily.

"Are you coming with us to St. Albans, David? We could take you to the Cathedral, if you've never been," he offered.

"Oh, do come, David!" Emily urged. "That would be great fun."

"I couldn't possibly intrude on your family reunion," he protested, embarrassed.

"Don't be silly!" Emily said fondly. "You're practically one of the family."

"No, really. I couldn't."

"Well, what can I do for you, then?" Gabriel asked with good humor. "We want to leave by mid-morning, don't we darling?"

Emily nodded.

"I'd like to speak to you," David replied awkwardly. "It's . . . well, could we talk in your study?"

Gabriel looked puzzled, but not annoyed. "Of course. If you don't mind, darling?"

"Go right ahead, you two. Have your secret chat. But just don't be too long about it!" she said with a smile.

They went into the study and sat down. "Now, David, what's this all about?" Gabriel inquired genially.

David felt acutely uncomfortable. A woman was dead— why was Gabriel so cheerful? "About Mavis's . . . death," he began.

Gabriel frowned. "What about it?"

"I've been thinking about it. Has anything . . . struck you, Gabriel?"

Folding his hands on his desk, Gabriel looked at him and said formally, "I have just finished speaking to the police about Mrs. Conwell's death. It is their conclusion, based on the postmortem examination and other evidence, that her death was . . . self-inflicted. That is to say, she hanged herself."

David stared at him. "Hanged herself? But you don't believe that, do you?"

"What reason would I have to disbelieve the police?"

"But surely . . . she was murdered? I mean, why on earth would Mavis kill herself ?"

Gabriel spoke slowly and deliberately. "The police spent the day in the church yesterday. A great deal of evidence has come to light. There's no reason why I shouldn't tell you. It would appear that Mrs. Conwell had been . . . appropriating church funds for her own use . . . for some months. There have been some discrepancies that various people have noted, and a page has been removed from the current ledger book. Mrs. Conwell's fingerprints were found on the book."

"Mavis stealing money! But if it's been going on all this time, why should she kill herself now?"

"The Quinquennial Inspection is due to begin within the next few days. The police believe that she panicked and tried to cover her tracks, and when she realized that it wouldn't work, and she was bound to be discovered, she couldn't face the shame."

"Is that all the evidence they've got?"

"Not at all. The sacristy door was locked, and the key was in Mrs. Conwell's pocket."

"But you know very well that doesn't mean anything! The door can be locked from the outside as well as the inside, and according to Daphne, half the people at St. Anne's have got a key."

Gabriel looked pained. "David, I do think you should let the police do their job. They have found no evidence at all to point to . . . murder. The position of the body, the lack of signs of a struggle—all perfectly consistent with suicide."

David took a deep breath. "But you know better, don't you?" he said softly. "You know she was . . . the blackmailer."

Gabriel recoiled. "Are you suggesting that I killed her?"

"No, of course not. I know that you were at the vicarage when she was . . . killed."

"Then what do you mean?"

"That you weren't the only one she was blackmailing. That she was playing a dangerous game, and it backfired on her. It all fits, Gabriel. And you believe it too." As he said it, David realized that there was no other explanation for Gabriel's ebullient mood and behavior: He believed that he was no longer in any danger.

Gabriel struggled for control. "The police are satisfied. They are not pursuing the case any further."

"Did you tell them about the blackmail letter?" David demanded.

"There was no need. It was nothing to do with . . ."

"Bloody hell, Gabriel! It had everything to do with it! Mavis Conwell attempted to blackmail you!"

"How can you be sure of that?" Gabriel challenged him. "What proof do you have?"

"No proof," admitted David, more quietly. "But it all fits. She had the motive—she hated . . . queers, and especially queer priests."

Gabriel winced at the description. "Perhaps. But how would she have known about . . . Peter?"

"I'm not sure," David began, then the thing he'd been trying to remember during the night came to him in a flash of memory. "Wait. She's been to Brighton—I saw a souvenir ashtray in her house. Obviously she met someone in Brighton, somebody who knew Peter. That's got to be it."

"Even if that were true," Gabriel said, "and I'm not saying it is, why does that mean she was murdered? She could have been the blackmailer, and committed suicide."

So that was what he wanted to believe, David reflected. Gabriel, too, had come to the conclusion that she had been his blackmailer, but had convinced himself that that fact was irrelevant to her death. He thought about it for a long moment. "But Gabriel, if she killed herself over money, why couldn't she have just taken some of the proceeds from the fête, before the money was counted? No one but Mavis knew how much was coming in. It was all there, I assume? All the fête money? It tallied with the ledger sheet?"

Gabriel looked at him. "There was no ledger sheet," he said guardedly. "There was just over eighteen hundred pounds on the table."

"No ledger sheet?" David tried to assimilate the implications of that statement. "But that means . . . that means that someone was in the sacristy after I left! The person who murdered Mavis Conwell!"

"The police are satisfied," Gabriel repeated stubbornly. "Leave it, David. You can only cause problems by stirring up all these questions."

David's legal training, his strong sense of justice, asserted itself. "How can you ask me to leave it?" His voice neared hysteria. "A member of your congregation is dead. Another member of your congregation murdered her. Someone else she was blackmailing. Someone else with a secret to hide. I intend to find out who it was! With or without your cooperation! With or without your permission!"

Gabriel raised his voice for the first time. "The police are satisfied! The investigation is closed!"

"I don't give a damn about the police!"

"Why don't you go home now, David? Forget about it all!"

"All you care about is your bloody reputation! You don't care about justice, about the truth!"

Gabriel had regained his self-control. "The police are satisfied," he repeated in a soft, steely voice. "And would you please lower your voice? My wife might hear you."

"The police can go to hell. And you can go to hell, *Father* Neville!"

* * *

Emily paused outside the study door, about to offer the men coffee. Though she couldn't hear their words, something in the quality of their voices made her hesitate. This was no friendly discussion, she realized. In spite of herself, she remained for a moment. Their voices were now raised in real anger, and several words resonated through the door: murder, police, secret, blackmail. Troubled, she retreated to the kitchen to puzzle about what she'd heard. Gabriel and David rowing. What did it all mean? Gabriel had been so . . . cheerful this morning. What could David have said to make him so angry?

After a few minutes she heard the front door slam. When there was no other sound, she went to investigate. The door to the study was open, and Gabriel was sitting, rigid, at his desk. His face was white and set, and his hand was clenched around the paperweight as though he were ready to hurl it through the window.

"Gabriel, what's wrong? What's happened?" she asked with concern, entering the study hesitantly.

"Nothing," he replied evenly, relaxing his body with a great effort and replacing the paperweight on the desk. "Nothing at all."

"But David—he was shouting at you."

He laughed tightly. "David tends to—overreact sometimes, that's all. He thinks that Mavis Conwell was murdered."

"And was she?"

"No, of course not. The police have closed the investigation. They're quite satisfied that it was suicide."

"But why should he care? He scarcely knew her. Why is he so upset?"

"God knows. David's a funny chap. I stopped trying to understand what makes him tick a long time ago." He said the words lightly, but there was something in his voice that set off an alarm in her brain.

"He was shouting something about . . . blackmail," she said slowly. "Won't you tell me what it's all about, Gabriel? I'm your wife. If you're in any sort of trouble . . ."

"Don't be ridiculous," he snapped. "You're overwrought. He didn't say anything of the kind. Why should I be blackmailed?"

Emily turned and left the room in a kind of daze. Why, indeed? She went back into the kitchen and gripped the counter edge, taking a deep breath. She knew her husband well enough to know quite clearly that he was not telling the truth. What was Gabriel hiding? Why was he lying to her? What was the terrible secret he felt he had to protect her from?

It was something that had started a long time before today, she was sure. David. How was he involved?

If Gabriel wouldn't tell her, maybe David would. She had to know.

Chapter 25

Then thought I to understand this: but it was too
*   hard for me,*
Until I went into the sanctuary of God: then
*   understood I the end of these men . . .*
*   Psalm 73:15–16*

The way Gabriel had said David's name, just now; the look on his face . . . Emily thought of it again, as she walked across the road from the vicarage to the church. Suddenly her conscious mind apprehended, with an icy shock, something that her unconscious must surely have known or suspected for a very long time. Gabriel . . . and David.

She knew, somehow, that she would find David in the crypt chapel. He turned to her light step as she came down the stairs. Still trembling with anger, he tried to calm himself as he saw the haunted, strained look on Emily's face.

"David, can we take a walk in the park? I need to talk to you."

"Of course," was all he said.

They walked in silence for a long time as Emily tried to summon the courage to frame the question that must be asked. Her need to know was now greater than her overwhelming desire not to know. When they'd passed Peter Pan, Emily abruptly pulled him down on to a bench and looked searchingly into his face.

"David, we're friends, aren't we?"

"You know that we are."

"If I ask you a question—a difficult question—will you promise to answer it?"

A trickle of fear reached his heart. "If I possibly can."

"David . . . were you and Gabriel . . . lovers?"

He caught his breath sharply, but managed to maintain eye contact with her. "Don't you think you ought to ask Gabriel that?"

She looked away suddenly, biting her lip. "You've just answered my question."

He regarded her mute misery for a long time. "Emily, I . . . that is, what do you want to know?"

Her voice was almost inaudible. "When? Where? For how long? Please, David. I have to know."

"Let's walk," he suggested. She walked deliberately, head down and hands in her pockets. At her side, David matched his pace to hers and kept his eyes straight ahead.

After a moment he began. "It was in Brighton. He was the curate at St. Dunstan's, and I was a server. We got to know each other. We . . . fell in love." He sensed rather than saw her flinch. "I didn't know what was happening at first. I was very innocent." He rushed on, thinking of Gabriel's lack of innocence. "I was twenty-eight years old. Gabriel was a little younger. It lasted . . . for about three years. We were very discreet. No one else ever knew. It ended . . . when he came to London, to St. Anne's. I never saw him again."

She touched his arm gently; he stopped and faced her. "I'm glad, if it had to be somebody . . . that it was you, David," she said awkwardly. He waited, hoping and praying that she wouldn't ask him if he'd been the only one; he didn't know how he would answer. Above all, he didn't want to tell her about Peter Maitland. Misunderstanding his silence, a look of painful comprehension crossed her face. "You still love him, don't you?" she whispered.

"I've never loved anyone else." It was said simply, without self-pity.

Her quick mind, stunned as it was, reached the next inevitable conclusion with a surge of sympathy for him, sympathy that showed on her face as she said softly, "How you must have hated me."

He managed a smile. "For ten years. Silly, wasn't it?"
"Oh, David." They resumed walking, in silence.

* * *

Eventually they arrived back at the church, and went down
to the chapel together. "What are you going to do now?"
David asked. "You really should talk to Gabriel."

Emily couldn't bear the thought of facing Gabriel now,
while this knowledge was so new to her. "Not now," she
said swiftly. "I need time . . . to think. To try to understand,
to make sense of it all. I thought I knew him . . ." Her voice
broke. She hadn't cried till now, but the realization of her
short-term dilemma was too much for her. She wept, and
David, who was unused to women's tears, held her gently,
stroking her hair, reflecting bitterly on the irony of the
situation.

When her tears were spent, she raised her eyes to him.
"Will you help me?" she appealed.

"Anything that's in my power," he promised.

"I need to get away for a few days. I just can't face him
now." Her voice trembled again.

He understood her need to escape. "Where will you go?
To your parents?"

"No, not there. I need to be alone, where I can think."

"What about the children?"

She bit her lip. "They'll be fine with my parents for a
few more days. I just can't . . ."

"No, of course not," he said, thinking quickly. "I could
take you to a place I know—a community of Anglican
sisters, just outside London. They'd look after you, and you
wouldn't have to talk to anyone."

"Oh, David, would you?" She looked at him with
gratitude.

"Of course. I think that would be best. You can stay as
long as you like, and when you're ready . . . well, when you
want to come back, I'll come and get you."

"And you won't tell Gabriel . . ."

"Not if you don't want me to." I don't think I'll have the chance, he added to himself. Not after the way we parted.

"I must write him a note—so he won't worry," she said. David found her a piece of paper, and she wrote, "Dear Gabriel, I have a lot of thinking to do, and am going away for a few days. Please ring my mother and ask her if she will keep the children for several days longer." She hesitated, then added, "Don't worry about me, and don't try to find me."

* * *

Emily sat quietly beside him in the car. After a while David spoke. "How did you . . . I mean, what made you . . . why now?"

She smiled ironically. "After all these years, you mean? Yes, I must seem pretty stupid to you."

"I didn't mean that."

She thought for a moment, then explained, "I heard you shouting. I was concerned to hear the two of you rowing. So I asked Gabriel what it was all about. He wouldn't tell me anything. It was nothing, really. Just something in the way he talked about you. Suddenly everything . . . well, it all made sense."

"And you never suspected anything before."

"Never. I was so naïve when I met him. And from the very beginning, our relationship was so . . . so physical. I just never dreamed." It was David's turn to flinch. "I suppose I didn't want to know, really," she went on, clinically. "He was the first man I ever loved, and he told me I was the first *woman* he'd ever loved." She laughed bitterly. "I just didn't ask the right questions. I wanted to believe it. It's silly now, when I think about it. To imagine a man as . . . beautiful, as . . . passionate as Gabriel, could reach the age of thirty . . . That he was waiting around for me, all that time . . ." She sighed. "I wanted to believe it. That was my only excuse."

"Don't blame yourself."

She closed her eyes. "How very foolish you must think me."

* * *

It seemed like something from another world, the rambling house set on the edge of rolling green hills. Emily felt enveloped by its tranquillity even before they were in the door. Perhaps it was just that shock was setting in, she realized; she was drained of emotion now, and just wanted to rest.

David was so kind. He took care of the technicalities: He spoke to the head of the community, who was apparently a longtime acquaintance, and arranged for an open-ended stay for her in one of the rooms set aside for retreatants. Emily sat by numbly while he did all the talking. Finally it was time for him to take his leave of her.

"You'll be all right here, Emily," he said awkwardly. "They'll take care of you. And you can stay as long as you need to." She nodded. "When you're ready to ... come back, just ring me at Daphne's and I'll come for you."

"You won't tell him?"

"No, of course not." He took her hand; it was like ice. He squeezed it. "Listen, Emily. If there's ever anything you need, anything I can do for you ... you know where to find me. I'll come in a minute if you need me."

She looked up at him with gratitude. "I'll be all right, David. Don't worry about me. And—thank you. For everything."

A sweet-faced nun came forward. "I'll take you to your room now, Mrs. Neville." Emily was silent as they passed down the corridor. "I'm Sister Mary Grace." She opened the door to a small, plainly furnished room. "If you ever need to talk to someone, just ask anyone to find me for you. Any time." With a sympathetic smile, she left Emily alone in the room.

Emily sat on the bed. That was all she wanted right now—to be alone.

Chapter 26

Who will rise up with me against the wicked: or
who will take my part against the evil-doers?
                                        Psalm 94:16

Having left Emily in the capable hands of the good sisters,
David set off on the return journey into London. He very
quickly became tangled in traffic, but his thoughts were in
such turmoil that he scarcely noticed his lack of progress on
the road.

He was more than ever determined to follow through on
his threat to Gabriel to investigate Mavis's murder. He
hadn't much liked the woman, but it went against his lawyer's
instincts to let a murderer go scot-free, just because the police
were too incompetent to recognize a murder when they saw
one. To be fair, he reasoned, it wasn't entirely the police's
fault—they didn't know about the blackmail. Damn Gabriel.

He felt an enormous need to talk to someone about it. It
was clear that he could no longer talk to Gabriel, and even
if Emily were available it would hardly be fair to burden her
with it. Lucy? He considered the possibility carefully. He'd
like to tell Lucy. She would be a good listener, and would
probably be able to offer some helpful insights. But she was
entirely too close to the situation. Her protective feelings for
Emily would get in the way, and her dislike for Gabriel
would predispose her to think the worst of him. And how
could David explain to her his own place in the scheme of
things? No, it would never do.

Daphne. That was the only possible answer. Daphne
would listen, and not pass judgement. With her incisive

understanding of people and her vast experience of crime novels, she could be of real help in puzzling things out. She knew all the people involved, and could probably shed some light on them in a concrete way. And he could trust Daphne. Of that he was sure. He could trust her completely with his innermost secrets. And he'd have to begin with his innermost secrets, or she'd never understand what was at stake.

Once that decision was made, he became impatient with the traffic. He wanted to talk to her now. He hoped she'd be home when he arrived.

He was in luck. She was in the kitchen, boiling the kettle for tea. "Just in time," she greeted him with a smile. "I wasn't expecting you for tea."

"I suppose you'd think it was too early for something . . . stronger?"

"Whatever you like," she agreed, switching off the kettle and reaching for the whisky. "Has it been that sort of day?"

"Absolutely."

"Do you want to tell me about it?"

"I'd like nothing better," he confessed, leading the way to the sitting room.

Daphne made herself comfortable and looked at him over the tops of her glasses. "Fire away," she urged.

David sat awkwardly on the edge of his chair, twisting the glass in his hands. "I don't know where to begin."

"The beginning is generally as good a place as any," Daphne suggested with an encouraging smile.

"The beginning. Well." He took a gulp of whisky and tried to relax in the chair. "We've known each other a long time," he started, self-consciously. "Oh, hell, Daphne! I just don't know how to tell you this. I've never told anyone before in my life."

"Told anyone what?"

"Well, it's just that . . . that is to say, there's something about me that you don't know. I don't . . ."

"Do you want me to make it easier for you?" she drawled. "Are you trying to tell me that you're gay?"

His body sagged in relief and amazement. "Daphne! How long have you known?" he gasped.

"Probably a lot longer than you have, if you must know. I always had a feeling you were . . . that way inclined."

"My God. And you never said a word."

"It was none of my business, was it?" she said imperturbably. "The question is, why are you telling me this now?"

"That's another difficult thing to explain. It has to do with Gabriel."

"I thought it might."

"You know about . . . me and Gabriel?" He stared at her. She smiled calmly. "I guessed. As soon as I met Gabriel. There was something about the way he talked about you, and about the way you talked about him. It was obvious there'd been something between you. Obvious to me, anyway," she added quickly, to forestall alarm. "I don't think anyone else has guessed. No one else around here knows you as well as I do. Anyway, I didn't see you very often during those years you were in Brighton. I had a feeling you might have . . . met someone special."

David felt limp. "I'm speechless. Daphne . . ."

"Well, go on. What's the problem?"

"When you wrote and asked me to come, to see about the chapel . . ."

"Yes."

"Gabriel wrote at the same time. He said he needed my help."

"I rather thought it might be something like that," she mused. "He came round here to see me one night, the night we decided to invite you to come and help with the chapel. I wondered what was up. He jumped at my suggestion so eagerly, and he was most anxious to conceal from the parish that you knew each other. So what was it all about? And does he know that you're telling me now?"

"No, he doesn't. I'll get to that. The day after I'd arrived, after early Mass, he showed me a letter he'd received. I suppose you'd call it a blackmail letter."

Daphne raised her eyebrows. "Blackmail?"

"Yes. It didn't ask for money, but there were . . . certain demands. I can't really tell you what it was about, but suffice to say that it was written by someone who'd found out . . . something . . . about Gabriel's past. Nothing to do with me," he added quickly. "But he thought I might be able to help him find out who'd written the letter."

"And did you?"

"I thought I had, a few days ago. But since then . . . well, I think it's quite clear that it was Mavis Conwell."

She nodded thoughtfully. "Certainly that would be right up her street, if the subject matter was what I think it was."

"Yes. When you said, last night, that blackmail was a motive for murder—well, everything fell into place. I realized that she'd probably been killed by someone she had blackmailed."

"Surely you're not suggesting that Gabriel . . ."

"Good Lord, no!" he denied too quickly. "That's unthinkable, as well as being impossible—he was at the vicarage helping with teas when she was murdered."

"Then who . . ."

"I believe that she was blackmailing someone else, as well as Gabriel."

"What do the police say?"

He sighed. "That's the problem. The police believe she committed suicide! They've closed the case."

"But they don't know about the blackmail, presumably?"

"No. Gabriel didn't tell them, naturally enough." David poured himself another drink. "This morning he and I . . . we had a terrific row." He closed his eyes for a moment at the memory. "I'm sure he believes that she was the blackmailer—he was so relieved, so cheerful. But he's convinced himself that she wasn't murdered."

"How does he reckon that?"

"Well, apparently she's been pinching money from the church."

Daphne gave a low whistle. "Is that so?"

"Yes. That's mainly why the police think it was suicide. Remorse, fear of exposure, all that. And Gabriel's buying it. At least he says so."

"And you think . . ."

"That she was murdered. By another blackmail victim.

After all, if she was blackmailing one person, why not more than one?''

"Why don't you go to the police?"

He shook his head. "I've thought about it. But it really would be damned awkward, without any evidence, now that they've closed the case."

"So what are you going to do?"

"I want to make a few discreet inquiries, like I was doing before, about the blackmail."

"To what end?"

"I'd like to find out, if I can, who murdered Mavis Conwell. What I'm looking for is someone with a secret—a secret worth killing to protect. I'm not pretending it will be easy..."

"It could be dangerous, David," she warned, "if this person has killed once..."

"I know. I'm not going to ask you to help me, Daphne. I wouldn't put you in that position. But I need someone I can talk to about it. Two heads, and all that. You know the people, you know the setup. What do you think? Will you be my sounding-board?"

"You're not going to relegate me to that role, now that you've brought me this far! We're in this together now, David."

"So you think I'm right?"

"I think that between us we can come up with an answer that makes more sense than the police's solution. And then... well, we'll see, won't we?" Daphne topped up her glass, then settled back. "That *is* decadent, drinking whisky at four o'clock in the afternoon. Cheers, partner," she saluted him.

"Where do we start?"

She thought for a moment. "I don't suppose we can do much today besides explore some of the possibilities. Let's try to think who might have something to hide. Something that Mavis might find... of interest."

"Do you think it has to be a man?"

"I think it probably is," Daphne replied. "From a purely practical standpoint, it would take a fair amount of physical strength to . . . well, to hang someone. Lifting the weight, and all that. Mavis wasn't a particularly big woman, but just the same . . . I don't think I could have done it, and I don't know many women who could.''

''Well, that makes it easier, if we can eliminate all the women.''

''Mavis would have been much more likely to be interested in the . . . secrets . . . of the men, anyway, I should have thought. Think about her obsession with 'manliness,' and lack of it, in the Church.''

''The servers,'' David said, thinking out loud. ''She despised them. She seemed to think they were all suspect, because of Tony Kent. Tony. Everyone seems to know he's gay.''

''Yes, but that's the point. Everyone does know it. He's never made any secret of the fact.''

''Unlike others we know,'' David said with a wry smile. ''Maybe it's the difference between his generation and mine, or perhaps just his upbringing and mine.''

''Well, it might be worthwhile talking to Tony, anyway. He may well know something that could help us.''

''I'm having lunch with him tomorrow,'' David remembered suddenly.

''That could be useful.''

''Roger Dawson. I can't imagine him having any guilty secrets. He seems as dull as ditch water to me.''

''But you know about still waters running deep,'' Daphne cautioned. ''Don't dismiss him on that account.''

''What does Roger Dawson do?''

''He's some sort of a minor civil servant. Works in the local DSS office, I believe.''

''Hm. Well, I'll find out probably more than I want to know about Roger Dawson soon, too. I'm going there for dinner on Wednesday,'' he said with a grimace.

''Now *that's* suspicious in itself! I wonder why they've asked you? The Dawsons have never been well-known for their hospitality!''

''I'm sure I'll find out in due time. But I don't think we have to worry about the Dawsons.'' David held his glass up to the light and squinted through the amber liquid as he worked through the possibilities in his mind. "How about Cyril?" he asked.

"I shouldn't think so. I don't think he'd be physically strong enough, in the first place. I'd say the same about Venerable Bead. And Cyril's too . . . candid for me to believe that he has any terrible secrets. I mean, everyone knows how he feels about Emily! And he doesn't seem at all embarrassed that it should be that way."

"Do you know who I'd like it to be?" David confessed. "Miles Taylor. I just don't care for the bloke. What secrets is he hiding?"

"Funny you should ask that," said Daphne, with a speculative look. "As a matter of fact, there is something distinctly suspicious about Miles Taylor."

"Tell me."

"Well, you know that he used to be organist at Selby Cathedral."

"I had heard," he said, rolling his eyes.

"Yes, I suppose it would be difficult to be around Miles for five minutes without learning that fact," she acknowledged humorously. "Anyway, Miles left Selby very suddenly about five years ago, and came here. Now, St. Anne's is a lovely church, and has a lot to offer a musician, but it's not a cathedral."

"No . . ."

"And there have been a few people who have wondered why a man with Miles's talent would have left a cathedral to come here. It's rather a step down in the world of a cathedral organist."

"Does anyone know why he left Selby?"

"He never talks about it. But I think there's something in it, something he's hiding."

"I wonder." David looked very thoughtful.

"Secrets," Daphne mused. "Everyone has them, I suppose."

"Even you, Daphne?"

She smiled enigmatically. "Even me. The things we think other people wouldn't understand . . . It's all perception, you know. The faces we show to the world..." Suddenly practical, she sat up. "We must make a plan. You will have lunch with Tony tomorrow, and talk with him. See what you can find out."

"I'd like to talk to the manly Craig, if I could. I'm not suggesting that he had anything to do with the murder—Mavis would hardly have blackmailed her own son, after all! But I might learn something about Mavis and her preoccupations from him. I don't know how I'd manage it, though. He's not exactly the sort one would pay a sympathy call on!"

"As a matter of fact, I'll be seeing Craig Conwell tomorrow," Daphne revealed with satisfaction. "He's coming in to discuss the arrangements for the funeral with me and with Gabriel."

"Excellent. Then I'll leave him to you—he's your assignment for the day."

"Then what?"

"I would dearly love to have a word with Miles Taylor. At the moment, my money's on him."

"I doubt that he'd be very forthcoming. You know how he is. Well, you can see him on Wednesday at the recital, anyway." Daphne suddenly looked very sheepish, then burst out laughing.

"What's so funny?"

"Oh, David. I've just realized something. Miles Taylor is the one person who couldn't possibly have killed Mavis!"

"Why not? If this motive turns out to be anything..."

"No, David, you don't understand! Miles was playing the organ, wasn't he?"

"Yes," David said slowly. "The recital had started when I left Mavis alive in the sacristy..."

"And he was still playing when Venerable opened the sacristy door an hour later! Whether you like it or not, David, Miles is in the clear!"

"Damn," said David, crestfallen.

Chapter 27

*Who imagine mischief in their hearts: and stir
   up strife all day long.
They have sharpened their tongues like a serpent:
   adder's poison is under their lips.*

                                        Psalm 140:2–3

The workmen were due to begin their repairs in the crypt chapel on Tuesday morning, David remembered. He'd promised Lady Constance that he would oversee their labors. So the morning before his lunch with Tony went by quickly, with scarcely time for thoughts of murder and blackmail. But inevitably before the morning was over, Venerable Bead puffed his way down the stairs to find out what was happening, his little eyes bright with curiosity. "Oh, I wondered if the workmen had started," he addressed David.

"Yes, just this morning. It's going to take some time, I think. The work is very delicate."

"Well, when you have to leave London, you can leave it in my hands," Venerable said with eagerness. "When are you going back home?"

"I've got a month off from work," David replied vaguely. "So I can stay a bit longer if necessary."

Venerable stood for a moment observing the workmen. "Mind you watch what you're doing!" he said sharply to one of them at some imagined infraction. The man glared.

David stepped in quickly to distract the old man's critical eye. "That must have been quite a shock for you on Saturday, finding the body."

"Oh, it gave me quite a turn, I can tell you! Not what I

was expecting to see, when I went to get ready for Even-song!" He was enjoying himself immensely, David could see, and he wordlessly encouraged him to go on. "Terrible, the sight was! I've never seen anything like it! She was hanging from that long bracket, the one for the statue of Our Lady, and the chair was knocked over on the floor. Her eyes were staring right at me! And she was all limp, and her tongue . . ." He shuddered deliciously, and demonstrated the expression on the dead woman's face. Venerable Bead's fund of stories had been enriched immeasurably—he'd be dining out on this one for the rest of his life, David thought.

* * *

When the time came, David was glad of the chance to escape from the church, and from the daunting prospect of the weekly lunches in the church hall.

Tony lived in a flat outside St. Anne's parish in Notting Hill Gate, not far from the Portobello Road. David had known the Portobello Road fairly well in his early days in London with Daphne, but hadn't been there for years, so he self-consciously consulted his A to Z before setting off. He was glad he'd done so, as Monday's overcast skies had turned at last to steady rain, and the pavements seethed with umbrellas. A taxi passing too close to the curb soaked his trouser-legs, and he cursed silently.

Tony seemed glad to see him. "Hope you didn't have too much trouble finding it, David. You look like you could use a drink. Sherry? Or would you prefer whisky?"

David looked at him gratefully. "You read my mind. Whisky, please." While Tony fixed the drinks, he observed the flat with interest. It was really only one room, cleverly divided into areas for sitting, cooking and eating, and sleeping. The sleeping part consisted of a loft, reached by a ladder and containing an oversized bed. The walls of the sitting area were lined with bookcases, and the whole flat was dominated by a sophisticated stereo system with multi-ple speakers. It was decorated with innovative but simple good taste. "I like your flat," he said sincerely, crossing to the purpose-built record shelves for a browse. A little Vivaldi might be just the thing, he thought, but he was disappointed: The record collection seemed to be dominated by rock music by people he'd never heard of.

"Sorry about that," Tony apologized, turning and seeing his furrowed brow. "My . . . flatmate . . . has rather esoteric tastes in music, I'm afraid. The sound system is his. I like a bit of jazz, myself—my records are there at the end."

David thought he might just about be able to endure jazz, if he had to. Tony put on some Dave Brubeck, turned the volume down low, and they sat on the low-slung chairs with their drinks.

"Your . . . flatmate's not here?" David asked conversationally. "Ian, I think his name is?"

"Ah, so someone's been talking, have they?" said Tony tensely.

"Only Venerable Bead," David reassured him.

"That's all right, then." Tony relaxed. "No, Ian's at work."

"Oh, isn't he a teacher, too? I just assumed he was."

"No. Ian . . . well, he drives a taxi."

"Ah! Maybe he's the one I have to thank for this, then!" David surveyed his damp ankles ruefully.

They both laughed, and the potential awkwardness was dispelled.

"The flat really is lovely," David reiterated. "Have you lived here long?"

"About six or seven years, I suppose. I've gradually fixed it up the way I like it."

"You're not actually in St. Anne's parish here, are you? Did you used to live in the parish?"

"No, I'm not a native Londoner. I grew up in Croydon—there's a good High Church tradition there, as you may know, so when I moved to London to teach, I looked around for a church nearby with the proper churchmanship. St. Anne's was just what I was looking for, and they happened to need servers very badly at that time. So I've been there ever since. It's suited me very well, and it's quite close by."

"I would have thought St. Anne's would never suffer from a shortage of servers."

"Well, not too long before I came, they'd lost the two oldest Dawson boys, Nick and Ben. They'd gone off to university. Venerable says they were both pretty good servers— very conscientious, anyway."

"But Francis?" David prompted. "You said you had a tale to tell about him."

"Oh, Francis. You haven't met him, have you? He's absolutely gormless. And as a server . . . Well, let's just say his career was short-lived but memorable."

"What on earth did he do?"

"He very badly wanted to serve. I wasn't keen on having him—I knew how clumsy he was, but Gabriel insisted that I at least give him a chance."

"Fair enough, I suppose."

"I gave him plenty of training, and thought he might be able to start as an acolyte. But the very first Sunday, he bent too close to the candle, and set his hair on fire!"

"That must have been quite a sight!"

"It was at the high altar, so I don't think too many people saw it. I'll never forget it, though! Next I tried him as crucifer—I thought that would be safer. But he led the procession off in the wrong direction. There wasn't anything that anyone could do but follow him. So much for being crucifer."

"You didn't let him be MC, did you?"

"Just once. He opened the book at the wrong page, and Gabriel read out the wrong collect. He wasn't very amused—I think he was beginning to realize he'd been too charitable in his assessment of Francis's abilities."

"So that was the end of his career?"

"Oh, no. He went out with a mighty bang. Literally. His ultimate ambition was to be thurifer, so I thought I'd give him a go at it on a weekday, at a Saint's Day service. I figured he couldn't do much harm there, but I was wrong. He was swinging the thurible, and got up such a good head of steam that he let it go. It went flying, with incense and charcoal landing all over the sanctuary carpet in flames. Gabriel didn't miss a beat. He stomped it all out while he intoned the Gospel. But that was well and truly the end of Francis's serving career. Gabriel put his foot down, so to speak." Tony shook his head. "You've got to laugh."

"Are those the only boys in the family?"

"Yes. Then there are the three girls. Bridget, Clare, and Teresa. Thank God no one has ever seriously suggested allowing girls to serve at St. Anne's, or Teresa would be the first to sign up! That girl is completely clueless."

"Well, I shall certainly look forward to my dinner with the Dawsons—it should be worth a great deal in entertainment value. I'm even promised a chance to meet the famous Francis!"

"You're going to dinner at the Dawsons?"

"Yes, tomorrow. Didn't I tell you?"

Tony looked amazed. "Well, I never. I can't imagine what that will be like. The Dawsons never have people over for a meal."

"Really?"

"No. Their meanness is legendary when it comes to hospitality, or lack thereof. You know, whenever I've been at their house for a meeting—servers, or whatever, the big event is the unveiling of the sacred Postman Pat biscuit tin. I think it must be a family heirloom. It's brought out with all due ceremony, and everyone present is invited to help themself to one biscuit, and one biscuit only."

"Maybe I'd better eat before I go."

"That wouldn't be a bad idea, probably! Speaking of food, though, are you ready for some lunch?"

"Any time."

"It isn't anything fancy," Tony warned. "Just plain food—not the airy-fairy sort of thing you'd get from Lucy Kingsley," he added, tongue-in-cheek, and watching surreptitiously to see his reaction.

David refused to be drawn. "I imagine you're a very good cook," he said blandly.

That proved to be true, and the tales of the Dawsons resumed over an excellent steak and kidney pie.

"Have you noticed Roger Dawson's liturgical ties?" Tony asked. "Probably not. It's a lot more noticeable when you get the whole family there, wearing their ties in seasonal colors."

"Do you mean to tell me the Dawsons wear neckties in liturgical colors? Every day?" David inquired, bemused.

Tony laughed. "Not every day, no. Just on Sundays and Feast Days. We've had a pretty long spell of green ties now, except for gold on the Patronal Festival. But if you're still here next week for the Feast of the Assumption, you'll get to see the rare blue tie, in honor of Our Lady."

"I don't believe it."

"Oh, it's true all right."

"But what about the women?"

"The girls generally wear hair bows, and Julia wears a silk scarf. There's no one more properly Catholic than the Devout Dawsons."

After lunch they relaxed over coffee. David had tried very hard to think of a way to introduce the subject of the blackmail letters in a natural way, but finally he gave up and plunged in. "Tony, you may think this is a strange question. It *is* a strange question, but I have reasons for asking it."

"Go ahead," Tony said, somewhat apprehensively.

"It's just . . . well, I wondered if you had any knowledge about . . . that is, do you know anyone who has received any . . . threatening letters? Letters that might have been written by Mavis Conwell?"

Tony stared at him in amazement. "How did you know?"

"Know what?"

"About the letter?"

"You've had a letter?"

"Yes, of course. How did you find out?"

David took a deep breath, stunned. "Tell me about it, please."

"It came—oh, a fortnight or so ago. Maybe longer."

"Have you kept it?"

"No. It was—horrible. I tore it up and threw it on the fire."

"Did you know it was from Mavis?"

"I assumed it was. I threw it away, and tried to forget about it."

"But what . . . can you tell me what it said?" Tony looked stricken. "I wouldn't ask if it wasn't important," David added gently.

"It said . . . that I was a disgrace to the Church."

"But there was a threat?"

"Yes." Tony hesitated fractionally, looking down at his clasped hands. "About Ian."

"I don't understand."

Tony turned and met his eyes. "Ian is only nineteen," he said in a low voice. "I could go to prison."

* * *

Walking back to Daphne's in the rain, David went through the Portobello Road market to look for a florist. The flower sellers on the market, discouraged by the weather, had long since packed up and gone home, but he found a florist shop around the corner. Roses for Lucy, he thought. Long-stemmed roses, the color of her hair. He chose them with a feeling of anticipation. Tonight he'd give her the roses, and they'd listen to Mozart, and he'd forget about murder for a few hours.

In the meantime, though . . . He picked out a sturdy bunch of mixed summer flowers for Daphne, and went back for tea.

* * *

"So how is the manly Craig taking his mother's death?" David asked while the tea steeped. "Prostrate with grief, is he?"

"He doesn't seem to be particularly bothered," Daphne said in her detached way. "He didn't have much to say for himself, but he's not especially verbose at the best of times."

"When will the funeral be?"

"Next week—probably Tuesday. I think the inquest will be Monday, and they'll release the body for the funeral then."

"Are there any other relatives?"

"I believe that Mavis had brothers and sisters, but there's no one close enough to be involved in the planning. Craig wants it as simple as possible, he says. Actually, he wants it as cheap as possible," she added cynically. "It will be a plain Prayer Book funeral, no frills at all."

"No servers?"

"No." Daphne laughed. "This is the other interesting bit. He says he doesn't want any servers—not even a crucifer. He said that his mother hated 'those poofs' and wouldn't have wanted them 'prancing around' at her funeral!"

"And what did Gabriel say about that?" David smiled in spite of himself.

"He didn't say a word, but he looked extremely pained."

"I should think he did."

Chapter 28

Upon an instrument of ten strings, and upon the lute: upon a loud instrument, and upon the harp.

Psalm 92:3

Daphne had already finished her breakfast and was nearly done with the newspaper by the time David emerged, yawning and rubbing his eyes. "Would you like a cooked breakfast?" she offered.

"No thanks, Daphne. I really can't have you waiting on me all the time. Just toast and tea will be fine."

"You must have been out quite late last night. How was the Mozart?"

"Oh, splendid," he replied with a reminiscent smile. "The worst part was queuing in the rain. I swore it was the last time I'd ever do that—and I'm too old to stand through a concert, anyway."

"I thought you said you were going to go again tomorrow night."

"Yes, but I've splurged, and bought seats in the stalls. It will be worth it."

"Are you going to the organ recital today?" she asked.

"Yes. Do you want to come?"

"No, thank you. I heard a bit of the one on Saturday, and a little of Miles goes a long way with me."

He frowned pensively. "I really wish I could pin the murder on him."

"Well, you can't. We've established that. Have you had any further thoughts on what Tony told you?"

"I've been thinking about it. I think that the fact that he was open about the letter he received puts him in the clear. If he'd murdered her, he wouldn't have told me about the letter."

"Not necessarily. He might have been trying to throw you off the scent. After all, you didn't actually see the letter. You don't know what it really said."

"Oh, Daphne, your mind is too devious for me. Is there anybody I can cross off the list of possible suspects?"

"Yes, Miles Taylor," she chuckled.

* * *

The sun had returned, at least intermittently; Lucy was waiting for him outside the church, shading her eyes against the bright light. "You're early," he greeted her.

"Yes, it was such a pleasant day that I couldn't really get started working, so I came out and walked over through the park. Anyway," she confessed, "I didn't get up very early this morning, so there wasn't time to do much painting, even if I'd been inclined."

"I didn't either," David admitted. "Poor Daphne, I don't know how late she waited up last night."

"You couldn't talk her into coming with you today?"

"No, she wasn't all that keen."

Lucy hesitated. "Emily won't be coming today, either."

"Oh?" David said, as noncommittally as possible.

"No. I had a letter from her in this morning's post. You know I said last night that I hadn't talked with her since Saturday? Well, apparently she's gone away for a few days."

"By herself?" he asked, hating himself for his dishonesty.

"Yes." Lucy didn't say any more, and he could only

guess at how much Emily had revealed to her. Not very much, he surmised. Lucy would be loyal and discreet, but surely Emily wouldn't have . . .

People had been steadily streaming past them into the north porch of the church. Now Beryl Ball approached, shuffling up in her moonboots. But instead of going past, she stopped and looked at David, then at Lucy, with her magnified eyes. "You just can't stay away from the women, can you?" she asked maliciously. "When I wouldn't have you, you went after that whore the Vicar's wife. She's not particular—she'll take any man! But she's gone now, isn't she?" she announced with triumph.

"Is she?" David said faintly.

"You know she is—that's why you've got this one now! You're a sex maniac, that's what you are!"

"How do you know she's gone?" Lucy asked.

"The Vicar told me himself! Yesterday, at lunch. I asked him where she was, and he said she'd gone off to take care of a sick relative. But I knew he was lying. She's gone for good, is that one. Run off with another man. No better than she should be, I always said." She nodded her head vigorously. "Sick with worry, the Vicar looked. Not that I didn't warn him, before he married the slut. I told him it would end in tears." Beryl looked back and forth between them, daring them to challenge her, then grinned suddenly as a new thought occurred to her. "To tell the truth, I wouldn't be a bit surprised if it was Mavis's boy that she's run off with! He wasn't half upset when I turned him down on Saturday! It was my new hat, you see—he just couldn't resist me in it. But I told him no, and he must have run off with her instead!"

"Miss Ball," said David finally, "I don't really think—"

"You can count on it. That's just what happened," she interrupted, with a self-righteous thrust of her dentures, and shuffled off into the church.

David had a guilty pang at the thought of Gabriel, sick with worry. Should he say something to him, just to ease his mind? No, he decided. Emily's needs were more important at the moment. She'd never forgive him if he betrayed her trust.

* * *

To David's disappointment, the penultimate piece of the program was the same piece—the Great G Minor Fantasia and Fugue—that Miles had performed on Saturday. Apparently he had not practiced it in the meantime, David noted; he was making exactly the same mistakes. The mistakes were not glaring ones, but they were evident to anyone who knew the piece well, and they grated. After several minutes, he whispered to Lucy, "Why don't we make our escape now? I've heard enough of this." She nodded agreement, and they slipped out of the north porch.

"Why don't you come to my place for some tea," Lucy suggested. But David made no reply; stopped in his tracks, he was staring with disbelief at Miles Taylor, who leaned nonchalantly against the church, smoking a cigarette.

"Come on," she urged. "Miles is just cheating again," she added in a whisper. "He must have the Great G Minor on the computer. You know, the machine that plays the organ for him."

David turned to stare at her. He deliberately marched her around the corner of the building, out of Miles's hearing, and said slowly, "Would you please repeat what you just said?"

"I said he must have the Great G Minor on the computer. Surely you knew about his fancy machine—he brags about it enough. He loves all that high-tech gadgetry, you know. And this is the latest thing."

"And what exactly does this machine do?"

"It plays the organ for him. I'm not sure about the technical details. But apparently it remembers all the registrations, and the key-strokes, and plays it back exactly—actually plays the pipes, just as if he were sitting at the console. Miles is a chain-smoker, surely you've noticed that. He can't get through an hour without a cigarette, so he's got some of his favorite pieces stored on the machine, and he usually puts at least one of them on every recital program, so he can sneak out and have a cigarette. When he's having a real nicotine fit, he doesn't have to play a note himself. Most people never know the difference.''

David closed his eyes and leaned against the warm stone. "Lucy, you're wonderful."

"Why, thank you. I think you're rather nice yourself. But to what do I owe that compliment?''

"I can't really explain now. But I need to have a word with Miles. Would you mind going on ahead and putting the kettle on? I'll be along in just a few minutes.''

"Whatever you say. See you shortly, then." With a quizzical look over her shoulder, she departed, and he watched her graceful walk as he had watched her the week before, the day they'd met. Only a week? he thought. Impossible.

* * *

The rest of the recital seemed to take hours, though in reality it was less than ten minutes. David waited at the back of the church in a fever of impatience while the applause went on, the organist took repeated bows, and finally descended to feed his ego on the adoration of the Fan Club.

But David reached him first, with a smooth smile. Flattery would get him everywhere with this man, he had decided; the direct approach would never work.

"Mr. Taylor—may I call you Miles?—that was a splendid program!" he enthused.

Miles turned to him, beaming. "I'm glad you liked it. It was rather good, wasn't it?''

"Splendid! Splendid!" he repeated, steering Miles past the waiting women and leading him outside. "It's a very fine instrument, isn't it?''

"Well, it has its strengths. Of course there are little problems that only an organist would understand. You're not an organist, are you?''

"No, just an appreciative listener," David gushed.

Condescendingly, Miles explained, "It's a fine organ. But some of the registrations just don't—well, I mustn't get too technical.''

"I suppose no organ is perfect, but it's the mark of a professional to be able to work with the imperfections to achieve such a magnificent sound!"

Miles's thin chest swelled. "You're right, of course. Though I must say that the organ at Selby Cathedral is as close to perfect as I've ever found. Sheer heaven, that organ. Mechanical action, beautiful voicing, incredible stops. Absolutely perfect for contemporary music."

"Of course, you were at Selby. That must have been a wonderful experience for you."

Miles flung out his arms in an expansive gesture. "Yes, those were the best years of my life! That magnificent organ! The wonderful music! And the choir—brilliant!" He beamed seraphically in nostalgic remembrance.

Having led him so satisfactorily up the garden path, David was ready for the kill. "St. Anne's is so lucky to have a man of your...experience," he said ingenuously. "Tell me, how did you come to leave Selby for St. Anne's?"

The smile froze on Miles's face, his eyes glittered behind his spectacles, and his arms dropped to his sides. "I'm afraid that as a nonmusician, you couldn't possibly understand. Now I really must be going. The ladies will be so disappointed if they don't have a chance to see me. Do come again next week, won't you?"

David watched his retreating back with satisfaction. Daphne had been right: He was definitely hiding something. But Daphne had been wrong about the other thing. Miles Taylor was not off the list of suspects, not by a long shot. At the moment, he was well ahead of the pack. With a thoughtful shake of his head, David resumed his journey towards Lucy and tea.

Chapter 29

Lo, children are the fruit of the womb: are an
heritage and gift that cometh of the Lord.
Like as the arrows in the hand of the giant: even
so are the young children.
Happy is the man that hath his quiver full of them:
they shall not be ashamed when they speak with
their enemies in the gate.

Psalm 127:4–6

Tea had stretched out over the afternoon, and the Dawsons had invited him for the unbelievably early hour of six, so David barely had time to stop at a wine merchant's to pick up a bottle and to call in on Daphne before hurrying to his dinner date. She told him how to find the Dawsons' house—a semi-detached, a few streets away from Mavis Conwell's terrace—and promised to wait up for his return, intrigued by his hints of revelations to come. "I can't imagine that you'll be very late," she called after him.

He was not really looking forward to this evening, David reflected, wondering again why he'd been invited. The Devout Dawsons were not his cup of tea. According to Tony Kent, the Dawsons were totally without any sense of humor, and paradoxically it was that quality alone that made them amusing, in an entirely unintentional way. But with people who took themselves so seriously, any temptation to share the joke, as it were, would have to be firmly suppressed. He practiced looking solemn, and pious. He hoped it would be a short evening. Five minutes late already—damn. With the Dawsons, he didn't imagine that six meant anything but six sharp.

Julia Dawson opened the door to him with her customary anxious expression.

"I'm so sorry I'm late," he began as he handed her the bottle of wine.

"We were beginning to worry," she said, ushering him in. "I was afraid you'd got lost, and Roger thought perhaps you'd had an accident." She announced his arrival in the lounge. "It's all right, he's here."

A small dog of indeterminate breed appeared as if from nowhere and hurled itself at David's legs, yapping frantically. David liked dogs, but he didn't much like the look of this one. Shaggy and unkempt, it resembled the business end of a well-used mop. "Ignatius!" Julia shrieked. "Leave the man alone! I thought I'd shut you outside!" She grabbed the dog by its collar and dragged it away. "I'm so sorry, David. Ignatius doesn't like strangers," she apologized over her shoulder. He stood a moment, bemused, then entered the lounge.

Roger Dawson rose, and extended his hand. Teresa, sitting in the corner, turned her head away in embarrassment at David's acknowledgement. And then there were the introductions to Francis, the man enshrined in serving lore forever.

Francis Dawson was pretty much exactly what David would have expected. Unprepossessing, in the honored family tradition. He wasn't tall, but neither was he short. His hair was the color and texture of wet straw—David had to bite his lip to suppress a chuckle at the thought of that hair blazing away, ignited by a candle; he could just imagine the look on Gabriel's face. Francis had mild blue eyes, not as protuberant as Teresa's, and his mother's thin, pointed nose. A tuft of scraggly beard gave him the illusion of having the vestige of a chin. His voice, when he spoke, was soft and diffident.

Julia returned, breathing heavily. "Do sit down, David," she urged, then struck by her own presumption, added anxiously, "May I call you David?"

"Yes, of course . . . Julia."

"Now, what would you like for your tea?" she addressed

her children. "Remember that we have a guest. Would you like fish fingers and chips? Or beans on toast?"

"Spaghetti on toast?" suggested Teresa hopefully.

Julia shook her head. "I'm afraid we're out of tinned spaghetti."

"Fish fingers, then," Francis said, and Teresa agreed. "After all, we have a guest."

Julia looked to David for his approval; he could only nod mutely. Tea, he thought. Not dinner—tea. No wonder they'd said six o'clock. With all those children stretched over so many years, they'd apparently never got into the habit of eating dinner like civilized adults. And they clearly didn't realize that the children had grown up. He shuddered inwardly at the thought of frozen fish fingers, but had to admit that they were preferable to the alternative of beans on toast. At least he wasn't too hungry—he mentally blessed Lucy, and the lovely sandwiches and cakes she'd fed him that afternoon. He gave up any hopes he'd cherished of being offered a sherry, and sat back to await his fate.

Filling the time until the food was produced proved to be a little difficult. Roger Dawson had the disconcerting habit of refusing to make eye contact: All his remarks were addressed to David's left shoulder. Teresa huddled in her chair, trying to make herself disappear. That left Francis as the most likely source of conversation.

"So, Francis," David began heartily. "What do you do?"

"I'm at university," he replied. "I've finished my first year."

"He's followed his big brother Nick to the University of Sussex," Roger added in his dry, slightly raspy voice, overlaid with a faint sibilance. "We're proud of our boys."

"And what are you reading?"

"Philosophy and Artificial Intelligence."

David hardly knew what to say to that. "That sounds an interesting combination," he managed.

"Yes."

There was an awkward silence, then Roger asked his son a question about his course-work, and they carried on a two-sided conversation for several minutes. That gave David the opportunity to observe the room surreptitiously. He concluded that it resembled nothing so much as a corner of the Shrine of Our Lady of Walsingham, a place he loathed, finding it tacky and tasteless. There was actually a statue of Our Lady of Walsingham, smirking child on her lap, surrounded by red and blue votive candles, on the mantel-piece; the walls were covered with cheap reproductions of bad religious paintings, adorned with old palm crosses. And the furniture was covered with dog hair—long, dingy-grey hairs. David inconspicuously, he hoped, picked a few off his trouser-legs.

Mercifully soon, Julia reappeared to announce the meal. They trooped into a dining room dominated by a huge family-sized table; places were set around it at widely spaced intervals. Passing the salt could be interesting, David envisioned.

The fish fingers were fully as appalling as he had imag-ined, but surprisingly the addition of Julia to the gathering improved the conversation considerably.

"I'm so sorry about Ignatius," she began. "He really is a very naughty little doggie." She put her head to one side, listening to the persistent and hysterical barking from some-where outside. "Do you like dogs, David?"

"Yes, very much," he replied without thinking, then, afraid she would interpret his reply as an invitation to bring Ignatius back, quickly changed the subject. "How did your cake stall do at the fête?"

"Oh, very well indeed. We sold out before the afternoon, and took in nearly five hundred pounds. It's the best we've ever done."

Unthinkingly, he responded, "Mrs. Conwell said that the fête had raised more money than ever before. When I saw her in the sacristy," he added lamely, when he saw their horrified faces staring at him. Julia's mouth hung open like a fish, and her chin trembled. Roger licked his lips nervously. Francis looked blank, but Teresa had at last, bizarrely, come alive. Her eyes glittered avidly.

"I heard that when Mr. Bead found her, her lips were blue, and her eyes were popping out," she whispered intensely, in the first complete sentence David had heard her utter.

Startled, he said, "Yes, I believe that's true."

"Teresa! That's quite enough!" her mother quavered. "Poor Mavis! How could you be so callous!"

Teresa looked down at her plate, but not before David caught the look of satisfaction in her eyes.

"David," Julia appealed to him. "Has Daphne said anything to you about the funeral arrangements?"

"She mentioned that there were some preliminary plans. I think it's to be next Tuesday."

"At St. Anne's?" Julia asked, her eyes wide.

"That was certainly the impression I got."

"Shocking!" was Roger Dawson's reaction, addressed to the potted lily on the sideboard.

"Why..."

"A suicide! A woman who killed herself—to be given a Christian funeral, and her ashes buried in consecrated ground! I just don't believe it!"

"Whatever can Father Gabriel be thinking of?" Julia added with a shaking voice.

Teresa raised her eyes again. "Maybe it wasn't suicide," she announced with relish. "Maybe it was . . . murder!"

* * *

After a sweet of tinned fruit with ice cream, they returned to the lounge. David wondered how soon he could decently escape, but Julia had other ideas. "We thought you might enjoy looking at some family pictures," she suggested, hauling out a mammoth album.

"Oh, yes, that would be lovely," David lied. He settled the album on his lap. Julia and Roger flanked him on either side of the sofa, and Teresa returned to her chair in the corner. Francis disappeared, and shortly David could hear the faint sound of a television from somewhere else in the house. Outside, Ignatius's frantic barking had transmuted into a steady howl.

He opened the album to be confronted by a mind-numbing array of Dawsons, at all stages of life and in every possible combination. There were baby Dawsons— unmistakably Dawsons, all of them—in prams, in cots, in push-chairs. Toddler Dawsons in the park, on the beach. Dawsons in school uniforms. Dawsons in cassocks and albs. Dawson dogs, of course, each one more unappealing than the last. And innumerable Dawson relations. "That's Uncle Edmund," Julia pointed out.

"He's dead," Teresa said in sepulchral tones. "He got run over by a train."

Dawson cousins, Dawson grandparents. "Grandmother Dawson," indicated Roger.

"She died last year," added Teresa. "Blood poisoning."

Dawsons on holiday, Dawsons standing in front of churches. David occasionally stopped to ask a question, to identify a person or place.

He looked at a photo of two young Dawson girls, dressed in virginal white with wreaths of flowers in their hair, posed in front St. Anne's with another little girl, similarly attired. "Bridgie and Clare," Julia explained, "after they were in the Procession of Our Lady one year. The girl with them is Cecily Framlingham's daughter."

"But she died," Teresa announced. "She drowned, on holiday at Bournemouth."

"How terrible," said David. He turned the page and looked at a picture of the Dawson he had come to recognize as Nick, sitting with a good-looking young man who was clearly not a Dawson, not even a Dawson cousin.

"That's Nick and his roommate, his first year at university," Roger explained.

Teresa opened her mouth, and David anticipated her words. "He's dead, too. He . . ."

"Teresa, that's quite enough of your morbid stories," her mother said shrilly. With a sulky yet venomous look, Teresa got up and left the room. Julia turned to David apologetically. "I'm sorry about Teresa. You know how teenagers are."

"Yes, of course." And David settled back for yet more of the pictorial Dawson chronicles.

* * *

"Poor David. They didn't even offer you a drink?" Daphne sympathized later.

"Not a drop. Not a sherry before . . . the meal—I won't call it dinner—and the bottle of wine I took disappeared without a trace. Nothing after, either. Just a cup of insipid instant coffee."

"Well, no one said it would be a fun evening," she said, pouring him a generous whisky. "But did you actually find out *why* they'd invited you?"

He laughed. "Eventually. After an agonizing evening of looking at family pictures, they finally got around to the reason for the invitation."

"Which was . . . ?"

"They were after some free legal advice, of course. I should have suspected it! It was something to do with Grandmother Dawson's will—they were just too mean to pay a solicitor, and thought I could help them."

"Of course," Daphne chuckled. "That makes perfect sense."

"They're the strangest family I've ever met." He shook his head, remembering. "Roger gives me the creeps, the way he never looks straight at you. Julia seems like she's always about to burst into tears. Francis—well, gormless is the right word for him. And that girl . . ."

"Teresa?"

"She's the most peculiar of all—she's a right little ghoul. What a household."

"Does that mean you're not going to invite them to stop for a visit on their next trip to Walsingham?" Daphne asked with a straight face. "They go on the National Pilgrimage every year."

"Yes, I'm sure they do," he groaned. "Promise you won't tell them where I live."

"I'll draw them a map to your front door, unless you stop all this Dawson talk and tell me right now what all this is about Miles! I've been sitting here all evening trying to decipher your hints!"

"Ah." He smiled, immensely pleased with himself, and leaned back in his chair.

"What on earth have you found out, David?"

"Only that Miles is no longer off the list of suspects. He's back at the top of the list!" She looked dubious but fascinated, as he went on to explain his discovery about the organ-playing computer, and his subsequent conversation with Miles.

"Oh, David. This changes everything."

"Absolutely."

"He could so easily have gone down the stairs from the console—they're right there in that corridor—and nipped into the sacristy without anyone seeing him. All the while the organ was playing. How long is that piece, by the way? The one he had on the computer today?"

"Twelve or thirteen minutes, I suppose. That would give him plenty of time. Or he could even have taken longer if necessary. Lucy says he can program in a whole sequence of pieces for the machine to play. I should have known," he added. "When he 'played' the Great G Minor today, all the mistakes were exactly the same, just like a recording. I just thought he hadn't practiced."

"But how could you have known about the machine? I certainly didn't, though I suppose I should have. I just never pay that much attention to Miles and his antics."

"Lucy says it's the latest thing. Emily told her that he went to the PCC and said he had to have it, and threatened to quit if he didn't get it."

She snorted. "Thank God I'm not on the PCC. I'm afraid I wouldn't have been keen to spend that kind of money, just so Miles could have a smoke! He probably spun them some plausible tale about being in the forefront of technological progress . . ."

"But the question is, Daphne, what do I do now? He's hiding something, but there's no way I'm going to find out what it is. Not here in London, anyway."

"I think you'll have to go to Selby," Daphne said practically. "That's where the answer is."

David nodded. "Yes, you're right. The sooner the better, I suppose. Will you come with me?"

She thought for a moment. "I don't think I should; you don't know how long it will take, and I need to be here on Sunday. Anyway, it's better for me to stay and keep an eye on things here."

"I can't go tomorrow," he remembered. "I'm having tea with Lady Constance, and I wouldn't want to stand her up."

"And don't forget stall seats at the Proms tomorrow night."

"Of course. But Friday—I can go on Friday. You'll have to help me think of a strategy. Miles Taylor may think he's clever, but between us, Daphne, we'll outsmart him."

Chapter 30

Forsake me not, O God, in mine old age, when I am greyheaded: until I have shewed thy strength unto this generation, and thy power to all them that are yet for to come.

Psalm 71:16

The contrast could not have been more marked, David reflected, between yesterday and today: between the tasteless clutter of the Dawsons' lounge and the understated elegance of Lady Constance's drawing room, between the nasty frozen fish fingers and the tasty finger sandwiches, between, indeed, the twitchy peculiarity of the Dawsons and the calm patrician aura of Lady Constance herself.

He had found Lady Constance looking rather tired, the lines on her face more pronounced than on previous meetings, and he inquired with concern. "It's nothing, young man," she reassured him. "Old age, that's all. I find I tire so quickly these days. It's a terrible thing to get old."

"But it's better than the alternative," he replied lightly.

"Sometimes I wonder," she said softly, but the smile belied her words.

"Perhaps Saturday was too much for you," he suggested. "Walking around in the hot sun."

"Perhaps," she agreed. A shadow fell over her face. "A terrible business, that, on Saturday. It has quite upset me."

"Oh, Mrs. Conwell's . . . death. Yes, it was. But you said she was a dreadful woman."

"And indeed she was. But . . . I certainly never wished her dead. For the woman to take her own life like that—how desperate she must have been. That must surely be the worst thing in the world, to feel so . . . trapped, that to make such a choice seems the only way out." Lady Constance's voice was soft and troubled, and David was touched by her deep empathy with a woman she hadn't even liked.

"But are you sure she took her own life?"

She looked at him with surprise. "Father Neville came to see me on Monday. He explained what the police had found—that Mrs. Conwell had been taking money from the church, and when faced with . . . exposure . . . she had . . . hanged herself. Is there any reason to believe . . ."

Impulsively, he leaned forward. "Would you feel any better about it if she hadn't killed herself? If . . . there was another explanation?"

Lady Constance was alert, intent. "Young man, what do you know about this? Please tell me."

He was already beginning to regret his impulse, but decided that there was no reason not to tell her, if it would somehow lessen her distress. "I can't tell you the details," he explained, "but I have very good reason to believe that Mrs. Conwell was murdered."

"Murdered!"

"Yes. I believe she was."

"But have you told this to the police?"

"No, I haven't. I didn't think they'd listen to me, without any hard evidence. But I've been making . . . certain inquiries myself, and I think I'm getting close to an answer. When I have something concrete, then I'll go to the police. The inquest isn't until next week, so the case is still technically open, even though they're not pursuing it.''

"But what have you found out?"

David hesitated. "I can't say, until I'm sure myself, or at least until I have some proof. I'm going to leave London for a few days, to do some . . . research elsewhere, but I hope to be back by the beginning of next week.''

She smiled with an effort. "I hope this doesn't mean that the chapel is being neglected," she said lightly.

He answered her smile, and matched her tone. "Not at all, Lady Constance. I have it well in hand.''

"Very good. What can you tell me about it?"

"The workmen began on Tuesday," David explained. "I was there all morning to get them started, and showed them exactly what to do. They're very good, though, and seem to know what they're about. This morning I checked on their progress. They've done the damp-proofing where necessary, and are working on the replastering.''

"How long will it take?"

"I'm afraid that once they've done the plaster, which they ought to finish within a day or so, they'll have to leave it for six weeks before they can apply any paint to that bit. But there's still a few days' work for them now with the other painting, and the gilding. Some of it needs retouching. That's a very tricky business.''

"You will be able to supervise that?" she asked with concern.

"Yes, next week. I'll be back by then. I'll make sure they do it properly," he reassured her.

Her face relaxed into a smile. "It's very good of you, Mr. Middleton-Brown, to humor an old woman like this. You must think me very silly to worry about it so.''

"Not at all.''

She looked out the window, in the vague direction of St. Anne's. "That church means a great deal to me," she explained softly. "My husband and I—we never had children. St. Anne's has been almost like my child. I care very much about what happens to it.''

"I understand.''

"Yes, I believe you do." She looked at him shrewdly. "You're a very sensitive young man. You love beautiful things. I trust you . . ."

* * *

After the sandwiches, after the scones, when the maid had brought in the cakes and a fresh pot of tea, David led the conversation around to the subject of Miles. "I went to the organ recital yesterday," he remarked casually.

"Oh, you did? Did you find it enjoyable?"

"Yes, indeed. The quality of the music at St. Anne's is most impressive."

"In spite of the Director of Music sometimes," she replied somewhat tartly. "Though that's not really fair of me. My taste in music and his are very different, I'm afraid."

"Why, what does he like?"

Lady Constance sniffed disparagingly. "Modern music. Dissonant noise, I call it. He's forever pestering the Vicar to let the choir sing things that were written five minutes ago. I'm afraid I don't approve of things that haven't stood the test of time. As long as I have anything to say about what happens at St. Anne's, you won't be hearing the music that Mr. Taylor prefers."

"And he complains about that?"

"He complains about it all the time. Not to me, you understand," she added with a wry smile. "He's not that reckless."

"What do you mean?"

"Mr. Taylor may be a somewhat outspoken young man, but he's not stupid. He's never less than completely courteous to me. I think he would dearly like to number me among what Mrs. Neville quaintly calls his 'Fan Club.'"

"And are you among them?" he asked boldly.

"No. I'm not as easy to get around as someone like Mary Hughes. I can see quite clearly what he's up to."

"And what is he up to?" David queried with an innocent air.

"Come now, young man. You're not that naïve. Mr.

Taylor is what one might call an opportunist. His primary concern is always what's best for Miles Taylor, and nothing else. He has all the time in the world for the elderly ladies at St. Anne's, especially if they have a bit of money and no one in particular to leave it to when they're gone."

David admired her candor, and her shrewdness. "Has he been successful with many of them?"

"Oh, yes. He's had several rather nice little legacies over the past few years, both for the music fund and for himself personally. And I wouldn't be a bit surprised if Mary Hughes were to make him her primary heir. She thinks he's marvellous."

"Is Miss Hughes well off?"

"Well enough. She has a private income, and a house in Kensington. That would suit Mr. Taylor very well, I'm sure."

David spoke even more frankly. "Has he tried . . . to make up to you?"

"He's tried, all right. He's revoltingly ingratiating to me, and that I can't abide. He hasn't quite had the cheek to invite himself to tea, but he's dropped enough hints." She smiled suddenly. "No, you're much more my style, young man. And I do hope you'll come again."

"Of course, whenever you like," he replied.

She closed her eyes briefly. "Let me see. Today is Thursday. Could you come next Wednesday? That's the Feast of the Assumption, so we'll have to make it lunch—if we're going to Mass in the evening, there will be no tea for us that day."

"I'll look forward to it," he said, taking the hint and rising. "And now I think I had better leave you, Lady Constance. You're looking a bit tired."

"Please forgive me, Mr. Middleton-Brown, but I am suddenly quite weary." She put her hand to her head. "And a bit dizzy." She rang for the maid as he bent over her with concern. "No, young man, it's nothing for you to worry about. Molly, would you please see Mr. Middleton-Brown out, and then help me upstairs?"

As she opened the door for him, Molly hesitated for a moment; David sensed that she had something to say. "What is it, Molly?"

"I wouldn't normally say anything, sir, but . . ." The girl spoke in a troubled whisper.

"Yes?"

"Lady Constance, sir. She's not been herself lately. She's really not well."

"She *is* an old lady, Molly."

"But she accused me of pinching her cameo brooch, sir. And I never."

"You're sure, Molly?"

The girl was indignant. "Course I'm sure. She'd just put it in the wrong drawer, was all. She found it the next day."

David smiled and patted her arm. "Don't worry about it, Molly. Old people often forget things. My mother was the same way. Lady Constance knows you wouldn't take her brooch . . ."

"Thank you, sir. But . . . I just thought as you ought to know, that's all. Her ladyship sets a lot of store in you. If you could kind of keep an eye on her, like . . ."

"Yes, I'll do that. I'm very fond of Lady Constance, Molly. Thank you for telling me." He didn't mean it as empty reassurance; he was genuinely concerned about Lady Constance's health.

But as David reached the end of the street, he was already thinking ahead to the evening, and Lucy.

Chapter 31

*For he maketh the storm to cease: so that the waves
thereof are still.
Then are they glad, because they are at rest: and
so he bringeth them unto the haven where they
would be.*

Psalm 107:29-30

In his favorite armchair in Lucy's sitting room, David was relaxed but by no means sleepy. The concert had been excellent, and the late supper at a cozy French restaurant, accompanied by a couple of bottles of champagne, had been delicious. Now he swirled the brandy around in his glass, and inhaled its aroma with sensuous pleasure. He glanced idly around the now-familiar room, realizing in a strange detached way that it was only a week since he'd first sat there, stroking Sophie.

Lucy was smiling at him from her chair. She was looking especially beautiful tonight, he thought. She was wearing black; it was the first time he'd seen her in a dark color, and he found that the contrast with her fair coloring only emphasized her loveliness. Tonight had been the first time, too, that he'd been conscious of being seen with her. Though they hadn't seen anyone that they knew, he had been aware that other people were looking at her, admiring her, and he'd been proud to be with her.

Sophie, who had been sleeping elsewhere in the house, materialized silently and jumped on his lap. She arched her back luxuriously, kneaded his trouser-leg with her paws, and curled up in a small orange ball, purring loudly. He automatically put a hand on her silky fur.

Lucy, too, was relaxed, after the music and after the champagne. He has nice hands, she thought, watching him stroke Sophie. Not for the first time, she noticed that his fingernails were chewed down to the quick. "You ought not to bite your nails," she said, without thinking.

He was not offended. "You sound like my mother," he replied good-humoredly.

She stretched and pushed back her hair. "You never talk very much about your mother," she said. "Tell me about her. What was she like?"

He thought for a long time before answering. "It's difficult to say. A very strong personality. Domineering, I suppose you'd say. She always ran my father's life, poor man."

"And your life? Did she run it, too?"

"Well, she tried. I was a great disappointment to her. I was never as rich or successful as she wanted me to be." He paused for a moment, looking into space and reflecting.

"It's funny, isn't it? She always said that she wanted me to have a backbone, to be independent, but of course all she really wanted to do was control me, mold me in her image. She said that she wanted grandchildren, but she wouldn't have known what to do if I'd married and moved away from her. And she always said that I was a failure, and should be making more money, but whenever I talked about selling the house and moving . . ."

Lucy said gently, "It sounds like you have a lot of unresolved feelings. Your life with her must have been very difficult."

He'd never talked about these things with anyone before. Suddenly he was telling her everything: about the constant belittlement, the sense of failing to live up to expectations, about the petty-minded morality and ugly middle-class values and all the resultant guilt, about the anti-intellectual snobbery that he'd battled against to go to university and educate himself. His mother had been extremely pretentious in her own way, but had always dismissed his more cultured tastes as "just showing off." And his churchgoing she had found effeminate and unnecessary. "You can be just as good a Christian in your own home as you can in a church full of hypocrites," she'd often said.

"I loved my mother, but I never liked her," he blurted out at the end, and as he said it he knew it was true. He felt cleansed, freed by the admission and the realization.

Lucy had said very little, but somehow she'd been with him through every step of his confession. Suddenly, fancifully, he imagined that Lucy was like a deep pool of tranquil water, hidden in some leafy glade. He could cast his problems, like stones, into her calm depths, leaving not even a ripple on the serene surface.

"But you never talk about yourself," he said. "I want to know everything about you."

"What do you want to know?" she asked calmly.

He was emboldened by the rapport that had grown so naturally and so warmly between them. "Emily said that you'd been married. Tell me about that. Who was he? What happened?"

Perhaps it was the champagne that made her unusually candid, or perhaps it was the incredible feeling of affinity between them. She looked into space thoughtfully, winding a strand of hair around her finger. "His name was Geoffrey. It seems like such a long time ago. I was very young—only eighteen." Lucy tossed her hair back. "As you know, my father is a Vicar in a rural parish, in Shropshire. I was the only girl in the family, with three brothers, and I was very protected. You can imagine." She smiled. "All those wholesome country values. My experience of life was quite limited. But I always wanted to be an artist. When I was eighteen, I left home and went to art college. I met Geoffrey there. He wasn't like anyone I'd ever known—certainly nothing like my family. We had nothing in common except art, but that didn't matter to me. He was brilliant, and I was dazzled by him. We married very quickly, and of course it was a disaster. It only lasted a few months. I haven't heard from him in years." She added frankly, "It almost seems like something that happened to someone else, maybe in a book that I read a long time ago."

It was David's turn for silence. After a few minutes he said, "And after that? A beautiful woman like you, surely. . . Have there been other men?" He marvelled at his own daring, and thought perhaps he'd gone too far. He wasn't even sure why he was asking: Was it only simple curiosity?

But she, too, was finding release in honesty. "A few," she said. "There was one, quite a while ago now. He ran an art gallery, and I met him when he had an exhibition of my works. We lived together for over a year."

"What happened?" he asked when she paused for a sip of brandy.

"He left me for another artist. A man," she finished candidly. "I was pretty devastated. It was worse than the divorce. We'd been together a lot longer than I'd been married to Geoffrey, and—well, I don't know. It didn't do much for my self-esteem."

He stared at her, stricken, but she just shrugged. "It was a long time ago. But it put me off men for quite a while—it was years before I got involved with anyone after that. Then a couple of years ago I met this chap." She laughed ruefully. "Believe it or not, I met him queuing for the Proms. I used to see him most nights in the queue, and we'd often have a chat, or sometimes a drink in the interval. One night I invited him back to the house for a drink after the concert. They'd played the Dovořák Cello Concerto," she explained, as if excusing herself. "We were both pretty emotional after that. He . . . well, I let him stay the night." She stopped, then went on matter-of-factly, "I was lonely. It had been a long time. It just happened." Her face was in shadow as she paused again. "Anyway, after that, we saw a lot of each other. We both enjoyed music, and we got on very well. It looked as though there might be a future in it. I even took him round to the vicarage for dinner once. After the Last Night of the Proms, he told me that he had a wife in Manchester. I never saw him again." Lucy smiled, without self-pity or bitterness. "And there you have it. The story of my love life. Oh, I've been out with other men, of course," she added. "But those were the ones that mattered— the ones I cared about."

David gripped Sophie so hard with his fingers that she gave an angry yelp, jumped up, and with an annoyed lash of her tail, disappeared. He was overwhelmed by a jumble of emotions. First of all, he was incensed on her behalf at the treatment she'd received from these men—it just wasn't acceptable to use people like that, and especially someone as vulnerable as Lucy. And he felt her pain keenly, empathetically. Though it was all in the past, there were clearly lasting scars: How she must have suffered. Finally, he realized with surprise, there was a large element of jealousy in his reaction. He was improbably jealous of those men she'd spent time with, had cared about, had . . . slept with. He didn't want to think about it.

After what must have seemed like a very long silence, he simply said, "Thank you for telling me. Can I have another drink?"

The atmosphere eased. They had more brandy, and talked about inconsequential matters, and later she put on some music and they simply sat and listened.

Sophie had forgiven him and returned to his lap, and David was completely at peace. His body melted into the chair; he felt that he never wanted to leave that chair again. It was at that moment that the idea entered his mind for the first time: Why should he leave? Why couldn't this go on forever? Why shouldn't he . . . marry Lucy?

Marry Lucy. It pounded in his brain, in time with the music. He couldn't think properly—not now. Not with the music, and the brandy, and this room, and Lucy so near. Marry Lucy. He'd think about it tomorrow. And now . . . if he didn't leave now, he never would. He put Sophie off his lap and stood up. "It's very late. I must go."

He lingered by the door, not really wanting to leave, knowing he must. "In the morning I'm going away for a few days," he told her. "Business. But I'll be back as soon as I can. And then . . . well, I think there are some things we need to talk about."

She stood close to him, not touching him but smiling into his eyes and willing him to make love to her. Almost without volition, he entwined his fingers in her hair, and brushed her soft, fragrant cheek with his lips. "Good night, my lovely Lucy," he murmured. And then he was gone.

Chapter 32

I am weary of crying; my throat is dry: my sight faileth me for waiting so long upon my God.
                                                    Psalm 69:3

In the middle of a lovely dream, Emily turned over and reached for Gabriel. He wasn't there; she awoke with a start and all the pain flooded back. The vividness of her dream made the reality even harder to bear. She was not in her own comfortable bed, with her husband curled up warm beside her; she was alone in a hard, narrow bed. And this was not their spacious room, with the wallpaper they'd chosen together, and their lovely antique furniture: This was a small cell, whitewashed and sparsely furnished. Her eyes focused on the plain wooden crucifix on the opposite wall. It was her fourth morning waking in this bed.

She'd spent much of the last three days here in this room, on her knees in front of the crucifix, lying on the bed thinking, or sitting in the hard chair writing: writing to Lucy, writing to the children, writing endless letters to Gabriel and tearing them up. But now she felt that she needed to escape from the confines of this room, the room that had seemed such a welcome refuge a few days ago. She pulled on her jeans and shirt and slipped down the hall quietly to the chapel.

The chapel was as unadorned as her little room, with its white walls and its large, stark crucifix. But somehow its simple piety, so different from the gilded gothic splendor of St. Anne's, was just what she needed at this moment. It was empty when she entered; she knelt near the back and poured out her heart in prayer. After a while the tears started to flow, and though she tried to choke them back at first, she was soon overwhelmed with misery. I should go back to my room, she thought, and rose to go. Her eyes blinded, she almost ran into a nun who was just coming in.

"My dear," said the nun with concern. "Are you all right?"

Emily blinked, and recognized the sweet-faced sister who had been so kind to her on her arrival. "If you ever need to talk . . ." the nun had said that day. Suddenly it seemed the only thing to do. "Oh, Sister." She took a deep breath. "Sister Mary Grace, isn't it? I'd really like to talk to you. But if you're busy . . . maybe later . . ."

"There's nothing more important right now," the sister said firmly, putting her arm around Emily and leading her to a small private room, furnished with only two chairs. "Now, my dear. What is it that makes you so sad?" she began, proffering a clean white handkerchief.

With an effort, Emily controlled her tears. She wiped her

eyes and blew her nose, and looked gratefully at the nun. Sister Mary Grace was of an indeterminate age—she could have been anything from thirty to sixty—with smooth, unlined olive-toned skin, compassionate eyes, and a kind smiling mouth. Emily felt that nothing she could say would shock or upset this calm, gentle woman. "Sister, I've made such a mess of my life, and I don't know what to do."

"Why don't you tell me. Start at the beginning, if you like."

The beginning. When was that? Ten years ago? Or longer?

"My husband is . . . well . . . I don't know if I should . . ." She hesitated.

"Nothing you say to me will go any farther than this room, my dear. You don't have to be afraid to tell me anything."

"My husband is a priest." The nun nodded encouragingly. "We've been married for nearly ten years. I love him very much. I've always thought he was everything a priest should be, and everything a husband should be."

"Then you've been very fortunate."

"Yes, but now I've found out that I didn't know him as well as I thought I did. From the very beginning. He lied . . . no, he didn't lie to me. He just didn't tell me the truth." Her mouth twisted at the fine distinction. "I was very foolish. I took him at face value, because I loved him and because I wanted him to be the man I thought he was."

"That's only natural."

"But he never was what I thought he was. That's what hurts me so much—realizing that for ten years, I never really knew him." She sat silently for a moment, searching for the courage to tell the story. "My husband was thirty when I met him. A bachelor. I did think it a little unusual that a man of that age . . . well, I asked him if he'd ever thought of marrying before. He said that he hadn't—that there had never been another woman in his life before he met me. I believed him. I wanted to believe him. I wanted to think that I was as unique and special for him as he was for me."

"And it wasn't true?"

"Oh, that part of it was true, I think. As far as it went. But I didn't ask the other question, because it never occurred to me, and he didn't tell me.'' The sister waited; finally Emily went on. ''He didn't tell me that he had been in love before—with a man.'' There, it was out. Still the sister said nothing. ''I know a lot of gay people; some of them are good friends of mine. I don't have a problem with it at all, in theory. But . . . he didn't tell me. And I don't really know how I would have handled it if he had. He never gave me a chance to try to understand, to come to terms with it. I loved him very much—I don't think it would have made a difference. But I don't know. My marriage: It's been very happy. But has it been based on a lie? Has he really ever loved me at all?'' The last terrible question came out on a sob.

''Have you asked your husband that question?''

Emily looked at her, horrified. ''Oh, I couldn't! Not yet, anyway. I don't know if I could bear it . . .'' She wept.

The sister squeezed Emily's hand until she regained control and was able to go on.

''My dear, have you been wrestling with this by yourself all this week? Why didn't you come to me sooner?''

''I just couldn't. I was in shock. I had to try to sort it out, to make sense of what's happened and my feelings about it.''

''What you haven't told me is how you found out about this. Did your husband tell you?''

''No, that's what makes it worse. He's in some kind of trouble—I know it. But he wouldn't tell me, so it must have something to do with all this. He's been distracted and upset for weeks, and still I haven't understood. I've been so stupid, so insensitive to him.''

''How did you find out?'' Sister Mary Grace repeated patiently.

''Finally, I just . . . guessed, I suppose. The other man. The one my husband . . . loved. I think my husband is being blackmailed about their affair. I'm not explaining this very well,'' she apologized. ''The other man came for a visit about a fortnight ago. I'd never met him. I'd heard his name, as an old friend of my husband, that was all. I didn't suspect—why would I? He's a nice man, David. I like him very much. But then he and my husband—they had a row about something. I overheard a bit, just enough to make me think about it. I asked my husband. He wouldn't tell me anything. I think that's when I knew, suddenly. It was just an intuition. I had to be sure. So I asked David. He was honest with me, admitted they'd been . . . lovers. I don't blame David," she burst out. "I don't blame him for loving Gabriel. Why shouldn't he love him? And he's been hurt too, poor David. I don't blame Gabriel for loving him. But why didn't he tell me? Why didn't he tell me?"

"Only he can answer that question, my dear. You must ask him. You must go to him and ask him."

"I just can't. Not yet. Please let me stay here a little longer."

"You can stay here as long as you like. But it mustn't be for much longer, my dear. Have you given any thought at all to how your husband must be suffering without you, not knowing where you are? I'm sure he loves you very much."

"Oh, poor Gabriel!" Emily wailed. "I've been so selfish! Thinking only about myself!"

The sister took both Emily's hands in hers, and gazed at her with compassion. "Perhaps not yet," she agreed. "Before you're ready to hear the answer from him, there's something you must ask yourself."

"I don't understand what you mean."

"You must ask yourself who you really are angry with. The things you've told me—you're in a lot of pain right now, but there's also a lot of anger there. And what I'm hearing is that you're angry with your husband, for not being honest with you. But mostly you're angry with yourself, for not understanding him better, for having unrealistic expectations of your relationship, for not asking the right questions, for failing him somehow, for being hurt even. And the anger brings guilt. My dear, you are full of guilt."

"Yes," Emily admitted.

"You must come to terms with that. Before you talk to your husband, you must come to terms with yourself. You must forgive yourself before you can forgive him."

Emily covered her face with her hands.

Chapter 33

Thou art fairer than the children of men: full of grace are thy lips, because God hath blessed thee for ever.

Psalm 45:3

"I think that the Three Swans looks your best bet," Daphne concluded, poring over her AA hotel guide. "It's right in the marketplace, very near the cathedral. And they've got a car park."

"That sounds fine," agreed David.

"Would you like me to ring and book a room for you?" she offered.

"Don't bother, I can take my chances." He reconsidered. "Well, actually it might be a good idea. That way you'd know for sure where you could reach me, in case there are any developments here."

"You never know. Miles might make a dramatic confession, and jump from the church tower."

"Ha. Well, anyway. I *will* answer the phone if you ring. But don't expect me to ring you, no matter what happens," he warned.

"I know better than that. Using the telephone is against your religion. But I've never known why."

"I'm not even sure of that myself," admitted David. "I must have been bitten by one when I was a child."

"How long do you think you might be away?"

"Probably not more than over the weekend. I'll be back when I'm back, is all I can say. Don't rent out my room while I'm gone!"

Daphne shook her head. "Never think it! All shall be kept in readiness for your return."

"Will you light a little candle in the window each night?"

"Get out of here."

"I'll see you in a few days, then, Daphne." She lifted her cheek for his affectionate kiss, and watched him from the window until his brown Morris was out of sight.

* * *

Negotiating Friday morning London traffic, and then finding his way to the A1, required all David's concentration; once he was in Hertfordshire he began to think about where he might eat lunch. He couldn't abide the multitudinous roadside restaurants that proliferated along the A1, with their identical synthetic food. Stamford would be nice, he thought—the George ought to serve a decent lunch. That was nearly halfway, and would be a good break. It was a pretty town, too, with its church spires, its twisting streets and its warm beige stone buildings. If he wasn't in a hurry to get to Selby, he might easily spend some time there exploring the churches.

Lunch plans thus disposed of, his mind turned to the subject he'd been avoiding since last night's brainstorm. It was time to think about it. He asked himself, finally, the big question: Should he marry Lucy Kingsley?

She was a beautiful woman. It would not be true to say that her beauty, which was so much more than skin-deep, left him unmoved. On the contrary, his response to it was deeply emotional, as it would have been to a stirring performance of Bach's B Minor Mass, the Sistine Chapel ceiling, or an exquisitely fashioned piece of silver.

He wished that he wanted to make love to her. But physical lovemaking had never been that important to him. Even with Gabe—especially with Gabe—the emotional closeness, the tenderness, were more important than their physical expression. No, sex wasn't all that central to his life. If it had been, he realized, he would never have lived for twenty-eight years before discovering his orientation, would never have been able to live the last ten years celibate

as a monk, would not now be able to contemplate the step
he was so seriously considering. And he was considering it
very seriously indeed.

He thought about the implications for his lifestyle, the
changes that would take place in his life on a practical level.
The house—it certainly wouldn't suit Lucy as it was now.
But she could redecorate it. It wasn't a bad house—it had
potential, anyway. Once they'd eradicated all traces of
Mother, Lucy could make it a showplace, with her exquisite
taste. The money was available, and she could do whatever
she liked. He'd be quite happy to leave it to her, or they
could work on it together. Make it reflect both of them. That
might be nice. She'd need somewhere to work. The attic
room could easily be converted into a studio for her, with a
skylight added. Or if she didn't like the house, he could sell
it and they'd find something else, get a fresh start. Maybe
something in Norwich, with its easy access by train to
London. They'd keep Lucy's house in Kensington, he
imagined. She'd probably want to keep it. They could go to
London for the weekends, so she could keep up her weekly
visits to the V & A. It would be nice to spend weekends in
London: They could go to concerts, art galleries and the
theatre, eat at good restaurants.

Maybe Lucy wouldn't want to live in Norfolk at all—
perhaps she wouldn't want to leave London. Well, he could
always find a job in London. That wouldn't be difficult.
And to be quite honest, having a beautiful, accomplished
wife wouldn't do him any harm in furthering his career.
He'd loved living in London when he was younger. Moving
to London would be fine. He'd see more of Daphne, of Emily.

And they could travel. He'd seen a fair bit of England,
especially during his years of travelling with Daphne, but
his dislike of travelling alone had kept him from spending
time abroad. With Lucy he could go to Italy, as he'd always
wanted to do. Perhaps she'd been there before and could
show him all the art treasures. They could go to France, to
Switzerland, even to Greece or Egypt.

But whether they lived in Wymondham, in Norwich, or
in London, he would no longer have to be alone—that was
the main thing. He hated living alone. He loathed preparing

meals just for himself and eating by himself, almost as much as he hated dining in restaurants alone. If he married Lucy, he would never have to be alone again.

He tried, then, to imagine what life would be like with Lucy as his wife. It was one thing spending time with someone when you were on holiday, as he was now. But to live with them, every day. . .

He wasn't at his best in the mornings, David realized that. He hoped that Lucy would be able to make allowances for that. He'd be more than willing to make an effort: He'd get up and make the tea, and bring her a cup in bed, as he had for years with Mother. He didn't require much breakfast, or much in the way of conversation in the morning, so she could lie in as long as she liked.

The evenings would be lovely. When he came home, they'd have a glass of sherry together and a chat. She'd talk about her day, and show him the painting she'd done. He could tell her about all the annoying people he'd had to deal with, and she'd soothe him with sweet reasonable words. Now there was no one to calm him down—he could only brood, and feel even worse. Then when they'd relaxed, they'd have a delicious dinner, and a good bottle of wine. They'd prepare the meal together: He enjoyed cooking when he didn't have to do it by himself and for himself only, and it would be great fun working with someone as accomplished in the kitchen as Lucy was. After dinner they'd retire to the sitting room, where they'd spend a companionable evening talking or listening to music. Perhaps they might read to each other—Jane Austen, or Barbara Pym, something deliciously entertaining and not too demanding. They might have a drink, a brandy or a whisky.

And later, after the long companionable evening, when he went to bed with . . . his wife: He supposed it wouldn't be so bad, though he couldn't really imagine the act. At least he didn't find the idea repugnant, only uninteresting. So that would be all right. If he were lucky, he might even get to like it. Gabe apparently had, at least enough to convince and to satisfy Emily.

It all sounded wonderful, too good to be true. What could he be leaving out of his calculations? It suddenly occurred to him that he had never asked himself what his feelings for Lucy really were. Did he . . . love her?

Lucy made him happy. It wasn't the wild, blood-pounding joy he'd found with Gabe, but that kind of happiness belonged to youth, and could never be recaptured. It was a quiet, contented sort of happiness. Her serenity, her tranquillity enveloped him with a feeling of well-being. He felt that he could be with her forever, and never tire of looking at her, listening to her, laughing with her. Wasn't this love, or at least a kind of love? He was so used to defining love in terms of his feelings for Gabe that he wasn't sure.

But did it really matter, after all? They could be happy together, he was sure of that. Lucy had a salutary effect on him; he thought that he was a nicer person when he was with her. As far as he could tell, there was every indication that she was fond of him; she even seemed to find him attractive, for some unknown reason. And he knew that whatever name you attached to it, he was very fond of her. Wasn't that enough? He and Lucy weren't a couple of kids. They were both too mature to be hung up on romantic terminology. He had been offered a chance of happiness that was as unexpected as it was enticing. Wouldn't he be very foolish indeed to turn his back on it?

Chapter 34

One deep calleth another, because of the noise of the waterpipes: all thy waves and storms are gone over me.

Psalm 42:9

David counted the cathedral bells as they tolled; one, two, three, four. In a few more hours he could get up. He had not stopped to consider the consequences of the guidebook term "very near the cathedral" in choosing his hotel. The cathedral bells were very pleasant to hear in the evening, sitting in one's room, but in the wee hours of the night they were less than welcome.

Not that it really mattered, he reflected. He'd complained about the room he'd been given—he would have preferred a view of the cathedral to a view of the car park—but had been told it was the only single room available at such short notice. And now the lack of a view had paled into insignificance beside the room's more noticeable drawback. It was located adjacent to the boiler room, and the clanging of the water-pipes had provided an unmusical counterpoint to the striking of the bells throughout the night. To top it off, the rumble of thunder had recently been added to the cacophony, and a few moments ago a terrific storm had let loose its fury on the cathedral city of Selby, in the East Riding of Yorkshire.

Why couldn't Miles Taylor have been organist in a more civilized place? David asked himself savagely. He hadn't been to Selby for years, and belatedly he remembered why. It was really nothing more than a small Yorkshire market town, elevated to city status by virtue of its magnificent abbey cathedral. There were no decent restaurants—it didn't even rate a mention in the *Good Food Guide*—and David had been reduced to dining on fish and chips. Tomorrow night—tonight, he amended, remembering the four bells—he didn't know what he'd do. Drive into York, maybe. He certainly wasn't going to be staying in Selby any longer than absolutely necessary. If he couldn't find out something tomorrow—today—he'd be inclined to give it up as a bad job.

He'd only had one tenuous lead in his search for Miles Taylor's hidden past. After Evensong, he'd lingered near the organ during the final voluntary. Close to the entrance to the console was a board with a list of the cathedral's past organists, their names painted in red, and he'd studied it with ostensible interest as a fresh-faced young man emerged from the console.

"The voluntary was excellent," he remarked as the young man passed him.

The young man stopped. "Oh, did you really think so?" His round face went pink with pleasure.

"I've rarely heard it performed so well," David replied gravely.

"Oh, well. I wasn't sure about the registration in the final bit. But if you say it was good . . ."

"It was superb. Are you the organist here? Mr. . . . Moffat?" he added, looking at the board.

The young man smiled in a flustered fashion. "Oh, good heavens, no. Just the assistant."

"You're certainly very accomplished for an assistant. How long have you been at Selby, Mr. . . . ?"

"Thompson. William Thompson. I've been here for nearly three years now."

Damn, thought David. "Well, I'm sure you'll be going on to bigger and better things very soon, Mr. Thompson." He looked again at the board, and said casually, "I see that Miles Taylor was organist here before Mr. Moffat. But that was before your time."

"Yes. Though of course I've heard plenty of stories about Miles Taylor. He was a real legend around here."

"Then I suppose there are still people in the choir who remember him?"

"Oh, yes. Why? Do you know him?"

"I've heard of him," David hedged. "His name . . . in musical circles, you know . . . the friend of a friend . . . that sort of thing."

"I see. Well, you won't find anyone here at the moment who knew him—the choir is on holiday. That was a visiting choir at Evensong, you realize."

"Yes, of course." David hadn't really thought about it.

"Of course, the person to talk to about Miles Taylor is Miss Somers. I don't believe she was here at Evensong tonight—she's getting on in years now, and doesn't always make it." The young man turned his head guiltily as a man in a cassock beckoned frantically from the transept. "Oh, excuse me, Mr. . . . um. I really must go. Frightfully nice to meet you.''

And the young man had scurried off, leaving David little more enlightened than he'd been previously.

Now, as the wind-driven rain lashed the window, its wooden frame rattling in the onslaught, David recalled again the young man's words. Miss Somers. He'd had enough hints from Daphne, and from Lady Constance, about Miles's predilection for wealthy old ladies. Was Miss Somers one of his conquests? Or one with whom he'd failed? Someone like Lady Constance, who saw through his manoeuvres and his facile charm? If he could, he would like to meet this Miss Somers.

* * *

To David's dismay, his alarm clock had been left on the bedside table of Daphne's spare room, so he marked time by the striking of the bells until they tolled seven; having nothing particular to get up for, but no compelling reason to remain in bed any longer, he rose, showered, shaved, and dressed. The room's shower, as he would have expected, was less than efficient, and he endured alternating trickles of hot water and jets of icy spray. But the kettle provided in the room seemed functional, and he decided to fix himself a cup of tea. Too late he realized that it would have to be made in the cup, with a tea bag, and that the only milk available was of the powdered variety. Giving up in disgust, he went down to a breakfast of runny scrambled eggs on soggy toast.

The day could only improve, he decided, leaving the hotel immediately after breakfast. The night's storm had been short-lived in its intensity, leaving the sky a bright, cloudless blue. David walked along by the river for a long while before heading back to the cathedral.

Selby Abbey was a splendid building, he reflected as he approached. Unfortunately, its monastic past meant that it was stranded in the middle of the town with no cathedral close to insulate it from traffic. The monastic buildings had all been knocked down, leaving only the church, which had survived as a parish church for several centuries before its elevation to cathedral status in the late nineteenth century. In the meanwhile, building had gone on all around it.

But inside the cathedral, one of the best-preserved monastic churches in the country, it was easy to forget its surroundings. There were several small clusters of tourists looking about, and near the south transept entrance a party was forming up around a guide. David decided to join them.

The guide was a small, elderly woman with untidy hair, bright eyes, and a strong Yorkshire accent. She was giving an account of the founder of the abbey.

"I suppose you can say that this is an institution founded on a theft," she said. "When Benedict fled from his abbey in France, he pinched the finger of St. Germanus, and that became the chief relic of the new abbey he founded here, in 1069. But Benedict didn't take kindly to others following his example—at least not that example. When two monks were caught stealing some silver, he had them castrated! He was so unpopular that he was finally forced to resign."

Sounds like a jolly chap, David reflected. He probably would have approved of his church employing a bloke like Miles Taylor.

When the tour was over, David stayed behind and spoke to the guide. "Thank you for a most interesting tour. What a fascinating history this place has!"

"Is this your first visit?"

"No, but I haven't been here in nearly twenty years. It's a splendid building." The woman smiled and nodded in agreement. On an impulse, David asked her, "Do you know a Miss Somers?"

"Yes, of course. Everyone at Selby knows Miss Somers. Why, is she a friend of yours?"

He thought quickly. "No, but someone from my local church knows her—a distant relative by marriage, I believe. They asked me to look her up." He smiled ingratiatingly, and, he hoped, convincingly.

"Well, if you want to see Mildred Somers, just come to Evensong this afternoon. She never misses it on a Saturday.

If you'll come up to the chancel with me now, I'll show you where she always sits.''

David looked at his watch. Only a few more hours to kill in Selby before Evensong.

* * *

There wasn't even a market in Selby on a Saturday. Walking aimlessly through the streets of the town, David resorted to people-watching. Everyone he saw seemed to be in pairs: teenaged couples, spotty and unattractive to anyone but each other, smooching unashamedly on the street corners; young married couples, their arms entwined; middle-aged and older husbands and wives, less affectionate but comfortable together as they accomplished their weekend shopping in tandem. Even the swans on the river were in pairs, he noted glumly: Swans, he knew, mate for life. For the first time since his mother died, David realized, on an emotional level, how very alone he was.

He spotted a Teleflora sign in a florist's window. Without stopping to think about what he was doing, he opened the door of the shop and went in; the bell on the door roused the clerk from dreamy contemplation of a potted fern. "May I help you, sir?"

"If I were to place an order now, could something be delivered to London this afternoon?"

"I don't see why not. What would you like?"

"Roses. Long-stemmed roses—a dozen. No, make it two dozen."

"Red roses, sir?"

"No, not red. Not pink. That sort of peachy-gold color. You know the color I mean." He wrote Lucy's name and address on the form the clerk handed him.

"And the message on the card, sir?"

David smiled a bit self-consciously; he was new at this sort of thing, after all. "Lucy, will you marry me?" He added, "No signature. I think she'll know who it's from."

Chapter 35

*Whoso hath also a proud look and high stomach: I
will not suffer him.*

Psalm 101:7

David was back with plenty of time to spare before Evensong. He went into the cathedral gift shop and bought a souvenir book with colored pictures of the cathedral to take back to Daphne. As an afterthought, he selected a couple of picture postcards, one of the west front of the cathedral and one of the high altar, to send to Daphne and Lucy. I'll be back before they get them, he thought, but at least it's a gesture. I should have done it yesterday.

"Did you need stamps for those, sir?" inquired the helpful young woman who took his money.

"Yes, that would be most useful." She smiled at him in a very friendly way and he was emboldened to ask her a question. "Do you know... a Miss Somers?"

"Yes, of course. Everyone does."

He hesitated. "You must think me frightfully ignorant, then, but who *is* she? Why does everyone know her?"

The woman laughed easily. She was younger than Lucy, but there was something about her laugh that made David think of Lucy, and miss her. "She was an institution around here for years, that's all. Miss Somers was the secretary to the Provost for as long as anyone can remember. Everyone knew that she really ran the cathedral—Provosts came and went, but Miss Somers remained."

"And now?"

"She finally retired, a year or so ago. She didn't want to, I can tell you. But they gave her no choice."

A customer behind David made an impatient noise, and he looked around guiltily. The woman laughed again. "Here I am, standing here gossiping when there are people to be served. I'll probably get the sack." She didn't look too bothered at the prospect, so with a quick nod of thanks, David moved away from the till.

He took a seat in the choir stalls, strategically chosen so that he could observe Miss Somers when she had arrived. He knelt to pray, and when he looked up again, she was there.

Formidable was the word. The only thing really reminiscent of Lady Constance about her was her erect carriage. She sat ram-rod straight, her eyes closed. Her hair, which remained quite dark with just a few streaks of grey, was parted in the center with military precision, and scraped back into a tight bun at the nape of her neck. Her eyebrows were pencilled on in thin lines above steel-rimmed spectacles, and her mouth had a no-nonsense set to it, even in repose. She had large ears, made even more prominent by her severe hairstyle, and in their fleshy lobes she wore, incongruously, oversized gypsy-like gold hoops.

Today's visiting choir, from a parish in the diocese, had more enthusiasm than skill, and David found himself unable to concentrate on the service. He watched Mildred Somers discreetly, from under half-closed lids, and wondered what she could tell him about Miles Taylor. She didn't look at all the sort of person to be taken in by Miles, and that would affect the manner in which David approached her.

In the end he decided on the direct approach. After the service, as she got to her feet with the aid of a stick, David waited to catch her eye. "Miss Somers?" he began tentatively.

"Yes?"

"So sorry to disturb you. I was told that you were the person to speak to about a former organist here, Miles Taylor."

She looked wary. "Why? Are you a friend of his?"

He thought quickly. "No, not at all. It's just that . . . well, a friend of mine is a churchwarden in a parish that's thinking of employing Mr. Taylor, and he asked me if I might make a few discreet inquiries. Nothing official, you understand. I thought you might be the best person to ask, on that sort of basis.''

She nodded, her earrings bobbing, and sat down again, gesturing for him to sit beside her. "Yes, of course, Mr. . . .''

"Middleton-Brown.''

"Mr. Middleton-Brown. I'll be happy to help in any way I can, of course. What did you wish to know about Mr. Taylor?'' Her voice, when she spoke the name, was decidedly frosty.

"Forgive me, Miss Somers, but you don't sound very enthusiastic about him.''

She flashed him an acerbic glance. "Clever boy. No, I have to tell you that I never got on with Miles Taylor.''

"Could I ask why?''

"Well you might ask. For one thing, the man was far too fond of himself for my taste. If you didn't know how wonderful he was, he would be happy to tell you, at great length. And I couldn't abide his arrogance.''

"Did he know his job?''

"His, and everyone else's too, if he was to be believed. He thought he knew better than anyone how the cathedral ought to be run. As far as the music was concerned, he was in charge, and there was no arguing with that. But worship, and administration—those things were none of his affair, but he couldn't help interfering, putting his oar in. No, I didn't get on with Miles Taylor.''

David could well understand that, if the man had been foolish enough to try to meddle in this woman's sphere of influence. "He was organist here for . . . several years, I believe?''

"Yes, four years.''

"And he left about five years ago?''

"That is correct.''

"Might I ask . . .'' he hesitated delicately, "about the circumstances of his leaving? Were there any . . . causes?''

Miss Somers fixed her gaze on the organ console just above them. "There were . . . disagreements about the music. He was very keen on experimenting with new things, and the Chapter felt . . .''

"But that's not the real reason, is it?" David asked gently but firmly. "You just said that he had final authority as far as music was concerned."

She compressed her lips, and regarded him keenly, shrewdly for just a moment. Making up her mind, she nodded again suddenly. "Yes, I think you . . . your friend . . . have a right to know. I don't know what Mr. Taylor has told anyone about why he left here, but it could have a direct bearing on someone's decision to offer him a post." David held his breath and waited, not daring to speak. "The truth is that Mr. Taylor falsified his credentials when he came here." David let his breath out in a long hiss, almost a whistle. Miss Somers raised her eyebrows significantly and went on. "We never questioned it initially, of course. You do take a lot on faith in this business, if you'll forgive the pun. In this particular case, that was a mistake. Miles Taylor lied to the Cathedral Chapter, to the Provost, to me. When it all came out, he tried to deny it—he was very brazen about it. We finally had no choice but to dismiss him, and to warn him that if he tried for another cathedral post, we would have to apprise them of the situation."

"I see."

"In the end he went to a parish church in London. They never asked for a reference—I suppose they thought they were lucky to be getting someone of his caliber. I don't know what we would have told them if they had asked. Is he still there, do you know? Somewhere in Kensington, I believe?"

"Yes, I think so."

"And this church that's considering him . . . ?"

"I doubt very much if they'll be interested, when they've heard this," he said hastily.

Miss Somers nodded again, satisfied.

* * *

So old Miles had lied about his credentials. Gabriel might be very interested to hear that, and so might the police.

He sat in a little café drinking a cup of tea. It was quite stewed, and obviously made with cheap tea bags, but at least they'd used fresh milk, and it had to be an improvement over what he could have made himself in his hotel room. He'd return to London first thing in the morning. He was half tempted to go back tonight, but he'd already had the young man at the hotel reception book him a table for dinner at a restaurant in York, a restaurant that had been quite favorably reviewed in the *Good Food Guide*. He'd have a good meal tonight and first thing tomorrow he'd go back.

* * *

Gabriel tossed sleeplessly in the comfortable bed. Never in his life had he had problems sleeping, until this week. His head hurt. He got up and took some paracetamol tablets; if he'd had sleeping pills, he would have taken them. At the first morning light, he rose and went downstairs to make himself a cup of tea.

There was a white envelope on the carpet, just inside the door. As he picked it up, his heart lurched apprehensively. The envelope had a familiar shape. He went into his study for his letter-knife and slit it open with mounting dread.

The letter was on the same paper as before, neatly typed.

> This is to remind you. You have until the end of the day on Wednesday, August 15, the Feast of the Assumption, to resign. It would be very foolish of you to ignore this warning.

PART III

PART III

Chapter 36

When thou with rebukes dost chasten man for sin,
thou makest his beauty to consume away, like as
it were a moth fretting a garment: every man
therefore is but vanity.
Hear my prayer, O Lord, and with thine ears
consider my calling: hold not thy peace at my tears.
Psalm 39:12–13

David probably would have sworn that he hadn't slept a
wink all night, between the water-pipes and the cathedral
bells, but the jangle of the telephone jolted him awake.
Damn, he thought. Time to get up already. Without his
alarm clock, he'd asked the hotel reception desk for a
wake-up call, so that he would be sure of making early
Mass at the cathedral and thus could get an early start back
to London. He hadn't actually believed that they'd carry out
his request, so his second thought was mild surprise at their
efficiency. He reached for the receiver. "Yes?" he growled.

The voice on the other end was tentative. "David?" He
didn't recognize it, but it clearly was not his wake-up call.

"Speaking."

"David, this is Gabriel."

Suddenly he was wide awake. Gabriel's voice sounded

strained—not like him at all. David replied cautiously. The last words they'd exchanged had hardly been cordial. "Yes, Gabriel?"

"I'm so sorry to disturb you. I rang Daphne, and she gave me this number where you could be reached. I wouldn't bother you like this, but . . . it's rather important."

It must be, for Gabriel to be ringing him in Selby at seven o'clock on a Sunday morning. "What is it?"

"David . . . there's been another letter. This morning."

"What on earth do you mean?"

"Another blackmail letter. Like the first one."

David struggled to comprehend Gabriel's words. "But that's impossible. Mavis is dead."

"You were wrong. Mavis couldn't have written the letters. I tell you, I've had another one."

"But that's impossible," David repeated stupidly.

"David, please come back." Gabriel paused awkwardly. "I'm sorry about . . . the way we parted last week. About the things we said in anger. I need your help now, more than ever. Please come back."

"I'll be there in a few hours." David hung up, then stared at the telephone for a moment. Gabe needed him. Again.

* * *

Gabriel must have been watching for him from the study; he opened the door before David could ring the bell. "Come in, David. Let's go into the study."

Once they were out of the dim light of the entrance hall, Gabriel turned to face him. "I'm glad you've come," he said simply. David caught his breath at the change in Gabriel's appearance. It had been less than a week since he'd seen him, in this room, but Gabriel had altered subtly yet noticeably in that week. He was immaculately groomed and attired as always, but he looked tired and—yes, older. There were tiny lines around his eyes where none had been before, and a pinched look around his mouth. This business has really hit him hard, David concluded, with a stirring of compassion.

Gabriel gestured him to a chair, and sat himself as usual at his desk. He seemed at a loss for words.

"Show me the letter," David said, without preliminaries. This time there was no need for concealment; there was no one else in the house. The letter lay folded on the desk, and Gabriel handed it to him silently.

David studied it for a moment. "It does seem to be from the same person," he admitted at last. That destroyed his pet theory, formulated on the drive from Selby, that there were two blackmailers. "So it wasn't Mavis. I was wrong. I'm not much of a detective, am I?"

"We were both wrong," Gabriel said with a bitter smile.

"Then who?"

Gabriel shook his head hopelessly. "I wish I knew. I've been over and over it in my mind, and I just don't know. And time is running out."

"Three days, give or take. What are you going to do?"

Gabriel looked at him pleadingly. "Won't you help?"

"All right, what are *we* going to do?"

"Thank you, David." His smile, though strained, was genuinely grateful. "Isn't there any way you can find out? You've been to Brighton—was there anything . . ."

David covered his face with his hands and thought hard. It was difficult changing gears like this, back to Peter Maitland and Brighton. "You'll have to help me, Gabriel. You'll have to think about this. Before, you didn't tell me anything about his background, his friends. I know nothing about him that would lead me to someone who knew him, someone to whom he might have mentioned your name. Did you ever meet any of his friends?"

"No, that wouldn't have been a good idea." Gabriel looked away. "And it wasn't that kind of relationship."

David suppressed a pang. "Try to think. Did he ever mention any friends—*anyone* he knew . . . by name?"

Gabriel furrowed his brow in concentration. "It's been so long ago. I can't remember. He had a sister somewhere, but I don't know her name. Maybe it was Kathy, Karen, something like that. His roommate's name was Dominic, I think. And I think he talked about someone named Anthony. Is it really that important?''

"I have nothing else to go on. And time, as you said, is running out.''

They talked around in circles for a long while. Gabriel was too upset and bewildered to be of any real use; finally David said, "I will do my very best. But it's so difficult on my own—I really haven't been a very clever detective so far. May I ask for Daphne's help?''

Gabriel was horrified. "Tell Daphne? What would she say? What would she think of me?''

David hesitated. "She already knows about . . . us. I didn't tell her—she guessed. And I don't believe she thinks the worse of either of us because of it. Daphne is discreet, you know that. And she never judges. It would be a great help to me to be able to talk it over with her: Daphne's very shrewd about people. I won't tell her all the details, just the bare facts.''

"If you think it's best, then.'' Gabriel nodded listlessly, playing with the paperweight. "I don't care how you do it, but just find out by Wednesday.''

"I'll do my best,'' David repeated gravely and, he hoped, reassuringly.

Gabriel roused himself. "Would you like a sherry? Or maybe a cup of tea?''

"I'd love a sherry. I didn't stop to eat.''

"Then you must be hungry. I haven't eaten, either. Maybe I can find us some food—you stay here.''

David was happy to remain, and occupied himself looking around the study. It was a lovely room, with the Queen Anne desk and the Persian carpet. He glanced at the photo of Emily and the children. Dear Emily—he wondered how she was. He must go to see her and find out. He browsed for a few minutes among Gabriel's books. Some of them he remembered, but many he did not. Gabriel's reading habits had always been catholic, with a small "c," so amongst the books on theology and exegesis were a sprinkling of the classics, and a few modern novels. And there, under "N," were Gabriel's own books; David took them down and looked at them with interest. *Transubstantiation: An Anglican Perspective*, followed by *Sacramental Confession: A Spiritual Imperative*, by Fr. Gabriel Neville, MA Oxon. He was surprised that he hadn't seen them reviewed in the *Church Times*. They looked suitably learned, but written with a certain popular appeal for a particular brand of churchmanship. He returned them to the shelf almost guiltily as Gabriel, bearing a tray, pushed the door open.

"I found a tin of tuna," he announced, indicating a plate of inexpertly made sandwiches. "Would you like a sherry first?"

"Yes, please."

"Amontillado?"

"Lovely."

They sipped sherry and munched sandwiches almost companionably for several minutes. They were both so hungry that the sandwiches tasted rather good. Gabe had never been much use in the kitchen, David recalled. But then, he'd never needed to be. There'd always been someone else to keep him fed: the succession of cooks at home, at boarding school, at university, at the clergy house in Brighton, then the housekeeper at St. Anne's vicarage, and finally . . . Emily. He wondered how Gabriel was faring without her on a purely practical level. Probably not too badly, if the story he'd concocted about Emily nursing an ailing relation had gained very wide circulation amongst the ladies of the parish.

"Would you like a piece of cake?" Gabriel asked, confirming his suspicion. "I think I've got a bit left from the one Mrs. Framlingham brought me the other day."

"No, thanks. I'm fine."

"She—Mrs. Framlingham, that is—said that she'd seen you at the Royal Albert Hall with Lucy Kingsley," Gabriel remarked casually.

"Oh, did she?" was David's calm reply. Interfering old cow, he added to himself furiously. None of her bloody business.

"You've been seeing rather a lot of Lucy Kingsley, from what I hear."

"And who are all these sources of information who are taking such an interest in my life?" Although he struggled to keep his tone light, his voice was beginning to take on a hard edge.

"Various people. In a parish like this, it's bound to happen. Let's just say that people have noticed. Don't get me wrong, David—I think it's great," Gabriel remarked heartily. "It's about time you found yourself a nice wife and settled down."

"A wife?" His expression was dangerously calm; Gabriel should have been warned.

"Yes. I can't recommend marriage too highly, David. Have you thought about it at all? Lucy would make you a good wife. She's an excellent cook, and good company, and quite pleasant to look at. You could do much worse."

David struggled with himself for a moment before replying. "How dare you," he said, very quietly. "How dare you presume to tell me what I should do with my life?"

"I only meant . . ." Gabriel stammered, startled. "I just want you to be happy, David. I just thought . . ."

"Anyway, I don't see that you're exactly a walking advertisement for the joys of wedlock. You seem to have cocked up your marriage pretty badly," David said brutally.

The face that Gabriel turned on him was white, as he struggled with a dawning realization. "You know where Emily is, don't you?"

"What if I did?"

"If you know, David, for God's sake tell me! Don't you know that I can't live without her?" There were tears in his eyes.

David looked at him for a long moment. He knew then that Gabriel's haunted look, the changes he'd noted in him, were caused by Emily's absence, and not by the second blackmail letter. Gabriel had suffered, was still suffering, and he hadn't been able to share his agony with anyone. He must love her very much. David knew then what he had to do. Emily might never forgive him, might not understand why he'd done it. But Gabriel deserved a chance.

"Yes, I know where she is," he said. "And I will tell you."

Chapter 37

But lo, thou requirest truth in the inward parts:
and shalt make me to understand wisdom secretly.
                                        Psalm 51:6

David had been walking aimlessly in the park for a long time—he had no idea how long. So many things crowded his mind, demanding attention: the blackmailer, Gabriel, Gabriel and Emily. Lucy. He had to talk to Lucy.

It was Sunday afternoon. He would find Lucy at the V & A.

He went to the gallery where she'd been working at closing time the week before. She was there, alone in the gallery, intent on her sketch pad. David stood immobile for a long time watching her. There was such grace in her every movement, her every gesture, and as she paused momentarily, unconsciously to push her hair back from her face, he felt his chest constrict painfully. She was so very beautiful, sitting there on a bench at the V & A with her red-gold curls shimmering in the late afternoon sunlight. He felt that he could not bear what he now had to do. His nerve failed him, and he half turned to go.

The movement caught her eye; she looked up and saw him, and her face illuminated with pleasure. David thought that as long as he lived he would remember that look, as if a light had been switched on inside her. In a continuous fluid motion she rose and came to him, checking herself at the last moment as she saw the expression on his face. "Hello, David."

"Lucy." He smiled, painfully, and took her hands in his. "How have you been?"

"All right. I missed you. How was your trip?"

"Fine. The weather was miserable, the food was awful, and the bloody pipes banged all night and kept me awake, but aside from that . . ."

She laughed. His heart constricted again, and he dropped her hands. "Listen, Lucy, we have to talk," he plunged in. It was now or never. "The roses I sent you . . . I thought I meant it, but . . . I just can't do it. I feel terrible about this . . ."

She interrupted him softly. "You don't have to say anything, David. Let's just leave it. We've had some lovely times together, so let's not spoil it now by saying anything we'll be sorry for."

"But I want to make you understand why . . . it has to be this way. It's not you, Lucy, it's me that's the problem."

"I do understand," she affirmed, raising her eyes squarely to meet his. "You're a lovely man—you deserve the best that life has to offer. I know it sounds terribly trite, but I hope that someday you'll meet somebody special and he'll make you very happy."

"How . . . how did you know?"

She laughed quietly, wryly. "I've known a lot of men, remember? I told you once that all the good blokes around my age were either married or gay. You're a damn good bloke, and you're definitely not married."

"You knew all along."

"I suspected. And the other night I knew for sure, when I wanted you to stay, and you wouldn't . . . couldn't."

"I didn't know that you wanted me to stay," he breathed with wonder.

"That's just it, isn't it? You didn't know."

"Then why . . . I was going to . . . I asked you to marry me!"

"Ah, David." She touched his cheek with great tenderness.

"I was going to say no. I was very tempted, but I would have said no."

"But why?"

"Don't you see, David? Marriage with you . . . well, it would have been very nice. Comfortable. An end to being alone. But that's not enough. There always would have been . . . something missing. It would have been a mistake for you, and it would have been a mistake for me."

"But, Lucy, I do love you." As he said it, he knew it was true.

She smiled into his eyes. "Yes, I believe you do. But maybe not in the right way, or maybe not enough. Marriage isn't a game, David. It's not an escape from anything—not even from loneliness. Some of the loneliest people in the world are married. Your loneliness is inside you, David, in a place I could never reach."

His eyes filled with tears; he found he couldn't speak.

"I've been there before," she went on. "Years ago I married for all the wrong reasons, trying to escape from my past, from . . . myself. It didn't work. But at least I've learned from my mistake. I won't do it again. And I care about you too much to let you . . ." She smiled through her own tears. "But let's not close all the doors yet, David. Please?"

His voice, when he finally spoke, was choked. "Lucy Kingsley, did anyone ever tell you that you were a wise woman?" He took her gently in his arms and, for the first and possibly the last time, kissed her on the lips, with a kind of love and with infinite regret.

Chapter 38

They that sow in tears: shall reap in joy.
He that goeth on his way weeping, and beareth
  forth good seed: shall doubtless come again with
  joy, and bring his sheaves with him.
                                                    Psalm 126:6–7

Emily was drowsing in bed. She'd spent much of the past two days sleeping, a healing sleep, and when she woke she thought about her past, and her future. Soon she would have to make some decisions and face the future, whatever it held. But first, in this limbo-like present, she must try to come to terms with the past, her past and Gabriel's.

In thought she'd gradually worked her way back through the years, the years of happy memories. The last few years, when the children were small, and needed so much attention and love. Before that, the incredible joy of their birth, after they'd both wanted them for so long. And the not-so-happy memories of the time before that, when she'd lost the baby, and disappointed Gabriel so terribly. But always, through it all, the love they'd shared . . .

Outside her window it was a golden August afternoon. It was on just such an afternoon that he'd first asked her to marry him. Emily closed her eyes.

It was his afternoon off, and they'd driven out into the country for a walk. They'd known each other only a few weeks. At the top of a hill, he suddenly stopped and said, "Emily, I want to marry you."

Breathless after the climb, and with surprise, she replied, "I just don't know, Gabriel. I have other plans for my life. I never counted on meeting you—I need some time to think about how you fit in. There's Cambridge, and the fellowship . . . I'm just not sure yet."

But later, back at the vicarage, the housekeeper away, he took her in his arms and kissed her, and from that moment on nothing else mattered. He'd kissed her before, but this time he meant business. His lips, his arms around her—she didn't want him to stop. He didn't stop. Afterwards, in bed, he smiled down at her, tenderly brushing a strand of dark hair from her cheek. "Now you'll have to marry me, my darling Emily." And, looking into his eyes, loving him, of course she said yes.

It was just after that, she recalled now, that she'd asked him the question: Why hadn't he married earlier? "Because I've never met a woman like you before. You must believe me, my love—you're the first woman I've ever loved." Had there been even a shadow of concealment on his face when he'd made his reply? She couldn't remember. She got up and splashed some cold water on her face at the basin, trying to stop the racing of her pulses at the vivid memory of his lovemaking. She scrubbed at her face with the rough towel, squinted at herself in the small mirror, and ran a comb through her tousled hair. Perhaps she'd go out in the garden and get some air.

There was a quiet tap on the door. "Mrs. Neville, there's a man here to see you," said a soft voice. David, Emily thought with a smile. It would be nice to see David. She turned as the door opened.

Gabriel! Her heart lurched with a wild joy and she instinctively moved towards his open arms, but she checked herself in time and retreated. "No, Gabriel. That would be too easy." She faced him across the narrow bed. "What do you have to say to me?"

He looked at her, stunned. "Say to you? Don't you understand, Emily? I've come to take you home."

"I'm not sure I'm ready to go home, Gabriel. There are a lot of things we have to talk about first."

His hands dropped to his sides. "All right, then. Let's talk."

"How did you find me?"

"David told me . . ."

She laughed harshly. "I should have known that you men would stick together."

"It wasn't like that. He didn't want to tell me—I begged him. He finally realized how important it was—that I should at least have a chance to see you."

"Did he also tell you why I left?"

Gabriel looked away. "Yes. But you must believe me . . ."

"How can I know what to believe, when our marriage was based on a lie?" she asked with heart-rending honesty.

"I never lied to you, Emily."

"No, you didn't, did you? 'Economical with the truth' is the phrase they use these days, I think. 'The first woman you ever loved,' you said. I suppose I was naïve not to ask about the other half of the human race." The bitterness in her voice touched him on a raw nerve.

"Don't you understand? I couldn't tell you—I was terrified of losing you. I didn't think you'd be able to accept it, to accept *me*, to believe that I'd changed and that all I wanted was you."

"Did you have so little faith in me, then?"

"You were so young, so innocent. I couldn't take the risk that you . . . would be disgusted by my past."

She was silent for a moment. She'd asked herself so many times over the last few days how she *would* have reacted. "And since then?" she asked finally. "Surely you could have found a moment, over the last ten years, when you might have told me. It wasn't fair of you to deny me that knowledge, not all this time. I just can't help feeling that our marriage has been a dishonest sham."

He recoiled. "Never that, Emily. Don't the last ten years mean anything? I've loved you, I've been faithful to you for ten years. David and the others—it was all a very long time ago."

She looked as if she'd been struck, but her voice was deadly quiet. "Others? There were others? How many?"

Oh, wonderful, he thought. "Didn't David tell you? I assumed . . ."

"No."

"Not many. Before David. Three, four... several. David was the only one who really mattered."

"Oh, Gabriel, it's all too much. How can you expect me to believe anything you say any more?"

He sat down heavily on the bed, burying his head in his hands. At last he raised his face, wet with tears, and said in an anguished whisper, "How can I make you understand? I'm so sorry that I've hurt you. I was foolish, and selfish. But I didn't want to lose you then, and I couldn't bear to lose you now. I love you, Emily. Please come home with me." She'd never seen him cry before, not even when she'd lost the baby. His tears reached her as his words could not, and in the end she was comforting him, stroking his head and murmuring her love.

* * *

In the car, on the way home, he told her everything: about David, and how he'd loved him, about the others, and finally about Peter Maitland, his death, and the blackmail letters.

She cried a little, but her love for him was very strong, and his honesty meant everything to her; by the time they reached the vicarage he had gained the most stalwart ally he could have. "If only you'd trusted me sooner," she said. "So much pain could have been avoided."

He took her hand, lacing his fingers with hers. "I think I can face whatever happens, now that I've got you back. Don't ever leave me again, my love."

Chapter 39

Daphne probably wouldn't know he was back in London,
David thought: He'd left his car in front of the vicarage, and
unless she'd been down to St. Anne's for some reason that
afternoon she wouldn't have seen it. In any case, he didn't
think he could face her—or anyone he knew—just yet. He took
the Tube to a far-flung corner of London and found a quiet
pub where he could sit in a dark corner and drink anonymously.

Daphne wasn't expecting him. She looked over the tops of
her spectacles in surprise when he let himself into the flat.

"All right, what is going on?" she demanded immediately. "Why was Gabriel trying to reach you? What's so
urgent that he'd ring here at seven o'clock on a Sunday
morning, looking for you?"

David sat down and put his feet up. "It's a long story."

"We've got all night. Do you want a drink?"

"Actually, I'd like something to eat, if it's not too much
trouble. I haven't had anything but a tuna sandwich all day.
And a few glasses of whisky," he added candidly.

"I could grill you a chop, if you like."

"Thanks. That would be lovely."

"Come through to the kitchen, then. You can talk to me
there."

He followed her to the kitchen. It was a fairly small
room, so to stay out of her way he leaned against the door
jamb and watched her as she quickly and efficiently put

together a meal for him. Dear old no-nonsense Daphne, he thought. What a treasure. Maybe I should marry *her*. But then there's no reason why she would have me, either, he reflected in a half humorous, half self-pitying way. By now he'd almost forgotten that he'd done the rejecting—that he'd decided he couldn't possibly marry Lucy. He remembered only that she'd said she wouldn't marry him. And he remembered that he'd said he loved her. It all seemed quite extraordinary, and a very long time ago.

"If you aren't going to tell me about Gabriel, maybe you'll tell me about your trip," Daphne prompted him. "Did you find out anything about Miles?"

"Yes, I certainly did." He told her with great relish about Miss Somers, and the circumstances of Miles's departure from Selby Cathedral.

"But that's incredible! It really does give him a motive for murdering Mavis, if she'd found out about it, and was blackmailing him about it."

David shook his head sadly. "That's what I thought, but unfortunately it didn't happen that way. It would seem that we've—I've—been barking up the wrong tree all along, so to speak: Mavis wasn't the blackmailer."

Daphne, on the way to the table with the plate of food, stopped in her tracks and stared at him. "Not the blackmailer? How on earth do you know?"

He sighed and took the plate from her. "That's what Gabriel was in a flap about this morning. He's had another blackmail letter, and it obviously didn't come from Mavis."

Daphne sat down at the table. "I think you'd better start again. Gabriel's had another blackmail letter?"

"Yes, today. And it was very clearly from the same person who'd written the first one. So that means Mavis couldn't have written either one." He looked a bit sheepish. "It's my fault—I was the one who assumed she was the blackmailer. I just jumped to the wrong conclusion, that's all. So all this business about Miles has been in the nature of a wild-goose chase."

"In other words, the blackmailer is still alive."

"And has nothing to do with Mavis's death."

Daphne chewed on her lip for a moment, thinking. "So where do you stand now? What does Gabriel want you to do?"

"He wants me to find the blackmailer. And there isn't much time—the deadline he's been given is Wednesday."

"This Wednesday?"

"I'm afraid so. The Feast of the Assumption."

"Can you tell me what it's all about, or would Gabriel rather you didn't?"

David smiled. "I told him that you and I work as a team, and if he wanted my help, he got yours as well."

She returned his smile, gratified. "Thanks, partner. So what is it about?"

He thought about how to begin. "As I told you last week, the letter was about something that happened before Gabriel came here. Just before, in fact. There was a boy in Brighton—his name was Peter Maitland—who drowned. Gabriel had . . . known him. Gabriel has reason to believe that the boy committed suicide, though the verdict of the inquest was accidental death. I think he felt in a way responsible—he might have been able to prevent the boy's death, but didn't. I think it upset him more than he's willing to admit."

Daphne nodded gravely.

"After that, he was anxious to leave Brighton, and got the living here through some connections he had, quite quickly. But apparently someone has found out about what happened—someone at St. Anne's."

"What is the threat?"

"That unless he resigns from St. Anne's and from the priesthood, he'll be exposed. The letter said that they would inform the Bishop, the national press, and . . . Emily."

She raised her eyebrows and whistled soundlessly. "The national press. After the smear job they did on Norman Newsome, Gabriel wouldn't have a chance. Just a hint of a juicy scandal like this, even if it's ten years old, and they'd be howling for his blood."

"Poor old Norman Newsome only had a few fantasies about choirboys, and look what they did to him," David mused. "I can just imagine the meal they'd make of Gabriel."

"Right," said Daphne, businesslike. "What have we got to go on? Who could have known about this boy?"

"That's the difficult bit. Gabriel says he never told anyone, and I have no reason to disbelieve that. I don't know who he would have told, anyway." He added, so quietly that she almost didn't hear, "he didn't tell me, and I knew him better than anyone. At least I thought I did."

With a quick look of sympathy, she went on. "Then the boy must have told someone. He must have mentioned Gabriel's name to a friend, a relative, a teacher..."

"Yes, that's what I thought. Before, that is. Before Mavis died, and I got side-tracked down that blind alley."

"And did you find anything? You went to Brighton, didn't you?"

He frowned, trying to remember. "I thought it was Miles," he said. "Funny, isn't it? Poor old Miles! I keep trying to pin everything on him!"

"Why did you think it was Miles?"

"I found the death notice in the local paper. It implied that Peter Maitland had been a student at Selby Cathedral School, even that he'd been a chorister there. Naturally I thought of Miles—I thought that Peter must have confided in him. I was all ready to tell Gabriel that I'd found his blackmailer, then the next day Mavis was killed, and Miles didn't seem relevant any longer."

"Did you get a copy of the death notice?"

"Yes, if I can remember what I did with it...I don't suppose I threw it away."

"Well, finish your meal, and then you can look for it. Anything else?"

"There was a newspaper report of the drowning, and an item about the inquest. Not a great deal to go on."

"So what we're looking for is a connection between this boy Peter Maitland and someone at St. Anne's," Daphne summarized.

"Exactly. And we have three days to find it. Tomorrow morning is Mavis's inquest, so we can't do much till after that."

"You'll have to go, you know. They'll want you to give evidence, pinpointing the time when you saw her alive."

"Bloody hell. Well, I suppose it can't be helped."

"Anyway," said Daphne, "you're forgetting something else. You know that Mavis was murdered, because of the missing ledger sheet. You weren't the last person in that sacristy. So even if Mavis's murder had nothing to do with this blackmail . . ."

"She *was* murdered! Well, I'll just testify about the ledger sheet being missing, and then it will be the police's business to find who killed her."

Daphne leaned back in her chair. "So we'll forget about Mavis, and concentrate on the blackmailer."

A few minutes later, David had located the photocopies of the newspaper articles, slipped into the pocket of his suitcase for safekeeping over a week ago.

Daphne read them in silence, concentrating on every detail that might be of importance. "Are you quite sure that Miles isn't involved? It does say Selby," she pointed out.

"I'm not sure about the timing, but it doesn't look promising. I'm sure Miss Somers said that Miles had been at Selby for four years, and she would be very precise about things like that. If he's been here at St. Anne's for five years, that would mean that Peter left Selby before Miles arrived." He frowned, remembering. "In fact, I spent a great deal of time studying the board with the list of past organists at the cathedral, and I'm positive that Miles didn't start there till the year after Peter died. Unfortunately."

"Then Miles is out. Again."

"It looks that way."

Daphne scowled. "Croydon," she said. "Do you know anyone in Croydon?"

Something teased at David's mind. "I can't think. There's someone who's recently mentioned Croydon to me."

"Maybe it will come to you, if you don't try too hard."

"I'm just not thinking very clearly tonight. I'm sorry. Do you think I could have that drink now?"

"Of course. Help yourself." She looked at him intently. "Are you all right, David? You really do look unwell."

He poured himself a drink and sat down. "It's been a long day. I've driven two hundred miles, and have had rather too much to drink. I've had a row with Gabriel, and . . . oh, hell. You don't want to hear my problems."

"Of course I do." She dropped the clippings and came over to him, bending over him clumsily. "Tell Auntie Daphne all about it," she urged with a self-deprecating smile. "My shoulders are very broad—along with the rest of me."

Oh, why not, he thought. It would be good to tell someone about it. And Daphne had always been a good listener.

"It's about Lucy," he began. "Lucy Kingsley."

Daphne sat down across from him and leaned forward. "Yes?"

"I . . . well, as you know, I've spent rather a lot of time with her since I've been here." Daphne nodded. "She's a beautiful woman, we have a lot of interests in common, and I've enjoyed her company. Last week, before I went to Selby, I thought . . . well, I thought that maybe it would be an idea for me to marry her."

Daphne's face remained impassive, and David, looking into his glass, didn't see that she gripped the arm of her chair. "Yes?"

"I thought about it a lot while I was gone. It seemed like a very good thing to do. I hate living on my own, you know. And even though I . . . well, I thought the other things wouldn't matter so much."

"Did you ask her?"

"Yes, I sent her some roses, and on the card I . . . But today . . . well, when I was talking to Gabriel, he said that he'd heard rumors about us—about me and Lucy." Daphne nodded; she too had heard talk. "He tried to talk me into marrying her, said it would be a good idea, that I needed a wife. That's when I knew I couldn't do it."

"I see."

"Do you see?" he demanded passionately. "Do you really? Gabriel—that was the one thing I couldn't cope with. Gabriel. After everything we'd . . . been to each other. I know it was a long time ago. I know he's got Emily now. But damn it, how could he tell me I should find myself a wife?"

Daphne bit her lip and resisted the impulse to reach out and touch him. "So what did you do?"

"I went to see Lucy. To tell her." He sighed deeply. "It was all for nothing in the end. She said that she wouldn't have married me anyway. I don't suppose I ever had any reason to think she would. After all, what on earth would I have to offer to a woman like that?" Laughing bitterly, he added, "I'm pretty hopeless, aren't I? I'm a failure as a detective—haring all over the country on a false trail. And I'm a failure as a . . . lover—I couldn't even manage a proper renunciation scene."

Daphne swallowed, cleared her throat, and asked quietly, "Do you love her?"

"That's the damndest part of it. I think I do."

"And have you told her so?"

"Yes."

"Then why wouldn't she marry you? Doesn't she love you?"

He closed his eyes, remembering. "She made a long speech about marriage not being an escape from anything, not even from loneliness. About not wanting to make the same mistake twice. It all made sense, but it hurt like hell."

"It sounds to me like she's a very perceptive and sensible woman," said Daphne. "You weren't going to marry her, anyway," she added reasonably.

"No, but . . . oh, I don't know, Daphne. None of it makes any sense at the moment. Give me some good advice. You can tell me now to forget about her, and get on with my life."

The expression in her eyes was unreadable. "No, I won't tell you that. I don't think you should burn your bridges, not just yet."

"That's funny. That's almost exactly what Lucy said. I'm not sure what it means." He took a gulp of his drink. "Thanks for listening, Daphne. You're a real friend."

Unable to meet his eyes, she leaned over and patted his hand awkwardly.

Chapter 40

The ungodly are froward, even from their mother's womb: as soon as they are born, they go astray, and speak lies.

Psalm 58:3

The room where the inquest was being held was not large, and it was nearly full when David and Daphne arrived, a few minutes before ten. Although the case was not a sensational one, it was sufficiently bizarre to have attracted a fair crowd of thrill-seekers, in addition to the interested parties.

When they'd found seats, David spent the remaining minutes before the opening of the inquest studying the crowd. Venerable Bead was there, of course, in the front row: Fairly bursting with self-importance, he continually turned around to see who else was there. Cecily Framlingham, dressed in black and looking fairly subdued, sat with Mary Hughes near the back. And David was not surprised to see Teresa Dawson there with her mother. Teresa had also dressed in black for the solemn occasion, but she looked anything but subdued: She was virtually licking her lips in anticipation. David didn't see Craig Conwell, but assumed he'd be there.

"Did you see Teresa?" Daphne whispered.

David nodded. "She's enjoying herself already."

"So is Venerable Bead."

"But where is Beryl Ball?"

"Oh, she'll be here. She wouldn't miss a show like this."

But she hadn't arrived when the inquest opened. Craig Conwell was the first witness to be called. He came from the back of the room, hands in his pockets and shoulders hunched, and when he was seated he seemed ill at ease. The questions he was asked were of a perfunctory nature, attempting mainly to establish his mother's frame of mind before her death.

"She seemed OK to me." He shrugged. "Just like usual. Of course she was always getting worked up over something, but that was the way she was."

"And was she 'worked up over something,' as you put it, that morning?" asked the coroner.

Craig shrugged again. "Oh, just some bill in the post. I think it was the phone bill. She said she couldn't afford to pay it."

"And when exactly was this?"

"Saturday morning, early. About eight o'clock."

"She left the house shortly after that?"

"About half past. To go to that church fête. She was a big shot at the church."

"That was the last time you saw your mother, when she left the house at half past eight on Saturday morning?"

His eyes darted around the room at the watching faces. "Yeah, that's right." David wondered if he had cultivated the Americanized drawl, or if it was just a reflection of a television-influenced youth.

"Thank you very much, Mr. Conwell." Craig returned to his seat at the back.

Next the coroner called David to give evidence. This, too, was fairly routine. He was asked to verify his statement to the police, particularly regarding the time that he'd left Mavis. This line of questioning had just begun when the door opened and Beryl Ball walked into the room. David saw that she was dressed entirely in pillar-box red, except for the green moon-boots. He stopped in mid-sentence; people became gradually aware of her as she made a stately but purposeful progress up the center aisle. She nodded and waggled her teeth knowingly at Craig Conwell as she passed him, then headed straight for the coroner's chair. She thrust her hand and her teeth out simultaneously; taken totally aback, he took her hand and shook it cordially. She turned to David with an exaggerated wink, then hobbled to an empty chair in the front row and sat down with a flourish.

The coroner regained his composure, and the attention of his audience, after a brief struggle. "So, Mr. Middleton-

Brown, you left Mrs. Conwell in the sacristy at approximately four forty-five."

"No later than that, certainly. Possibly a few minutes earlier."

"And you are satisfied with your statement as it now stands?"

David hesitated. "With the statement, yes. But there's something I'd like to add—something that I think is rather important."

"Yes, Mr. Middleton-Brown?"

"I was asked by the police to look around and confirm that the sacristy was as it was when I left it. In fact, something was missing from the room, but I only realized that later."

"And what was that?"

"The ledger sheet on which Mrs. Conwell had recorded the hourly totals for the money she was counting. It was on the table when I was there, and I assumed that the police had it, along with the money. But I . . . was told later that no ledger sheet was found."

"Is that all?"

"Yes, but—"

"Thank you, Mr. Middleton-Brown. You've been most helpful."

People were becoming anxious for what was undoubtedly the centerpiece of the day's proceedings—Venerable Bead's testimony. There was a noticeable stir of interest as Percy Bead's name was called. Teresa Dawson was leaning forward so far in her seat that she was in danger of falling off.

"Mr. Percy Bead?"

"That's right."

"I'd like to ask you a few questions about that Saturday afternoon, the fourth of August. What was your business in the sacristy?"

"I was getting ready for Evensong."

"Doing precisely what?"

"Well, I was going to put out some fresh candles. I'm not the Sacristan, you understand, but . . . well, I like to help out when I can. And I saw that the candles were getting rather low."

"Interfering old busy body," Daphne muttered.

"And Father Gabriel likes me to lay his cotta out for him—sometimes I give it a quick press before he comes in."

"So what time was it precisely when you went to the sacristy?"

"Just after half past five. I looked at my watch, and wondered when the organ recital would finish. Evensong starts at six, and I like to be ready in plenty of time."

"You found the door locked, I understand. Were you expecting it to be locked?"

"No. It usually is, of course, but I assumed that with Mrs. Conwell in there . . ."

"And you have a key."

"Yes, of course." He looked affronted at the question. "I have a position of great responsibility at St. Anne's."

"Could you describe what you saw when you entered the sacristy?"

Teresa Dawson's eyes glowed as Venerable Bead launched with great relish into his description of the lolling head, the blue lips, the staring eyes, the limp body.

"And you knew that she was dead."

"Yes, of course I did."

"You didn't touch or move the body?"

"No."

"What did you do?"

"I went immediately to the vicarage to fetch the Vicar. I thought he'd know what to do."

"Going back a bit, Mr. Bead. The . . . object around Mrs. Conwell's neck. How would you describe it?"

"She was hanging on a black girdle." Some of the older and more secular members of the audience chuckled with discreet amusement; Venerable Bead glared. "A girdle," he amplified with dignity, "is a sort of rope belt, worn with an alb."

"And this . . . girdle. It was kept in the sacristy?"

"Yes, in a drawer."

"Mrs. Conwell would have known this?"

"I should have thought so."

"Thank you very much, Mr. Bead."

The rest of the inquest was an anticlimax. Cyril Fitzjames was called to answer a few questions about the church finances. He launched into a complicated explanation of the bookkeeping system; he became hopelessly entangled in his own verbiage and had to begin again. David's attention wandered and he idly watched the woman who was making the transcript of the proceedings. What a waste, he thought. All those words. Next week they'll be forgotten, and the transcript will be filed away somewhere with thousands more just like it, and no one will ever look at it again. Unless . . . He sat up straight as an idea came to him, and he was in a fever of impatience as the inquest wound down with expert testimony from police, doctors and pathologists, all concluding that the state of the body was perfectly in keeping with suicide. He hadn't heard a word since Cyril Fitzjames was speaking, and so he was possibly the only person in the room who was surprised when the coroner announced a verdict of self-inflicted death.

"Suicide?" he exclaimed to Daphne as soon as they were outside. "Is he mad? Didn't he listen to what I said about the ledger sheet?"

"He must not have thought it was important. All the expert witnesses agreed."

"Fine experts they are! Honestly, Daphne!"

"Well, I suppose the funeral goes ahead tomorrow."

David looked at his watch. "I don't have time to worry about this now, Daphne, there's something I need to do. I may be back quite late tonight. But promise you'll wait up for me. I shall need your clear brain by then, I think."

Chapter 41

When thy word goeth forth: it giveth light and understanding unto the simple.

Psalm 119:130

David's last trip to Brighton had taught him a lesson; this time he took the train from Victoria, and arrived by mid-afternoon.

It was with a degree of reluctance that he approached his old offices. He hadn't been back since he left Brighton nearly ten years ago. Things were bound to have changed.

The first change was evident on the outside: Graham's name, on a brass plate, was now among those of the partners. He and Graham had started with the firm at just about the same time, nearly fifteen years ago, and now Graham had received his reward for faithful service.

David paused for a moment outside, contemplating Graham's name, and summoning the courage to enter those doors again.

The interior looked much the same as he remembered, though the girl answering the phone at the desk was not familiar. She looked about eighteen. She would have barely been out of diapers when he was here, he realized with a faint shock. When she'd finished dealing with the phone, she turned to him with an inquiring, professional smile. "Yes, sir?"

"I wonder if Mr. Crawford is free?"

"Do you have an appointment?"

"No, I'm afraid not. I'm an old friend. I was hoping he might have a minute to see me."

"You might have rung," she reproved. "Mr. Crawford is a very busy man."

Suitably chastened, he persevered. "I am sorry. But would you ask Mr. Crawford if he could see Mr. Middleton-Brown, just briefly?"

With a disapproving look, she rang Graham's office. "Mr. Crawford will see you," she told him a moment later. "He'll be down in a moment."

"Thank you very much." He smiled at her in a conciliatory way, but she turned away and applied herself to some papers while he waited.

He didn't have long to wait. Graham burst into the reception area, a delighted smile on his face. "David, my dear chap! What a lovely surprise! What brings you here?" He clasped David's hand warmly.

"I came to see you. Have you got a moment?"

"For you, old chum, any time! Is this official, or shall we pop out for a drink?"

"Oh, please."

"The pub round the corner is open all afternoon now. I love

these new licensing hours! Miss Morris, please take any messages that come in for me. I'm not sure how long I'll be."

David couldn't resist a slightly triumphant look at the disgruntled receptionist.

"Where did you get her?" David asked as they went around the corner. "What happened to old Miss Bradgate?"

"Miss Bradgate, bless her, retired a few years ago. Michelle's not so bad when you get to know her—she just takes her responsibilities very seriously."

"I suppose that's no bad thing. But for a young girl she's damned intimidating."

"You've always been easily intimidated, David." They reached the pub and went up to the bar. "What are you drinking, my good man?"

"Whisky, please. I'm not driving today."

Graham ordered the drinks, then turned to him. "How did you get here?"

"I came down by train from London."

"Damn, it's good to see you, David. It's been a long time."

They appraised each other for a moment while they waited for their drinks. Graham looked decidedly middle-aged, David thought. He'd always been boyishly handsome; now his fair hair had thinned noticeably and his hairline had receded well back from his forehead. The moustache also made him look older. David assumed that Graham was drawing similar conclusions about him.

"So, how are things?" David asked. "How are Fiona and the children?"

Graham grimaced. "To tell you the truth, David, Fiona and I have split up."

David could have kicked himself. "I'm so sorry. I didn't know."

"No, of course you didn't." Graham paid for the drinks and led the way to a table. There was an awkward silence as David tried to think of something to say; Graham finally answered the unasked questions. "Things hadn't really been right between us for quite a while. I moved out this spring, and a divorce is in the works."

"I'm really sorry. I always liked Fiona." David remembered

all the occasions when Graham's wife, feeling sorry for a
lonely bachelor, had included him in family get-togethers.

"Yes, so did I," Graham said with a wry shrug. "Don't
ask me what went wrong. But there you are."

"Where are you living? It's a good thing I didn't go to
the house to find you."

"I've taken rented accommodation here in town for the
time being, until I get myself sorted out."

There was another pause. "And the children?" David asked.

"James is at university now, and Sarah is still at home
with Fiona. She's entering her last year at school this
autumn, doing her A Levels."

"Good Lord. I still think of them as being about this
high." David indicated the height of a small child.

"They probably were, the last time you saw them. God,
it has been a long time! How has life been treating you?
You're still in Wymondham?"

"Yes." He paused. "Mother died about two months ago."

"Now it's my turn to say I'm sorry. I didn't know."

"No."

"Are you keeping the house?"

"For the moment. Like you, it's a bit soon to decide
where I go from here."

"Well, if you ever want to come back to Brighton,
there's a job for you at the old firm. I can guarantee that."

"Thanks, but I doubt it somehow." David smiled.

"Is there . . . anyone special in your life right now?"
Graham asked discreetly. Graham, bless him, had never
pried into his private life, for which David had always been
grateful. Fiona had occasionally tried to fix him up with one
of her single friends, but Graham had shielded him. David
wondered whether Graham suspected the truth—he'd have
to be pretty naïve not to—but Graham had never said a
word to indicate any possible suspicions.

"No, not really." On impulse he added, "I met a lovely
woman recently. I thought . . . anyway, nothing has come of
it. Nothing will," he finished, embarrassed.

"Oh, you never know, old chap." Graham looked interested and, yes, possibly a bit surprised. "I must say, I'm

rather enjoying the single life myself. There are a lot of women out there—God, I had no idea! All those years of marriage, and now... well, it's a whole different world! Women these days aren't ashamed to take the lead, to let you know what they want!'' He smiled a self-satisfied smile.

"Another drink?" David suggested. "Or do you have to get back to work?"

"Bugger work. It's not every day I have a chance to see an old friend."

"I won't tell Miss Morris you said that," David said over his shoulder as he went to the bar.

Graham lifted his glass when David returned. "Cheers. So, David, what brings you to Brighton? It's a damned odd time for a social call, if I may say so."

David took his measure carefully before replying. Except for the inevitable physical alterations, Graham hadn't changed since he'd last seen him. He thought he knew the best way to approach his problem. "I want to ask you a favor," he began. "I need you to do a bit of spying for me."

Graham immediately looked interested. He'd always been fascinated by espionage, devouring spy novels in his spare time. He'd sometimes lamented the fact that he'd missed out on a career in MI5. "Yes? What sort of spying?"

"It's a delicate matter," said David temptingly. Graham leaned forward. "I need some information from the transcript of an inquest."

"But they're not available for public inspection. You know that."

"That's where the spying comes in. I need you to infiltrate the coroner's office and take a look at this transcript for me."

Words like "infiltrate" were calculated to pique Graham's curiosity.

"Is this top-secret stuff?" he asked eagerly.

"Top secret. Very important, too."

Graham leaned back. "The coroner's office. I just might be able to manage that. There's a sweet girl who works there—Denise. I have reason to believe that she might be willing to bend the rules a bit to do me a favor." He nodded in satisfaction.

David smiled. "I knew that your charms would come in handy some day."

"When do you need it?"

"Uh . . . tomorrow," David replied, "if that's not asking too much."

"That should be no problem," said Graham expansively. "Tell me what you need to know."

* * *

David had declined an invitation from Graham to stay and join him for a meal, promising to return at an early date. The train was not an express, so he had time for a quick meal from the buffet car. "East Croydon," came the near-unintelligible announcement over the loudspeaker, and David stopped in mid-bite. Croydon. Of course.

He was back in London much earlier than he'd anticipated, and walked the short distance from the Tube station to the flat quickly, full of his new revelation. Daphne was not at the flat when he arrived; he got himself a drink and settled down impatiently to wait for her.

She was surprised to see him back already when she returned. "I've been down at the church getting things ready for the funeral," she explained. "I didn't think you'd be back yet."

"No, neither did I. Hope you don't mind."

"Of course not. Have you eaten?"

"More or less." He grimaced. "I had a bite on the train. Delicious British Rail cuisine."

"Train? Where have you been, then?"

"Brighton."

Daphne looked interested. "Have you got a lead?"

"That remains to be seen. Just a little idea I had—I'll tell you when and if it pans out."

"Be that way."

"Oh, it will probably come to nothing. But I'll tell you what I *have* remembered: I remembered who was talking about Croydon. Just as you said, it came to me when I wasn't thinking about it, tonight when the train went through East Croydon.''

"Tell me! Who was it?''

"It was Tony Kent, last week when I had lunch with him. He mentioned that he'd come from there—talked about the High Church tradition he'd grown up with.''

"Well, well.'' Daphne sat down. "So Tony comes from Croydon.''

"I've been thinking about this all the way back. Tony is about the same age that Peter would have been . . . if he'd lived. They might have known each other.''

"Tony Kent.'' Daphne considered the possibilities.

"Wait a minute,'' David said slowly. "Tony. What is his proper name, do you know? Is it Anthony?''

"It could be, I suppose. You just never know with nicknames. I've never heard him called anything but Tony, but it probably is Anthony. Why?''

He rubbed his forehead. "Did I tell you? I asked Gabriel if he knew the names of any of Peter's friends. He couldn't remember much, but he did mention that Peter had a friend called Anthony.''

Daphne looked at him for a long moment. "You might be on to something, my boy. You just might be on to something.''

* * *

Later, they discussed the morning's inquest. "I just can't believe they still think it's suicide,'' David groaned, shaking his head. "After what I told them about the ledger sheet.''

"The ledger sheet,'' said Daphne. "Let's think about the ledger sheet. Why would anyone take it?''

"To hide something?''

"To hide what? Something about the figures on the sheet.''

"Like . . . that they didn't tally with the money on the table!'' David exclaimed, with dawning comprehension.

"Exactly!'' Daphne agreed.

"And they wouldn't have!'' he added, his excitement

increasing. "I just remembered—Mavis told me when I saw her that they'd already raised over two thousand pounds! I'd forgotten completely that she'd said that!"

"And how much was there when the body was found?"

"I think Gabriel said it was around eighteen hundred pounds."

"So someone took some of the money—not enough that it would be obvious as robbery, and took the sheet so that no one would know any money was missing."

"And they wouldn't have known that she'd told me about the two thousand pounds . . ."

Daphne nodded. "It fits perfectly. The murderer goes in the sacristy, kills Mavis, takes some of the money and the ledger sheet, and makes it all look like suicide. If they'd taken all the money, it would have been obvious that it was murder."

"Then who?" asked David.

"Who, indeed? That's the question."

"Someone she would have let in the sacristy, someone who could have got behind her unawares . . ."

"Someone who needed money. Maybe not a lot of money, but . . ."

"Craig," stated David. "We ruled him out as a possible murderer before, but that's when we thought the motive was blackmail. But if the motive was money, theft . . ."

"But would he kill his own mother for a couple of hundred quid?" Daphne asked.

"From what I've seen of that young man, I wouldn't find it a bit hard to believe. He probably would have killed her for tuppence. She had to have been a frightful parent—there must have been a lot of bottled-up hostility on his part."

"We're forgetting something," Daphne put in reluctantly. "Craig wasn't at St. Anne's on Saturday. He said he wasn't, and no one saw him there."

David sat very still for a moment, searching for an elusive memory. "Oh, yes they did," he said slowly. "Beryl Ball saw him."

"How do you know?"

"She said so, a few days later. Before the organ recital. It was one of her usual stories—I wasn't paying much attention. You know, about every man in London being after her body. She said that Craig had wanted her. *On Saturday,* she said. On Saturday."

"Maybe it was earlier in the day. Or later."

He thought a bit longer. "No. It was then, all right. When I left the sacristy and went through to the organ recital, I met Beryl Ball in the corridor."

"And the little outside door was unlocked."

"Yes. Craig could have—must have—come in right after I left."

They stared at each other. "Good Lord," said David at last. *"Good Lord."*

Chapter 42

Save me, and deliver me from the hand of strange children: whose mouth talketh of vanity, and their right hand is a right hand of iniquity.

Psalm 144:11

Daphne had gone to the church early, to make sure that all was in order for the funeral, so David walked to St. Anne's alone. He looked automatically at the vicarage as he passed; Emily was just coming out of the front door, so he stopped and waited for her self-consciously. He'd heard from Daphne that she was back, but had not yet plucked up the courage to seek her out; he told himself he'd been too busy.

She smiled at him without reservation. "Good morning, David."

"I'm glad you're still speaking to me."

"Of course I am."

He plunged in immediately. "Emily, I want to apologize

252 / Kate Charles

for betraying your confidence and telling Gabriel where to find you. It was very wrong of me, but my only excuse is that I thought I was doing the right thing. I should have contacted you first, and asked your permission to tell him.''

She put her hand on his arm. ''It's all right, David. I was a little upset at first, but it all turned out for the best.''

''He was so devastated. I thought—well, I felt that if you saw him like that, you'd know how much he cared.''

Emily turned grateful eyes on him. ''That was very . . . unselfish of you, considering how you feel.''

''He does love you very much, you know,'' said David impulsively. ''I knew it that day.''

She smiled. ''Yes. We're not out of the woods yet, Gabriel and I, but things are better between us now than they've ever been. For the first time in our relationship, he's been totally honest with me.''

''I'm glad, Emily. I mean that. You deserve all the happiness . . .''

''Thank you, David. I know what it must cost you to say that.''

They walked towards the church together. ''You're going to the funeral?'' he asked after a moment.

''Yes. I thought I really should go.''

''The children?'' he inquired.

''We fetched them yesterday morning, first thing. Oh, it was good to see them again! For us all to be together again, as a family!''

''Where are they now?''

, ''They're too young for an ordeal like this. I've taken them to Lucy's for an hour or so.'' She looked at his profile closely as she said the name. He kept his face impassive. How much had Lucy told her of what had passed between them? Very little, if he knew Lucy—she was always disinclined to talk about herself. He didn't want to think about Lucy now.

Venerable Bead was at the back of the church, solemnly passing out hymn books and prayer books. He regarded this particular funeral as his personal property, by virtue of his role in finding the body; ordinarily, he would have been among the first to condemn Gabriel's decision to allow a church funeral for an apparent suicide, but he wouldn't have missed this for the world. Cyril Fitzjames, as the surviving churchwarden, assisted him; he would have contrived to give a set of books to Emily, and possibly have a word with her, but Venerable Bead was too quick for him.

Emily and David sat together near the back; it was early yet and the church was just beginning to fill up. At the front of the nave, in front of the rood screen, was a bier, ready to receive the coffin. "So they didn't bring her in last night?" David whispered.

"No. Craig didn't want it, and Gabriel wasn't very keen either, under the circumstances."

They watched the other mourners arrive. Teresa Dawson led her parents as far towards the front as she dared. Cecily Framlingham, in a black pill-box hat, seemed genuinely grieved, leaning on Arthur's arm. Miles Taylor began playing soothing chords on the organ and Mary Hughes nodded approvingly as she entered and found a seat. Not surprisingly, Tony Kent was nowhere to be seen. Just before the appointed hour, Lady Constance, holding herself very erect and looking straight ahead, walked slowly down the center aisle and sat near the front; David thought that she appeared very frail indeed. Then Craig slouched in, looking thoroughly bored. The people with him, leading him to the front row, were apparently aunts and uncles, siblings of Mavis. And at the very last minute, Beryl Ball hobbled down the aisle, sheathed in rusty black from head to toe. She smiled and nodded to the assembled congregation, and took a seat in the front row, on the opposite side from the family.

There was a hush, then Gabriel's resonant voice sounded from the back of the church. "I am the resurrection and the life, saith the Lord: he that believeth in me, though he were dead, yet shall he live: and whosoever liveth and believeth in me shall never die." He swept solemnly up the aisle, majestic in a cope of rich black brocade, followed by the somber men with the coffin on their shoulders. "I know that my Redeemer liveth, and that he shall stand at the latter day upon the earth . . ." They rested the coffin on the bier and

Gabriel turned to face the congregation. "We brought nothing into this world, and it is certain we can carry nothing out . . ."

He read the psalm.

> I said, I will take heed to my ways: that offend not in my tongue.
> I will keep my mouth as it were with a bridle: while the ungodly is in my sight.
> I held my tongue, and spake nothing: I kept silence, yea, even from good words; but it was pain and grief to me.

David and Emily exchanged a look; nothing could have been less applicable to the dead woman.

"For man walketh in a vain shadow . . ."

* * *

After the service, Craig was nowhere to be seen among the family, gathered in the north porch to greet the mourners. David caught a glimpse of him lurking around the corner outside the church, smoking a furtive cigarette; on impulse he made a hurried excuse to Emily and strolled up to him.

"Hello, Craig," he greeted him. "May I offer my condolences on this very sad occasion?" The words were perfectly straightforward, but his voice held a hint of irony as he observed the sullen young man.

Craig eyed him suspiciously. "Who are you? I've seen you before, haven't I?"

"I was at the inquest yesterday. I saw your mother a few minutes before her . . . death. My name is Middleton-Brown."

"Oh, yeah." Craig took a drag of his cigarette and observed David through the smoke as he exhaled.

David's expression never altered. "Why didn't you tell the coroner that you were in the church that afternoon? In the sacristy, in fact?"

Craig went white, and choked on the cigarette smoke;

David waited patiently while he prolonged his coughing to cover his agitation. "I wasn't," he said finally, belligerently.

David decided to bluff a little. "I saw you," he said calmly. "You came in that side door, and you went into the sacristy. The door wasn't locked—I'd just left there myself. I saw you. So did Beryl Ball. You know she did—you saw her, too."

"You mean that crazy old bag in the funny hat?" Craig said without thinking.

David smiled and Craig blanched. "That's right, Craig. You saw her, all right. Why did you kill your mother? Was it just for the money? I know that you took the money. And you took the ledger sheet, because you thought that without it no one would know that any money was missing."

Craig no longer looked defiant. His hand, as he raised the cigarette to his lips, was trembling. "I didn't kill her," he said at last. "Yes, I was there." He hesitated. "I don't know how you know so much, man, but I was there. And I—I took the money. And the piece of paper. But I didn't kill her—you have to believe me!" His voice had become a high-pitched whine. "She was a miserable old cow, but I didn't kill her! She was still alive when I left that room! She locked the door behind me, and then she . . . she hung herself. I know she did! I didn't kill my mother! Please don't go to the cops, man! They'll think I did it! That's why I couldn't tell them I'd been there. Please, man! I'll give the money back, if that's what you're after, only please don't tell the cops!"

* * *

David went to the sacristy then, and found Daphne putting away the funeral cope. "How did you manage to keep Venerable Bead from doing it for you?" he asked.

"With great difficulty," she chuckled. "But I think he's followed them to the crematorium."

David told her, as succinctly as possible, about his confrontation with Craig.

"What are you going to do?" she asked.

"I really don't know. The police will have to be told eventually, of course, whether he gives the money back or not. But I'm not sure I believe him—I still think there's a good chance that the little sneak killed her."

"Then why would he admit he'd been here?"

"He had to. He thinks I saw him, and he knows that Beryl Ball did. But of course he wouldn't admit killing her, even if he'd done it."

"You'll have to go to the police."

"Yes, but not today. We've only got another day to get this blackmail problem solved. Then it will be time enough to deal with Craig Conwell."

* * *

It was late that evening when the phone rang. Daphne answered it. "David, for you. Graham Crawford."

He took the receiver. "Hello, Graham."

"Hello, David old chap. Sorry to be so late ringing—I had to take Denise out to dinner. Quid pro quo, you know. You owe me."

"I'm sure you'll get your own reward, if you haven't had it already."

Graham laughed. "Fair enough. But she came through with the inquest transcript that you wanted. Even made me a photocopy, the angel. I've put it in the post to you already. First class. No expense spared for you, old boy."

"You're wonderful, Graham. I knew you could do it."

"Can you at least tell me what it's all about?" he asked plaintively.

"Sorry, Graham. Too secret."

"Oh, well." Graham was philosophical. "I'm sure it's all in a good cause."

"Can you tell me the answer to a specific question? Maitland's roommate testified that there was no suicide note?"

"Yes, that's right."

"And the roommate was named in the transcript."

"Yes, of course. The roommate's name was . . . just a

second, I've got it written down here somewhere. The roommate's name was Dominic Dawson.''

* * *

"I got the idea yesterday that the transcript of the Maitland inquest would tell us his roommate's name. I thought that might shed some light, give us a lead. But I don't understand. Dominic Dawson," said David slowly, trying to make sense of it. "Peter Maitland's roommate was Dominic . . . Dawson."

"Do you mean Julia and Roger's son Dominic?" Daphne asked, puzzled.

"They have a son Dominic? I know Francis, of course, but I thought the others were Nicholas and Benedict. Nick . . ."

"Oh, Nick's not Nicholas, he's Dominic."

David stared at her. "Dominic. I just assumed that Nick was short for Nicholas."

"As I said last night, you never know about nicknames, do you?"

"But . . . Nick! Daphne, I've been so stupid! Of course it had to be Dominic!"

"You should have known," she agreed bluntly. "Dominic, Benedict, Bridget, Clare, Francis, Teresa."

"They're not just saints' names, are they?" He shook his head at his own failure. "They're all founders of religious orders. Only the Dawsons could name their children like that . . . Even the bloody dog, Daphne! Ignatius! But I should have known! Nicholas just doesn't fit with the rest."

"But how did you know the Dominic part of his roommate's name?"

"Gabriel told me. He said that Peter's roommate was named Dominic." He rubbed his forehead. "Nick Dawson went to university in Brighton, to the University of Sussex, like Francis. I knew that—Roger told me."

"Nick's about the right age, isn't he?"

"Tony Kent said that Nick was around his age. We've already decided that Tony was about the same age as Peter."

David went for the whisky bottle. "This really does

explain everything, Daphne.'' Suddenly a picture flashed across his brain, a clear image of a good-looking young man with dark eyes, and he stopped in his tracks. ''My God, Daphne, I've seen his photo!''

''What?''

''Peter Maitland's photo! That interminable evening at the Dawsons! I saw his photo. It was one among hundreds—it seemed more like thousands. Nick and his roommate, they said. And Teresa said . . . he's dead. They were all dead, Daphne. How was I to know?''

She shook her head. ''The question is, now that you know, what are you going to do about it?''

''Tell Gabriel, of course. First thing in the morning. Then he can deal with it. I don't know what he ever intended to do, if and when I found the blackmailer—go and talk to them, I suppose. Try to convince them not to go ahead with their threats. Well, it will be up to him now.''

''Which Dawson do you suppose it is?'' Daphne asked. ''Roger?''

''Probably. I don't think Julia would have the nerve. And I doubt that Francis would have the brains.''

''Why now, do you suppose? After all these years?''

He shook his head. ''Maybe the Norman Newsome affair triggered it off. Or maybe the possibility of his promotion to Archdeacon. Or maybe they hadn't put everything together before now, and Francis found something out in Brighton . . .''

''Well, congratulations, David. You may have waited until the eleventh hour, but Gabriel's confidence in your abilities was well placed.''

''With a lot of help from you,'' he added with satisfaction. ''But I must admit, I am pleased. I've been down a few blind alleys, but this is finally one that takes us somewhere.''

Chapter 43

For thou, O God, hast proved us: thou also hast tried us, like as silver is tried.

Psalm 66:9

"I should have cleaned the silver yesterday," Daphne admitted over toast and tea on Wednesday morning. "But with the funeral, and all the excitement—I'm afraid I just didn't get round to it. I'd better get an early start on it this morning."

"Would you like a hand?" David offered. "I have a few hours free before my lunch with Lady Constance."

She smiled her gratitude. "I usually don't let anyone else touch the silver... but in your case, I'm prepared to make an exception."

"I'm honored." He raised his eyebrows ironically.

"You haven't really seen the silver, have you? We have some rather nice pieces."

"I'll look forward to seeing it. With everything else going on, it hasn't exactly been on the top of my list, but now that things are falling into place . . . well, I shall enjoy looking at some silver," he said with real anticipation.

"And cleaning it, don't forget."

"And cleaning it," David grimaced. "But on the way, I'd better stop at the vicarage and have a word with Gabriel."

* * *

"Oh, David, I'm sorry, but you've missed him," Emily said with a frown. "He's gone to Brighton, of all places."

"Brighton? Whatever for?"

"To preach at the noon Assumption Day Mass at St. Dunstan's."

"St. Dunstan's?" David repeated stupidly. "He never told me he was going to St. Dunstan's."

"No, he didn't know it himself until yesterday," Emily explained. "They had a last-minute problem, and thought of their old curate as a final resort. The churchwarden rang yesterday afternoon."

"But what happened?"

She laughed. "Apparently a certain Area Bishop of the London diocese—I need mention no names—was scheduled to do it, but he discovered at the last minute that he was double-booked. He couldn't be at Walsingham and in Brighton at the same time, so poor old St. Dunstan's drew the short straw, and got Gabriel instead."

"I dare say they've got the best of it," David responded. "Gabriel's a much better preacher than the Bishop of . . ."

"But Gabriel doesn't have a mitre, and that's what they all come to see. Or am I being cynical?"

"Give him time," smiled David. "Your husband will wear a mitre one day. But when is he coming back? I need to see him."

Emily looked at him searchingly. "You have good news for him, don't you? Oh, David! I knew you could do it! He'll be so relieved! He was in such a state this morning—it was all I could do to get him to go, in the end, with this thing hanging over his head."

"When will he be back?" he repeated.

"Probably not much before the Mass here—it's at half past six. He's gone in the car, and you never know what the traffic will be like. But as soon as he comes in, I'll tell him to ring you."

"If he doesn't catch me, tell him I'll see him before the service. Or after."

"You can't tell me who it is, can you?" she asked curiously. "No . . . I don't really want to know. Not yet."

At that moment they were interrupted by a small body hurling itself at Emily's legs. "Mummy! Viola's taken my teddy—again! Can't you make her stop?"

"Sebastian, darling. We'll deal with that in a moment. But now, won't you say hello to your Uncle David?"

The boy looked up at him with frank curiosity. Looked at him with Gabriel's dark-lashed blue eyes: It was a most extraordinary sensation for David, who had not really been prepared for it. "How do you do, Uncle David," said the little boy solemnly, extending his hand. Sebastian clearly had also inherited his father's self-assurance.

David took his hand, recovering himself quickly. "It's very nice to meet you at last, Sebastian." Instinctively he bent down on a level with the boy. "May I meet your sister, too?"

Sebastian looked scornful. "Oh, you wouldn't want to meet her. She's just a *girl*."

"Girls do have their uses, Sebastian," Emily said fondly, her hand on his tousled dark head.

* * *

Daphne opened the safe with her own key; David waited in anticipation as the items of silver came out on to the table, one by one. "It's a shame we can't leave the candlesticks on the altar all the time," Daphne commented. "But that would be asking for trouble. So many London churches have lost their best pieces that way."

"How sad. Country churches, too, from what I hear. They have to be so careful these days. So many churches are locked all the time now." He leaned back in the chair. "Remember the good old days, Daphne? When we used to travel the countryside, and never find a locked church in a whole week?"

She nodded briskly, not looking at him. "We saw some lovely churches."

He caught her hand impulsively. "Daphne, what do you say? Let's do it again! That trip to the West Country that we never took—do you fancy giving it another go?"

She stopped. "Well, I don't know. At my age . . ."

"Your age! You're only twenty years older than I am— you're in the prime of your life!"

Only twenty years, she thought. "I suppose I could get away from this place for a few days."

"Of course you could. Venerable Bead would be more than happy to fill in for you, I'm sure. Oh, let's, Daphne."

"I never could say no to you, David. Almost never, anyway." At last she smiled at him. "Yes, I'd like that."

"Great. We'll set a date before I leave."

She put her head in the safe before she asked, "And when are you leaving?"

"Maybe tomorrow. I'll have a word with the police about Craig, then . . . well, there's nothing to keep me here after that. I've taken advantage of your hospitality long enough."

"You know I've enjoyed having you," she said, her head still hidden in the safe.

* * *

Most of the silver had been inspected, appreciated, and cleaned. "I've saved the best for last," Daphne confessed. "The festival thurible, only used for high days and holy days. The other one we use every Sunday, but this one is special." She brought it out with pride. It was an extremely handsome piece, hand-fashioned of solid silver and very heavy.

David's eyes lit up. "I say. That is splendid. Where did it come from?"

"Lady Constance, of course. She gave it a couple of years ago, in her brother's memory. I think it might have been his: He was a priest, you know, and undoubtedly a man of taste."

"Of course." He screwed one eye up and examined the hallmark with the other. "Definitely a man of taste. Just like his sister." He started. "What time is it, anyway? I don't want to be late for lunch with Lady Constance."

Daphne consulted her watch. "You've got plenty of time. But go ahead if you want to—this is the last thing I've got to do."

"Wait a minute." He lifted the pierced lid of the thurible. "When's the last time this was used? There seems to be something inside."

"It shouldn't be incense, or charcoal. I certainly cleaned it out after the Patronal Festival, and it hasn't been used since. What is it?'' Daphne's bent head joined his over the thurible.

With two fingers he extracted a charred piece of folded paper. ''It looks like someone was trying to burn something in it.''

Daphne was indignant. ''Well, it certainly wasn't me! Of all things!''

He looked at the paper with a furrowed brow. ''What . . .'' It was charred around the edges, but relatively undamaged; he unfolded it carefully.

It was a letter, typed on ordinary paper. David looked at it with a sinking feeling of recognition.

> I have good reason to believe that you have been taking money from St. Anne's. You have abused your office of churchwarden in a most shameful manner, and I will not stand by and allow that to happen. You must resign your office, and repay the money you have taken, before the Feast of the Assumption, or I will inform the Bishop.

Daphne took it from him. ''David! I don't believe it!''

''It's true, all right,'' he said softly, shaking his head. ''I was right that her death had something to do with the blackmail. But Mavis wasn't the blackmailer—she was one of his victims! She must have tried to destroy the letter that day, the day she . . . died.''

''She must have put it in the thurible and lit it, then shut it in the safe, not realizing that it would soon go out without oxygen. And then . . .''

''And then, Daphne . . . she killed herself.'' He sat immobile for a very long moment, staring at the paper; when he spoke again, his voice was very quiet, very measured. ''Oh, Daphne, I've been so frightfully stupid about this whole business. I've been wrong about everything, all along the way. I've looked at it all the wrong way up. But now . . . now I understand everything. Or nearly everything . . .''

Chapter 44

There be some that put their trust in their goods
and boast themselves in the multitude of their
riches
But no man may deliver his brother: nor make
agreement unto God for him;
For it cost more to redeem their souls so that he
must let that alone for ever;
Yea, though he live long: and see not the grave.

Psalm 49:6–9

He had stopped along the way and bought several bunches of freesias. Lady Constance opened the door herself, looking a bit stronger than she had on Tuesday. "You remembered that I liked freesias. How very kind of you, Mr. Middleton-Brown."

"How are you feeling today, Lady Constance? Better than last week, I hope?"

"Yes, thank you. The lovely weather...well, it does make one feel better. And I do find your visits a tonic, young man. I hope you'll be staying in London for a long time."

"I'm afraid not, Lady Constance," he said regretfully. "I'll be returning home to Wymondham tomorrow. I've been here nearly three weeks already—that's a long time to impose on Daphne's hospitality, and I've accomplished what I came to do... with the chapel."

She looked genuinely distressed. "You must come for regular visits, then," she said. "You will always be welcome to stay in this house. I'm sure you would be more comfortable here than at Miss Elford's."

"Thank you, that's most kind."

* * *

They had lunch in the garden. Lady Constance's garden was surprisingly large, and received the afternoon sun. They sat in the shade of a tree, as it was a very warm afternoon. Lunch was a smoked chicken salad, with a chilled bottle of white wine—a very good wine. "In your honor, young man," she pointed out. "On the very sad occasion of your last day in London."

If I didn't know better, I'd almost think she was flirting with me, David thought as she raised her glass to him. He looked at her, almost as if for the first time. She must have been quite a stunner when she was young, he reflected; he tried to imagine her, with the silver hair dark, and the beautifully modeled features unlined. The beringed hand in which she held the glass was purple-veined now; once it must have been smooth and white. Like Lucy's, he thought with a quickly suppressed twinge.

"How is the work progressing on the chapel?" she asked him. "You're satisfied enough to leave it?"

"Oh, yes. The workmen are excellent, they don't need any help from me. I watched them start the gilding yesterday. They're doing a superb job."

"I can't thank you enough for your part in it," she said warmly. "I've wanted to have it done for several years now, but no one had the expertise to supervise it. It's a memorial gift for my brother," she added. "I shall want to have a plaque put up to say that the restoration was done in his memory. I would have liked to have had it finished by now—he died two years ago today."

"I saw the silver thurible you gave in his memory. It's an exquisite piece of work."

She smiled. "Lovely, isn't it? I'm glad you've seen it. Edward bought that himself, quite a few years ago. I thought it right that St. Anne's should have it, and use it."

Apparently Lady Constance did not find it too painful to talk about her dead brother, so David encouraged her. "He was a priest, I understand?"

"Yes, he was—an excellent priest. One of the old school, brought up when things were done properly, and nothing less was tolerated."

"I'm surprised that he didn't have the living at St. Anne's; I would have thought that you would have wanted him here," David probed.

"Nothing would have pleased me more," she admitted. "I tried so many times to persuade him to take the living here. How I wish he had . . . Over the years, he sent us a few of his protégés"—she gave the word its proper French pronunciation—"but of course that wasn't the same as having dear Edward here."

"Why didn't he want to come?"

She smiled in fond remembrance. "He was a keen boatsman, and didn't want to leave the sea. I don't think he ever lived more than five miles away from the sea in his life." Her eyes followed the progress of a bird from tree to tree at the end of the garden, but her mind seemed elsewhere for a time, until she began speaking again. "Edward was everything a priest should be: loving, compassionate . . . and holy. My brother was a very holy man. If he had any fault, it was that he was rather too inclined to think the best of people, even in the face of evidence to the contrary."

"Surely that's what priests are supposed to do?"

She sighed and shook her head. "This is the real world, young man. People aren't always what you would wish them to be. A priest, of all people, ought to understand that fact."

* * *

It was a perfect afternoon in high summer. They sat for a long time over their lunch, enjoying the warmth of the sun. A few butterflies fluttered desultorily over the multicolored flowers of the garden, but otherwise it was very still, with barely a breeze to stir the leaves of the trees. The heavy scent of the roses blended with the smell of freshly cut grass to make a powerful perfume. The maid brought them raspberry mousse in stemmed crystal dishes, but afterwards Lady Constance waved away the coffee. "Too hot for coffee today, Molly. Bring us some mineral water instead. With lemon, please. Unless you'd like more wine?'' she addressed David. ''But I think we've had rather too much wine already.'' The sunlight through the tree dappled her pale mauve dress with gently moving shapes, and gave her skin an even whiter cast than usual. She stretched out a hand towards David. ''I do hope you don't feel that you have to run off immediately, young man. I'd like you to stay for a while.''

''Of course I'll stay,'' he reassured her. ''I just don't want to tire you. Perhaps you ought to have a rest before the service this evening.''

''Ah, yes. The Feast of the Assumption of Our Lady.''

''I'm looking forward to it,'' he said. ''I haven't seen a proper festival service in St. Anne's. I'm sure they do it very well.''

''Yes, Father Neville makes sure of that.'' A small smile curved her lips as she looked beyond David at the garden. ''Proper appearances mean a lot to our Father Neville.''

''He certainly did the funeral beautifully yesterday,'' David said deliberately.

Lady Constance sat up even straighter, and turned her gaze from the butterflies. She looked penetratingly at David. ''Last week when you were here, you told me that you thought Mrs. Conwell had been murdered. You said that you were doing some investigations on your own. Can you tell me what you've found?''

He held her gaze steadily. ''I was wrong,'' he said, firmly but gently. ''I realize now that she killed herself. In many ways it was more . . . comfortable to believe that someone else had done it. Suicide is such a terrible act—it's difficult to think of someone being that desperate. And sometimes it's even more difficult to comprehend the . . . forces that would lead someone to make that choice. But I've come to understand that Mrs. Conwell was under more pressure than anyone knew.''

She looked away, finally. ''I see,'' she said softly. Somewhere a bird burst into full-throated song. Neither one moved for a very long time; at last Lady Constance stirred. ''Perhaps it would be best for you to go now, young man. I am rather tired, and I have a letter that I must write this afternoon.''

David stood. He bent over her, taking her hand in both of his. ''I'll see you at Mass this evening, Lady Constance, but I'll take my proper leave of you now. Thank you so much for this lovely afternoon, and for the many kindnesses of the last few weeks. It has been a real privilege to know you, and I shall always remember with pleasure the time we've spent together.'' His words were formal, but there was real warmth behind them.

She looked up at him; her eyes met his in a searching look. ''It is I who must thank you, Mr. Middleton-Brown. Your kindness to an old woman has been . . . more than I deserve. I'm very grateful for that.''

He raised her hand to his lips in silent tribute, then turned away. She watched his back until she could see him no longer.

Chapter 45

As soon as they hear of me, they shall obey me: but the strange children shall dissemble with me.
The strange children shall fail: and be afraid out of their prisons.

Psalm 18:45–46

Craig Conwell didn't have a job, as far as David knew, so there was a chance of finding him at home in the afternoon. With a little thought, he was able to remember how to find the Conwell house.

He rang the bell. After a rather long delay, just as David was about to give up, Craig opened the door to him. The young man was looking rather unwell; his skin had an unhealthy pallor, and this intensified when he saw David.

The hand clutching a can of lager trembled. "Go away and leave me alone," he muttered, swinging the door shut.

David put a foot in the door. "Good afternoon, Craig," he said smoothly as he forced the door back open. "Mind if I come in? I won't take up much of your valuable time, but I have something important to say to you. I think it's something you'll want to hear."

"Suit yourself." Craig shrugged, giving up. He turned and slouched into the room on the right of the entrance hall, without looking to see whether David was following. When David entered the room behind him, he was already slumped in a chair, swigging lager from the can.

David looked at the room in amazement. Mavis had been a house-proud woman, just like his own mother. But ten days after her death, she probably wouldn't have recognized her own sitting room: It bore no resemblance at all to that tidy room he had seen on his visit with Daphne. There was an indefinably musty feeling about the room, as though it hadn't received any fresh air in ten days. In spite of the warmth of the day, the windows were shut and the curtains were drawn; it felt oppressively hot. And strewn about the room were bits of dirty crockery, some containing half-eaten food; David looked with disgust at the dried, curling remnant of a cheese sandwich and the attendant flies. Everywhere there were empty beer cans, and ashtrays overflowing with cigarette butts. The television was on; already Craig's eyes were fixed on the antics of cartoon animals.

David crossed the room and switched off the television. Craig scowled, but couldn't be bothered to argue. Removing what looked like a collection of dirty clothing from one of the chairs, David sat down opposite Craig and leaned forward. "Craig, I want you to listen to me. I know now that your mother wasn't murdered."

Craig shot him a triumphantly venomous look. "I told you so."

"Yes, and you were right. She killed herself."

Craig lit a cigarette and took a long draw. "So, tell me something I don't know."

"What I want to know, Craig, is *why* she killed herself."

"How the hell do I know? She was taking money from the church, wasn't she? I guess she had a guilty conscience." He spoke the last two words with a sneer of distaste, as if it were a particularly nasty social disease.

David drew back and looked at him. "She took that money for you, didn't she?"

"So what? A guy needs money to live. Since Dad died, there just hasn't been that much dough around. And she was too busy being Mrs. Bloody Churchwarden and poking her nose into other people's business to go out and get herself a job."

"And you couldn't get a job? You're an able-bodied young man," David said with ill-concealed contempt.

Craig shrugged nonchalantly. "I tried it for a while, but I just couldn't stick it. They wanted me there every day at nine o'clock, for God's sake. I couldn't be bothered. Anyway, it was up to the old bag to support me—I didn't ask to be born, did I?" He puffed on his cigarette and blew a cloud of smoke at David.

David shook his head in despair at the young man's callous selfishness. "What are you going to do now? Now that she's dead, and can't support you any longer?"

"Maybe there's some insurance, I don't know." He lifted his shoulders. "If not, I'll just sell the house. I can live for a long time on the price it'll fetch. Get myself a bed-sit somewhere. I'll manage."

"No one's going to buy the house looking like this," David couldn't help remarking, as he glanced around at the filthy squalor. Craig merely shrugged. "Maybe one of your girlfriends would like to come in and clean it up," David added maliciously.

"Yeah, maybe," Craig nodded thoughtfully, flicking some ash on to the carpet.

Leaning forward again, David said abruptly, "But what I want to know, Craig, is why your mother *really* killed herself."

"I told you. It was because of the money."

"It couldn't have been just the money. Not even the

money you took that day. I'm surprised that she let you have it, by the way. How did you talk her into it?''

Craig smirked. ''I didn't talk her into it, I just took it. When she wasn't looking. I figured a rich church like that would never miss a couple of hundred quid.''

''Why *did* you go there that day?''

''To get some money. I knew she was counting the dough and figured I could talk her out of a fiver. I never figured there'd be so much cash! She got all self-righteous with me, and said I couldn't have any of it. So as soon as her back was turned, I just helped myself to a bit of it. She never knew.''

''Until you were gone, and she missed the ledger sheet.''

''No, I didn't take it then.''

David stared at him. ''When did you take it?''

''Later. A few minutes later. I got to thinking about it, and figured I'd better take that piece of paper, or somebody would twig. So I went back.'' He paused. ''I went in. She was . . . dead. Hanging there. So I took the paper and got the hell out of there. I took her handbag, too, just in case there was any money in it.''

''But you said she'd locked the door behind you when you left!''

Craig looked defiant. ''She did. I . . . had a key cut. I took all her church keys out of her handbag once, and had copies cut; you never know when something like that might come in useful. And it did. I locked the door behind me when I left.''

''What have you done with the keys?''

''I threw them in someone's rubbish bin, along with the handbag—there was no money in it, anyway,'' he added in disgust.

David suddenly remembered the brown vinyl handbag, sitting on the desk in the sacristy during his visit there. And that evening it had been gone. He berated himself for being so unobservant.

He turned his attention back to Craig, who was lighting another cigarette. ''Craig,'' he said firmly. ''There's something you're not telling me. What in God's name did you say to your mother when you were there? What did you say that would make her kill herself, in those few minutes before you came back? If she didn't even know you'd taken that money..."

Craig didn't respond right away, and when he did speak he didn't answer the question directly, but said in a self-pitying whine, "You just don't know, man. You don't know what it was like, living with her." He tilted the beer can back and poured the last few drops down his throat, then tossed the empty can on the table with its fellows. "You don't know what it's like having a self-righteous old bitch like that trying to run your life."

David looked at him with loathing, but there was a kind of pity there too. "That's where you're wrong, mate," he said in a soft, steely voice. "I know exactly what it's like. I've been there, too. Now tell me the truth, or I'll have the cops here so fast..."

Craig jerked into an upright position. "Not the cops!"

"Then tell me."

Slumping back down, Craig turned his head away under David's relentless stare. Unwillingly, he began. "It was the bloody phone bill. She was at me in the morning about it. Then that afternoon she started in on me all over again." He picked up a beer can and absently crushed it in his fist.

"What about the phone bill?"

"It was too high, she said. She couldn't afford to pay it. She wanted to know who I'd been phoning. Girlfriends, she said." He laughed mirthlessly. "She thought she knew everything, the old cow. She said I'd been ringing girlfriends. That's what she wanted to believe."

David held his breath; he had a premonition what was coming.

"I was really pissed off with her then. I thought, what the hell. She thought she knew everything!" His voice shook; he pulled the tab off another can of beer and took a deep swallow. "I told her it wasn't a girlfriend I'd been calling—it was a boyfriend. I told her all the details. I enjoyed that, enjoyed seeing her cover her ears with her hands, say that it wasn't true, that I was just making it up to get at her. She cried a lot. In the end she believed it." He paused and smirked, the smoke wreathing his head. "I knew that she was upset, but I didn't think the stupid cow would go and kill herself! I was surprised when I went back in and saw her hanging there. But I guess that was the one thing my mother couldn't live with—the idea that her son was a bloody queer."

David stared at him; suddenly, improbably, he was filled with empathy for this troubled young man. What would his own mother have done? "Craig..." he began, not sure what to say.

Sneering, Craig laughed at him. "You believed me! So did she, the gullible old cow! And killed herself over a lie!" There was no mirth in his laughter. "Me, a queer? Give me a break, man! Not in a million years!"

Chapter 46

Thou hast turned my heaviness into joy: thou hast put off my sackcloth, and girded me with gladness. Therefore shall every good man sing of thy praise without ceasing: O my God, I will give thanks unto thee for ever.

Psalm 30:12–13

Kissing the cross on his stole, and putting it around his neck, Gabriel automatically said the set prayer to himself. But the prayer in his heart was wordless: a prayer of thanksgiving for his deliverance. His vesting for the Mass was nearly done; he turned with a radiant smile to take the cloth-of-gold chasuble from the hovering Venerable Bead.

He'd only had time, after his hurried return from Brighton, for a brief word with David, but that had been enough. He

was free. David had done it somehow. Gabriel knew none of
the details, not even the name of his blackmailer. But he
had David's assurance that the threats would not be carried
out. He wasn't even going to need to confront anyone. It
was all over. David would come and see him tomorrow, and
tell him the whole story. But for now, that was enough—it
was all over.

The sun was still high in the sky; its light streamed through
the west window as the sounds of the Palestrina introit
soared to the roof: *'Assumpta est Maria in caelum.''*

In his stall, Gabriel closed his eyes and absorbed the
beauty of the music. It would be a long service: The
Palestrina "Missa Assumpta est Maria" was nearly thirty
minutes long, apart from anything else. They were very
fortunate to have a choir capable of performing a Mass like
that, Gabriel reflected. He opened his eyes and observed
Miles Taylor, conducting the choir with characteristic enthusiasm, his long arms flailing away. What a very peculiar
man, always moaning about something and wittering on
about contemporary music. But one could put up with a
great deal of personal eccentricity for the sake of music like
this.

After the Kyrie, during the Gloria, Gabriel took the
thurible from Johnnie—or was it Chris?—and censed the
altar reverently. The puffs of fragrant smoke rose to join the
music, high above their heads. Then came the first lesson—
read by the curate he'd borrowed for the occasion from a
neighboring parish—followed by the psalm.

> Thou hast loved righteousness, and hated iniquity: where-
> fore God, even thy God, hath anointed thee with the oil
> of gladness above thy fellows.
> All thy garments smell of myrrh, aloes, and cassia: out of
> the ivory palaces, whereby they have made thee glad.

The servers moved out of the chancel: Johnnie, swinging the
thurible, with Sebastian once again beside him with the
incense boat, Chris with the processional cross, flanked by

two acolytes, and Tony, bearing the large book. Gabriel came forward to intone the Gospel, and for the first time he was able to see the congregation. It was a respectable crowd. Most of the regulars were there, he ascertained with a quick glance. And, inevitably on these festal occasions, the numbers were swelled by a few out-of-town punters, drawn to St. Anne's by the music, or the ceremonial, or something else indefinable.

Gabriel was not aware, even as he was delivering it, that tonight's sermon was anything out of the ordinary. He'd given it once already that day—how fortunate for St. Dunstan's that he'd had one prepared—so the delivery was practiced and the words flowed smoothly. But it was his overwhelming sensation of joy and relief that infused it with special power, and made it a sermon that the parishioners of St. Anne's would later talk about as one of the finest they'd ever heard. Even the Dawsons admitted as much. Roger Dawson flaunted his Mary-blue tie that night, disgruntled that Gabriel had once again not allowed them to take the statue of Our Lady of Walsingham around the church in solemn procession. And cloth-of-gold vestments were all very well and good, but by all rights Our Lady should have blue and silver.

After the Credo, and the Prayers of Intercession, the congregation made their corporate Confession. "Forgive us all that is past; and grant that we may serve thee in newness of life . . ." As Gabriel made the sign of the cross and spoke the words of Absolution, he felt personally cleansed, and ready for a fresh start.

The offertory party came forward then. Usually, for a festival service such as this, it was the privilege of the two churchwardens to bring the elements to the altar. But there was now only one churchwarden. Cyril Fitzjames's jowly countenance was transformed by a rare smile; he had asked Emily to assist him. Viola went in front of them, proudly and carefully bearing the silver ciborium with the wafers. As they entered the chancel, she couldn't resist a sideways look of pure triumph at her brother.

The sun dipped lower; the light coming through a west

window had a dreamy golden quality, trapped in the clouds of incense that now filled the church.

"Though we are many, we are one body..." All those unique individuals, somehow united in this place, and at this moment. And then, once again, they were all coming up to the altar to receive communion. Gabriel experienced a sense of *déjà vu* as he waited for them to kneel: It was so like the Patronal Festival, such a short time ago, yet so unlike. So much had happened in the intervening weeks, and so many things had permanently changed. For one thing, there was no Mavis. Someone else was missing, too—he couldn't quite think who. Gabriel noted each person as he administered to them. The servers received first: Tony Kent, Johnnie and Chris, Venerable Bead, the acolytes, and little Sebastian, bowing his head for his father's blessing. Miles Taylor, still for just a moment. Hobbling up ahead of everyone else, Beryl Ball, grinning at him and wiggling her dentures. The Dawsons, Roger, Julia, Teresa and Francis, defiant in their blue ties and bows. A horde of white-haired old ladies, led by Mary Hughes. Cecily Framlingham, staring with pointed satisfaction at the flowers as she came up. Reliable, unflappable Daphne. "The body of Christ," he said to each one. Cyril Fitzjames came near the end, with Emily behind him. His own beloved Emily, and their daughter. And David. Dear David. He hadn't been here that other time.

When he'd reached the end, Gabriel realized who was missing. He hadn't given communion to Lady Constance.

Chapter 47

For he seeth that wise men also die, and perish together: as well as the ignorant and foolish, and leave their riches for other.
And yet they think that their houses shall continue

> *for ever: and that their dwelling-places shall*
> *endure from one generation to another; and call*
> *the lands after their own names.*
>
> *Psalm 49:10–11*

David was up very early the next morning. He hadn't slept particularly well, and he was anxious to get to the post before Daphne arose.

The letter was there on the mat, as he had expected. He picked it up and made sure that it had his name on it, then took it to his room to read in privacy. Opening his curtains, and seeing that it was a beautiful clear morning, he decided to postpone the moment for a bit longer. He shaved, dressed, and packed his case, to save time later, and went out into Kensington Gardens, as he had on his first morning in London, nearly three weeks ago.

Although there were few people about, he avoided the publicly visible benches, found a spot in the grass, and leaned against a tree. It was going to be another hot day; already the sun had evaporated the dew and the grass was quite dry. Sitting on the grass in a park was not something he'd been particularly fond of before he met Lucy, he thought, then put the thought away from him quickly. He still wasn't ready to think about Lucy.

He examined the envelope carefully before opening it. It was square, and made of a heavy bond paper; the writing was much as he would have expected, spidery and fine yet definite, the letters well-formed and not in the least wavery, reflecting the writer's personality.

David slit the top with his pocket-knife and extracted a rather thick sheaf of papers. The writing paper itself was not perfumed, but it exuded a faint scent of lavender. David sighed and unfolded the letter. It was dated the previous day, August 15.

My dear Mr. Middleton-Brown,

I am sure you know why I am writing this letter—perhaps you are even expecting it. At any rate, much of what I have to tell you will come as no surprise to you. But after your kindness to me,

I owe it to you to tell you the whole story, so there will be nothing left unexplained.

You are aware, I am sure, that I have been unwell lately. I have suffered from spells of dizziness, and feelings of depression. These leave me quite exhausted and frightened. But more frightening still have been periodic episodes of dementia and paranoia, during which I have, apparently, done things about which I later have no recollection. My servants assure me that this is so, and there is other evidence. It would seem that recently I have written several letters during these spells. I do not remember writing these letters, but, with my customary thoroughness, I have kept carbon copies which I have later discovered. All of the letters seem to have been prompted, in my subconscious, by my concern for the future of St. Anne's Church, but that does not excuse the abominable things that I said in them.

One of them, of course, was to Mrs. Conwell. I don't know how you discovered the truth about her death, but you are a very clever young man to have done so.

Not so long ago I began to suspect, from various discrepancies, that someone was taking money from St. Anne's. There were few people in a position to do this, and from conversations with Mrs. Conwell and others I concluded that she was in fact the person. It was a simple matter for me to do a check of the books, and to confirm my suspicions: I of course have a key to the sacristy, where the ledger books are kept. The discrepancies were fairly minor, but her attempts to cover her tracks were crude. I meant to confront her with the evidence, and to ask her in a reasonable fashion to restore the money. But events took a different course.

As you are aware, I profoundly regret Mrs. Conwell's death. I never meant for her to take her own life, but I accept full responsibility for it. Mrs. Conwell died because of the letter I wrote—that fact seems inescapable, and nothing will explain it away. The guilt is mine.

The second person to whom I wrote a letter was young Tony Kent. I had been worried, in the light of the Norman Newsome affair, that his living arrangements might lead him into trouble, and thus cast discredit upon St. Anne's, where he holds a position of great responsibility. I find Tony Kent a very pleasant young man, and profoundly regret any embarrassment or pain that I might have caused him.

Then there is the matter of Father Neville. I am not sure whether you know about this or not, though I suspect that you may—as I said, you are a very clever young man. But I shall tell you about it in any case, and perhaps you will tell him as much as you think is right. I rather think that your acquaintance with him is of longer standing than I have been led to believe.

In this instance, my concern for St. Anne's was only part of the underlying cause. Just as important was my love for my brother Edward.

Just over ten years ago, the living at St. Anne's was vacant. Edward was nearing retirement age, and was happily settled in his last parish in Lewes, so I'd given up hope of his accepting the living himself. But he rang me one day and said that he had a candidate for me—a very bright, very promising young priest in the diocese, one of his protégés. The man had been serving a curacy in Brighton, but was ready, even anxious, to move on. I don't need to tell you that priest's name—Father Gabriel Neville. Father Neville came to see me, and I was very impressed, but my brother's recommendation was all I needed. I trusted his judgement. As there was a vacancy, the appointment went through very quickly and Father Neville was installed here inside of two months. Up until about two years ago, I was very happy with him as a parish priest, and felt that he served St. Anne's ably. I also very much like and approve of his wife, whom I have known all her life, and feel that she has been a great asset to him, and to St. Anne's.

Over two years ago, my brother fell gravely ill. Edward and I had always been very close, and I felt that I wanted to care for him myself. I tried very hard to persuade him to come to London, where he could be close to Harley Street and receive the best private treatment available. But he didn't wish to leave his parish, and I respected that wish. So for several months I nursed him through his final illness.

He had a terrible disease, and he died a very protracted and painful death. Even now I can scarcely bear to dwell on it, but it is important for you to understand. He was in much pain, yes. But the worst part of it was that he was not himself by the time the disease had truly taken hold. After he lost the use of his limbs, he was still aware of what was happening. It was about that time that I contacted an organization that makes it possible for people to die peacefully—and when they are ready—rather than waiting for disease to do its worst. They provided him with the means to accomplish that. But Edward wasn't ready to make that choice then, and after that—after that he lost his mind. It was a terrible thing, and as I said, he was not himself. He said things that Edward would never have said. It was appalling to hear him, day after day. At first I thought he was just hallucinating, and that the things he was saying were coming out of some dark corner of his imagination. But as he repeated himself, I realized the truth behind what he was saying.

He talked about a boy named Peter Maitland, who had drowned. And about a young priest who had come to him, his spiritual director, for Confession, with that death on his conscience. He had tried to help that priest, first by hearing his Confession, then by counseling him, and finally by helping him to find a new position and to start a new life. Of course that priest was Gabriel Neville. My brother believed in him. He believed that he was a good priest, and deserved his help. But at the end of his life, the tragic things he'd heard in that Confessional came back to haunt him and torture him.

In his right mind, my brother would never have broken the seal of the Confessional, I can assure you of that. But his disease robbed him of his reason, and so I learned things I never wanted to know about my own parish priest.

I've lived with this knowledge for two years, and have done nothing. Consciously, I knew that Gabriel Neville was not to blame for my brother's distress, but subconsciously I suppose I held him responsible. I knew it was the disease, but if Edward hadn't had that burden to bear...

And now I can see my brother's dementia, in the form of paranoia, exhibiting itself in me. I can assure you, though, that at the moment my mind is very clear, and I know exactly what I am doing.

I nursed my brother, and know very well the symptoms of his disease. Although I have not been to a doctor, I recognize these symptoms in myself, and know that I have contracted the disease that killed my brother.

You will surely realize that when you receive this I will be dead. I am assured that it will be a peaceful and painless death, unlike my brother's. Edward lost his mind before he could make the choice to end his life, and that was not a decision I could make for him. But I have kept the drugs that the society sent him. I make my choice in full possession of my mind, and knowing that it is proper for me to do so. Mavis Conwell died because of an action I took, and that is not something with which I can live. The remainder of my life would have been short and painful, and I might have done more regrettable things, caused pain to others. It is best that I go so.

There is one other matter I need to mention, though I am almost embarrassed to do so. It is the matter of my will. I have no family left, and have always intended to leave the bulk of my estate to St. Anne's. This is still my intention. But since I realized that I was terminally ill, I have been most grieved by the thought of my beloved home being sold, and probably converted into flats. This is surely what would happen if I were to leave it to St. Anne's. This house has been in the Oliver family for generations, and deserves a better fate than that. Therefore, I am going to ask you to look after my house for me. As I've come to know you over the past few weeks, I've realized that you have a rare appreciation for beauty, and the taste to match. And so I will trust you with my house. I have just written a codicil to my will, which has been signed and witnessed by my servants. It gives you my house, along with a capital sum in trust, the income from which should be more than sufficient for its upkeep and maintenance, on the condition that the house is not sold in your lifetime. You need not live in it, if that is not convenient for you, but only look after it. I hope this is not too great a burden for you, and that you will care for it and love it as I have.

I ought to tell you not to grieve for me. But I am a selfish old woman, and I would like to think that you might grieve, just a little. Good-bye, my dear young man, and thank you again for your kindness and your sensitivity.

It was signed with a flourish: Constance Oliver.

David sat under the tree as the sun climbed higher in the sky, the tears wet on his cheeks.

Chapter 48

*My covenant will I not break, nor alter the thing
that is gone out of my lips: I have sworn once
by my holiness, that I will not fail David.*
                                    Psalm 89:34

David parked his car in front of the vicarage. He'd said his farewells to Daphne; his case was in the car and all that remained was the final interview with Gabriel. Although he hadn't allowed her to read the letter, he'd told Daphne everything—about Craig, and about Lady Constance; he felt that he owed her that, after all her help and support. But he was as yet undecided about how much he needed to tell Gabriel; perhaps he'd just see how their conversation went. He didn't know whether Gabriel would even have heard yet of Lady Constance's death: If not, he didn't want to be the one to tell him, especially if there was a chance that the death could be construed as accidental, or occurring from natural causes. Lady Constance deserved his discretion, and his silence.

Emily and the children were on their way out as he arrived, bound for Kensington Gardens and the Round Pond, if Sebastian's sailboat were any clue. The children waited impatiently while David took his leave of their mother.

"I'm so glad you caught us before we left!" she said. "I couldn't bear the thought of your leaving town without saying good-bye."

He smiled. "I would have waited, Emily."

"David." She took his hand. "I can't thank you enough for what you've done for him—for us. You've been a real friend to both of us."

Embarrassed, he looked away.

"Mummy, can't we go now?" Sebastian demanded.

"Just a moment, darling. I'm saying good-bye to your Uncle David."

"Is he going away?" Viola asked, staring at him with frank curiosity. "Where's he going?"

"Uncle David lives a long way from here. He's going home. It might be a long time before we see him again."

"I wouldn't be too sure of that," he said with a smile. "Remember that first morning I was here? You said you'd come to Wymondham to see me."

"And so we shall, if you still want us."

"Please do, soon. And I'm sure I'll be back in London," he added. "I have a lot of friends here now." He frowned, thinking of Lady Constance, then of Lucy.

She looked at him inquiringly, not sure how much she could say. Finally she ventured, "Lucy?"

Again he looked away, then forced his eyes back to hers. "Lucy," he said. "Tell Lucy... Tell her I'll be in touch," he finished awkwardly.

Emily nodded. "I'll tell her."

As Sebastian and Viola looked on balefully, they regarded each other for a moment, neither one quite knowing how to say good-bye. Suddenly Emily threw her arms around his neck. "Dear David," she said softly. "I'm so glad we've become friends."

"It took ten years, but..."

"It was worth waiting for." She kissed him on the cheek, then disengaged herself. "Take care of yourself, David."

"You take care of yourself. And... take care of Gabriel."

"I will."

"Mummy, let's go now," Viola insisted. "Or I'll tell Daddy that you were hugging Uncle David," she added slyly.

Emily laughed. "I don't think your father would mind. Good-bye, David. Gabriel's waiting for you in the study."

"Good-bye, Emily."

* * *

Gabriel paced up and down the study restlessly. "There are so many things I don't understand. I think you'd better start at the beginning."

"Which beginning? Your story, or Mavis Conwell's?"

"Start with Mavis. Was she murdered, or not? I still don't know."

"No, she wasn't murdered. She killed herself, just as the coroner said, just as the police said."

"Then why. . ."

David gave a self-mocking laugh. "It was my blind stubbornness. I got it into my head that she was murdered, and nothing would convince me otherwise. Not even the evidence."

"The medical evidence at the inquest was quite clear. There was no indication that it was, or could have possibly been, anything but suicide."

David looked sheepish. "I'm afraid I wasn't listening during that part. My mind was made up."

"So what made you change your mind?" Gabriel asked.

David answered indirectly. "Did you ever have one of those kaleidoscopes when you were a child?"

"Yes. Sebastian and Viola have one now. You turn it around, and the shapes change." He looked puzzled.

"My problem was that I was looking through the wrong end of the kaleidoscope," David explained. "I was looking in the back end, and all I could see were bits of colored glass falling about. No pattern, no sense to it. Just bits of colored glass. But when I turned the kaleidoscope around, and looked through it the proper way, all the bits of colored glass formed a pattern, and the pattern made sense."

Gabriel nodded. "I see. So Mavis's death had nothing to do with the blackmail."

"No, that's not true at all. It had a great deal to do with it. But I was looking at it backwards, assuming that Mavis must be the blackmailer. It was only later that I realized the truth—Mavis was also being blackmailed."

"Good Lord." He stopped in his tracks, then sat down at his desk. He considered this knowledge a moment. "What about?"

"About her taking the money. She was threatened with exposure to the Bishop."

"Of course. So that's why she killed herself. She couldn't face the humiliation of public exposure. Poor woman."

David hesitated. "It wasn't quite as simple as that. There was also . . . Craig."

"Craig?"

"Yes. She was taking the money for him, of course. She was terrified of him, for some reason—I saw her absolutely cowering one day, when he came looking for her at St. Anne's, demanding money. I think he's a pathetic snivelling little creep, but he frightened her." He made his mind up, and continued, "He went to the sacristy that afternoon."

"The afternoon of the fête?" Gabriel frowned. "No one's ever said they saw him that day."

"Beryl Ball saw him. She told me so, and he's admitted it. He took some money—about two hundred pounds—and the ledger sheet, so no one would realize that anything was missing."

Gabriel rubbed his chin thoughtfully. "I see. So that's why she killed herself."

David didn't meet his eyes; he didn't want to say any more, but he was uncomfortable telling less than the whole truth. "Yes. He's admitted it all to me, and promises to give the money back, if only we won't turn him over to the police."

"You agreed to that?"

"I told him it would be up to you."

Nodding, Gabriel assented. "That seems reasonable to me. As long as we get the money back, it need not be a police matter. I'll deal with Craig myself." He paused.

"But how did you find out that she was being blackmailed? That was jolly good detective work!"

"Not at all," David disagreed with a self-deprecating smile. "That was the easiest part of all—I had it handed to me on a silver plate. Or in a silver thurible, to be more precise."

"What?"

"Just before she . . . hanged herself, Mavis tried to destroy the blackmail letter. But she bungled it, otherwise we would never have known. She tried to burn it, in the festival thurible. But she shut it in the safe before it had properly started burning."

"And didn't realize that the fire would go out quite quickly," Gabriel reasoned. "Good Lord."

While he sat in stunned silence, David thought carefully how to go on, anticipating the next question. It wasn't long in coming. "So can you tell me now? Who was the blackmailer?" Gabriel turned puzzled blue eyes on him.

After a moment's hesitation, David said simply, "Lady Constance."

There was a sharp intake of breath, and a look of incomprehension. "Lady Constance?" he said, after a long pause. "But how . . . ? Why . . . ?" Gabriel massaged his forehead with the palms of his hands. "I really don't understand. I don't understand how she could have found out about . . . Peter Maitland. He wouldn't have told anyone who knew Lady Constance . . ."

"No, but *you* did."

Gabriel stared. "I never told a soul. I swear to you, David . . ."

David smiled a bittersweet smile. "And that's what had me looking in the wrong end of the kaleidoscope all this time. There was one person you told—your spiritual director."

"But I didn't *tell* him! I made my Confession, of course, but that . . ." He stopped. "Lady Constance's brother," he said slowly. "I made my Confession to Lady Constance's brother. But the Confessional is sacred—he would never have told anyone something that was revealed to him under the seal of the Confessional."

"I should have realized," David mused, glancing up at the bookshelves, and Gabriel's book, *Sacramental Confession: A Spiritual Imperative*. "Of course you would have made your Confession. And I should have figured out that you had a connection with Lady Constance to get the living at St. Anne's so quickly. I knew about her brother. But I just never put it all together. I was so busy looking for someone Peter Maitland might have told . . ."

Gabriel, stunned, listened to his musings without saying a word.

David explained it to him then, about the illness and its effects, and Lady Constance's reaction on receiving the knowledge, and the circumstances under which she'd written the letters. Gabriel sat in silence, shaking his head, and turning the paperweight around and around on his desk. He asked no questions after that, so it was not necessary to evade; Gabriel would find out about Lady Constance's death in due time, when he was safely gone.

Finally, Gabriel asked one last question. "Is it really over? I mean, you're sure she'll take no further action."

"I can say with certainty that you have nothing more to fear from Lady Constance," David replied. "She would never have followed through with the threats she made in the letters."

Gabriel sighed. "That's that, then."

"Yes, that's that."

He turned to David. "How can I thank you? Without your help, I don't know where I'd be right now. David . . ."

Embarrassed, David looked down at Gabriel's hands. "You don't have to say anything, Gabriel. I'm glad I was able—" He stopped suddenly, staring at the paperweight, his throat constricting. It was a smooth rock, about the size of a fist, but curiously shaped like a heart. He'd seen it on Gabriel's desk on all his previous visits, but this was the first time he'd actually looked at it. In an instant he was transported thirteen years back in time.

They looked into each other's eyes.

"I don't understand what's going on, Gabriel," David said softly. *"I'm afraid."*

"You should never be afraid of love, my darling David." When David said nothing, he went on gently, *"I do love you, you know. But I won't rush you—you must choose the time."* Still David was silent. *"We don't have to talk about it now if you don't want to. Let's take a walk."*

It was an unseasonably warm afternoon in late autumn. The season for holiday-makers and day-trippers had long since ended, and Brighton beach was virtually empty except for the two young men. Not daring to touch, scarcely daring to look at each other, they walked along the rocky beach for what seemed like miles, speaking hardly at all. David was intensely, acutely aware of Gabriel's nearness. He felt more alive than he ever had before, as half-realized, long-denied feelings came to the surface at last.

Finally, in the early dusk, David stopped suddenly, bending down. He plucked the heart-shaped stone from the beach and held it in the palm of his hand, feeling the weight of its smooth coolness.

"I love you, Gabriel . . . Gabe," he said, shyly, extending his hand.

Gabe touched the rock with a finger, then took it from his palm. *"I'll treat it with care,"* he promised, putting it in his pocket.

There was no one else in sight. Gabe kissed him then, and for a long moment they clung together on the deserted beach.

Gabriel followed his gaze; he held the stone up with a bemused smile. "No, David, I haven't forgotten," he said softly. "No matter what you may think, I've never forgotten."

It was David's turn to be speechless. Finally he said, "All these years. You've kept it all these years?"

"Yes. You can't just forget the kind of love we had, David. Things change, and life goes on, but there are some things . . ."

David found it hard to speak. "But . . . Emily."

"Yes, Emily." Gabriel's voice was gentle. "I told you once that you can't live in the past. And we live in a world that forces us to make choices. I regret that fact, but I don't regret the choice I made. My life is with Emily now. She's my present, and my future. I love her very much. I can't really explain it to you—my love for Emily is . . . different. It's very real, but it's different. And it in no way replaces what we had, or invalidates it. You were very special to me, David. You still are, in a certain way. Nothing will change that. I think Emily understands that, and accepts it, and I hope that in time you'll be able to understand it too. Our love was real, David. And I'll never forget it."

David stood, swallowing hard. "I think I'd better go now, Gabriel."

Gabriel rose too, and offered his hand, his lips curving in a painful smile. "You can call me Gabe."

* * *

David sat in his car for a long time—he had no idea how long. For ten years he'd clung to the knowledge—the certainty—that Gabe loved him. Over the last few weeks the question he hadn't dared to ask himself was whether it were true, or just a figment of his imagination that he'd needed to believe in. Now he had his answer: his affirmation, and something more. In a funny sort of way, he'd got Gabe back. He'd lost him completely, bafflingly, for ten long years, but now he'd got him back, and nothing could take him away again.

Suddenly, unbidden, a picture of Lucy came into his mind, painfully vivid—lovely Lucy, with her serene secret smile and her rosy corona of hair. He found that he couldn't bear the thought of never seeing her again. Without a conscious decision, he started the car and turned south towards Kensington instead of north towards Wymondham. It was Thursday—Lucy would be at home, painting. As he approached the entrance to her mews, he slowed the car, then went on to the next roundabout, and made his way north. Not yet, thought David Middleton-Brown. Soon, I'll get in touch with her. But not yet.

Epilogue

Hope thou in the Lord, and keep his way, and he shall promote thee, that thou shalt possess the land: when the ungodly shall perish, thou shalt see it.

Psalm 37:35

It was a Sunday late in September, with the first crisp hint of autumn in the air; St. Anne's Church was celebrating the feast of St. Michael and All Angels. Before Mass, Gabriel Neville, in a snow-white chasuble, stood at the front of the nave. Beside him was St. Anne's newly elected churchwarden, Roger Dawson, who paused momentously, inflated with self-importance and the gravity of his task. Unconsciously he wrung his hands. "I have an announcement to make," he intoned in his dry, raspy voice. "The Bishop of London would like me to announce that as of next January first, Father Gabriel Neville will be the Area Archdeacon." He waited for a moment for the message to sink in, then continued. "I'm sure you will all wish to join me in congratulating Father Gabriel, and wishing him all the best for the future. He will be very much missed here at St. Anne's."

From the front row, Emily smiled at Gabriel with love, and with pride.